NO PEACE
FOR THE WICKED

GUY HALLOWES

National Library of Australia Cataloguing-in-Publication entry

Creator: Hallowes, Guy, 1941- author.

Title: No peace for the wicked / Guy Hallowes.

ISBN: 978-0-6484790-7-9 (pbk.)

Series: Hallowes, Guy, 1941—author. Winds of change; bk. 3.

Subjects: Anti-apartheid movements—Fiction
Apartheid—Fiction.
Botswana—Fiction.
Angola—Fiction.
South Africa—Fiction.

Dewey Number: A823.4

Cover design by Designerbility www.designerbility.com.au
Layout by OMNE www.omne.com.au

Published by OMNE www.omne.com.au

DEDICATED TO
THOSE BRAVE PEOPLE,
WHO FOUGHT AND DESTROYED APARTHEID.

Contents

CHAPTER 1

Kamau was dreaming of his mother Rafiki; she was down by the river washing clothes in the warm sunlight and he was playing in the clear water and skimming the occasional stone across the river, watching it skip five or six times over the water.

He tried to stay asleep and continue his beautiful dream, knowing somehow in his half sleep that when he woke up harsh reality would hit him like a sledgehammer.

After a few minutes he gave up the unequal struggle. In the halflight of the dawn he could see his grandmother herding the twenty or so goats out of the hut. They were always herded into the hut at night to protect them and create warmth for the occupants. Kamau was sleeping in his grandfather's village in the Thika area of Kenya, at six thousand feet above sea level, where the nights were often frosty and the mornings misty and cold.

Kamau watched idly as his grandmother quickly swept the earthen floor of the hut, mainly of the droppings from the goats; then she put some kindling on to the ashes of the fire and blew life into it. The hut was round, about forty feet in diameter, made from rough hewn planks with the cracks filled with mud. The roof was neatly thatched and there was one door and no windows. Apart from the bed in which Kamau slept, there was another bed, where his grandmother slept, screened from the rest of the hut by blankets hung from the roof timbers. The rest of the hut was scrupulously neat, with pots and pans stacked in one area, a pile of wood for the fire in another and an old wardrobe and chest of drawers in another (rejects from some white household).

As the flames from the fire grew brighter, it suddenly hit him. Today was the dreadful, ghastly day that the Wazungu (white people) were going to hang his beautiful, kind mother Rafiki. At ten years old he didn't really understand why they wanted to do this to her. He sat up in bed, suddenly throwing aside the rough blankets. His grandmother came over and sat on the side of the old iron bedstead and made soothing noises in her native Kikuyu. Kamau tried not to cry and the emotions surged through him.

"What is the time?" he asked.

"Just after six," was the quiet response.

They both knew that six a.m. was the appointed hour for the execution. Kamau was silent for a few moments.

"Is she dead now?" he asked.

"I suppose so," was the answer.

For almost twenty minutes they both just sat there, holding each other, with tears trickling silently down their cheeks. Rafiki's mother and her son.

They said very little. All the words had already been said over the past two or more years since Rafiki had been wounded and captured, and then there had been the ordeal of her trial and conviction. The British had always been determined to make an example of her. She had really stood no chance of escaping the gallows once she had been captured.

"I hate all the Wazungu and I will kill them all," whispered Kamau.

Then he felt ashamed; his father was a white man and he loved him dearly. Peter Lawrence, his father, had spent every ounce of his strength in trying to save Rafiki from the gallows.

"Except Munyu (Peter's Kikuyu name)," he added.

His grandmother squeezed him and said nothing. She loved this little brown boy, the child of her daughter Rafiki. She knew he was exceptional. He had his father's strong build and his mother's charm and intelligence. She knew that in a Kenya where opportunity was equal, he would rise to the very top. It seemed that that was not to be, if Rafiki's execution was anything to go by.

After a little while, the grandmother got up and cooked them both a small amount of oogie, a liquid gruel made from posho (maize meal). Kamau had dressed and gone out of the hut. Along with the other boys in the village, he often helped herd the goats and his grandfather's cattle, which were kept in the boma (thorn-bush enclosure) outside the hut for the night. Kamau was not on duty that day because of Rafiki. The other boys hardly knew what to say to him. They herded out his grandfather's cows and goats along with those belonging to the other villagers, to graze the nearby hills. Kamau returned and ate his breakfast silently.

Kamau had spent many years in this village, during the time of the Mau-Mau emergency in Kenya. He had been born on Naseby, his father's farm in the "white highlands". But before his memories began, his mother and he had been snatched away from Naseby, by Mau-Mau colleagues of Rafiki. Before she met Peter Rafiki had been inducted into the Mau-Mau and had taken the oath. Her commitment to Peter Lawrence, especially after Kamau was born, meant that her fellow workers on Naseby had told her nothing of their plans and when they all deserted Naseby to fight in the forests, she had been given no choice and had been spirited away to join them.

The memories that Kamau had of the years in his grandfather's village were happy. He had spent most of his time with Wainaina, his grandfather, and his grandmother. Rafiki had always been around but kept tearing off on her little motorbike. As Kamau grew older he began to understand that Rafiki's job was to organise food drops for the Mau-Mau fighters in the forests; so she raced about on back roads often at night and organised other Kikuyu women, mainly employed on white owned farms, to carry food to certain designated places in the forests. He had one very bad memory from when he was about three, of being carried off into the forest by some evil men who were opposed to his mother's activities. There had been a lot of terrifying noise and shooting in the forest and all the evil men had been killed.

Other than that, his life had appeared to be tranquil; he had some education from a local white missionary, he saw his mother most days and he was very much part of the village, not at all conscious of his coffee-brown skin although all his peers were much blacker in appearance. His mother's activities were not often discussed, but he got the distinct impression that his grandfather Wainaina disapproved both of her support for the "Mau-Mau baboons" as he called them when provoked, and also of her liaison with Kamau's father, the M'zungu (white person) Peter Lawrence. None of this prejudiced Wainaina's attitude towards Kamau, which was always kindly. Wainaina made very sure that Kamau was brought up strictly within Kikuyu traditions, despite the ministrations of the missionary.

The dangers to which Rafiki had continuously exposed herself only became obvious to Kamau after she was badly wounded by the British security forces and then captured and imprisoned. The nightmare had really started once she was put on trial and it became clear that the British would execute her if they could possibly manage it.

Since Rafiki's imprisonment, Kamau's father Peter (Munyu to the Kikuyu) had reconciled his differences with Wainaina and he, Kamau, had spent the last few years with Peter on Naseby, where Peter had engaged a Mrs. Smith and the local correspondence school to try to plug the large gaps in his education.

Peter had fearlessly led the defence of Rafiki in the Kenya Supreme Court, despite being vilified by the local, white controlled press and the white community in general. Wainaina had helped where he could but he recognised the truly superhuman effort that Peter had put in and it was no fault of Peter's that the trial had ended in Rafiki being condemned to death.

Kamau spent the rest of the morning wandering disconsolately round the village. He didn't know what to do with himself. Inside he was seething and starting to blame himself. "Surely there was something I could have done," he thought. The others in the village were equally despondent; Rafiki was one of theirs too. After midday his grandmother called him for his midday meal of ogalie (maize meal cake) vegetables and a small amount of goat's meat; he shared the meat with one of his grandfather's scrawny dogs. Just as they were finishing the meal, they heard the sound of a vehicle, Peter's pick-up truck, Kamau was certain, tearing up the hill towards the village. It came to a screeching halt on the outskirts. Hardly the sort of behaviour Kamau expected from people coming back with his mother's dead body, he thought. As he went through the doorway of the hut and out towards where the vehicle was parked, he heard Peter and Wainaina yelling in Kikuyu:

"They stopped it, she's free, and she's not dead!"

Kamau ran out to the pick-up and into his father's arms. He was completely bewildered.

"What, what?" was all he could say.

Then Peter told him the whole story. "London stopped it, London stopped it at the last minute," he repeated excitedly. "She'll be free in a few days."

Kamau had thought London was a place, so he was even more confused; London must be a person too.

Wainaina was busily telling the rest of the village what had happened.

After about half an hour Kamau, his grandmother, Wainaina and Peter all clambered into the cab of the pick-up and a dozen of the younger men leapt into the back of the vehicle.

"Where are we going?" asked a now very confused Kamau.

"To the prison, to see Rafiki," said Peter happily.

Peter drove at breakneck speed back to Nairobi. The young men in the back all took up the chant that had been the rallying call at Rafiki's trial: "RA, RA, RA, RAFIKI!" they yelled all the way into Nairobi.

There were many other groups in cars, pick-ups and on the street, all yelling the same chant and some were yelling: "JOMO KENYATTA, JOMO KENYATTA!"

"Who is he?" asked Kamau.

"The Kikuyu leader," said Peter diplomatically; "He will be released from prison soon as well."

They raced to the prison and then Peter told them, "I will talk to them; you all stay here."

Half an hour later he came out and took Kamau and his grandmother by the hand and led them into the prison. "They didn't want to let us in, they all still seem utterly confused," he said. "Anyway, they've now agreed to a ten minute visit."

They were led into a grubby little room, where only days before Kamau had thought he had said his final goodbyes to his mother. After what seemed an interminable wait, Rafiki was led into the room. Kamau flew to her; he wanted to touch her, to feel her, to make sure all this was real. He was prized away after a few minutes and her mother was allowed to hug her daughter.

Too soon the visit came to an end and they were ushered out of the prison.

"When can she come home?" asked Kamau.

"Soon," was the answer from Peter.

Several weeks later, after many frustrating bureaucratic delays, the day came when Rafiki was to be released. As Peter confided to Wainaina: "It seems that they cannot bear to think that they are going to lose her forever. Somehow if they keep her in the prison, all this will turn out to be a bad dream and they will be able to go on with their vile plan to execute her."

Eventually an executive order came from the Colonial office in London that Rafiki was to be released immediately and Peter and Kamau went to pick her up at the prison.

The family spent a night at Wainaina's village and then made their way back to the farm, Naseby. To start with Kamau would not let his mother out of his sight and he often returned from whatever he was doing to touch her and feel her.

Kamau's lessons with the correspondence school and Mrs. Smith continued. Mrs. Smith was very sensitive to both Kamau's needs and those of his mother and suggested that Rafiki might want to supervise her son's lessons.

"No, no." Rafiki said laughingly. "He is only just behind where I think that I finished; my education was, as you know rather rudely interrupted.

Anyway during the past few years you seem to have got him under control, so I don't want to spoil anything."

At the time that Kamau came to live with Peter on Naseby after Rafiki had been captured the family had decided that the farm school could not possibly provide the required level of education that they, and Peter in particular, was determined that Kamau would have. Peter felt guilty enough in regards to Kamau and he was determined that no effort would be spared to give him the best opportunities he possibly could.

The schools that Kamau's half-brothers John and before him Robert had attended, were still closed to Kamau since they were reserved for white children only. At ten years old Kamau did not really understand this, but as he grew up he was determined that all the forms of discrimination that he had suffered because of the colour of his skin should be fought and eliminated. [John and Robert were also Peter's children; their mother had been killed in a horse riding accident, years earlier.]

John went to a Government boarding school in Nairobi, still called "The Duke of York". Kamau hated to see him go away for what seemed like ages and he really loved the all too short school holidays, where John was happy to spend his time with Kamau. During Rafiki's trial and imprisonment John had taught him to ride and to shoot, and as he grew older he became a better horseman and a much better shot than his gentler older brother. "Kamau is much more like Robert," Rafiki observed. Kamau barely remembered Robert, who was now studying in England. He had a sense that Robert had been hostile to him, for reasons that he did not understand.

Peter, Rafiki and Wainaina had decided that Kamau should not lose his Kikuyu roots he had so painfully acquired while Rafiki was part of the Mau-Mau, so he spent one weekend a month in his grandfather, Wainaina's village.

Peter was determined to spend as much time as possible with his talented and surprisingly well adjusted son; he still felt guilty that he had not spent enough time with his eldest son Robert and certainly Kamau had been lost to him, for the years of the emergency, when he did not really know where Rafiki and her son were. The lessons were a priority; Peter knew that within a short time all the restrictions in relation to school attendance would be lifted and Kamau would be allowed to go to the previously all-white schools. Kamau always raced through his lessons in double quick time and Peter taught him to drive the tractors, so when the tractor drivers knocked off Kamau was able to take one of them out and continue the work. Peter could trust him on his own from the age of about eleven. He also taught him how to run the milking, twice daily, so he was able to drive to the milking shed on the tractor and save Peter and Peter's nephew Ken, who was actually running the farm, much time.

All the Kikuyu on Naseby had left years before, when they just disappeared one night, kidnapping both Rafiki and Kamau. Peter had of necessity replaced this labour with Wakamba families, who were not involved in the Mau-Mau rebellion. Robert and John had always played soccer with the children in the farm village and John and now Kamau continued that tradition; both John and Kamau became quite fluent in the Kamba language as a result.

Peter and Ken had bought some soccer balls and through the farm school on Naseby had encouraged the children to play informal games both on Naseby and on the neighbouring farms the school serviced. Most of the farmers had welcomed the advent of the school, now some ten years earlier, but there were some diehards who had always opposed the set up of the school, although their own labour sent their children there. One afternoon John and Kamau and some of the children from Naseby, had quite innocently gone over to a nearby farm, unbeknown to them owned by one of those who had long opposed the creation of the school, to play an impromptu game of soccer with the local kids. The game had been in progress for a few minutes when there was a flurry of shots in the air over the heads of the players. The kids shrieked, some of ran away into the nearby huts and the bush and some just lay down on the bare earth of the pitch. A very angry white farmer came into view brandishing a rifle. "I will not have my farm crawling with thieving black hands, the take over has not yet happened." He then spotted John. "And as for you, John fucking Lawrence you and your wog-loving father have not been welcome here for more than ten years. Get off my land and take all your black friends with you." He then saw Kamau. "I suppose that you are that abomination that was born to that black whore of a mother of yours and the wog-lover Lawrence. Your mother should have hanged, and for my money your father should have as well. Now get off and I do not want to see any of you again." He brandished his rifle and the Naseby kids scuttled off the pitch and down the road back home.

The incident was discussed, with both Peter and Rafiki, when they got home. Both Kamau and John were visibly upset and Rafiki wept when she was told the story. At the time Kamau did not understand much of what had been said, but the incident remained with him and had an influence on his commitment to tackle the question of blind racial discrimination. He began to understand that he would be the subject of this type of prejudice for the rest of his life.

Peter said to them all later at dinner: "As you all know, a part of the settlement for independence will be the acquisition of many of the white owned farms, including this one. We will then settle land starved Africans on these farms. This is a very sensitive issue and many of the whites are having trouble getting used to the idea that they will have to start again somewhere else."

"You mean that we will all have to leave Naseby?" asked Kamau.

"Yes, we are going to live in Nairobi," answered Rafiki, "Which means that you, Kamau, will go to a primary school there and John will be able to attend Lenana [the new name for the Duke of York] as a day scholar if he wants but he may wish to continue as a boarder."

"What is Dad going to do, without the farm?" asked John.

Peter smiled.

"The Mzee {meaning old man, which was the common sympathetic name used for Jomo Kenyatta} has asked me to be a minister in the new government; I am to be the Minister of Agriculture and I will be responsible for settling people on this farm as well as many others."

"If we don't live here, where will we live?" asked Kamau. He was excited about his new school but he found all this change too much to absorb all at once.

"We have seen a very nice place in Karen, which is about ten miles outside Nairobi, near Lenana. We will call it Sattimma," said Rafiki.

"Oh yes," said Kamau. "That's the highest peak of the Aberdare Mountains; we can see it everyday from Naseby."

The next few months were difficult for the Lawrences. Many of the farmers recognized that Peter had done them and white farmers in general an enormous favour by helping to create a mechanism whereby, they could, with some money, leave their farms to start again, either in Kenya or elsewhere. There were some, however, who had great difficulty in accepting any of the changes that were occurring; they blamed Peter for 'stealing' their farms and they accused him of engineering a better deal for himself than for the rest of the community. These were the same people who had accused Peter of betraying the white community when he and Rafiki became lovers and had considered Kamau's birth a disgrace. "Nusu-Nusu" they called him, meaning "Half-Half", that is half white and half black.

Peter responded to accusations that he was treated more favourably than others in the district by widely publicizing the arrangements for the acquisition of Naseby, which were no better than for anyone else in the district. The Lawrences were not invited to any of the numerous farewell parties, although some people did make a point of coming to say goodbye.

In the end Peter was glad to leave the district, although he shed a tear for the now broken dreams that he and Jenny, Robert and John's mother, had had seventeen years earlier. Peter now had his new ministerial responsibilities to look forward to; helping to create a more just Kenya for all to share in rather than the small white minority, as was the case until independence.

Rafiki, although she loved Naseby, was looking forward to being mistress of "Sattimma". She also hoped that the society in Nairobi would be more tolerant than the one in Ol'Kalou. She was ever mindful of the lack of medical facilities catering for the poor Africans and had already made moves to set up a clinic in Pumwani, which apart from being one of the poorest areas in Nairobi was also part of Peter's new constituency. She had emotionally left Naseby all those years ago, when she and Kamau had been kidnapped to fight with the Mau-Mau. Since she had left prison she had really been waiting for the new Kenya to emerge; and she felt that she had earned her place there.

John was happy that Sattimma was close to the school, he would have a choice between becoming a day scholar or remaining as a boarder. He was also looking forward to University in Britain. Peter had explained that he would never be able to inherit or be part of the dream that was to own a farm in Kenya. Life was before him, he was ready for a change.

Kamau was happy to be part of a whole family again. He knew that Wainaina's village was much closer to Nairobi than Naseby. Above all he really looked forward to attending a proper school for the first time in his life.

❋　❋　❋

CHAPTER 2

Kamau Lawrence did very well well at primary school. All things being equal he would have been head of school. The old prejudices still existed, however, and in his last year, although Kamau was a prefect, the head of school was a white boy. He supposed he should not feel hard done by; he had after all only been there for one and a half years.

Before he went to the school both his father and mother had told him that in all probability he would be victimised and discriminated against because of his colour and background. In particular his mother Rafiki had said to him, "Don't ever be a victim, don't ever feel sorry for yourself. If you find that happening, find a way to turn that into a positive situation. If you need help, I'm here for advice. If you forget that you're brown, the rest of the world will forget it as well; if you in any way emphasise your skin colour that is how people will think of you. You may not understand this yet but you soon will."

Initially Kamau was put into classes and sports teams well below his ability. Remembering his mother's advice, all he did was to try his very best, and within days or weeks he was promoted until eventually he was at the top in almost everything. In most cases this attitude worked, but when he applied to play rugby all the other boys laughed at him and he was only allowed to be the touch judge. Week after week he watched in frustration. The white boys all told him that it was well known that black children did not have the heart for tough physical sports like rugby and that he should try something else. Even the master in charge asked him if he would not like to do something else. He said "No," and waited. Then one day during a practice session one of the boys suffered a nasty tackle and was not able to continue. Much to the surprise of the players on the field Kamau took his place at centre three-quarter. Kamau had been well schooled by his father and had had a few impromtu games with the children on Naseby. His opposite number got the ball and before he knew where he was, Kamau tackled him; the ball went loose and Kamau picked it up and scored under the posts. There were some uneasy glances around the field. The very next play the ball came out to Kamau and he sidestepped two players and again scored. There was some whispering among the players on the opposite side and hostile glances at Kamau; he could see that something unpleasant was being hatched. He watched and waited. The ball came out to him very slowly this time and he could see three of the toughest, heaviest boys from the opposite side looming. He grabbed the ball, ducked a swinging arm and grubbered the ball so that his wing could follow up, which he did. As the wing was tackled, Kamau was on hand to pick up a difficult pass and he again scored. This went on all afternoon; none of the opposite side was able to lay a hand on Kamau and much to the master's amusement he scored at will. From then on he was included in the side and was quickly promoted to the school first fifteen.

Not long after he had established himself within the rugby fraternity he overheard a conversation, which indicated that some of the less tolerant boys were going to beat him up. There were five of them and they had decided that they would try to injure him just before a rugby match against another school. They did not want Kamau to play and this would have been his first time in the first fifteen for the school. He tried approaching one of the boys and said: "Look, I know what you and the others are up to; what's the problem?"

The boy just said: "Stay out of that team and you won't get hurt." Kamau tried to remonstrate with him but got nowhere. "We don't want blacks in that side," was all he got out of the boy. Kamau decided that he would have to deal with the situation as he found it. On the day before the match, the five followed him around for most of the day, waiting for an opportunity. Kamau took advantage of the situation and lured them into a passageway where only one of them could tackle him at a time. They tried to rush him and he ruthlessly smashed the leading boy in the face; the second one he kicked in the groin and the third received a powerful kick in the stomach and a blow to the face. The so-called leader of the group then reluctantly had to face up to Kamau, when a master came around the corner and stopped them. "You will all come to the headmaster's office now," he said.

"It's all his fault," stammered one of the boys.

"What, for being selected in the rugby team?" asked the master.

They all shuffled off to the headmaster's office, where the master reported that he had been aware of the conspiracy of the five boys to disable Kamau so that he could not play in the match the next day. "I'm sorry that I didn't get there sooner," he said to Kamau.

"Why didn't you report this to me or one of the staff earlier?" asked the head, looking at Kamau.

"I decided to deal with the situation myself," was the response. "I have had to deal with more difficult situations than this in the past. I was doing fine actually, as you can see." He smiled.

Kamau played in the rugby match and the five conspirators were made to spend their Saturday gardening under the supervision of one of the masters, who would much rather have been watching the match.

Kamau's reputation grew and grew and within six months of being at the school he was courted by most of his fellow students and his talents was recognised by the school in general. During that time he did not specifically make friends with one racial group or another; his friends came from a wide range of different people. Where he saw discrimination he dealt with it himself.

To his delight, Robert, his half brother living in London, had started corresponding with him just after he went to the primary school. During his final year he told Robert of his frustrations at not being made head boy. Robert himself felt that he had been hard done by and not been made head of school for much the same reasons. "Don't let it get to you," he advised. "Sooner or later, your obvious talents will be recognised and they will not see the colour of your skin."

Now almost fourteen, Kamau was about to go to Lenana high school, which had been called the Duke of York in the days before Uhuru (freedom). [Lenana is the lesser of the two peaks on Mount Kenya.] This was the school which both his white half-brothers had attended.

In the meantime he had to go through the Kikuyu initiation ceremony with his age group at his grandfather Wainaina's village.

The boys, all of his age, were each given a large warm blanket; in days gone by this would have been a skin. The girls were part of the ceremony too but did not have to dress down since the clitorectomy that had been performed on previous generations was now forbidden. There were about forty children all told.

Kamau won the boys' race to the sacred tree, so he became the leader of his age group. All the children's heads were shaved and they were smeared with white and red ochre.

During the first two days of the ceremony there was a multitude of ceremonial dances by both the boys and the girls. The parents, including Peter and Rafiki, drank beer and fussed over their offspring, who were all on the verge of adulthood. Kamau was much admired, especially for his athletic prowess; he could run faster and jump higher than any of his peers.

On the third day of the ceremony the group was taken to the river in the early morning. They were all made to strip, both boys and girls together, although the girls were allowed to keep their little leather aprons on. They then had to sit in the near freezing river for about thirty minutes. The freezing temperature numbed their bodies so they would not feel any pain from the knife they would shortly have to endure. The girls were also made to participate to keep faith with the tradition, although there was now no operation. When they left the river the boys and girls were separated. The girls went to a large hut in the village; the boys were wrapped in their blankets and taken to a clearing in the forest where the mondo-mogo or witchdoctor was waiting.

The boys were made to sit on the ground naked except for their blankets. Kamau was the first to be operated on, he now being the leader of the group. It was really important that there should be no outward sign of any pain during the operation. Anyone who grimaced, drew a sharp breath or worse, made any kind of sound, would be vilified for life as a coward. Kamau opened his blanket; the witchdoctor held Kamau's penis in one hand and with a sharp razor in the other removed most of the foreskin; the foreskin was then tied in a knot on the right hand side of his penis.

Kamau felt no pain; he watched in fascination. The operation took less than thirty seconds and then the mondo-mogo moved on.

Kamau took little notice of the rest of the ceremony, although he did notice when one of his peers yelled out during his operation. Kamau now examined his penis. He couldn't believe his eyes —his precious, precious willy was now a bleeding, gory mess, and there was his foreskin in a little knot on the right side of his penis (this protrusion is called ngwati). He wondered if it would ever recover. As a concession to modernity one of the mondo-mogo's assistants bathed him with dettol and then wrapped the injured member in leaves, which had healing properties. He wondered if he would ever be the same again; certainly sex was the very last thing on his mind.

The people running the ceremony allowed eight days for healing, during which time the children were given instructions on various adult issues, particularly the practice of ngweko where the boys and girls were encouraged to lie together without actually having full sexual intercourse.

Kamau's wound healed quite quickly and he was an avid listener to all the initiation talks, especially the ones dealing with ngweko. He really liked the look of the girls in his age group, especially Wamboi who was the girls' leader.

Eventually Peter and Rafiki returned to the village and took Kamau back to Karen. Kamau had paid regular visits to his grandfather's village ever since he had gone back to live with his father on Naseby when Rafiki was in jail. Wild horses would not keep him away now; he had every intention of fully participating in ngweko when his penis had properly healed.

When he asked Peter what the little knot—ngwati, the remains of his foreskin—was for, he got a very non-committal answer. He received a much more straightforward answer from Rafiki. "To enhance the sexual pleasure of the woman," she said. He shyly asked her if she had been through the traditional women's ceremony.

"I went through the ceremony but my father refused to let them do the operation on me and about half the girls in our group also escaped it. We had much more fun than the group who had the operation," Rafiki added knowingly.

"They taught you about ngweko?" Rafiki asked her son in a matter of fact way.

"Yes, of course."

"Well you make the most of that, it will teach you about your body and also it is a great bonding exercise with your age group. Whatever happens in later life that age group will always be close to you."

Kamau, although a day scholar, managed to find the occasion to show his recently altered appendage to his peers at school. Many of the other Kikuyu at the school had had the same operation so they were all able to trade stories and admire each other's operations.

Once a month Kamau made his way to Thika and Wainaina's village where he joined his age group. The group played all sorts of games, running and jumping for the boys, dancing for the girls. Encouraged by tradition they all paired off as the evening wore on. The boys stripped completely naked but the girls were obliged to wear their little leather aprons, which normally just hung down protecting their modesty. During ngweko, they were obliged to tie the two strings dangling from the bottom of the apron round the back to the belt or string holding the apron round the waist. The purpose of this was to cover up the female genitals, making full sexual intercourse impossible whilst the apron was in place. Whilst Kamau spent many happy ngweko hours with Wamboi, his favourite, they were encouraged by their elders to play ngweko with a variety of partners.

At first they all played by the rules and whilst they as a group managed to extract more and more sexual pleasure from the activity, Kamau and some of the other boys became bolder and bolder.

John came to the rescue. One day when Kamau was explaining to him the details of ngweko, John put his hand in his pocket, produced a packet of condoms and explained to Kamau what they were for.

Next time Kamau went to the village he was determined to try his new knowledge out. He had brought enough condoms for the whole group but he thought he had better try it out first with Wamboi.

The whole process was explained in the best detail that Kamau could muster once Kamau and Wamboi had retired to their bed. Wamboi was very doubtful, but was eventually persuaded to take her apron off altogether. Kamau as it turned out was a very sensitive lover and he pleased Wamboi greatly, again and again. Even during ngweko they were not allowed to spend the whole night together, so when the group reassembled and the boys went back to the thiringa or men's hut, he shared his knowledge with all the other boys and gave them each a packet of condoms. During the next eighteen months the group became very sexually experienced, especially for a group of teenagers. In the traditional society, many of them, by this time, would have become married and started to raise families. Many of this group, however, were in a similar position to Kamau where they had their sights fixed on higher education and university. Marriage was the last issue on their minds.

During his first year at Lenana, although at first he was a day scholar Kamau had to board on one or two occasions when Peter and Rafiki went overseas on official business. At that time it was traditional for the younger boys to clean shoes and make beds for the prefects (a practice called fagging).

When Kamau was told of this practice his reaction was, "I will not clean anyone's shoes or make anyone's bed but my own. My people have cleaned enough shoes and made enough beds to last ten centuries."

On the first day, when he arrived at the dormitory for junior boys and was given a pair of shoes to clean, he simply handed them back.

"I will not do it," he told them, 'you can do anything you like."

The housemaster explained that it was part of the tradition of the school. Kamau was unmoved. Eventually in desperation they told him that unless he cooperated he would be beaten. He took the shoes he was given and with the help of a stick covered them in dog droppings. He apple-pied the prefect's bed and then put a large toad in the bed for good measure.

When the prefect came to bed, there was a very unsavoury smell around the place. "No matter," he thought, "we'll find out what that is the morning." When he tried to get into bed he stepped right on the toad and then leapt out of bed at the speed of light, yelling. All the lights were put on and eventually the housemaster was called.

"Did you do this?" he asked Kamau.

"I've told you, sir, many times, that I will not participate in this nonsense; I do not care what tradition it violates," he responded.

"I'm going to have to beat you."

"Then I insist on seeing the headmaster," said Kamau.

The housemaster hesitated. Kamau Lawrence was the outstanding athlete and scholar of his age group in the school. His father was a minister in the new government and he was aware of the disadvantages that Kamau had suffered in his earlier years. After much discussion it was agreed that Kamau was excused 'fagging' duties. Within a year the practice was banned at the school altogether; it caused too much dissention, particularly when much of the intake at the school was black and Indian and necessarily almost all the children at the top of the school were white, as a result of the previous "whites only" policy.

In his early days some of the less tolerant children tried to make fun of Kamau by calling him "Nusu-Nusu", the Swahili for half-half, referring to his parentage. He took a very firm line with anyone using this expression, and most of them immediately backed down and apologised. He did get into one or two fights with the more recalcitrant tormentors and he always won his fights. In time nobody dared use the expression.

Kamau progressed well at Lenana and became a leader at the school, as he was in his age group at his grandfather Wainaina's village.

By the time he was fifteen Kamau was playing in the first rugby fifteen and had become one of the stars of the school.

During one of the matches Kamau received a bad gash on one of his legs. He was bandaged up very caringly by the daughter of the one of the housekeeper/matrons at the school. He supposed she was about seventeen; Kamau was absolutely smitten. He sought her out after the game. "Joanne Black," she introduced herself. He didn't see her for a few weeks, until he had occasion to spend more time in the boarding establishment while Peter and Rafiki were away at a conference in Addis Ababa.

After a brief chat he said, "When can I see you again?"

She looked at him coyly.

"How about the cricket pavilion after prep tonight?"

So it was set.

After prep Kamau stored his books away and then unobtrusively went out the back way. He ran to the cricket pavilion. He walked around it and looked at his watch. Ten minutes late.

"Damn," he said to himself, "she must have thought I wasn't coming." He waited another ten minutes and then was just about the give up when a voice called.

"Over here."

A wraith-like figure emerged from behind the cricket sightscreen.

"I've been watching you," she said.

"I thought you had gone since I was late," he said.

They sat on the roller and chatted and held hands.

"Kiss me," said Joanne.

Kamau had never kissed anyone; although he had seen people kissing in the movies, it wasn't part of the Kikuyu tradition and certainly not part of ngweko.

She giggled at his clumsy efforts.

"Here, let me show you."

Kamau was a quick learner and he got the idea very quickly. He tried to put his hand up her shirt.

"Not so fast, not so fast," she whispered. "I must go soon, otherwise I'll be missed; I'll see you tomorrow." She slipped away.

They met regularly at the pavilion but their activities were confined to kissing despite all Kamau's considerable efforts. Then one evening things seemed to be different. He put his hand up her dress, expecting to have to remove her panties. There were no panties; he touched her now damp, soft, furry mound. She moaned.

"Here," she said. "Use one of these." She handed him a condom.

"It's O.K., I have my own," said Kamau.

"Oh."

He gently removed her dress and all his clothes and they lay on top of them in the damp grass. Kamau, due to his ngweko experience, was a very accomplished lover and he pleased her greatly.

They hastily got back into their clothes; it was just a bit cold to be running about naked at night. Nairobi is about six thousand feet above sea level.

They walked back towards the main school buildings area.

"Bit cold out there tonight," volunteered Kamau.

"Mm," said Joanne.

"Is there somewhere warmer we could go?"

"I'll tell you what," Joanne said brightly.

Kamau looked at her enquiringly.

"Just come to my room, it has a door from the garden."

"What about your mother?" Kamau asked.

"We don't have to worry about her, she'll be reading or listening to the radio," Joanne said.

The next night Kamau crept through the little garden to the flat occupied by Joanne and her mother. The curtains were open and he could see Joanne pottering about in her bedroom. He tapped quietly on the French door; Joanne skipped over and opened it. She put her finger to her lips.

"Shh, we'll have to be quiet. Mum's asleep in her chair," Joanne giggled.

They drew the curtain, locked the door and made the most fantastic love that either of them thought imaginable.

Joanne was intrigued by the knot or ngwati made from Kamau's foreskin by the witchdoctor.

"No wonder you are so good, I suppose this little thing really helps," she said, holding his appendage in one hand and stroking it.

"I suppose," he said.

This went on for about a week and then one evening Joanne's mother went past the door just as Joanne was in the middle of the best and biggest orgasm she had ever experienced.

"Joanne, are you alright?" called Mrs. Black.

"Yes, fine," she said in a strangled voice.

"Can I come in?"

"It's locked, I'll let you in, in a minute," said Joanne.

The doorhandle was tried.

Joanne just pointed to Kamau and then under the bed. He scrambled out of bed with all his clothes and crawled under it. The bedspread hid him comfortably. Joanne slipped on a nightie, grabbed a book and unlocked the door. Her mother looked in suspiciously. She had noticed her daughter's particularly happy demeanour of late and wondered if any of the boys in the school were taking notice of her. The sooner she went to that finishing school in Switzerland, the better, she thought.

"Everything alright?" Mrs. Black asked sweetly.

"Fine, Mum, yes."

"I thought I heard you cry out."

"Just a sad part in this book." Joanne waved the book about.

Mrs. Black now definitely smelt a rat. Joanne, as far as she knew, never read a book from one year's end to the next, and the book she was holding was a book of poems by T.S Eliot.

"O.K., see you in the morning, I'm going to bed."

Joanne shut the door again and locked it once she heard her mothers' footsteps going down the passage.

She tore off her nightie again, Kamau emerged from under the bed and they continued where they had left off before the interruption.

Kamau wasn't able to get away the next couple of nights, but Joanne's mother remained on full alert.

The next night when Mrs. Black heard the key turn in the lock of Joanne's room, she crept up and listened outside the door. There were muffled sounds for a few minutes, and then the sounds were unmistakable. Someone was screwing her daughter. She crept away, remembering her own first youthful experiences at that age. She was not going to let her precious daughter make the same silly mistakes that she had made. She was going to find out who this fellow was, and he would be in serious trouble. The next day she removed the key from Joanne's door and hid it.

Kamau, as usual, arrived at about nine and after a few preliminaries; they were in the midst of making love when Mrs. Black burst in. Joanne had looked around for the key to her room but didn't bother much; she was too keen to get into bed with Kamau.

"Got you, you little bugger!" Mrs. Black grabbed at Kamau's foot.

He leapt out of bed and frantically tried to put his clothes on, with Mrs. Black slapping him and pushing him around.

"Mum, stop, stop, let him get dressed," yelled Joanne.

Mrs Black was furious; she couldn't believe her eyes. Her daughter, with a black man—well, a brown man. She was disgusted although she couldn't help admiring Kamau's athletic looking body while he was getting dressed. By this time Kamau was fully dressed and Joanne had put on her nightdress.

She shook her finger at Kamau.

"This is going to the headmaster, and you will be expelled, I am sure. I knew we should never have opened schools such as this to riff-raff like you.

Now get out of here."

Kamau left by the front door this time. He knew he was in trouble; he wondered how he could escape being expelled. He was completely shattered; his whole life could be destroyed by a silly piece of self-indulgence. Then he had an idea. Instead of going back to the dormitory he went to see the headman of the large labour force the school employed. Most of the labour were Kikuyu including the headman, and they knew Kamau very well, but he was surprised to see Kamau at such an hour.

"What's the problem?" Kamau was asked after he had been admitted to the man's small house.

Kamau explained the predicament and how he had been caught by Mrs. Black. He then explained that in his, Kamau's, view all he was doing was practicing ngweko as he had been taught to do in his home village. The fact that his partner, on this occasion, was a white girl and not in his village age group was conveniently ignored. A shrewd look came across the headman's face.

"And you want me to explain the practice of ngweko to the headmaster in the morning?"

"Yes," Kamau looked relieved, "Also your wife."

The headman would do anything to help Kamau; he could see that people like Kamau were the hope of the new Kenya and it was important that they were educated like the Wazungu.

"Mrs. Black said she would be in the headmaster's office after assembly at eight thirty tomorrow morning, so if you could be there at that time I expect you will be able to see him soon after that," said Kamau.

Kamau respectfully bade his host farewell and ran back to the dormitory.

The next morning a very agitated Mrs. Black, with her daughter, button-holed the headmaster just as he went into his office. Mrs. Black explained the situation.

"So you see he just has to be expelled, now, today. We can't tolerate this sort of thing here," she concluded. "We should never have let them black bastards into our schools; they just lower the standards all the time".

"Mummy, that's not fair," said Joanne.

"Quiet, you've been enough trouble for one day."

The head was in a quandary. With any other boy he would not have hesitated, but Peter Lawrence's son was another matter. Besides being the son of the Minister of Agriculture, Kamau was already the outstanding sportsman and scholar of his year, and was likely to be head boy in his final year. If he, the headmaster could possibly find a way out of this he would.

He looked at Mrs. Black shrewdly; he was fairly certain that Joanne was born out of wedlock and the "husband" she spoke of did not really exist. He sympathised and supposed she didn't want her beautiful daughter to make the same mistakes she herself had made.

Kamau was called in; he'd been hovering outside.

"Explain yourself Lawrence," said the head. "Mrs. Black has already given me the background."

"I just need to explain the Kikuyu custom of ngweko," said Kamau.

"Go on."

Kamau explained the circumcision ceremony and the subsequent practice of ngweko. He of course omitted to say that ngweko did not permit full sexual intercourse. He knew that all whites, including the head, would assume that if a man and a woman lay down together alone, full sexual intercourse would ensue.

Mrs. Black kept interjecting with, "Disgusting!" and "What else would one expect from a bunch of black savages?" She was ignored.

"Lawrence, this all seems rather farfetched; do you have any proof?" asked the head.

The head could now see a glimmer of light at the end of the tunnel.

"Sir, I just saw the headman and his wife going past; they are Kikuyu, they would be able to explain," said Kamau.

The head looked at him shrewdly. He went out and found the headman and his wife hovering.

The head explained in Swahili that he needed to understand more about ngweko.

The headman nodded and then he and his wife gave a masterful performance. Without once looking at Kamau they told the headmaster almost exactly what Kamau had just told him.

Mrs. Black understood exactly what was being said; she was flabbergasted.

"You're going to let him off aren't you?" she fumed. "I found him in bed fucking my daughter and he's going to get off scot-free, just because he's black and just because of some disgusting tribal ritual he and his disgusting parents have encouraged him to be part of."

"You're forgetting yourself, Mrs. Black," the head said quietly. He was quite taken aback by her language, which perhaps betrayed more of her origins than she was ever prepared to let on.

Kamau kept a completely straight face; Joanne glanced at him.

"Please leave us," the head looked at Kamau, Joanne and the two African servants.

"Mrs. Black, please listen to me," said the head when they were alone.

She looked at him.

"I know this is difficult for you. It's difficult for all of us but I must do what I think is best for the school."

She made no response.

"I'm not going to expel Kamau. There is something in this ngweko thing, although perhaps not as much as has been made out. You also have to make allowance for Lawrence's background. His mother was almost hanged a few years back; his father had a very bad time in the emergency."

"All of his own making," interjected Mrs. Black.

The head held up his hand.

"Hear me out, please," he continued. "Kamau is a very fine young man; as you know, he is the outstanding athlete and scholar of his year; he has and will continue to bring great credit to the school."

Mrs. Black burst into tears.

"I wanted so much for her, and now this!"

"I know it's disappointing, but it's not the end of the world. Presumably she's not pregnant and you are sending her to a finishing school somewhere, aren't you?" he looked at her.

Mrs. Black brightened up.

"Yes, Switzerland in six months time," she said.

"O.K, I will deal with Lawrence; I hope you can leave it at that," he said hopefully.

"Yes, I understand your point of view, but he'd better stay away from her or else," she said defiantly.

"He was going home anyway this week; his parents are back in town."

They shook hands.

Mrs. Black went out.

The others looked at both her and the headmaster expectantly.

"Lawrence, come in, the rest of you can go," said the head.

"I'm really disappointed in you," he said to Kamau in a rather unconvincing manner.

Kamau hung his head. He was about to get out of it scot-free, he could tell. For once in his life, his origins and brown skin had created an unfair advantage.

"I'm sorry, sir," said Kamau. Inside he was elated.

"I'm not even going to beat you," said the head, "but I will talk to your parents."

"Thank you sir."

He was dismissed.

A few days later when Kamau was at home he spoke to Peter and told him exactly what had happened.

"I wondered what the head wanted; he's coming over for a drink tomorrow night," Peter said. "Apart from that he was non-committal."

Rafiki was contemptuous.

"He can sleep with black girls and this is fine, but do the same with a white girl and there's all this fuss. Imagine what fun the press would have with all that."

"He's a bit young; anyway, I imagine the headmaster is aware of most of those issues," said Peter.

"He's not too young for a Kikuyu, that's what ngweko is all about," responded Rafiki.

"I get the feeling that he goes further than ngweko allows," argued Peter.

"We always went further than ngweko allows," said Rafiki triumphantly.

Kamau had no intention of letting his relationship with Joanne wither. He went to see Kinua, who had built a stone cottage on the property next to the garage, which he now owned.

"Ngweko, you said," said Kinua doubtfully, "with an M'zungu? [White person]"

Kamau nodded.

"I will speak to Sarah," he said, "There is a small spare room now that Karanja has gone away."

Kamau was elated. When he next went to school, he managed to slip Joanne a note without anyone seeing.

"Meet me at Kinua's garage on Sunday afternoon."

Joanne read the note.

So they continued their happy liaison until Joanne left for Switzerland six months later. Nobody was any the wiser.

Kamau was entirely happy during his time at Lenana, except for one ghastly episode when he was kidnapped by some people who were hostile to some of his parent's activities. Due to the quick action of the police and his parents he was rescued, physically unharmed. The incident made him wary of unckecked authority and after that he took nothing for granted always hoping for the best in people but being prepared for the worst.

There were no other rivals to Kamau becoming the head boy of the school when the time came. He became head boy and easily managed to gain a place at Oxford University.

When he was appointed head boy he had a very happy letter from Robert congratulating him. "I knew that one of us earned that honour," the letter concluded, "and I really am glad it was you." Kamau knew that from that point he had a real friend; his own brother.

Chapter 3

Robert had gone to England with the objective of distancing himself from his African background. Since his mother had died in a horse riding accident and his father had taken up with Rafiki he, Robert, felt that he had been marginalised in the Kenya white society. He considered that his ability and character had gone unrecognised. By rights he should have been head boy of his school and rugby captain, but none of these honours had come his way and he had had to fight for the few honours that were bestowed on him.

In contrast, Robert's life in England was one of privilege. He had spent three years at Oxford where he obtained a first in law and he had played for those three years in the Oxford rugby team, the last as captain. It seemed like a dream compared to the previous ten years in Kenya where his father was reviled because of his relationship with Rafiki. Robert was now completing his articles with a firm of solicitors in London: Barnes, Ramsey and Hawthorne. Since he left Oxford he had found a regular place in the England rugby side. Robert's aunt (his dead mother's sister) Louise and her wealthy husband Giles had provided a home for Robert in their large luxurious house in Belgravia, where Robert stayed when he was down from Oxford. The Dingley-Ferris's also had an estate in Oxfordshire, Dingley Hall, and Robert and some of his friends were guests there on a regular basis. Robert especially enjoyed the fox hunting in which he excelled due to his riding skill learned on Naseby.

After Oxford Robert had spent a year living with his aunt and uncle but he had recently moved out into a small bed-sitter in Egerton Gardens in Knightsbridge. The contrast between the bed-sitter and the Dingley-Ferris mansion in Belgravia was marked. The bed-sitter had a washbasin and a small gas ring, apart from the bed and the yellowish, faded, illfitting curtains, which let the light in from the street. The toilet and bathing facilities were shared; a couple of inches of hot water in the bath required a shilling in the gas meter. Still, Robert was happy enough. He was a constant visitor at the Belgravia mansion where he was a more than welcome guest at the frequent dinner parties held there. Robert met many of the high and mighty in the English establishment there and his membership of the England rugby side gave him credibility, which he used to the full. Robert was pleased with the independence that his little bed-sitter created; it meant that he was able to bring the occasional girlfriend home, away from the prying eyes of his aunt Louise. Louise knew him very well; she had stayed with them on the farm in Kenya for a year after her sister Jenny's death.

Robert had recently met Jessica Hawthorne, after one of his rugby club matches in London. Robert only found out after their third date that Jessica was the daughter of one of the partners in the firm he worked for. Jessica, for her part, was relieved that Robert liked her for herself and not because her father was a partner in a leading firm of solicitors. Quite early on in their relationship Robert and Jessica had been invited to Dingley Hall for the weekend. There was to be a meet of the local hunt on the Saturday morning and then Robert had been told of a dinner party on the Saturday night.

Jessica was used to a very solid, middle class lifestyle but was quite unprepared for the Belgravia mansion and the Bentley. Dingley Hall was quite the most exquisite place she had ever seen. Giles drove the Bentley through a set of wrought iron gates onto a bricked driveway. The double storey house was covered in ivy. From what she could see there were several living rooms on the ground floor, all beautifully furnished. Robert carried her suitcase up to a bedroom on the first floor. Louise had firmly put Robert in the only bedroom on the ground floor.

Dinner that evening was very charming, with Giles telling Jessica the history of the house and what he had done to have it restored to its full glory. By ten o'clock they had all decided to call it a night, as they needed to be up before six to be ready for the hunt the next morning. Robert, sitting on his bed was wondering how soon he could creep up the stairs when the door quietly opened and Jessica, dressed in only a very flimsy nightgown flew into his arms.

"What kept you?" she pretended to pout.

"I was just waiting for the coast to be clear and then I was on my way up."

They had only recently become lovers and Robert was very pleasantly surprised by her forthrightness. They made the most passionate love and just as the early dawn light crept into the room, Jessica left Robert's warm bed and returned to her room.

Robert dressed and went out to the stables. His own horse, a large thoroughbred, was already saddled up. The horse snickered at him, and Robert gave him the carrot that he had brought along specially. Robert then went to see Jessica's horse, which the stable hand was busy attending to.

"Good morning, Fred," said Robert.

"Morning, Mr. Robert."

"How's this horse?" asked Robert.

"She's all right; I've had her out a couple of times myself. Bit nervous at times, but she should be O.K. I understand the lady who is riding her is reasonably experienced."

"Yes, I think so," said Robert non-committally. He could see he'd better keep his eye on the situation.

The morning started off without incident and soon the hunt was in full flow. Robert could see that Jessica was handling the horse well, especially over the jumps. He stopped worrying and started admiring Jessica's pretty behind as she took the horse through its paces. The hunt had gone through a good three mile chase, the fox had been caught and killed by the hounds and everyone was just catching their breath when suddenly Jessica's horse went berserk; it probably caught a whiff of the smell of blood. The horse bolted with Jessica frantically tugging at the reins trying to stop it. Robert instantly saw what was happening and within seconds he had his horse going at full gallop. Jessica's horse was headed for nearby trees; Robert pressed his horse for further effort. "Dear God, this is going to be tight," he thought. About twenty yards from a large overhanging bough Robert caught up with Jessica; they didn't have time to slow down so he rode up alongside her and jumped from his horse to hers. He only just had time to push her down and duck himself when the branch swept over the top of them both. He was able to grab the reins of Jessica's bolting horse and quietly brought the animal under control. They stopped; Robert still had the reins of his own horse over his arm. Jessica was as white as a sheet, and was shaking like a leaf.

"She…… she just took off," she stammered.

"I saw that, it may have been the smell of blood," said Robert.

Robert kissed her gently on the cheek.

"It's okay," he said, "its okay now. If you can bear it it's better to stay on the horse, otherwise you may lose your nerve altogether."

Robert manoeuvred the horses together again and then quietly slipped back onto his horse.

"How do you do that?" asked Jessica nervously.

"Practice, years of practice," Robert smiled. He was still holding the reins of Jessica's horse.

The rest of the hunt trotted up.

"Everything O.K?" asked Giles anxiously.

"Yes, now it is," said Robert," That horse seems a bit skittish, I'll take her out in the morning to see what the problem is."

Louise came up. Robert looked at her. Years earlier she had tried to stop Robert and his brother John from playing dangerous games from the backs of horses at Naseby.

"See, all that practice eventually had some value," Robert smiled

Louise nodded and smiled.

They went back to the stables. On the way home Robert made Jessica take one or two of the smaller jumps, which she did nervously.

Robert described the incident to the stable hand.

"I'll take the damned horse out in the morning on her own," he told him.

After a shower and a late lunch, Robert went up to Jessica's room. He found her fast asleep in bed. He left her and went looking for Giles, who he found in the library.

"Where did you learn to ride like that?" asked Giles.

"On the farm. Mum started us off, but John and I did all sorts of crazy things with those horses. We had to entertain ourselves; as you know we weren't welcome elsewhere in the district much," said Robert.

Giles did not want to get into that discussion.

"Saved her life probably," then he changed the subject. "Look, I want to talk to you about tonight. We have rather a special guest coming."

Robert raised his eyebrows. He expected some member of the British Government.

"You know about the ANC?" Giles asked.

"Of course, the South African Government has just imprisoned Nelson Mandela and a number of people at a big trial there. Rivonia trial I think it's called."

Robert always tried to keep up with what was going on in Africa.

Giles nodded.

"I am responsible for investments all over the world including some substantial ones in South Africa," he said. "Change is inevitable there, so

I keep in touch with both sides- that is, the current government and the future government."

Robert raised his eyebrows.

"We have one guest coming tonight. He is a senior member of the ANC; I'll call him Trevor Mdantsane.

"I have to be very careful, I'm sure the ANC realise that I am talking to the South African government but at this stage the South African government have not been told I'm talking to the ANC."

"What's the objective, what are you trying to do?" asked Robert.

"At some stage both sides are going to have to talk. I may be able to act as a go-between and indeed provide a place like this where they can talk without people outside being any the wiser."

"And Louise?" asked Robert.

"She understands; with her South African background and her sojourn in Kenya with you, I think she understands," said Giles.

"What do you want from me?" asked Robert.

"Just listen."

"And Jessica?" asked Robert.

"I was going to ask you to send her back to London, but I've changed my mind after this morning," responded Giles.

Robert raised one eyebrow.

"You'll marry her, so she'd better understand from the beginning what she's letting herself in for," said Giles, looking at Robert intently.

"Well, that's far from settled," said Robert defensively," and I'm really trying to shake the dust of Africa off my boots forever."

Giles laughed.

"You'll never really shake the dust of Africa off your boots; none of us ever do, especially with your background. I've said my piece on Jessica—anyway, all I ask you to do is to listen. The settlement in South African may take a long time and someone of your age could be invaluable in a few years' time when I'm too senile to help." Giles smiled.

Robert was amazed. His vision of life at present was to play rugby for England, pass all his legal exams and to see as much of Jessica as he could. Giles was opening up a whole new vista and he wasn't at all certain that he wanted any of it.

"Mr. Mdantsane is here," said Giles. "Dinner is at eight."

Robert went to Jessica's room just before six. He tapped lightly on the door. "Come in."

Jessica was sitting in front of the mirror brushing her hair. She was stark naked.

"I hoped it might be you," she said. "I half expected you to come and see me earlier."

"I did, but you were fast asleep, so I let you be," said Robert; he kissed her.

"Make love to me, now," she whispered urgently.

Robert was out of his clothes in five seconds flat. They made the most delicious love.

"Thank you, thank you for this morning," said Jessica afterwards. "How can I thank you enough?"

"Shush," said Robert. "Don't talk about it. I hope I would have done the same for anyone. The fact that it was you makes it all the more special though." He kissed her.

Robert then went on to explain the dinner guest. Jessica knew little about the ANC and the Rivonia trial; she was intrigued.

Robert and Jessica made their way to the small lounge on the ground floor. Giles was already there, talking to a very well dressed, handsome black man.

Giles made the introductions.

"Mr. Mdantsane, this is Jessica Hawthorne and my nephew Robert Lawrence."

They all shook hands.

"I know of your father, Peter Lawrence," said Mdantsane. "A very courageous man, very courageous."

Then it all flooded back to Robert. He'd kept that part of his life frozen and compartmentalised away from him for the past four years or more. He'd only been back to Kenya once for a short visit. The presence of this black man opened it all up again. In spite of himself, he realised how he missed it, the wide open spaces, the cheerful people, the sun, the wild animals; his memories tempered as always by the hell he'd been through.

Louise came in looking poised and elegant. She greeted their visitor in what Robert assumed was Xhosa. The exchange was fluent.

"I didn't know you spoke Xhosa," said Robert.

"There are many things you don't know about me," said Louise smilingly." Our cook in Jo'burg taught me; she gave me lessons every day."

The men were dressed in suits and Louise and Jessica wore elegant evening dresses; Giles had obviously decided to make it a formal occasion.

The conversation for a while centred around language; Robert was able to show off his prowess in Kikuyu, some Kamba, and Swahili. Both he and their visitor were able to achieve common ground by comparing various aspects of the various languages they spoke. They were pleased to find many words with similarities.

"Of course the root of the language is the same, the Bantu, who were part of a migration southwards for hundreds of years. The Xhosa are the southernmost Bantu tribe and they eventually made it to the Great Fish River, only to be rudely interrupted by the white migration north in the past three hundred or so years." Mr. Mdantsane laughed at his own humour.

They went in to dinner.

During the dinner Mr. Mdantsane gave them all a brief history of the ANC, mainly for the benefit of Robert and Jessica.

"It was formed in 1912, soon after the British came to an accommodation with the Afrikaners in the Act of Union in 1910. This brought the Union of South Africa into being and completely disenfranchised the blacks."

"Until very recently the ANC was dedicated to non-violence, but this really meant the South African government was able to ignore us altogether. Since 1948 the Nationalists have introduced all these apartheid laws, which entrench discrimination against the black majority. So now we have an active military operation, 'Umkonto we Sizwe', started by Mandela."

Jessica was spellbound; as for Robert, he'd heard much of it before and the tone was familiar. He wondered what on earth the colonists had tried to do in Africa, except perhaps create a little piece of Europe there.

Mdantsane continued.

"Maybe when the white people came into the interior in South Africa they found an empty land. This was because Shaka, the great Zulu king, had devastated most of east and central South Africa in a process known as the mfecane, in creating the Zulu nation. The situation is very different now. Although the blacks are about seventy-five percent of the population, they have only thirteen percent of the land. We are patient; time is on our side, but we know that with ongoing population increases the ratio will get even better or worse depending on your perspective."

Jessica's knowledge of South African history was very sketchy and was confined to a couple of battles in the Boer War, namely Ladysmith and Mafikeng and the great British victory at Rorke's Drift over the Zulus. She briefly mentioned this.

Mr. Mdantsane looked at her.

"Have you ever heard of the battle of Isandlwana where the British side lost more than twelve hundred men?"

"No," said Jessica nervously.

"It was the day before Rorke's Drift and the British forces were caught in the open. Anyway, Rorke's Drift could have gone the other way. The British had run out of ammunition- one more Zulu attack and it would have been all over."

"Oh," she said quietly.

Giles nodded at Mdantsane as if to say carry on.

"Back to modern times. Interracial marriage, and indeed any kind of sexual liaison between races, is now a criminal offence in South Africa; whites may not mix with blacks, coloureds or Indians. Supposedly every member of the population is classified, but there have been some unfortunate consequences of this, where supposed white families have produced a "throwback" or a child that looks black or coloured. The child then gets reclassified and relegated to another category."

"Does this mean that you, Robert, would be white and your brother Kamau would be classified differently?" Jessica asked Robert.

"Yes, I suppose so," was the answer.

Mdantsane's curiosity was immediately aroused.

"Who is Kamau?" he asked.

"Kamau is my half-brother," answered Robert. "My mother was killed in a horse riding accident and, to cut a long story short, my father and Rafiki, who I'm sure you have heard of, had a son; they are now married."

"I didn't know about the son, but the rest of the story is well known." Mdantsane had noticed an edge to Robert's narration; maybe that was worth following up at some stage.

"Also all black people have to carry passes allowing them into the main urban centres,' Mdantsane continued. If they don't have a pass or if they lose their job they can be rounded up by the police and sent back to their homeland. In many cases the people in the towns and cities have never seen their supposed homeland; their passes, however, always assume residence in some tribal area or other."

"Who checks the passes?" asked Jessica.

'The police: on the streets, on buses; they even raid at night." Mdantsane became quite heated.

"Sounds like Nazi Germany," said Jessica quietly.

"Maybe the same," Mdantsane acknowledged.

"The black people are not allowed to perform certain skilled jobs, for example laying facebricks in a house is a job reserved for whites, coloureds, or Indians. No blacks may do such a job and whites cannot be supervised by a black under any circumstances.

"You mean black people are not allowed to work as bricklayers, carpenters and things like that?" asked Jessica.

"No, not in white areas," was the answer.

"White areas?" Jessica raised her eyebrows.

"The whole of South Africa is divided into areas: certain areas for whites, certain areas for blacks, certain areas for coloureds, certain areas for Indians. If you want to buy a house in a white area you have to prove you are white," answered Mdantsane.

"There must be a huge bureaucracy administering all this; it sounds just like Communist Russia," said Jessica.

"More than one third of all white jobs are with the Government and quasi-government operations like railways and electricity supply."

"Sounds just like the communist system," said Jessica firmly.

Robert just looked on. He thought he'd escaped all involvement in Africa but a sense of creeping inevitability came over him. Much of what Mdantsane had to say had applied in Kenya; it just seemed that the South Africans had institutionalised the whole process of keeping the blacks in their place.

"The religious justification for the whole apartheid system is contained in the Old Testament and I quote from the book of Genesis Chapter nine verse 25, "And he said, Cursed be Canaan; a servant of servants shall he be unto his brethren." Canaan being interpreted as representing black people. This is in turn is supposed to mean that black people in South Africa will always be servants of the whites and that it is God's will that this is so. The educational system is designed to achieve this end; there are separate educational facilities for each race from primary school to university and the majority of the resources go to the whites, with the blacks getting the fewest resources."

"The South African government is controlled by the Dutch people there, isn't it? What about the attitude of the English settlers?" asked Jessica.

"Afrikaans, not Dutch," corrected Mdantsane, "The English severed the Dutch connection when they took over the Cape in 1804; the Afrikaans language is loosely based on Dutch, though. The English provide some opposition but they don't really have the will or the power to be effective. The survival of their culture does not depend on the eventual outcome of the political evolution in South Africa. The English there will have to go along with whatever is decided between the Afrikaner Nationalists and the African Nationalists represented by the ANC."

"Only the ANC?" Jessica asked.

"Probably; we are the only party which has really attempted to include all races in our constitution, which in any event makes us illegal."

"Illegal?" asked Jessica.

"Yes, we are a banned organisation. Membership of the ANC is illegal, as is the organisation."

"What about free speech?" Jessica was horrified.

Mdantsane laughed.

"What about it? There are many laws that prevent free speech. For example, anyone can be imprisoned for ninety days without trial and after that they can be banned, which effectively means house arrest. They can't attend gatherings of more than two people, that is, themselves and one other and so on. When a loophole is found in one law it is quickly plugged and more draconian laws applied. Torture by the security police is commonplace. Also newspapers can be and are regularly censored."

Everyone round the table was silent, absorbed in their own thoughts.

Giles had remained virtually silent during the whole discussion.

"You see, the situation there can't really last, but there must be dialogue to resolve it and this business in Rhodesia really does not help, with Mr. Smith now declaring independence unilaterately," said Giles diplomatically.

"Why have we been told all this?" asked Jessica. "I think it's awful but what can I do? What can anyone do- what are you doing, Giles? You seem to have some influence," she went on heatedly.

Giles looked at Mdantsane.

"As Mr. Mdantsane knows very well, I talk to both sides. I frequently have ANC people here and just as often I have people from the South African government here as well. My fervent wish is that one day they will both be here together, it may take many years though; that is why you and Robert are here tonight," answered Giles.

"From what I've heard I'm not sure that I want to hear the other side of the story. Is there another side of the story?" asked Jessica.

Giles laughed and said, "Oh yes, there certainly is."

"History is of course on the side of the majority though," Mdantsane continued. "We, the blacks, will eventually gain power in South Africa. The nature of the black struggle in Africa is that time is on our side. Whether we succeed in ten years or fifty years actually does not matter, we will in the end succeed."

"Fifty years! How many people will be killed if it lasts fifty years?" asked Robert.

Mdantsane shrugged.

"Many people both black and white will die in this conflict."

Louise had remained silent throughout the meal. She had really concentrated on making certain everything was perfect.

Now Robert turned to her.

"What's your position on all this Louise?" he asked. "You were brought up in Jo'burg. You spent a year with us on the farm in Kenya; what do you think?"

Louise looked at him thoughtfully.

"I always felt that the blacks in South Africa were hard done by, although our own servants were well treated; we even paid for our cook's son to go to Fort Hare University. In the days before the Nationalists I suppose the expectation was that black political aspirations could somehow be accommodated through evolution. I don't really think anyone had thought about it too much though. The apartheid policies of the Nationalists, with them really trying to put the clock back and entrench white supremacy has really brought it all to a head. I hope there is some peaceful way of bringing about a black majority government in South Africa; the longer this goes on the more likely there is to be a bloodbath. But the march of history is inevitable; we have the changes that have occurred in East Africa as an indication. Maybe the same thing will happen throughout Africa- in fact I'm sure it will."

It was late when they all went to bed. Without even thinking Robert accompanied Jessica to her room, where he spent the night.

Robert stirred early in the morning.

"Where are you going?" asked a sleepy Jessica.

"I'm going to find out what the matter is with that horse you rode yesterday."

"Horse? You're worried about a bloody horse when all those people are dying and being tortured in South Africa?"

"I'm going to worry about the horse and South Africa. I'll see you at breakfast."

Robert went out to the stables; he gave his own horse a carrot and then went and saddled up Jessica's mount of the previous day. He trotted the mare out of the stable yard amid the protests of his own horse, which almost battered down his stable door in order to join him. Just as they were leaving the yard, while Robert was adjusting his stirrups, the horse gave three large bucks and Robert, to his fury, found himself sitting down on the stony yard; luckily he still had hold of the reins. The horse reared up and backed off, obviously expecting to be hit. Robert just got up quietly and after five minutes of coaxing managed to calm the horse down; he gave her a carrot. This time he was more cautious and he made all the adjustments to the stirrups before he remounted. The ride went quietly enough; Robert took the mare over several jumps and again the horse seemed to relax. Robert then decided to gallop the animal along a flat stretch of farm track. They were doing splendidly when the horse unexpectedly shied at a puddle. Robert ended up in the puddle. He was really glad there were no witnesses. He must be losing his grip, he thought. He scrambled back on the horse and quietly rode back to the stable.

Fred, the stable hand couldn't help laughing when he saw Robert covered in mud.

"Mean one, that," said Fred.

"Is this what she did to you?" Robert enquired.

"Much the same. I think she's just mean spirited," said Fred.

Robert left the horse with Fred and went back to the house.

He went into the dining room. Jessica and Mdantsane were deep in conversation, which stopped abruptly when Robert walked in. Giles and Louise were nowhere to be seen.

Jessica burst out laughing.

"Just look at you, did you fall off then?" she came over and hugged Robert.

Mdantsane looked at Robert warily.

"Well, I presume that you are going to clean up before you grace us with your presence," Jessica teased him. "Mr. Mdantsane and I were just continuing our conversation of last night; do you realise," she said," that black people are still being forceibly removed from land they have occupied for generations to make way for white farmers?"

"Yes I did know that," said Robert evenly.

He wondered what Mdantsane was up to.

"I'll be a few minutes," he said.

"Don't rush, I'm having a fascinating conversation," said Jessica gaily.

When Robert returned half an hour later Mdantsane was nowhere to be seen. Jessica was sitting there quietly finishing off her coffee. He kissed her.

"Where's our guest?" asked Robert.

"Oh, the car came for him; he's gone back to London."

"And Giles and Louise?"

"Giles came to see him off; I haven't seen Louise. I told him you'd fallen off that horse," Jessica teased him.

"And what did Mdantsane tell you?" Robert asked after he had helped himself to eggs and bacon from the hot tray.

"Much the same as last night. He talked about a childhood on a white owned farm near East London- how the farmer used to beat his labour including his own father; about his struggle to get an education, first in farm school then high school and eventually Fort Hare," Jessica rambled on."Robert, we've got to do something. I can't believe what I've heard in the last two days. Was it like this in Kenya?" she asked.

"Not on Naseby, but in many other places, probably yes. Not that my father was perfect. The living conditions of the farm labour were quite primitive," he answered.

He finished his eggs and put his hand on hers.

"Just listen to me for a minute, please," he looked at her. "There is much injustice in the world including South Africa. You don't really understand the situation; before you get in too deep please try to see all sides of the story. The South African government is totally ruthless, because they see this as a fight for survival. The ANC is also ruthless. If you get involved they will use you while it suits them and then you will be left to fend for yourself. Please, please try to understand the situation; it is very, very dangerous.'

She tried to withdraw her hand.

"We've got to do something for those poor people," she said quietly.

"Don't patronise them. They will run their own show and one more or one less white supporter will make no difference in the end. In many ways they prefer to deal with the hard line Afrikaners, at least they know where they stand. With the so-called liberal whites, whilst they sympathise with the blacks' cause they still feel they have to be in charge somehow; that they should be in a position of privilege or power even in an organisation run by blacks. It pisses the blacks off mightily," Robert continued.

"Tell me, what has Mdantsane said to you? Let me guess- has he asked you to act as a courier for messages to South Africa?"

Jessica looked sheepish.

"Yes, he mentioned something like that."

Robert nodded.

"Once you're in you will not escape. It's not something you can toy with and you will not necessarily be safe in England. The South Africans are bound to have agents all over the place. Please, please listen to me and be careful."

Jessica stood up.

"I must go and pack. Come and talk to me if you like."

Robert followed Jessica to her room and sat in a chair and watched her pack.

"My people have given a lot to Africa and I suppose in many ways have gained a lot," he started.

Jessica continued packing.

"The last few years have been a magic time for me. I really thought I was beginning to get away from it all. Talking to Mdantsane has brought it all back. You know my father built a productive farm there out of nothing, only to have it taken away from him. He now has a very senior position in the Kenya government but I really wonder how he fits in. He really understands the local culture, he is married to a Kikuyu, he speaks several of their languages, but he is not and never will be one of them. The same applies to me. I speak several African languages, my playmates from the age of about ten were all blacks, apart from John, but I am not of Africa, I feel much more at home here."

Jessica flushed. She said heatedly, "I'm not surprised you feel at home here with all this wealth and privilege surrounding you. There is a huge injustice occurring before your very eyes. You of all people are in a unique position to do something about it with your background and language skills and all you can think of doing is to cocoon yourself in the security of first world privilege. I'm damn well going to do something about it; you I am sure will make your own choice."

Robert's shoulders slumped.

"Maybe you're right, maybe I can't escape. Giles certainly thinks that I should be involved. We would not have been asked here last night if that wasn't so. Please don't rush into anything. If you really want to be of help and to be useful, you need to understand the situation better than you do now. I can at least help you do that," Robert pleaded.

"Maybe you can," she said evenly.

Robert put his arms around her and kissed her quietly. She melted into his safe strong arms.

"What's the matter?" he asked, kindly.

"Nothing. I don't know," was the quiet answer.

"Talk to me for God's sake. Tell me what you're thinking."

"I don't really know what I'm thinking, I do know that the last twenty four hours will change my life, that's all," said Jessica.

"Make love to me," said Robert.

He undressed her quickly and flung off his own clothes. He made the quietest and most sensitive love to her and he pleased her greatly.

Robert went to sleep with Jessica wrapped up in his arms. She looked at him intently. Robert was everything she had ever dreamed of. He was handsome, talented, and successful and was certain to do well in England with his ability and connections. He was also considerate and brave; he had probably saved her life. But was this all there was to life- marriage to Robert, a house, children, schools? Although she was also completing her legal studies she knew that his career would prevail while she looked after all the domestic issues. This African thing was her chance to do something different, to get out of the rut, not to play second fiddle to some man, and dedicate her life to his success just like her own mother had. She turned it over and over in her head. Was she being selfish? Were the injustices in South Africa anything to do with her? Was she thinking of getting involved just to serve her own needs? Did she really understand what was happening in South Africa? Could Robert help her, would he understand or would he just try to protect her? Damn, life was cruel, she thought. Twenty-four hours ago she had been deeply in love and thought she had found her soulmate; now she wasn't so sure.

The lovers missed lunch and the drive back to London was rather quiet, with everyone absorbed in their own thoughts. They dropped Jessica off first, and she thanked Giles and Louise for the weekend. Robert helped her with her suitcase, and carried it up to her flat.

At the door she kissed him quietly and said, "I've had a wonderful week-end, thank you so much; call me tomorrow."

"Can't I come in?" asked Robert.

"Not tonight. Giles and Louise are waiting in the car for you," she responded.

The door closed quietly and Robert went thoughtfully out to the waiting car.

"Everything all right?" asked Louise.

"Yes, I think so," said Robert.

"She seemed rather absorbed in her own thoughts on the way back," said Louise.

"That man last night and the whole business in South Africa have upset her," said Robert.

"She probably needs a bit of time and space to sort herself out. She's only young and to see her life more or less taken care of by marriage to you, Robert, is perhaps rather daunting," said Louise shrewdly. "Last night's conversation probably opened her eyes to other worlds as well. I think I understand her position perfectly and what she is going through."

Before they dropped Robert off Louise said to him, "Don't push her or you'll lose her, let her come to you on her own terms. I will call her in a few days and make sure she knows she can come to me anytime if she wants a shoulder to cry on; she may need one."

Halfway through the week Robert had been called in to his principal Mr. Hawthorne's office.

"I understand I have to thank you for saving my daughter's life," he said pleasantly.

Robert looked uncomfortable.

"That's a bit of an exaggeration- I merely prevented an accident," he replied.

"From what I hear there's more to it than that, anyway from myself and my wife, thank you."

Robert was about to go.

"There's one other thing. You never mentioned your relationship with Dingley-Ferris before," Hawthorne looked enquiringly at Robert.

"No, it didn't seem pertinent. I wanted to be accepted on my own merits," said Robert.

"Yes, of course," said Hawthorne. "You do realise of course that with such a person as a client the road to a partnership could be rather swift."

"Thank you for saying that; I expect Giles has a battery of legal firms all vying for a piece of the action. I've never discussed it with him," said Robert.

Hawthorne then changed the subject.

Trevor Mdandtsane was an extremely shrewd and ruthless operator. He was completely dedicated to the ANC and to achieving majority rule in his country. It was part of his job to find people to courier messages to South Africa but he was also aware of the wider issues. The Dingley-Ferris connection was vital to the ANC, who knew perfectly well that they could never win a full-scale military conflict with the South African Government. He did not want to upset Giles in any way but that Hawthorne woman had greatly intrigued him. She had after all given him both her home and office telephone numbers. On the way back to the capital he decided to play the Jessica card for all it was worth. He phoned her at work on the Monday following the weekend at Dingley Hall.

"Jessica Hawthorne." Jessica was expecting Robert to call.

"Ah, Jessica, this is Trevor here, how are you?"

"Fine, thankyou," she said with reservation.

"I just wondered if you wanted to follow up on our conversation over the weekend. As you know we need all the help we can get, especially from people with your background," he said charmingly and thought, "a little flattery will get you everything you want."

"Oh, what did you have in mind?" asked Jessica.

"Well, I've had a chance to dicuss the situation with my colleagues and we can take the possibility of our cooperation at least one step further," said Trevor guardedly. This was complete fabrication; nobody within the organisation had any knowledge of the identity of any of the couriers except Mdantsane himself.

"Yes?" she said questioningly.

"Well, if we could meet somewhere for, say, an hour, I can tell you what we have in mind and then we'll take it from there," said Trevor.

"We could meet in a pub somewhere," suggested Jessica.

"It needs to be more private than that," said Mdantsane.

"A restaurant then?" enquired Jessica.

"Still too public," was the response. "And you should not come here; I think it's under observation from South African security.

"Well you could come to my flat," said Jessica hesitatingly.

"Will we be alone?" asked Mdantsane. "I do not want any witnesses."

"What about Robert?" asked Jessica.

Mdantsane hesitated.

"I think this should just be between you and me," he said eventually.

"O.K." Jessica then gave him the address. "If you come at five this evening, my flatmates do not get home before six thirty, that should give us more than enough time," said Jessica finally. She didn't want him getting any ideas.

Trevor Mdantsane realised he had been finessed. He was hoping for rather more from the relationship than just arranging a courier but he realised that any further discussion on the subject would create unwanted suspicion.

Jessica arrived home at about fifteen minutes before the appointed time and quickly tidied up the modest second floor flat that she shared with two other girls. She took care that she looked smart in her business suit and she put some fresh lipstick on. At five minutes to five there was a knock on the door.

"He's early," she thought and she went to the door and opened it.

Jessica stood stock still for about five seconds, the blood drained from her face.

"What's the matter, seen a ghost or something?" asked Robert disarmingly. "Can I come in for a minute?"

"Yes, just a minute, I need to go out again before five," she answered.

"The office told me you had gone home early so I just popped in on my way to rugby training," said Robert as he pecked her on the cheek.

Jessica tried to gather her thoughts. If Mdantsane arrived now he would think she had set him up. Also, what would Robert think? Her only hope was to get rid of Robert quickly.

"You'll have to hurry, I've got to go," she snapped uncharacteristically.

"O.K, O.K. I just wondered if I could pick you up after practice, say at eight thirty. We could then have a quick bite round the corner," said Robert. He'd never seen her looking so flustered.

"Yes, O.K, see you at 8:30 then," she said hurriedly.

Robert tried to put his arms around her. She skipped out of his grasp and said, "I'll come out with you. I have an appointment with the doctor at five thirty."

"O.K, O.K, let's go then," answered Robert. Jessica collected her handbag and keys and they went out together. She prayed that Mdantsane would be late.

Robert had parked his car outside the flat.

"Can I drop you off anywhere?" he asked.

"No, no," she said hurriedly. "It's just around the corner."

He pecked her on the cheek, climbed in the car and slowly drove off.

Robert was non-plussed. Jessica was not exactly hostile but she clearly wanted him out of the way. He could not understand why. Then just in front of him one of him one of London's black cabs stopped and who should step out onto the pavement but Trevor Mdantsane. Now it started to make sense. Robert did a U-turn when there was a gap in the traffic and parked unobtrusively in a place where he could keep the main door of the building housing Jessica's flat under observation. Just as he had stopped the car he saw Jessica hurry back down the street, look guitily around her before she made her way into the building. A few minutes later he saw Mdantsane make his way up the street, carefully looking at the numbers. He also looked round and then disappeared into the same entrance.

"Now I understand," he said to himself.

Jessica just had time to calm herself down when there was a firm knock on the door of the flat. This time it was her expected visitor, the tall, suave, urbane and goodlooking Trevor Mdantsane.

She had had the presence of mind to boil the kettle.

"Would you like some tea, or perhaps a beer?" she offered.

"Tea is fine, thank you," said Trevor pleasantly.

Jessica poured the tea and looked at her visitor expectantly.

"Do you have a current passport?" asked Trevor.

"Yes, certainly, I only had it renewed a year or so ago," said Jessica.

"Look, an urgent job has come up; I need you to go to Johannesburg within a few days to deliver something. Do you think that you can do that?"

"I'll have to arrange leave from my firm but what do you mean by a few days?" she asked.

"Well, what I had in mind was you catching the BOAC flight from Heathrow on Friday night and returning here on Monday or Tuesday next week. You would have to deliver a package and bring one back," said Trevor.

Jessica was surprised to say the least. She had expected a long discourse on the aims and objectives of the ANC.

"You could call in sick," said Trevor helpfully.

"Don't worry about that," Jessica laughed. "I think I can manage a few days off."

Trevor then produced an economy class airticket, a very thick envelope and fifty rand in cash.

"I'm sorry we don't have much money for expenses," he said apologetically.

"That's O.K," said Jessica.

"When you arrive in Johannesburg I suggest that you book into one of the inexpensive hotels in the Hillbrow area. This key is for a postbox in the Braamfontein post office, which is not far away. Leave the package in there after four in the afternoon on Saturday. Check the postbox again on Monday morning. If there is a package there, collect it and return on the Tuesday morning flight. If there is no package, check again on Tuesday and in any event return on the Wednesday flight."

He gave her a key in an envelope with a number on it.

"That's the box number in the Braamfontein post office," he explained, "Any questions."

"No, not really, not at this stage," Jessica stammered.

"O.K, I'll be on my way then," said Trevor.

"There is just one thing," said Jessica.

"What's that?"

"What do I tell people—Robert for example? I can't just fob him off with any old story," she said.

"Tell people as little as possible," he answered.

"I'll probably have to tell Robert the truth," she said quietly.

Mdantsane said nothing. He got up, shook Jessica by the hand and went to the door.

"Best of luck," he said. "Call on this number when you return (he handed her a card) from a public phone since the number is probably bugged. When I answer just say 'I'll see you at Knightsbridge tomorrow.' I'll then call you at the office the following day. Got that?"

Jessica nodded.

He left.

Jessica was stunned with the speed of developments. The previous Friday she had barely heard of the ANC, now she was committed to acting as a courier for them. She was exhilarated and frightened. She was still sitting there twenty minutes later when her two flatmates came bustling in.

"You're early," said Jill. "My, you do look pensive, what have you been up to then? Tell us about the weekend, I'm dying to hear all the details. Robert Lawrence must be one of the must eligible bachelors in London and his uncle is certainly at the top end of the money business," she prattled on.

So Jessica told them about the weekend, about Dingley Hall and the hunt and how Robert had rescued her and about the Saturday night dinner, although she left out most of the details relating to the ANC. She just told them there was a black man there from some exotic African country. When she had finished Chloe said to her, "I'd be over the moon if any of that had happened to me; you seem a little flat and slightly depressed. Did anything else happen? Was Robert nice to you? Is something the matter?"

"No, it couldn't have been nicer; Robert and his aunt and uncle were charming," said Jessica. "It's just that—," she hesitated.

"Just what?" they chorused.

"Well, is this all life is about? I'm sure that Robert is in love with me, he seems to expect to marry me in due course although he hasn't actually proposed. But is that all there is to life… I don't know. Me, becoming Mrs. Robert Lawrence. I suppose I will have a few kids… is that all there is to life?" She stopped.

"Jessica Hawthorne," said Jill, "You are stark raving bonkers. If you scoured the streets of London it would be hard to find a better man than Robert. You don't know when you are well off." She smiled knowingly. "Frankly speaking, he can come and put his shoes under my bed any day of the week, you just give the word."

Jessica laughed. She liked the uncomplicated way her friend approached life.

"But I need more of my own personal identity; I'm afraid of being all caught up with being Mrs. Robert Lawrence," Jessica continued, "I need to do something for myself, for the world, for humanity."

"Well I've told you my opinion," responded Jill. "You should take the breaks where you can get them. You may well go and attempt all your high-minded ideas and by the time that's done, Robert will have found other fish to fry and you'll end up with some half-baked retread. You don't know when you are well off."

They all laughed.

"Dinner anyone?" asked Chloe.

"Robert is coming later, so leave me out," said Jessica. "By the way, I will be away for a few days from Friday; I hope to be back by Wednesday."

"Business?" asked Jill. Jessica had been away for a day or two from time to time in the past on behalf of her firm.

"Sort of," replied Jessica evasively.

"Where are you going?" asked Jill.

She hesitated and almost said 'Scotland'.

"South Africa," she said.

"South Africa?" chorused the other two.

"Wow, how exciting," said Chloe. "Now you are a real jetsetter."

"It's not very important," said Jessica. "They just need a responsible person to deliver something."

"Is Robert going with you?" asked Jill.

"No, I haven't yet told him, anyway he's playing rugby over the weekend," replied Jessica.

"You are going to tell him aren't you?" It was more of a statement than a question from Jill.

"Probably," answered Jessica.

Jessica went to her room and started to think about what she should take with her. She guessed the weather would be starting to warm up since the seasons were the opposite of the northern hemisphere.

Just after half past eight there was a knock on the door and Jill let Robert in. Robert had excelled at rugby practice and he had partly succeeded in putting out of his mind the fact that Jessica had deceived him. He hoped she would tell him what was going on. If she wasn't prepared to be open with him he would have to recognise that the relationship was not destined to flourish, and he would focus his attention on his rugby and legal studies.

They went to a small unpretentious restaurant nearby and while Robert tucked into a large plate of spaghetti, Jessica picked at a salad. Robert chatted on about his rugby and the prospects for the weekend game. Jessica responded appropriately but she was not her usual bright, sparkling self.

"Anything wrong?" asked Robert.

"No," she replied. Now was her chance, she thought; why didn't she just tell him everything? She couldn't; she knew that he would try to dissuade her and she couldn't face that at the moment, so she stayed silent. Robert held her hand and looked her in the eye.

"Do you believe that in a relationship such as ours we should try to be as open and honest with each other as possible?" he asked.

"I suppose so, but we don't own each other, do we?" Jessica responded defensively.

"I sort of understand what you are going through," said Robert. "Unfortunately just as I was driving off this evening, I saw Trevor Mdantsane arrive in a cab. He went into your building just as you did; the doctor's appointment was a fabrication. Can't you tell me what's going on?" he asked kindly.

Jessica's stomach went into a hard tight knot, but then almost involuntarily she blurted: "You are not to spy on me, Robert, you do not own me. I can and will lead my own life."

Robert said quietly, "I had no intention of spying on you, Jessica, you know that's unfair. I almost ran Trevor over and it was clear that he was going to see you. I thought we had something special going on between us. Maybe I was mistaken. I'll certainly let you lead your own life, as you put it. Until you can fully trust me, I'll leave you alone."

He still had hold of her hand and he said, "I don't pretend to understand all this. I still love you Jessica, I'm sorry. Come, let me take you home."

He paid the bill and left. Robert pecked her on the cheek and left her at the door of the building housing her flat. With a heavy heart he climbed into his car and drove off.

Jessica stumbled up the stairs, let herself into the flat and promptly burst into tears. Her friends fussed around her for a few minutes. She then told tem the whole story about the weekend, Trevor Mdantsane, the ANC and what she was going to do in South Africa. She eventually climbed into bed and cried herself to sleep.

The first thing she did in the morning was to phone Louise. They arranged to meet the next afternoon.

Jessica rang the doorbell at the Belgravia mansion at the appointed time.

Louise herself opened the door. The two women embraced briefly. Louise was casually dressed in slacks and a blouse. They had tea in a corner of the lounge where there was a patch of weak, watery autumn sunlight.

They talked of inconsequential things for a while and then Louise asked, "How's Robert?"

Jessica burst into tears and then told Louise of the break-up and the reaons for it and her trip to South Africa.

"Couldn't you have told im about South Africa?" asked Louise.

"Maybe I should have, but I knew he would try to dissuade me from going, I couldn't face that," said Jessica tearfully.

"Robert is coming to dinner tonight. I can see he is absolutely smitten with you, maybe it will work out in the end," said Louise hopefully.

There was a moment's silence.

"So what do you want to talk about?" asked Louise.

"Life, maybe," said Jessica.

Jessica then explained that while she was probably in love with Robert it seemed to her that there was more to life than marrying Robert in, say, two or three years' time and then riding for the rest of her life on his more or less assured success.

"It all seems so inconsequential," she added. "Marriage, house, children, schools, retirement, death, what the hell does it all add up to? I know I have brains. I want to make some sort of a difference somewhere and not just be wrapped up in Robert's life, his rugby, his legal practice, his children. And then that man on Saturday night, Trevor, he has real issues of life and death to deal with. Perhaps I can help him; maybe I can make a difference there."

"What does he want you to do? Apart from the trip this weekend." asked Louise.

"He wants me to be a courier for the ANC between here and South Africa. I know I can do it; I think I understand the risks," said Jessica.

"I'm sure you can do it, but you don't understand the risks," said Louise. "What did Trevor tell you?" She made no attempt to dissuade Jessica or to make any judgements, for which Jessica was truly grateful.

"Not much, just that every few months I would be asked to carry messages to South Africa, it seems very simple," said Jessica. "It seems the least I can do."

"Why do you want to be involved at all?" asked Louise.

"Being honest, I am doing this for myself as much as anything, just to prove that I can make a difference. I am also incensed by the injustices going on in South Africa, I can't believe what is happening to the blacks in particular," said Jessica.

"You must understand this is not a game. Both sides think they are dealing with the future of South Africa. If you are caught, and there's a high risk of that, the ANC will deny all knowledge of you and the South African Government, after a period of torture, will either kill you or leave you to rot in prison," said Louise." Do you understand that?"

"I think so," said Jessica.

"It's not something you should get involved in lightly. A change in the political landscape there is inevitable but it will profoundly affect the lives of many people, both black and white."

"I think I understand."

They went on chatting for a while.

"And another thing," said Louise.

"Yes?"

"Black men are inclined to treat women as chattels who do their bidding without question. Trevor will probably expect to sleep with you but it won't mean much. You will be expendable; the wider political issues will be what drives this thing. One well meaning white English girl more or less will mean nothing. If things go wrong you will be discarded as easily as a used condom."

Jessica shivered. She had no intension of sleeping with Trevor Mdantsane.

"Jessica, if you get into trouble, I'll be here for you or if you want any advice. You're a brave girl," Louise finished.

Robert buried himself in his rugby and in completing his legal studies. Occasionally he asked Jessica's father how she was and got a non-committal "Fine" as a response.

※　　※　　※

Chapter 4

The prizegiving on Kamau's final day at Lenana had been a triumph for him and for Rafiki and Peter.

Kamau had been head boy and had taken most of the coveted academic prizes. He had also been the outstanding sportsman of the year, indeed the past two or three years. He had captained the rugby side with flair and success.

Peter briefly reflected that Robert had achieved much the same things almost ten years earlier, the only difference being that Robert's efforts had not been recognised. He did not spoil the day by saying anything; Rafiki was beaming with pleasure and reflected glory. She could not have dreamed ten years ago of anything like this for her son, who was now going to Oxford to study law as his half-brother Robert had done.

Robert met Kamau at the airport. Giles had offered to have him picked up in the car but Robert had said, "No, it might give him ideas above his station." The "car" was Giles' Bentley. Peter had arranged for Kamau to get a British passport, which he was entitled to because Peter had not been born in Kenya.

"Besides, it may give you the opportunity to play rugby for England. Anyway we can get you a Kenya passport any time," he added.

The boys embraced shyly at the airport. Except for the colour of their skin they were very much alike in height and build. They were both over six feet tall and well built. Robert had blondish hair like his father and green eyes. Kamau had classically African crinkly black hair and brown eyes. They took the airport bus to the Cromwell Road air terminal.

Kamau had some recollections of London from when Peter and Rafiki had been married there almost ten years earlier. He noticed for the first time the mean looking terraced houses in the approach to London from the West. He was thankful that from his recollections of Giles and Louise's house it was rather more spacious. Kamau also noticed the green fields and the trees; the sun had been shining when they circled to come in to land and the beauty of the neat, orderly fields, the lush nature of the countryside, contrasted starkly with the dust and dry bush around Nairobi. He had seen a herd of contented looking cows grazing and remembered the many occasions when he had herded his maternal grandfather's cattle, with the yells, the red dust, the flies. He wondered how he would fit in. He looked at his now successful brother, almost a mirror image of himself but with a white skin and then at himself, a real product of Africa with a black mother and black grandparents. He shivered despite himself. Kamau was confident of his own abilities; after all no white boy had come anywhere near him in his school achievements. This, however, was a different environment.

Robert pointed out with great pleasure the various landmarks as they went by taxi from the terminal to Belgravia. Kamau's eyes almost popped out of his head as they slowly went past the windows of Harrods department store; the taxi at Robert's request took a detour past Buckingham Palace. Kamau remembered it vaguely from his last visit.

Kamau was pleased and intrigued by the welcome he was given at the Belgravia mansion. Louise hugged him warmly and his cousins Belinda and Angus were really anxious to make him welcome and show him around. Belinda was a stunningly beautiful dark haired girl of about sixteen, thought Kamau, and Angus, tall and good looking like his father, was two years younger.

Between them Robert, Belinda and Angus showed Kamau the sights of London. Belinda's friends in particular were intrigued.

"Cousin, how can he be your cousin?" asked one, "he's brown."

Belinda tried to explain.

"Kamau is not an English name, or even Scottish, Irish or Welsh," observed another.

Kamau's good looks and charm eventually won them over. He realised then that he was always going to be a bit of a curiosity in England, even more so when people started to understand his history. In some ways he envied his half-brother Robert who fitted in to the English scene seamlessly and had virtually become an Englishman.

Kamau was happy that his brother no longer showed any of the hostility that had shadowed some of his earlier years. They were able to have long and involved conversations in Kikuyu, which Robert particularly enjoyed. On the tube and buses this drew a few curious glances. Once to their surprise a fellow white fellow passenger joined in the conversation. He'd apparently been with the British forces during the emergency in Kenya and had picked up a few words of Kikuyu then.

In the fortnight before Kamau went to take up his place at Oxford, Robert had introduced Kamau to the rugby fraternity in London. Kamau had decided he wanted as far as possible to make it on his own and for this reason he joined a different club to the one that Robert belonged to. Kamau expected to play for Oxford, but when he was down from University he would play for the London club.

Oxford suited Kamau beautifully. He wasn't really a curiosity there since it was a melting pot of many people from all over the world, especially the British Commonwealth. He was a bit of a curiosity in the rugby world though; not many non-white people had ever played rugby for Oxford. His ability and charm enabled him to fit in very well and soon he was the regular choice for inside centre for the university. His reputation and ability also very quickly found him a regular place in the London club side he had joined.

During the Christmas vacation one of the regular fixtures was between Robert's and Kamau's respective clubs. The game was, as expected, very close and Robert, to his considerable chagrin, was outplayed on more than one occasion by his younger brother. He found himself on the wrong end of several of Kamau's very hard tackles. In the end Robert lifted his game and his side won narrowly. All the rugby club changing rooms had very large communal baths where the players gathered after the game. While they were cleaning themselves up, jugs of beer were produced and the inevitable songs were started. Robert's side had a very large, strong prop forward named Flynn who usually started the singing.

"An engineer told me before he died…" he started.

At that moment Kamau climbed into the bath next to Robert about ten feet away from Flynn. He had a mug of beer in his hand. The singing stopped.

"Get your black bollocks out of my fucking bathwater," yelled Flynn.

Kamau took no notice.

"Hey you, wog, didn't you hear what I just said. I said get your black arse out of here," he repeated.

Kamau started washing. Robert started to make a move to get up; he knew Flynn quite well, they had played rugby together for years.

Kamau put his hand on Robert's shoulder, "Leave this to me," he said quietly. "Just look after my beer."

By this time Flynn was towering over Kamau in his nakedness. He made a grab for Kamau's hair. In a split second Kamau had grabbed Flynn by his leg, unbalanced him and Flynn was lying with his head down in two feet of water with Kamau's foot on his throat. Kamau still held him by the leg. There was a great deal of splashing which gradually got weaker and weaker. Eventually Kamau motioned to Robert and between them they picked Flynn up and they dumped him none too gently with his head over the edge of the bath, his legs in the bath and his stomach propped up on the wall of the bath. Flynn was then violently sick, spitting up large quantities of water and beer. He lay there for some minutes and then with the help of a colleague crawled dazedly back to his place. There was a stunned silence; Kamau finished washing, took his beer and got dressed. There was no more singing.

Robert went up to the captain of his side. "If you intend to put Flynn's name on the team sheet next week, then you must leave mine off. I hope you understand."

"But—but he's our best forward," was the response.

Robert just looked at him.

"What's this fellow to you anyway? In the end no harm was done," said the captain.

"He's my brother," hissed Robert.

The captain was genuinely taken aback.

"Brother?" he stammered. "But he's black."

"We have the same father. Anyway, that's not the point; this sort of behaviour should not be tolerated. If I don't get a call from you by Monday night, I'll find another club." Robert was angry.

Robert sought Kamau out; he was with his own side, all of whom sympathised with Kamau.

"I think we should make ourselves scarce," said Robert. "Things could get ugly. I think Flynn and a couple of his like-minded friends are spoiling for a fight."

They left.

Robert joined another club. Many questions were asked about his move, but no answers were forthcoming.

Kamau had a very good rugby season with both Oxford and his London Club. He was eventually included in the England squad for training purposes. "Just to get to know the ropes," was how it was explained to him. He had no realistic expectations of playing for England that season, but he was obviously regarded as promising.

Kamau had played for the university against the touring South Africans (their last tour for more than twenty years as it happened). The South Africans won handsomely. Kamau had managed to play reasonably well and he kept out of trouble especially when it was clear that he, being black, was being targeted by some of the rougher elements of the South African team.

Two weeks before England were to play South Africa at Twickenham, Robert's partner in the three quarter line, who normally played outside centre, was seriously injured. Kamau was then drafted; he merited selection but there was no doubt the English selectors wanted to demonstrate to the South Africans their abhorrence for the racially biased nature of their society and their selection process.

When the team was announced the press had no inkling that Robert Lawrence and Kamau Lawrence named in the backs were related. All they knew about Kamau was that he was black and a student at Oxford.

Peter and Rafiki had contrived to come to England to watch what they assumed would be Robert playing for England against South Africa. Peter had arranged various press interviews to publicise the good things that were in his opinion coming out of Kenya. One of the interviewers had realised that Robert was Peter's son and at the end of the interview asked Peter about the match, about Robert and who he thought would win.

"I actually have two sons playing now," said Peter.

"Two?" the reporter was incredulous, "who's the other one?"

"The other centre Kamau Lawrence is also my son."

"But he's ..." The reporter was going to say black, then he remembered Rafiki.

Within hours the story was all over Fleet Street. The tabloids made all their usual sensational headlines; the Lawrences were badgered for interviews. They eventually agreed to one interview with Peter, Rafiki, Robert and Kamau all present. Peter's and Rafiki's roles in the Mau-Mau were dissected, Rafiki's near hanging, Robert's quiet role as one of the mainstays of the England side over some years and Kamau's sudden rise to prominence. Despite constant questioning the family hung together; in the end all the papers and television focused on the match.

Before the match Kamau was surprised at his lack of nerves. He felt he was lucky to be part of the game, but he knew he was very able and that he and Robert had an understanding that was almost uncanny.

After all the pre-match preliminaries Robert came to him and said, "You see their inside centre there."

"Yes, Hannes Roux is his name," said Kamau.

"I overheard him say that he was going to 'donner hierdie blerrie Kaffir' (kill that bloody kaffir) that means you," said Robert.

Kamau nodded and smiled.

"Well two can play at that game," said Robert. "You go high and I'll go low; he'll collect us at the same time as he collects the ball."

Kamau nodded.

Robert went to the open side flanker and explained what was to happen.

"With any luck the ball will finish up a yard or two behind Roux; make sure you're there to pick it up."

Twice during the early part of the match Kamau made a run and Roux tackled him hard and late. Both penalties were converted. Kamau was unhurt and unmoved. Then their opportunity came: the ball came slowly from a South African scrum twenty yards from their line. Roux received the ball plus Robert and Kamau virtually at the same time. Both the Lawrences hit Roux with the hardest tackles they could muster. The ball trickled away and was picked up by the flanker who went tamely in for a try under the posts. Roux was unconscious and was eventually stretchered off with concussion. The South Africans were down to fourteen men (this was before the days of the automatic replacement). They were stunned. Roux was supposed to be their head man; he was the one that set out to eliminate opposition players, not the other way around. After that Robert and Kamau had a field day, scoring a try apiece and creating many more opportunities. England won the game handsomely.

For a brief period the Lawrence brothers were feted extravagantly in the press as the saviours of England rugby. The season soon came to an end and the Lawrences were temporarily forgotten.

Jessica Hawthorne, although she had not seen much of Robert for a few years, knew about Kamau because of all the fuss in the press. She had made several trips to South Africa as a courier for the ANC. Her task was simple enough: she took the overnight BOAC flight via Nairobi to Jan Smuts airport in Johannesburg, spent a few days with friends there, deposited a package containing she knew not what in a postbox in the Braamfontein post office for which she had been given a key, went to various game parks and other tourist attractions in South Africa and then went home.

The ANC paid her airfares; Jessica paid for everything else herself. "For which the ANC is truly grateful," as Trevor Mdantsane told her.

She spent about ten days in South Africa on every trip.

"You must look like a real tourist," Trevor told her.

Jessica had never seen a black township.

"You must not draw attention to yourself," Trevor said. She knew no black people in South Africa.

"The Government keeps the races apart," said Trevor. "If you fraternise with the blacks there you will be no use to us, as the police will be on to you straight away."

The security police had identified her as a courier for the ANC on her second trip to Johannesburg. The ANC knew she had been identified by the time she took her third trip. The ANC used her to plant misinformation; the security police thought she would lead them to bigger fish. Jessica of course knew nothing of this.

The firm of solicitors for whom Jessica worked was unaware of her activities on behalf of the ANC. As far as they were concerned members of staff could use their holidays in any way they wished; nobody even knew that she went to South Africa. Jessica also helped the ANC in London as far as she was allowed. She wrote various pamphlets for them and represented them in certain minor legal matters. She attended various meetings, none of which told her anything she didn't already know. She never met any of the more senior ANC people except Trevor Mdantsane.

"It is better for security reasons that you don't know anyone," Trevor told her. "Then if you get arrested by the police in South Africa you can't tell them anything if you know nothing," he reasoned.

Jessica started to get frustrated, she really believed in the ANC cause, she felt she should have earned their trust, she had been an entirely reliable courier but beyond a certain point there was nothing. She wondered whether she would gain the inner circle if she became Mdantsane's mistress.

Trevor Mdantsane for his part wondered how much longer he could keep her as a courier. He could see her frustration, but there was no way that she could advance in the organisation.

"She has no knowledge of Africa, no contacts, no nothing. She will expect us to listen to her opinions. She is white, she is a woman," said one of Mdantsane's colleagues, "Trevor, maybe you will have to fuck her, keep her happy for a few more years." The colleague laughed uproariously. Trevor looked uncomfortable. He preferred large, lusty black girls himself.

"Why the hell didn't she just marry that Robert Lawrence?" said the colleague. "We are going to need the help of such people over the years when we start speaking to the Afrikaners."

Robert had seen Jessica once or twice in the intervening years. He could never understand why she had not allowed their relationship to develop.

Unbeknown to Jessica, Giles had continued to invite Robert to meet various members of the ANC at Dingley Hall. Robert had met the whole hierarchy of the ANC resident in the UK and many of the "other side" including a senior cabinet minister. He had a real grasp of the issues; mostly he kept his mouth shut. He knew his time would come, he knew he couldn't escape it.

As a result of his rugby exploits Kamau got to know many of the girls that somehow found their way into the company of rugby teams. Since he had been in England he had missed the company of his age group and the ngweko game they played. He had never found a replacement for Joanne Black although he'd had the occasional fling.

After one long party that went on long into the night at the conclusion of a club game Kamau was invited back to the flat of Jane, the girl he had spent the evening with, "for coffee," as the invitation went. There was no time for drinks, for coffee, for anything; within minutes of entering the flat Kamau and Jane were in bed having the time of their lives. As with all his white lovers, she eventually found Kamau's ngwati or foreskin knot and this gave him a chance to explain the initiation ceremonies he went through and some ideas of tribal life. During the night Kamau was woken up with the sound of someone being violently sick in the bathroom.

"That's probably that South African again; Annabel is absolutely besotted with him," murmured Jane.

"South African?" queried Kamau.

"You know, the rugby player, the one you knocked out." Jane was half asleep.

"You mean Hannes Roux?"

"Yes, that's the one; he's a stupid, ignorant beast as far as I am concerned," said Jane,"but Annabel seems to like him. Bet he hasn't got a…"

"Ngwati?"

"Yes, an ngwati on his willy," said Jane. She giggled. "I'll ask him in the morning."

"I don't think he's stupid or ignorant," said Kamau. 'That he is a beast I don't doubt." He wondered what Roux's reaction would be to finding that he was there in the morning.

"Who is Annabel?" asked Kamau.

"My twin sister, we're identical twins," was the response.

Kamau was due at Giles and Louise's home in Belgravia for lunch, so they got up in good time. Kamau cooked the breakfast: fried eggs, bacon—the works.

Just as they were finishing Annabel appeared. She looked just like her twin sister. Jane made the introduction.

"Smells good," she said.

"I can fix you some breakfast too," said Kamau.

"Yes please." She yelled down the passage, "Hannes, do you want fried eggs for breakfast?"

There was a muffled reply.

"Make that two," said Annabel.

Just as Kamau finished serving it up, Hannes Roux appeared, looking rather the worse for wear. He stopped dead when he saw Kamau and just stared.

"Good morning," said Kamau evenly.

Roux took in the scene: the twin sisters sitting at the dining room table and Kamau serving up the breakfast.

"Have you been here all night?" He asked Kamau belligerently.

"Yes; I know you have." Kamau smiled.

"In my country blacks get arrested for sleeping with whites," Roux growled.

"Hannes, don't spoil things," said Annabel, "come and eat your breakfast that Kamau has cooked for you."

"Ja, that's what Kaffirs do in my country, cook the breakfast, but they don't sleep with the white mistress first. It's against the will of God," he said unpleasantly.

"Your God, but not my God," said Kamau quietly, putting the plate laden with eggs on the table.

"Hannes, shut up or get out," yelled Jane. "You're a guest here; if you don't like the other guests then you can leave."

"I'm just going to fix that fucking Kaffir first," he muttered. He made a rush into the kitchen area and grabbed the frying pan, which was still full of hot fat from frying the eggs. The gas had not yet been turned off.

"Look out!" yelled Kamau.

Too late—the boiling fat went all over Roux's face and hands as he lifted the frying pan up to take a swing at Kamau.

Roux shrieked with pain.

"Oh my God, look what the silly bastard has done to himself!" yelled Annabel.

They called an ambulance.

Kamau tracked down the hotel where the South Africans were staying and within an hour one of the members of management was round at the flat.

The girls explained what had happened and where Roux had been taken.

Kamau and the girls were offered abject apologies.

"I'm sorry, sometimes people like him get carried away, they forget where they are," he said. "Is anything broken? Can I replace anything?"

"No, the only damage was to himself," said Annabel.

Just as he was about to leave the South African said, "Look, it would be better for all if this stayed out of the papers, so no police, no press, no reports. O.K. with you?"

"O.K.," said the girls.

"And you?" he looked at Kamau.

"There's nothing to be gained by going public on this. I hope Mr. Roux has learnt a lesson," said Kamau.

The man left.

The girls apologised to Kamau; the whole episode and the passions it revealed meant nothing to them; it was merely an unfortunate incident.

Kamau went to his aunt's place in Belgravia and explained what had happened over lunch.

Robert and Giles were aghast; Louise was more phlegmatic.

"You know what certain elements of that society are like," she said. "You must expect it to surface from time to time. Anyway, you were right to keep the press out of this; you never know when they might turn on you."

Kamau found out later that Roux would be severely disfigured for life: the left side of his face and both his hands would carry a distinctive white scar tissue.

Jessica had in the meantime contacted Kamau, who knew that something really unwholesome was going on in South Africa and that he, Kamau, was going to do something about it.

Several times she took Kamau to see Mdantsane. Kamau had heard some of the horror stories in Kenya from his mother and father but the stories that were coming out of South African made his blood boil.

"We have camps, training camps in Tanganyika," Mdantsane eventually told him. "When you are ready we can send you there."

"Mnn, yes, maybe when I have finished at Oxford," said Kamau.

Mdantsane nodded.

"Why can't I go to Tanganyika," pouted Jessica when she was told.

"You are white, you are a woman and you wouldn't last five minutes," Mdantsane told her unkindly. "You'd be raped and killed and your body dumped in the bush for the hyenas to eat. You are more valuable to us here."

Kamau and Jessica eventually had a long chat.

"You know even after all this time Robert still dotes on you, he just doesn't want a repetition of what happened last time, that's all. Why don't you call him?" said Kamau.

Kamau then went on to explain the weekends at Dingley Hall and the role he thought she could usefully play. "Robert has met most or all of the senior people in the ANC and many of the white South Africans. You don't seem to be able to get beyond the front room though."

"Why do you think that is?" said Jessica.

"You are a woman, you are white and you know nothing of Africa; it's just what Mdantsane told you," said Kamau. "Maybe you would be useful playing a role here dealing with what you do know."

"But I really want to help; I find all this so frustrating," she said.

"They don't want to be dominated by white people who don't really understand, don't you see that?" responded Kamau.

"You are almost white," said Jessica.

"I have spent large parts of my life as a tribal African," responded Kamau, "living in my grandfather's village. I've been through all the initiation ceremonies; I really am an African. There is a vast difference in people's attitudes. For example, one's first loyalty is to the village, and then to the tribe; the country is almost an irrelevance to most Africans. Here it is different; you are firstly English and you are loyal to your country, the rest comes far behind. You could not have fought two world wars if that were not so. The Kikuyu have never fought a war as a complete tribe, but there have been plenty of skirmishes between villages both of the same tribe and of other tribes. Africans do not understand, really understand, the concept of country; it is a European concept and quite a recent one at that—look at Germany and Italy for example. Even during the Mau-Mau uprising, most of the Kikuyu involved in the conflict were on the side of the British. And this is only one issue. You could never be an African. Even my father, though he understands a great deal of Africa, deep down is not an African."

"I think you should go and see Robert," said Kamau finally. "Maybe you will find some sort of solution there."

"I've promised them another trip," said Jessica.

"Be very careful, nothing in Africa is really what it seems to be on the surface," said Kamau.

Hannes Roux recovered quickly. He knew he would be disfigured for life but he didn't really mind that. He was actually a member of the South African security police. His job was to frighten people; his disfigurement would help with that.

The South African embassy had arranged for Roux to stay in London for a few months for plastic surgery to his hands and face. He used the time well. He knew several of the addresses in London used by the ANC, and for some sixteen hours a day he kept them under surveillance, mostly just by sitting in a car on the other side of the street.

One address in Finsbury Park gave him all he needed. His powerful camera took pictures of all who went in and out, including Jessica, Mdantsane and then finally Kamau, besides most of the hierarchy.

Roux's instincts had told him that sooner or later Kamau would appear. Kamau had won the first two battles with him; maybe next time it would be his turn.

"That stupid English bitch Jessica Hawthorne," he thought. "We've been on to her for a couple of years now; maybe we should pick her up next time she comes to Johannesburg." He smiled evilly at the thought.

CHAPTER 5

Oxford was good for Kamau; he was clever at his studies although he found the law somewhat dry. He had made his mark with the University Rugby Club and was now in the England Squad, his social life was very active and he had participated in a number of debates in the Oxford Union. The fact that he was articulate, obviously clever and held his own in any company and that he was black or at least brown made him very welcome in the liberal atmosphere at the university.

The easy success, the people fawning over him, worried him rather. He wondered why he deserved any recognition from these people at all. He noticed that people's first reaction to him—those who did not know him—was that they expected to patronise him. He concluded that the only possible reason for this was the colour of his skin; their first reaction was that he would be inferior to them. Initially this did not worry Kamau much, as he had coped with that attitude during most of his young life. The realisation then dawned on him that in England this would be the situation for the rest of his life if he chose to stay there.

Mdantsane and the ANC had continued to be a part of Kamau's life; he went to the home in Finsbury Park when he was in London and became well known among the leadership there. He often wondered why he was more welcome than Jessica and concluded that, as much as the colour of his skin it was the fact that he was of Africa and Africa was part of his soul. Robert had also become much more of a friend than when they were growing up. They were very alike both in ability and character. The considerable attempts that Robert was making to "shake the dust of Africa off his feet" as he put it amused Kamau; in unguarded moments Africa seemed, judging from the nostalgic comments that he made, just as important to Robert as it was to Kamau. On the face of things Robert was indeed becoming an Englishman; Kamau supposed that he, himself, could follow in those footsteps and pretend that the continuing political injustices, the poverty and the rotten administration of the newly independent states could just be put out of his mind. Kamau knew in his heart of hearts that this would never be an option for him; he would in some form or another be engaged in Africa for the rest of his life.

During one of his visits to the home in Finsbury Park Mdantsane again mentioned that they had set up a military training camp in what was now Tanzania (the merger of Tanganyika and Zanzibar). The camp was under the control of the ANC but the training was all in the hands of a cadre of Russian instructors. Kamau was to spend his university summer holidays in Kenya with his parents; Mdantsane suggested that he could spend some weeks of his holiday in the camp undergoing training.

Kamau flew to Nairobi at the start of the summer holidays, spent a few days at Sattimma with Rafiki and Peter and then in a small pick-up truck he had rented from Kinua made his way to the Tanzanian border at Namanga. Two days later, having reported to an address in Dar-es-Salaam, he found himself in a very dusty camp in an out of the way spot not all that far from the Tanzanian capital. He had told his parents what he was up to and although they were concerned they raised no real objections; their own history was too fresh in their minds. Rafiki had given Kamau an address in Dar, some expatriate Kikuyu who for some reason could not return to Kenya. He had left the pick-up there.

The camp regime was extremely harsh and although it was under an ANC commandant the Russians actually ran the place. The routine in the first four weeks was reveille at five am, a five mile cross country run, breakfast of mealie meal porridge at seven thirty, two hours of a drill practice on the very dusty parade ground, then after a break; weapons training which consisted of learning to strip and reassemble a Kalashnikov AK47 rifle. They were also shown how to prime and throw hand grenades, how to deal with explosives, making bombs, and then how to pack, prime and detonate explosives for various targets.

Kamau, as he had done all his life, learnt quickly and had no trouble in mastering the technical issues. He was fascinated with the mix of people in the camp: Xhosa, Zulu, Tswana, South Sotho, Venda, Ndebele and so it went on. Many of the people had lived in the black townships around the white cities in South Africa. The conditions described were similar to those in the slum areas of Nairobi with which he was familiar since it was where his mother ran her clinics and Pumwani, the largest slum, was part of his father's constituency.

To start with Kamau was treated with suspicion; the other members of his billet thought he was a South African Coloured (mixed race) because of his brown skin and shunned him. A genuine Coloured in the camp explained the social position of the Coloured community in South Africa as being somewhere between the blacks, who occupied the lowest position, and the whites who were on top. His natural charm soon overcame any doubts the people had and soon the conversation flowed quite freely albeit in a mixture of various Bantu languages and English. All of Kamau's colleagues in the camp had a rudimentary education, most had barely made high school, and they were envious and fascinated when Kamau told them he was at Oxford, studying law.

The camp was mostly tents, with six men to a tent. The toilets consisted of a large pit with a row of seats across the pit; sacking had been tacked onto some poles to obscure the view from the camp, the front of the toilets was open to the bush. There was a shower block with cold water only.

Weapons' training was followed by lunch, which consisted of mealie meal cake, vegetable and sometimes very tough meat, then the majority of the camp inmates were directed to building some permanent barracks. Kamau, however, spent the afternoons learning Afrikaans, which was necessary because if he ever went to South Africa he would be taken for a Coloured. Afrikaans is the native tongue of the Coloured population of South Africa and he would have to speak it fluently or his presence would create immediate grounds for suspicion.

The Afrikaans teacher was a pretty Russian girl in her mid-twenties. She thought she had come to the camp to teach Russian but there was really no call for that. Tanya spoke passable English but had absolutely no knowledge of Afrikaans at all, but between them and with occasional help from the one genuine Coloured person in the camp, she and Kamau made some progress towards learning the language. Kamau was amazed that such a person had been sent to the camp. One or two of the Russian instructors had their wives with them and the kitchen was run by a group of local Tanzanian women, but apart from that all the inmates were male. For the first week or two Tanya kept her distance and the lessons were strictly business.

Kamau had found the atmosphere in the camp very restrictive and on the first Saturday night he was there he and one of the other more restless souls in his tent had crept out to a local village they had seen in the neighbourhood. The people in the village spoke Swahili, the lingua franca of the region, and Kamau soon ingratiated himself with the headman. The headman undertook to get a message to Kamau's contact in Dar and he said he could keep his pick-up truck there at the village. During the week Kamau's Dar contact left the pick-up at the village and Kamau got a message regarding its whereabouts through one of the kitchen staff. Kamau was seen by the locals as a sort of Kikuyu, at least he was an East African and they had something in common with him. They found the South African blacks condescending in their attitude, supposedly looking down on what they considered to be unsophisticated rural peasants.

Once everything had settled down on the Saturday night, Kamau and five others crept out into the night and after making their peace with the headman they drove into the city. Dar-es-Salaam (Haven of Peace) in contrast to its northerly neighbour in Kenya of Mombasa (Isle of War) was a very sleepy, dull little place. They found a few bars and a disco but there wasn't a great deal going on. So by 3am they had found their way back to camp and into their tents. The main entrance to the camp had a proper guardhouse but the camp was almost open to the bush and was only patrolled in a desultory fashion by a local night watchman with a knobkierie and a spear, who was easy enough to avoid.

During the following week Kamau managed to get Tanya to talk a little about herself and what her social life was like in the camp. From the discussion he gathered it was almost non-existent although once a month most of the Russians went into Dar and had a meal at one of the hotels. On the pretext of having to fetch a book that she had forgotten Tanya and Kamau went to her room, which was a little cottage built of concrete blocks with a corrugated iron roof. It wasn't very elegant but was much more comfortable than Kamau's tent. The cottage consisted of a small sitting room with a kitchenette and a bedroom off that. There was a shower off the bedroom. Tanya was apprehensive and shy but within a few minutes Kamau had used his charm to persuade her to part with all her clothes and they made love until it was time for his Afrikaans lesson to stop.

The trainees played sport from four to six pm—mainly football, which Kamau was well versed in, having played the game with the children of his father's farmworkers on Naseby. The evening meal was much the same as lunch and by eight-thirty it was lights out. They had very little equipment but the instructors tried their best to ensure that the camp had the appearance at least of a military establishment with regular inspections ensuring that clothes were properly washed, boots cleaned etc. Additional duties were imposed on all those found out of line.

The afternoon excursions to Tanya's room became a regular feature of Kamau's days. He took precautions to ensure that they weren't seen by any of the Russian instructors. Kamau had told Tanya of his pick-up truck and his now quite regular excursions into Dar. It took quite a lot of courage for her to eventually accompany Kamau and some of his fellow trainees into Dar one Saturday night. She was afraid of being seen by her fellow instructors or others from the large Russian embassy in Dar; she also had some concerns about being seen in public with black people.

In days gone by Dar-es-Salaam was just a small fishing village until the Sultan of Zanzibar decided that it would make an ideal trading port for shipping. The cargo consisted mainly of slaves and ivory from inland, which was destined for his domains in the Persian Gulf. When the Germans colonised Tanganyika as it was called then, they had eventually moved the capital of their colony to Dar in 1871, from Bagamoyo, a few miles up the coast.

Tanya, Kamau and the others went to the usual bars and discos where they were starting to be well known and they had the time of their lives. Tanya had never had so much fun; the Africans were fun to be with and so lively compared to the very strict Russians in the camp. As before they crept back into camp before the dawn and since the next day was a Sunday Tanya and Kamau made their way to her little cottage.

They were waiting for the unsuspecting pair, six big burly Russians. As soon as they opened the door Kamau was felled by an uppercut to the jaw and Tanya was grabbed and manhandled into the sitting room. She was eventually tied to a chair and had to watch while Kamau was systematically stripped naked and beaten up. Kamau was then groggily made to stand and watch while each Russian took it in turn to rape Tanya. As the Russians left one of them came over to Kamau and said, "Russian women is for Russians only; you keep your lousy black cock for black women in future."

He then kicked Kamau in the groin; Kamau collapsed. An hour or so later Kamau managed to crawl into his clothes and stagger back to his tent, where his fellow inmates tried to patch him up as best they could.

The camp commandant was a Zulu, a member of the ANC, ostensibly the Russians reported to him. In fact they took little notice of him and took their orders from the KGB officers in the embassy in Dar. Kamau persuaded his fellow inmates to go to the commandant and try to get him to come down and see Kamau, which they eventually succeeded in doing. He was absolutely furious when he saw Kamau and heard the story but as he explained, his hands were tied; his job was to produce trained guerrilla fighters to fight the white regime in South Africa, and the Russians were needed for that. However, if the occasional Russian was found floating face down in the harbour in Dar he guessed that nobody would be any the wiser.

Kamau made a list of the Russians who had beaten him up, and the story of his beating and the reason for it was circulated throughout the camp with the list of people involved. During his remaining few weeks in the camp Kamau made sure that his persecutors were made fully aware that in one form or another they would be dealt with.

Amongst the other things he had become skilled at, Kamau was now a fully trained demolition expert; he was also able to prime the timing devices in hand grenades. On one occasion one of his Russian tormentors was conducting a grenade handling course, and Kamau was able to switch a grenade with the normal seven second fuse to one with a less than a two second fuse. He had warned all his fellow trainees what he was doing. The Russian was showing them what to do:

"Pull the pin, release the lever."

To his surprise the group scattered.

"Count, one…."

He almost got to two when the grenade blew up in his hand and blew his head off. The incident was put down to an unfortunate training accident.

A second Russian was seen by some of Kamau's friends going off with a prostitute from one of the bars they all frequented in Dar. His naked body was found the next day floating in the harbour with multiple stab wounds. None of the people in the training camp were suspects since none of them were supposed to be in the city at all.

At that point the other four Russians involved became really frightened and persuaded the Russian embassy on various pretexts to send them back to Moscow.

Tanya was never seen again. When Kamau asked where she was he got a very curt "Moscow" from one of the more approachable Russians.

In the eight weeks of his training Kamau had become a well trained guerrilla fighter. He was also extremely fit. Many of his colleagues in the camp, after a few more weeks of training and indoctrination, would be sent back to South Africa to fight with Umkonto We Sizwe.

Always one of the concerns of the people in the camps was whether any of their number was really an employee of the South African military sent to the camps to spy on them. The screening process to be admitted to the camp was extensive but notwithstanding that the South African security forces employed numerous blacks, and if they tried hard enough one or two would always get through the screening process.

One of the occupants of Kamau's tent was suddenly pounced on by camp security one day and his kit searched. They found numerous notes with all the names of the inmates of the camp, their origins and any other information that might be useful. Kamau was horrified to find that his name was on the list with very detailed notes about his origins and his career at Oxford. The man had come into Dar with Kamau on one or two occasions and although he was not really a friend, Kamau had certainly thought of him as a colleague. The man was tried and condemned to death within three days. Kamau was dismayed to find that his name had been drawn as one of the twelve to make up the firing squad. He tried to get out of it on the grounds that the man had shared a tent with him. He was refused and had to take part in the execution.

"Just remember Mr. Lawrence," he was told by the camp commandant, "that this man would have revealed you to the South Africans and would have had no compunction in being part of a firing squad with you as its target."

As usual they were all up at five am when the reveille was sounded. Kamau and the eleven others chosen for the squad, all took their now well-maintained Kalasknikovs and were formally issued with three rounds of ammunition each.

The man, with his hands bound behind his back, was blindfolded and placed against the wall of the rifle range. The firing squad lined up about twenty-five yards from him.

"Ready?"

The rifles were all raised.

"Aim."

Kamau noticed a wet patch on the front of the man's trousers as his bladder and bowels emptied in fear.

"Fire"

He was tempted to aim away from the victim but he remembered the commandant's words. He aimed for the heart. The volley of shots went off and the man slumped down on the ground, dead.

Another group had been assigned to bury him. Kamau noticed two other graves in the area.

The rest of the training went off without incident. Kamau had gone to the camp full of the innocence of youth and when he had finished he had been directly involved in the deaths of two people and heaven knows what damage had been done to poor Tanya. His mother noticed a very changed person when he returned and spent two weeks with them at Karen. It was as if Kamau had suddenly come of age and he realised that what he was into was no longer a game but a deadly serious business. He quietly envied Robert with his white skin and his apparent ability to shut the emotions and the commitment to Africa out of his life. Kamau knew he could never do that, he knew he would be in the front line of the battle in the South; the colour of his skin dictated that.

The story of how Kamau had spent his eight weeks was told to Peter and Rafiki a few days before he left the sanctuary of Sattimma. Kamau left nothing out.

Rafiki wept quietly in the bed in Peter's arms that night. "My poor baby," was all she could say. They made no effort to dissuade Kamau from his chosen course of action; they didn't want to and they knew it would be useless.

Kamau attacked his university studies with renewed vigour. As Mdantsane told him, "We have enough uneducated peasants; the South Africans have ensured that with their second or third rate levels of education for blacks there. We really need smart, properly educated leaders for the future."

Another thing the camp had taught him was that he had to learn to speak Afrikaans properly and he had to learn the slang and the inflections of the language in the way the Cape Coloureds spoke it. It would probably mean the difference between surviving and not surviving.

Before going to the camp Kamau had not realised that the Coloured population were really a race in South Africa. They spoke Afrikaans, the language of the white government, and were from the same stock as the white Afrikaners but because of the colour of their skin were rejected.

During conversations in the camp with his fellow trainees he had learnt about apartheid:

Separate trains.

Separate buses.

Separate living areas.

Separate entrances to post offices.

Separate park benches.

No mixed marriages.

Separate hotels and restaurants.

And so on and so on. He had witnessed discrimination in the Colonial era in Kenya but nothing like South Africa where it was entrenched in law. It made him angry to even think about it. He had also learnt that the African reserve areas that had been set aside in the last century were being set up as independent homelands, none of which had a hope of being viable, all of which were subsidised by the South African government and all of which were in the control of what were presented to Kamau as self-serving thugs.

He spent time talking about his experiences to Robert and discussing what he thought he could do about the situation. Robert just listened with admiration. He did not try to put him off.

⁂ ⁂ ⁂

Chapter 6

The ANC had been aware for some time that Jessica was known to the authorities in South Africa as a courier. They had used her to circulate misinformation on several occasions. They had never told Jessica or anyone close to her of this knowledge. She was surprised and hurt by the small role she played in ANC affairs despite her obvious sacrifices and her talent. She constantly hassled Mdantsane for more jobs and he continued to put her off. Jessica also began to wonder if she had lost Robert forever—the one man who had really meant anything to her. She had had a few short-lived affairs but they had all turned out badly for one reason or another.

Mdantsane had spoken to Kamau a few times in the past.

"We had always assumed that Jessica would marry Robert," he said. "She would be far more use to the ANC as a co-hostess for meetings in this country with our people and eventually with both ANC and the white Nationalists. All parties will have to talk sooner or later. This situation may go on for years, and if Giles Dingley-Ferris gets too old we will need the younger generation to continue to provide safe places for us to meet outside the public gaze. Jessica, I know wants to be part of the front line, but she is really no good at that. She is white and English. She sticks out like a sore thumb."

Kamau spoke to Jessica about her role and tactfully explained how she could be of real value to the ANC. Robert had retired from rugby and had now been promoted to partner in Barnes Ramsey and Hawthorne. Giles had also given him some legal work, which helped to cement his position. Since Robert's departure from the England rugby side Kamau had really made sure of his own position in the side. He managed on one occasion to invite both Robert and Jessica to a game at Twickenham to watch him play and then arranged a threesome to go to the London theatre and dinner. Eventually his tactics worked and within a short time Robert had forgiven Jessica for the hurt she had caused him and they were an item again.

The family had decided that before Kamau had graduated they should have one big family holiday together. Peter had some contacts in Botswana, everyone was keen to try to understand something about what was happening in Southern Africa generally and the ANC were interested in finding a way of having Kamau move in and out of South Africa.

Peter and Rafiki flew down to Johannesburg and met the rest of the party at Jan Smuts airport. Robert and Jessica as well as Kamau and John flew direct from London to Johannesburg. John, Robert's younger brother, had been at university in Scotland and was now studying to be an accountant in Edinburgh.

They all had to wait in the transit lounge. Robert, John and Jessica would have been allowed into South Africa, but Rafiki and Kamau would have had trouble and they were not sure of Peter's's status, although he was white and born in South Africa. Because of his history he may not have been a welcome visitor. So they had decided to stay in the transit lounge and wait for the Air Botswana flight the next morning.

The ten seat Air Botswana Twin Otter was almost full. The Lawrence party were tired and filled with their own thoughts. Peter looked enviously at the hundreds of orderly factories on the East Rand as the plane slowly gained height. He had never returned to the land of his youth, which he had left now more than thirty years previously.

"If only we had a modern industrial base like this," he pointed the factories out to Rafiki. "What a different place Kenya would be."

Rafiki had felt distinctly uncomfortable during their stop over in the transit area, aware of the hostile glances of some of the other passengers and the ever-present young white men in blue uniforms with "Suid Afrikaanse Polisie' on their epaulettes. She shrugged and smiled. "I hope we'd put the value all that creates to better use," she said.

Peter raised his eyebrows.

"It's not much use having all that value and all you do with it is to suppress a large part of the population," she added.

"No, I suppose not," added Peter.

Robert and Jessica were holding hands in the rear of the plane. They flew over the leafy northern suburbs of Johannesburg, dotted with hundreds of bright blue swimming pools; the only blot on the landscape as far as they could see was the horrid smokey township of Alexandra nestling up against the comparative luxury of the white areas.

Kamau was excited. "So this is where I will come, within weeks," he thought.

The plane levelled out at ten thousand feet so they had a good view of what was below. Johannesburg itself is at about six thousand feet above sea level. John, who had taken the trouble to study as much as he could about the country, said, "On the high veld here there is almost no rain from April until September or October. Jo'burg is warm and sunny during the day but in winter the temperature goes down below freezing at night."

It was now mid-July, the best time of year in the Botswana game areas.

John was quite tall at five foot ten, but slightly built with a shock of blond hair. He was very personable and the rest of the family loved him dearly. Although he was outshone on both the sports field, and in academia, by his brother and half brother he took all that in his stride. He was justly proud of their achievements but quietly and happily got on with what he was himself doing.

John continued, "The land gradually falls away as we go west, and gets drier." They crossed the Hartebeestepoort Dam and the Magaliesberg. Some of the land was obviously white owned farms but there were tracts of what looked like rural slums.

"Looks like parts of the Kikuyu reserve," muttered Kamau.

"In this case Bophutatswana," John informed them. "The South African government are trying to make it into a homeland, an independent country with something like a dozen separate unconnected blocks of land stretching from here into the Northern Cape. They are even building a separate capital for it outside Mafikeng, called Mmbatho. Apparently Mafikeng will remain in the so-called white area. And yes it is called Mafikeng of Boer war fame despite the British calling it Mafeking all these years."

They passed over the Marico, some of it thorn scrub, some of it well watered farm land near the Marico River. An hour or so after leaving Johannesburg they circled the Gaborone dam and touched down on the short tar strip that was Gaborone airport.

There was a crowd of people in the tin shed that was all there was of an airport building. Customs and passport formalities were completed without any trouble and the Lawrence party found themselves standing outside with their luggage in the bright winter sunlight.

A Toyota pick-up truck came bustling along and a man dressed in a sports jacket hopped out.

"Mr Lawrence?" he asked.

"Yes, Peter Lawrence," answered Peter.

"I'm Samisi, your counterpart here in Botswana."

Peter had made contact with the Government and in particular the Ministry of Agriculture in Botswana.

They loaded the luggage into the truck.

Peter and Rafiki got in the front with Mr. Samisi and the rest of the party hopped in the back. Peter was relieved with the lack of formality. When he had been told that the minister would meet him at the airport, he had hoped against hope that it wouldn't be a large entourage of official cars as it might have been back home.

Mr. Samisi explained that he preferred to use his own vehicle most of the time since it was less obtrusive. He also explained that he used the vehicle to visit his cattle post during weekends.

"Cattle post?" asked Peter.

"The land is all owned communally by the tribe, but we have a rule that with the permission of the chief, a person can sink a borehole for his own use provided it is at least five miles from any other borehole," the minister explained.

"So the person sinking the borehole effectively has the rights to the water and the land around it, without challenging the tribe's ownership of the land," said Rafiki.

"Exactly," said the minister. "I can take you to my cattle post at the weekend if you like," he offered.

"We'd like that," said Peter.

They were dropped off at the President Hotel in the centre of Gaborone.

"You and Mrs. Lawrence are invited to a dinner at State House this evening. I will pick you up about seven fifteen; you will need to wear a suit," said Mr. Samisi.

"Just you two, the rest of your family I am sure can look after themselves," he added.

The President Hotel had pretensions to being a capital city hotel and was located on a pedestrian mall in the centre of the town. The mall had a few seedy looking shops and Peter noticed that the British owned banks were prominent. They had arranged to stay at the President because it was Government owned. When they checked in, Peter said to Rafiki, "I have been in many hotels that have seen better days, but this one must have started life off being seedy. Look," he pointed to the walls and ceiling, "the roof leaks when it rains here; luckily for us that is not very often."

They really didn't care what the hotel was like; they had all their children with them and they were sure they would enjoy themselves.

Peter had arranged to hire two Toyota Land Cruisers plus all the camping equipment they would need. Robert and the others went to collect everything from a site in the industrial area. They would have a few days to make sure they had forgotten nothing and they had to make food purchases. Peter left the organisation of the trip, which was considerable, to Robert; he and Rafiki were going to make the most of their stay in Gaborone. Peter was keen to see some of the work done on dryland agriculture, which he was sure would have applicability in the dryer parts of Kenya. He had also made arrangements to visit the large meat processing plant at Lobatse to the south, which, much to his envy, had a licence to export beef to the European Economic Community. This was because Botswana had a very strict and very successful foot and mouth disease control programme, which meant that there was no chance of contamination in the meat being sent to Europe.

The dinner at State House was a delightfully informal affair, Peter and Rafiki were the guests of honour and apart from Sir Seretse Khama and his wife Ruth there were several other ministers there and their wives.

The President described State House as "The Woodpile." Peter had heard he had a quirky sense of humour and asked apprehensively, "The Woodpile?"

"Yes," said the President, "and I'm the nigger in."

All the ministers laughed uproariously, with Peter and Rafiki joining in. Peter just could not imagine the same thing or anything like it happening in any of the other African countries he had visited.

The President then went on to explain how his grandfather Khama III had somehow steered a course between the Boer Republics of the Transvaal and Orange Free State, prior to their defeat by the British in the Boer War, the British themselves and the predatory manipulations of Cecil Rhodes and his cohorts.

"Somehow he kept his head; he managed to get Rhodes and the British to build the railway line from South Africa to what was then Rhodesia through our territory which has helped development. Although we became a British protectorate we did not get a large number of settlers like you did in Kenya and we were very much left to our own fate. The British even administered the territory from Mafikeng in South Africa and we shared a

Governor with Swaziland and Basutoland (Lesotho) who lived in Pretoria. Somehow I think we are truly lucky, the British did nothing here except keep the Boers out so we have not had to undo anything since independence, not like Kenya and now Rhodesia (Zimbabwe). You were a settler yourself in Kenya weren't you?" he added looking at Peter.

Peter had long ago come to terms with the effort he had made in developing Naseby and then actually being personally responsible as Minister of Agriculture, for buying white owned farms and redistributing the land.

"Yes," he said. "As a young man I saw it as an opportunity to create an independent lifestyle for myself, and I put my heart and soul into developing the place. With the political development and the population increase my department has supervised the return of almost all the land that was once white owned to black Kenyans. There are a few large cattle ranches and tea and coffee plantations still in the hands of the original white owners. Maybe we've found a way to have the best of both worlds."

They talked about the President's marriage to Ruth, now Lady Khama, and the horror this had caused in both Britain and among his own tribe.

"The idea of a black man, even one like me who was the son of a chief, and British educated, actually marrying a white woman, was anathema to both the British and the people of Botswana, in particular my own people the Bamangwato, so we had a six year holiday in the Caribbean!" he laughed. "We had a wonderful time and two of our four children were born there."

He then went on to explain that he thought the secret of Botswana's success was that it was a genuine democracy, that corruption had been kept to a minimum and that apart from the diamond mine at Orapa and the copper mine at Selibe-Pikwe they were hopeful of finding more diamonds west of Gaborone and the industrial base was growing.

"We have the meat processing in Lobatse and now we have built a brewery here in Gaborone. We decided to let the Germans try their luck at running it, if they fail I am sure the South Africans will come and rescue us. I hope the Germans make a go of it; we need to continue to develop our skills independent of South Africa."

"How do you get on with the South Africans?" asked Peter.

"Actually quite well, we are part of the South African customs union together with Lesotho, Swaziland and of course South Africa; we are treated fairly. It is of course ironically in their interests to let us succeed," he went on.

Peter looked quizzically at him.

"It helps to justify their apartheid policy," he said. "What they are trying to do is to get all the black South Africans to belong to a homeland of some sort, and they want these homelands to be viable, like we are, so that they have some justification for their policy of separation."

"Surely you don't think it will succeed?" Peter said in a horrified voice.

"No, no, none of the so-called homelands is remotely viable and they are not complete countries. Bophutatswana, for example, is for our fellow Tswanas across the border and is run by a thug who is a puppet of the South Africans. It consists of a number of patches of land all over the place; the policy has no chance of succeeding."

"What will happen then?" asked Rafiki.

"Majority rule at some stage, hopefully without a bloodbath," was the answer.

When it was time to leave Sir Seretse said, "Look, I found out you were staying at the President. We can't have you staying in a dump like that; I've had all your things moved over here."

"We have our children with us," said Rafiki.

"Oh yes, they've helped move everything. They are here as well," said Lady Ruth.

Peter could see that one of the ministers was looking uncomfortable.

Khama went up to him and patted him on the shoulder.

"Come on, you know that place is awful, the roof leaks and the food is inedible; the sooner you can find people who know how to run hotels the better off we will be. What do we know about such things? We are cattle people."

Peter was amazed at such candour. He had no complaints.

Robert and the others were just going out of the front door when they all emerged from the dining room. The introductions were made.

"Just thought we'd check out the Holiday Inn," said Robert.

"Another dump," said the President. "The casino there brings plenty in taxes; I'm not really sure what it does for the local people though. Actually I am," he added thoughtfully, "there is no doubt it damages the social fabric, as people go and spend money they can ill afford in the place, then children starve. Still most of the money comes from South African tourists."

Robert, Jessica, John and Kamau went in one of the rented Toyota four-wheel drives to the Holiday Inn, which was less than two miles away. The place held no charm for any of them. The entrance was controlled by a large number of security personnel whose job it was to deter the hoi polloi from entering the hotel and particularly the casino, which was accessed through the main foyer of the hotel. From their observations it appeared that what the authorities would really have liked would have been for the locals not to come near the place or at least not come near the casino and leave the casino to the tourists. However almost all the visitors were whites from South Africa and nobody wanted the racial separation that was enforced in that country to persist in Botswana. In the end there was a sort of truce between the overworked security people and the locals; some locals were let in to play the slot machines, but the main gaming tables were kept out of bounds to all locals except the elite.

"We can certainly do without this sort of thing in Kenya," muttered Robert.

They lost a few Pula at blackjack and had then moved to a roulette table when Robert nudged Kamau.

"There's a fellow over there at the bar, who seems to be paying us an awful lot of attention," he said. "Somehow his face is familiar but I don't remember anyone with quite such a bad disfigurement."

"Hannes Roux," said Kamau. "I've had my eye on him for at least thirty minutes."

"Hannes Roux, you mean the rugby player, I don't remember him being quite so disfigured," said Robert.

"It was that accident in the flat with those girls a couple of years back," Kamau reminded him. "He dumped a frying pan full of boiling oil all over himself."

They both glanced across the small casino with three blackjack tables operating and the same number of roulette tables. The players were all small time, mainly business people in town for a few days, or tourists. The South African border was only twelve miles from Gaborone and Johannesburg only four or five hours' drive away.

"There's nothing for me here," said Robert, "but I do think we should buy our friend a drink, don't you? Maybe we can leave John and Jessica out of this though."

Kamau threaded his way through the smoke filled room towards the bar; Robert quickly passed by Jessica and told her what they were doing. She and John had a largish pile of chips in front of them and were quite happy to be left where they were.

Kamau in the meanwhile made his way up to Hannes Roux, who was sitting alone by the bar. The left side of Roux's face had a very disfiguring, livid, white scar from his hair to his jaw line. Kamau also noticed that his left hand had a similar type of scar. Robert joined them.

A pair of steely blue eyes stared at them from an expressionless face; eventually he reluctantly put his hand out and shook both Robert and Kamau's proffered hands.

"Ah, the Lawrences," he said in his gutteral Afrikaans accent, "I wondered if I would ever bump into you again."

"We're just here on holiday," answered Kamau. "We're going up to the swamps in a few days; my parents are with us."

"Oh, where are you staying?" asked Roux.

"Well," laughed Robert, "we were staying at the President but somehow the old man wangled a move to State House."

"State House, you mean the place Khama lives in?"

Roux was startled to say the least.

"Yes, that's the place," answered Kamau.

Roux had seen the four of them walk into the casino. He knew that Kamau and Jessica were active members of the ANC; he didn't know what Robert's involvement was and he couldn't place the fourth member of the party at all. Part of his job as a member of the South African security police was to meet with police agents in Botswana and identify ANC members living in the country, particularly identifying their residences. When his day's work was done he often repaired to the bar in the casino; he had assumed it was the last place ANC people would come to.

They talked a bit about rugby, both Robert and Roux had retired but Roux was aware that Kamau had a regular place in the England side.

"And what brings you to this neck of the woods?" asked Robert.

"This and that," said Roux. "Botswana is part of the customs union and I have to come up here on government business from time to time."

He obviously could not tell them what his real job was and certainly if the Botswana authorities found out what he was doing, there would be trouble. Roux made his escape soon after that and made extensive notes on the encounter.

Robert and Kamau finished their drinks.

"I don't like the feel of any of that," Robert eventually remarked, "he couldn't wait to get away, and his explanation of what he does here was not convincing."

"Who was that delightful looking character?" Jessica asked cheerfully. She and John had won about one hundred Pula.

"Rugby acquaintance," Kamau and Robert chorused.

"Hm, you're hiding something," she said, "he looked pretty unsavoury to me; are you sure he's not a diamond smuggler?"

They all laughed. Kamau told Jessica the story of the incident in the flat with the hot oil from the frying pan.

When they left the hotel they didn't see Roux in the shadows taking a reel of pictures of them with a specialised camera.

"What a dreadful place," Jessica said afterwards. "Still, we had fun, we won a few Pula."

John had told her that Pula meant rain, which in that dry desert country was a commodity in short supply.

The four of them thoroughly explored Gaborone and its surroundings over the next few days. Gaborone: a dry, dusty, place which had only come to life in recent times when it was decided that the capital of the newly independent state of Botswana would be located there. Prior to that it was merely a stop on the railway line that ran up the eastern side of the country. Almost all the traffic on the line was between South Africa and Rhodesia. John made it his business to find out all he could. He told them the town had sixty to seventy thousand inhabitants, one third of whom lived in a shanty town called Old Naledi, south of the city on the Lobatse road. There was a significant expatriate population, mainly British civil servants on contract to the Botswana Government. There were many embassies, such as Russian, Chinese and even Libyan; John guessed that Gaborone was a listening post for many of the countries who would be unable to have embassies in Pretoria.

They found their way to Mochudi, where they bought some local wool wall hangings and to Thamaga, where a German couple made wonderful pottery.

After a few days Peter had done all he wanted in Gaborone; they took their leave of the Khamas and set off up north.

Chapter 7

They left early in the morning, with Peter driving one of the Toyotas and Robert the other. As they had been told, the good tar road north from Gaborone suddenly petered out at Mahalapye, which was the first major settlement they came to in the hour's drive from the capital. Peter of course had his cameras and they had borrowed two rifles in Gaborone.

Both Peter and Robert were used to rough roads in East Africa but for a main road they had never seen anything like this.

"The German Government have provided money to tar the road all the way to Francistown, so while they are building it no money is being spent on maintaining the existing road," John told them. "There you can now see the construction equipment for the new road." He pointed.

Both Peter and Robert knew that the only way to deal with the rough road was to drive flat out, the theory being that the vehicle then rode over the bumps when it travelled at speed. Robert let Peter go a little way ahead to avoid the thick cloud of choking dust his vehicle threw up; they made the sixty odd kilometres to Palapye in short time and were thankful then to turn off the main Francistown road with its abundance of heavy trucks onto the less well used road to Serowe.

"Serowe is the capital of the Ngwato people. Khama's people," John told them. "It also has the reputation of being the largest village in the world with some twenty thousand inhabitants."

The party didn't stay long in Serowe since they were anxious to make as much progress as possible that day.

From Serowe the directions had been somewhat vague; all they had been told was to make certain that they took a right turn after Letlhakane otherwise they would be on the wrong side of the Botletle river.

"There is a ferry," said John," but my sources of information said that it belonged to the United Nations and was not available to anyone else."

They made their way into ever-drier country along increasingly ill-defined tracks. Every now and then they came to a fork in the road and it was pure guesswork which direction they chose.

On two occasions they came across makeshift barriers in the track, manned by old men who lived with their family and possessions in a nearby hut.

"Foot and mouth control," Peter said.

"A packet of cigarettes and a six pack of beer should stop him from wanting to look in our freezer boxes," said Rafiki.

"What about the foot and mouth?" asked Peter. Rafiki was just about to reply when she saw the twinkle in his eye. She just smiled and handed the contraband to the grateful man.

They all tried their considerable array of language skills on the gatekeepers and, when they got to Letlakhane, on a few of the villagers. Whilst they were able to make themselves vaguely understood, they still missed the vital right hand turn onto the Makgadikgadi Salt Pan. After driving for a few hours they could see the trees on the edge of the Botletle River on the right hand side of the vehicles, not the left as should have been the case.

They stopped to discuss the situation.

"We'd better try and find that ferry," said Peter.

As they had moved west the country had become obviously drier and less populated but they saw plenty of game: zebra, wildebeeste and numerous antelope. They drove on, and after some time saw the dust of another vehicle on the road ahead. Within a few minutes a well-kept Toyota Landcruiser appeared down the track.

"Can I help you?" asked the man in the truck.

"We seem to have missed a turn and are now on the wrong side of the river," said Peter. "I was hoping to find the ferry which is somewhere near."

"It's a private ferry," said the man defensively.

"Oh, we were told it belonged to the U.N," said Peter.

They all laughed.

"No, no, it belongs to a safari company, the one I work for," said the man, now more pleasantly. He had sized the Lawrence party up, and decided that there was no harm in them. At the same time the curious combination of black, white and coloured all in the same party had piqued his curiosity.

He introduced himself as Dan Blundell.

"I'll tell you what," he said, "I have to make a radio call to Maun and then I'll direct you to the ferry. I'm actually camped on the other side and provided my client has no objections you can pitch your tents over there as well."

A few minutes later they were on their way. Following the track, they eventually drove down a steep bank to the river where they saw the "ferry", which consisted of eight fuel drums strapped together with a few planks on the top as a platform. The contraption was pulled across the two hundred yard wide river on a single chain.

"You use this thing at your own risk," said Dan. "If your vehicle goes to the bottom of the river, it's your problem."

Peter nodded.

"Look, I'm having trouble with my vehicle, she keeps stalling," said Dan hopefully.

"I'll have a look at it," offered Peter.

The three vehicles were individually ferried across without mishap; Dan was lucky Peter was around because his vehicle stalled and was unable to move off the ferry until Peter had spent half an hour with his head under the bonnet.

Dan showed them to the camp and said, "I'll have dinner with my client and then maybe we'll come over for a beer later."

The Lawrences set their camp up expertly and within forty minutes they were all sitting around the camp-fire enjoying a beer. Peter and the boys were completely at home; Rafiki tolerated the situation although, like many Africans, she failed to see anything romantic in a rural setting.

"After all," she reasoned, "most urban Africans have spent their lives trying to get away from what they consider to be rural drudgery or penury."

What Rafiki liked was having Kamau and Peter's elder children with them again.

Jessica was totally fascinated. She'd been interested to see Gaborone, but this was different: this was the Africa of Livingstone and the explorers, and this was only the beginning.

Dan eventually came and sat with them on his own. His client was tired, he explained. He was fascinated with the group; in this part of the world the racial mix of the party was quite unusual.

"You come from Gabs?" Dan eventually asked Peter; he was judging from the vehicle licence plates.

"No, no, we're from Kenya, except Jessica who is from England; although all the young are in living England at the moment working or studying."

"Kenya—why are you down here then? I thought the game there was better than it is here."

"Not now, with all the poaching going on; in many places it's getting wiped out," said Peter.

Dan's curiosity was now working overtime. "What did you say your name was?" he asked.

"Lawrence," responded Peter.

Then it all fell into place. "Oh, I remember, you're the Minister of Agriculture there."

"Yes."

He looked at Rafiki and kept his mouth shut.

"And you two," he looked at Robert and Kamau, "have destroyed our rugby team from time to time."

They smiled at him.

They spent a few hours together; Dan told them where to go looking for game and what to look out for.

'The Makgadikgadi salt-pan absorbs most of the water coming from the southern end of the Okavango Delta via the Botletle River. The pan teems with game but drivers have to be careful to stay on the tracks,' Dan told them.

"A few people have got themselves bogged down, gone for help and found, when they returned a day or so later, that the vehicle had completely disappeared," Dan warned them. "They just sink through the surface and into the mud below, never to be seen again."

After what appeared to be a pleasant but inconsequential evening they all went to bed. Dan went to his radio set up and made a very special call on a little used frequency. He identified himself with his call signal "Botletle". The conversation was in Afrikaans.

Dan said: "Party of six, one black woman, her white husband, two white adult children, one coloured adult child, all named Lawrence, one white adult female named Hawthorne, over."

There was a short silence.

"I'll just get someone; please wait. "Over."

Another voice came on the line, and Dan repeated his message.

"Where are they from? Over," asked the voice.

"Kenya, but most of them live in England. Over."

"Do you know anything about them? Over," came the voice.

"Peter Lawrence, the father of most of the children, is the Minister of Agriculture in Kenya. Over."

"Anything more? Over."

"Two of his children have played rugby for England. Over," answered Dan.

"O.K, thanks, where are they going? Over."

"They will be in Maun in two or three days; tomorrow they are going onto the salt pan. Over," responded Dan.

"O.K, thank you. Over and out," came the voice.

The next day there was a conference in the bowels of the State Security centre in Pretoria. Hannes Roux and a number of other officers were there. The subject of the Lawrences came up. The conversation was all in Afrikaans.

"I bumped into them in the Holiday Inn in Gaborone," reported Roux.

"We're pretty sure that the coloured, Kamau, has attended an ANC training camp in Tanzania; we didn't get final confirmation as they got our man and executed him before he was able to return here," he continued.

"Also that Jessica Hawthorne has been acting as a courier for the ANC for some years now."

He produced the photographs taken outside the Holiday Inn in Gaborone.

"OK, I recognise these two," said a senior man excitedly. "They have played rugby against us."

"Yes, that's correct," said Roux.

"What about that Kaffirboetie (lit. Kaffirbrother, derogratory term for people with sympathies for black people) Lawrence and his wife?" asked the senior man.

"We have no evidence of any activity outside Kenya; they seem to be straightforwardly involved in trying to help that place," said Roux.

The senior man growled.

"They will wreck the place like they've wrecked everything else." They all knew he was referring to the African government there.

"What about this Robert Lawrence?" asked the senior man.

Roux hesitated.

"He has no direct contact with the ANC," said Roux eventually.

"But?" The senior man looked at him quizzically.

"Do you know who Giles Dingley-Ferris is?" asked Roux.

The senior man stiffened.

"That's the fellow who is trying to get some of our Kaffirboetie ministers to talk to the ANC in England."

"The very same," said Roux.

"What's he got to do with this lot?"

"Dingley-Ferris' wife is Robert and John Lawrence's aunt," answered Roux.

"How come?"

"Their mother, who died some years ago, was Mrs. Dingley-Ferris' sister. They were both brought up in Jo'burg," Roux continued.

"We must be very careful then," said the senior man.

"Maybe they are just in Botswana on holiday and will go back home afterwards," he continued.

"Maybe, but I doubt it. Botswana is an easy jumping off point for activity here. Kamau Lawrence will more than likely try to come in here and pass himself off as a Coloured," answered Roux.

"What about the language? He will have to speak Afrikaans," said the senior man.

"He's been having lessons in England. I think we can assume that he speaks the language reasonably," Roux said with some finality.

"Keep an eye on them then, but don't do anything without instructions."

"Yes, sir."

Before they left in the morning Peter went looking for Dan to say thankyou but was told that Dan and his client had left at four thirty am to look for leopard. Peter left him a note.

They drove through the pan making certain they stayed on the track. The place was absolutely teeming with game, the usual zebra, wildebeeste and many types of antelope and in the distance some buffalo.

"Watch for the vultures," said Peter.

"Vultures?" asked Jessica.

"Lions," they all chorused.

"When lions make a kill the vultures, who have fantastic eyesight, will see it and as soon as one vulture drops down to the kill all the others follow. They keep an eye on each other for miles around," Robert explained.

Rafiki saw them first.

"Vultures," she pointed, and there they were a few hundred yards off the road.

Peter got the binoculars out.

"Looks like a pride of one large male and six or seven females, can't see any cubs," he said.

Kamau and Robert walked a few yards into the bush off the track.

"Too soft," said Kamau. "We'll get bogged if we try to drive down there."

"We'll walk," said Peter. "Grab the rifles."

They had borrowed a .357 Magnum and a .360 Express in Gaborone. Generally they kept them well hidden since they were not supposed to have them in game reserve areas. Peter had no intention of shooting anything, but he felt more secure with the rifles about.

Peter took his camera. John and Kamau took the rifles. Rafiki was going to stay with the vehicles, which were now parked under a small tree on the side of the tracks, but Peter persuaded her to come with them. They tested the wind and then went in a big circle so they approached the lions downwind.

They crept to within about two hundred yards. The pride was as Peter had described it and yes, there were a few cubs about as well. They crawled and crept closer with Peter taking as many photos as he could. Robert held Jessica's hand; John and Kamau were on the edge of the group slightly in front. The lions appeared to take no notice; the male got up and stretched and then there was a throaty growl. The group lay flat. The lionesses kept chasing the vultures away in between mouthfuls of zebra.

When the party came within about forty yards of the kill the lions had had enough. One of the lionesses leapt up and came streaking at them.

John and Kamau both kept their heads. They had no intention of killing anything and almost simultaneously each put a shot over the head of the charging lioness, who by this time was less than twenty yards away. The lioness veered off and just kept going, to be followed quicklyby the rest of the pride.

Peter had got dozens of really good photographs, which he was pleased about. Jessica was thrilled; to have got this close to a charging lion was really exciting. Even Rafiki, who pretended to be somewhat disdainful of all this interest in wildlife, was excited. The lions disappeared over the horizon and the group went up to the half eaten zebra, which would now be given over to the vultures during the day and the hyenas and jackals at night.

"Poor lions," muttered Jessica, "they've lost their meal."

"Don't worry," said Peter. "There's plenty of game about, they will not starve."

They made their way back to the vehicle, and spent most of the day on the pan. Camp was made again on the bank of the Botletle.

The next day they made their way into Maun.

Robert found a telephone at Riley's Hotel in the town and organised accommodation for them at Island Safari, a hotel set up a few miles out of town. Peter meanwhile had gone into one of the safari companies, which had moved its base from Nairobi to Maun; the same one Dan Blundell worked with.

"I've organised mokoros to take us into the delta; they'll pick us up at Island Safari, the day after tomorrow," he told Robert.

Dan Blundell had already mentioned the encounter with Peter to the people at the safari company in Maun, so they were expecting him. Peter was well known to them as their operations had originated in Kenya. They didn't really approve of his activities during the emergency in Kenya, when he had seemed to take the part of the local Africans rather than the white settlers. Although they had got used to the idea of Peter marrying Rafiki, they along with the majority of settlers, would have been happy to see Rafiki hang. Peter was now a Kenya Government minister and supposedly powerful; they realised it cost them nothing to help him with his safari and they needed friends to protect their interests in Kenya.

The Lawrences made their way to Island Safari, which was located on the river out of Maun and consisted of a number of separate thatched bungalow type rooms dotted about the property and a main building which housed the bar and dining room. The hotel fitted into the landscape beautifully; it was located on the edge of the river, with the occasional mokoro drifting silently past, poled along expertly by the two-man crew.

They had dinner; afterwards Peter and Rafiki decided to watch a wild life film shown in an open-air cinema on the property. Robert and Jessica had an early night, thankful for a nice comfortable bed: making love on a camp bed within hearing of the rest of the party was not ideal as far as Jessica was concerned. John and Kamau were trying out the local Prinz Brau brewed at the German owned brewery they had seen in Gaborone. 'Yuck,' said John looking closely at the bottle in his hand, 'this is undrinkable.'

"Take a look at this," whispered Kamau.

Two pretty girls in their twenties had come into the bar followed by their parents.

"Give me the key," said John. "I think I'll just lock those rifles in the back of the truck out of sight; I'm uncomfortable with them in the room."

They had cleaned the rifles carefully once they got to the hotel. Kamau handed over the keys.

"Be careful of the fishing line," said Kamau.

"Fishing line?" asked John.

"There are some characters round here I don't like the look of. I tied some fishing line across the entrance to the room; if someone comes sniffing around they may trip over it, especially if they are in a hurry," Kamau replied.

John shook his head. "The things you think of," he muttered.

John walked the few yards to his room, shaking his head; as he approached he thought he saw a flash of light in their room and then he heard a low whistle. The light went out and just as John came to the door a figure came flying out and, as Kamau had promised, tripped over the fishing line and fell flat on his face at John's feet. John made a grab for him; but he rolled over and scampered away but not before John managed a good look at his face.

John went into the room, which looked almost untouched. He retrieved the rifles from under the bed, looked around, made sure the fishing line was in place, then switched off the light, and relocked the door. He carefully stowed the rifles in the truck well out of sight. He returned to the bar.

Kamau had edged closer to the two girls and was trying to converse with one of them.

"I'd like to introduce my brother, John," he said.

The girl burst out laughing, but found John's good looks immediately appealing.

"How can he be your brother? He's white, and you look like a Cape Coloured," she said insensitively.

"Same father," said John.

The other girl now joined them.

"Tracy and Jemma," they introduced themselves.

It took some time to convince the girls about John and Kamau's filial relationship.

"What d' you do?" Jemma asked Kamau.

"I'm at Oxford," answered Kamau.

The girls had been brought up in South Africa and were quite unused to meeting educated people of other races.

"And I suppose you play cricket for England," laughed Jemma, "Go on, tell me another."

Kamau smiled.

"No, but I do play rugby for England; I've played against South Africa and would again except for the boycotts."

The girls looked non-plussed. They turned to John.

"I suppose you also play for England," asked Tracy.

"No, I don't even play rugby and I'm at a less well known university in Scotland."

There was a lull in the conversation and John said to Kamau, "There was someone in the room; he fell flat on his face in front of me. I got a good look at him."

Kamau described him and where he and his two colleagues were sitting at dinner.

"How did you know?" asked John.

"I saw them gawping at us in the dining room," was the answer.

"What, someone in your room? You should report it to the hotel management," said Tracy. She was just about to march off and find the proprietor.

Kamau touched her arm.

"No, no, don't tell anyone, we'll deal with this in our own way," said Kamau.

Kamau kept his hand on her arm; she was surprised when he touched her but was quite happy for him to keep it there. Some music started up in the next room.

"Come on, let's dance," the girls got up.

John and Kamau's free spirit and exuberance soon charmed the girls. After a couple of hours Kamau saw John and Jemma moving off; John waved the room key behind the girl's back as a signal to Kamau. He seemed to be making equally good progress with Tracy who, after her initial hostility or indifference, had really fallen for Kamau's obvious charm and good looks.

It seemed that Tracy was totally aware of where John and Jemma had gone and once she and Kamau were outside she led the way quite confidently to the room which she and Jemma were sharing.

During the past few hours Tracy had almost forgotten that Kamau was not white. As they undressed each other she shivered in anticipation; all she could think about was holding that strong brown body.

Just as the dawn broke Kamau got a gentle poke in the ribs.

"Wake up lover," it was Tracy, "Maybe you should go back to your own place. I'll see you after breakfast."

Kamau could see that Jemma, looking rather sheepish, had just crept into the room.

"Maybe we could go fishing," suggested Kamau. "I'll see you at breakfast."

He dressed quickly and made his way back to his own room, remembering not to trip over the fishing line.

At breakfast Peter came bustling in.

"The four of us have hired mokoros and are going up river for the day. We thought you might be otherwise occupied," he said cheerfully.

"Where'd'ya get the boats from?" asked John.

"Oh, Dan Blundell's safari company, but the hotel can fix you up; ask at the desk. We'll see you at dinner," said Peter.

He left.

John went to the desk.

The girls came in looking fresh as daisies. Kamau groaned. "How do they do it?" he thought.

They greeted each other as if nothing had happened the night before.

"John has just gone to arrange a boat and a picnic lunch and some fishing rods," said Kamau. "You'll come, won't you?"

"Of course, but we'll just have some breakfast first." They sat down.

"Don't look behind you now," said Kamau, "but when you next get up, those two in the corner are the goons that were poking about in our room last night."

"They look like troopies (national servicemen)," said Tracy after she had made a trip to the buffet.

"Bit more than troopies," observed Kamau, "but you're on the right track."

The two 'troopies' as they had been described had been in Maun for a day or two before they had bumped into their quarry at Island Safari. They were actually trainees in the South African security police and had been told to keep an eye on the Lawrence party. The foray into John and Kamau's room was quite unauthorised and would have been frowned on by the higher authority had they known.

"Look at those tarts," muttered Danie in Afrikaans, "sucking up to that kleurling (coloured) bastard Lawrence. The next thing you know she'll be sleeping with him."

"That's illegal," said Kosie.

"Not here it's not," said Danie.

"It's against God's law," said Kosie defensively.

"Only in South Africa," said Danie.

"It's what the dominie (priest) says," Kosie went on.

"Shut up for a minute will you, I'm just trying to hear what they are saying," said Danie. Kosie was beginning to get on his nerves.

"Kosie, they're going in a boat up river; just go fix us with a boat and we'll follow them," said Danie, having overheard the conversation.

The two "agents" were like two peas in a pod; both were from the suburbs of Johannesburg and they were tallish and well built with unruly blonde hair. They were quite decent kids but were quite out of their depth in the wilds of Botswana. Their parents had been brought up on farms in the Western Transvaal but they had spent their whole existence in Johannesburg and had no rural skills at all. The atmosphere in the hotel resort was completely different to anything they had ever experienced and the apparent equality of black and white was totally alien.

Kosie came back.

"It's fixed," he smiled, "small boat with an outboard motor and some fishing gear."

Kamau and John loaded their own boat, which was a dingy with an outboard, and then went to call the girls. John noticed Kamau had put one of the rifles in the bottom of the boat.

"What do you want that thing for?" asked John. "I was hoping we could leave the guns behind."

"Instinct," said Kamau, "just instinct."

"I decided on a dingy instead of the mokoros," said John. "More private." He grinned.

They went off to be followed shortly by the two South African agents..

"I'll see if I can give them the slip," John said. He sped the boat up river and then found a small inlet where they hid. Sure enough, ten minutes later the agents whizzed past going at top speed.

"Should give us a few hours," muttered Kamau. They moved out of their hiding place and puttered quietly along the river which was clear and about six to ten feet deep. They were all wearing swimming costumes. Kamau baited a line for Tracy and while it was trailing away behind the boat, covered her with some sun tan lotion. He admired her natural blonde hair, her blue eyes and her beautiful figure with its freckled white skin. Suddenly the line jumped and would have gone in the water but Kamau quickly grabbed it. He handed it to Tracy.

"Just reel it in, there's a fish on the end," he said.

And there was; a small river bream.

He unhooked it and tossed it back.

"Hey, that's my fish," she pretended to pout.

"Too small," he grinned.

Jemma was equally pretty, but had black hair, brown eyes and her skin was quite dark.

"Touch of the tar brush I'm afraid, lady," laughed John. "What is it Zulu, or Xhosa, in your background?"

"Portuguese," she smiled," at least that's what I'm told, but since you ask I'll opt for Zulu."

"I'm going for a swim," announced Tracy, "to see if I can find the fish you so carelessly threw back." She got up.

"Don't," said Kamau, now quite serious. "I'll see if I can show you why."

"Why?"

"Crocs—just be quiet for a minute." Kamau took the tiller and very quietly moved the boat up river.

After about twenty minutes Tracy started to fidget. Kamau put his hand on her leg and then slowed the boat right down and pointed. They all looked but could see nothing; then they saw it as its mouth opened. A huge crocodile, about fifteen feet long, was lying on a sandbank. Kamau drifted the boat towards the animal to within about twenty yards. There was a quick movement and a mighty splash as the croc escaped in to the river.

Tracy went quite pale and clutched Kamau's arm. Nothing was said.

They found another little inlet and out of sight of the main river and lazily ate their lunch. John and Jemma disappeared and Kamau slipped Tracy's bikini off and made love to her in the grass. It was blissful, with not a cloud in the sky and a light breeze.

On the way home John said, "I wonder what happened to those two goons." They heard a lot of laughing and splashing and came round the corner to see both Danie and Kosie splashing about in the water.

"Stupid buggers," said Kamau.

Kosie had got back into the boat and Danie was half in with his legs dangling in the water when there was a splash and a yell and a large crocodile had grabbed Danie by one of his legs. Kamau didn't hesitate; he grabbed the rifle, took aim and fired. He hit the croc right in the back of the head. It released its grip and slipped back into the now bloody water. Kosie grabbed Danie and pulled him into the boat. John gunned the engine and covered the fifty yards that separated the two boats in a few seconds.

Kamau had put the rifle down and as the two boats touched, jumped into the other boat.

Danie's leg from the knee down was a real mess. Crocodiles attach themselves to their prey and then turn their bodies viciously to overturn or drown their prey. Danie was pouring blood. John grabbed a shirt and a towel and eventually between him and Kamau they stopped the flow of blood. Kosie just sat there with his mouth open.

Kamau looked around.

"What's your name?" he asked Kosie.

"Kosie."

"Look, Kosie, you and John take the other boat and go as fast as you can to the hotel. Get a doctor quick," Kamau ordered.

"Yessir," yelled Kosie.

John jumped into the other boat with Kosie and helped Tracy and Jemma into Danie's boat.

"Pass me all the warm things you can find," Kamau was giving all the orders.

"Ok, now go," he yelled.

John gunned the engine and in a flash they were off.

Kamau and the girls tried to make Danie as comfortable as they could. He then started the engine and they followed quickly, about twenty minutes behind John.

When they arrived at Island Safari there was a stretcher waiting with the hotel proprietor together with John and Kosie. They manoeuvred Danie onto the stretcher and then into the back of a Landcruiser.

John said: "There's a doctor in Maun, I'll go with this fellow. You bring Kosie and their kit; I expect they'll fly him to Jo'burg tonight." He was speaking to Kamau. The landcruiser sped off with the hotel owner at the wheel and John holding Danie down. Danie was now in severe pain although he had been given a shot of morphine at the hotel.

Kamau and the girls quickly helped Kosie pack up and then followed in one of their Landcruisers. Kamau retrieved his rifle.

They drove straight to the airfield where the doctor was waiting. By the time they arrived a plane had already been commandeered and the seats were being taken out so that it could accommodate a stretcher.

The doctor helped get Danie out of the Landcruiser and in the small waiting room at Maun airport had a look at his leg.

"Who tied this up?" he asked John.

"My brother, he's on his way," said John.

"Saved this fellow's life and probably his leg," he said. "Does he have medical training?"

"No, only first aid."

"Remarkable," said the doctor.

He gave Danie another shot of morphine and put him on a drip, then loaded him onto the aircraft just as Kamau arrived with Kosie and their baggage. Everything was loaded on to the plane.

The doctor came over to Kamau.

"Look, you saved his life," he said.

"I would have done the same for anyone," said Kamau.

"He shot the croc as well," added Tracy.

"Shot the croc?" asked the doctor.

The doctor looked thoughtful.

"My, my, where did you learn all that? Oxford?" he mused, "sounds more like the S.A.S."

Kamau just smiled.

Within two hours of the attack Danie was on his way to Johannesburg with Kosie and the doctor; another four hours later he was on an operating table.

When the plane took off they all quietly went back to Island Safari.

Peter and Rafiki met them as they returned and they went to Peter and Rafiki's room to hear the full story. They all crowded in; John, Tracy, Jemma, Robert, Jessica as well as Kamau, Peter and Rafiki. Kamau kept quiet, John and Tracy told the story.

"They were the two goons that were sent to watch us," said Kamau.

They all laughed.

"It looks as if their assignment came to an abrupt end," said Peter.

"Look, can we go somewhere else for dinner?" said Kamau. "I don't really want to have to tell this story over and over."

A few days later Kosie was in the basement room in Pretoria with Hannes Roux and some senior security officers. The conversation was all in Afrikaans.

"Well, Van Staaden, you made a real fool of yourself," said Roux.

Kosie remained silent.

"I said you made a real fool of yourself," shouted Roux.

"Yessir," responded Kosie.

"Ok, Ok, just calm down, let's just hear about all this," said one of the senior men more calmly.

Kosie told them.

"Why did you go swimming?" asked Roux.

"Well, we lost them," Kosie started.

"You mean they lost you!" shouted Roux. "You pampoen (pumpkin head)."

"Let me just understand all this," said the senior man.

"This fellow, a kleurling (coloured) has enough brains firstly to take a rifle with him, he then shoots a croc from more than fifty yards away standing up in a boat—we must bear in mind that he can't have had more than a split second to aim and fire, he then jumps into your boat and does a real expert job on Corporal Danie Vissers' leg. The doctor told me he can save the leg, thanks to the kleurling. He then organises you to go and get help. Anything else?"

Kosie told them about the abortive attempt to search Kamau's room.

"Shit, who trained this fellow, the British S.A.S?" asked the senior officer.

"No, the Russians in Tanzania, we've now had confirmation," said Roux.

"Well, we now know what we're up against. If that fellow Kamau had had any sense he would have let the bloody croc eat both of you. Now voetsak (get out)."

Kosie left.

The mokoros appeared to Rafiki to be tiny. There were three of these small narrow dug out canoes. The seats were just wooden slats and there was no shelter from the sun. It was winter time in Botswana but quite hot during the day. Peter, Rafiki and Kamau went in one canoe and John, Robert and Jessica in the other. The baggage, mainly all their camping gear, went in the third. Kamau and John had cleaned the rifles and put one in each boat; they supposed they weren't really allowed to take them but without saying anything to each other they had decided that provided they were all discreet nobody would care. Rafiki was not sure how much she would enjoy three days in this little dugout but she knew how much Peter loved the African bush and she was really hoping to renew her closeness with her only son Kamau, this young man who was so terrifyingly good at everything he did. Her eyes had been opened by the incident with Danie and Kosie; clearly he could use his power and skill to create and save as well as destroy. Each mokoro was manned by two local tribesmen, who poled the craft along the ill-defined waterways of the Okavango delta.

John had, of course, done his homework and told them all that the Okavango River rose in Angola and entered Botswana in the north-west at Shakawe. Much of the water flowed into and spread out over the huge area of the delta because the land was so flat. Some of the water found itself in the time of the annual flood flowing into Lake Ngami in the south west of the delta and some fed the Botletle River and the Makgadikgadi pan in the south-east. A small tributary fed the Chobe River in the north-east which eventually flowed into the mighty Zambezi.

"The extraordinary thing," added John, "is that about ninty percent of the water that comes in from the Okavango River in the north just disappears into the sands of the Kalahari Desert. The main flood comes in during April and gets here to Maun by July, so we will be seeing the delta at the height of the flood. According to the hotel the flood this year is about normal."

John and Kamau had said fond farewells to Tracy and Jemma. They had both exchanged their English addresses with the girls; Kamau didn't disclose that he was intending to spend time in South Africa.

The mokoros were owned and manned by some Wayeyi fishermen, who had found that taking tourists into the delta was a very useful supplement to their income. The Wayeyi or Yei are a Bantu tribe, so the language roots are the same as for the Bantu tribes in Kenya. Within a very short time the group (except Jessica who spoke no African language) had charmed the Yei and were exchanging a few words of their own language with the boatmen.

The boatmen poled the mokoros silently up the river and into the delta. Rafiki watched her two favourite men totally absorbed in what they were doing, taking photographs of the numerous birds and wildlife that was around every corner. She watched Peter, now greying but not really showing his sixty plus years, still slim and strong and weighing the two hundred pounds he weighed when she first met him, his six foot three frame carrying the weight easily. He needed spectacles to read but out here his long sight was perfect and he and Kamau operated his accumulation of cameras like two small boys playing with meccano sets. They were completely oblivious of the discomfort of the boat and Rafiki's observation. She watched her only child Kamau, dressed only in a pair of tatty shorts, his brown skin making him look the picture of health. Kamau was slightly shorter than Peter but well built and lithe and strong; after all the trials and tribulations of the past years Rafiki felt very fortunate in her family and her relationships in general. Rafiki looked at herself, and found that she also carried her middle age years well, her mother's Masai blood had given her her height, which at five foot nine was tall for an African and she was still quite slim. She wore jeans and a shirt and sandshoes on her feet and she was thankful for her large straw hat to keep off the sun. She wasn't that fascinated with the wildlife and camping but tolerated it to be close to her family. Somehow this trip felt special to her.

They had seen several evil-looking crocodiles and wide-mouthed hippos on the way as well as numerous Lechwe antelope, whose splayed hooves enable the animals to cope with the marshy ground in the delta. Rafiki marvelled at how the boatmen knew their way around; for her the delta was a confusing mass of water and reeds, the channel seemed to have no fixed course and clumps of reeds seemed to float past in a completely haphazard manner.

Suddenly the boatmen stopped and pointed; a small herd of elephant were crossing the river ahead of them, having to swim in the main channel.

The boatmen were able to get the canoes to within about thirty or forty yards of the beasts and Peter and Kamau in the front boat and John and Jessica in the other had a field day with their cameras. When he saw the elephants Robert had put his own camera down and picked up the rifle; he levered a round into the breach. His precaution was unnecessary; although the animals were aware of human presence they took no notice of the party and climbed out of the water and continued on their way.

They stopped for lunch and then at about four o'clock they landed on a small island and made camp. One of the boatmen signalled to Robert to bring his rifle and they went off for an hour and came back with a young Lechwe male.

Peter looked at Robert disapprovingly. "Surely that's illegal, this is a game park," he said.

"From what I can gather he says he has permission to hunt here since this is his traditional land, so it seems to be all O.K," said Robert. "At least we'll have fresh meat tonight." He grinned.

Peter grunted.

In the hour that Robert had been away an area of ground had been cleared and the three tents pitched facing what was now a blazing fire. Peter and Rafiki were sitting on deck chairs sipping cold beers; the others were making do with stones and logs as seats. Much to their fascination and surprise the boatmen were included as ordinary members of the party. Robert butchered the meat and Jessica organised vegetables; she had already wrapped potatoes in tin foil to put in the ashes of the fire.

They were all enjoying the last of the sunlight and were preparing to wrap up since the nights can be cold at that time of year in Botswana.

Kamau addressed Jessica very kindly. "Jessica, I don't think you should now be going into South Africa to deliver that message for the ANC; even if they didn't know before, the South Africans will now have every reason to be suspicious of you. They will pick you up and you may get hurt."

Jessica bridled; she had always been slightly jealous of Kamau's easy access to the ANC leadership and her own comparatively low status in the organisation.

"How the hell do you know what I'll be doing after this trip? It's none of your damn business anyway."

Kamau hesitated, "Look, I know that Trevor values you highly but I also know that he would prefer you and Robert to play the important background role of providing safe meeting places in England for the leadership of the

ANC and the Nationalists, when they come to their senses, so they can negotiate the political future of South Africa." He bit his tongue and wished he had not used the word background.

She flew at him.

"Stuff you Kamau; I'm just as much committed to change in South Africa as you are. I know I have a white skin but I don't want to be relegated to the background as you so aptly put it. This process may take another fifty or more years and you want me in the background knitting socks or something. Anyway I've told Trevor that after this trip I will start to act as the hostess with Robert at Dingley Park."

Kamau was not to be put off.

"Jessica, just listen to me: even if the South Africans were not aware of you before, as sure as a God made little apples they will be aware of you now. You will be picked up and searched as soon as you set foot in the country, then your cover will be blown and you will be no use in any role any longer-assuming, of course that you survive."

Jessica was not put off.

"This is the tenth and last time I will be doing this; just leave me alone. I will deliver the message and then get out."

Kamau looked imploringly at Robert; they didn't need to say anything. Robert would talk to her later.

They finished what was a delicious dinner and Kamau helped Jessica wash up. She was still cross with him but allowed him to put his arm around her.

"Please don't get hurt," was all he said. "Robert needs you and so does the ANC, and please understand that I know what I am talking about. These people are evil and will stop at nothing to protect their special white society."

She was silent.

They spent a delightful hour after that talking to the Yei boatmen. None of them, apart from Jessica, had ever been in a position where they couldn't communicate fully with their fellow Africans. Using a mixture of Kikuyu and Swahili, together with Peter's fluent Zulu, somehow they managed to piece together a conversation, and they talked about their families and way of life. The boatmen were pleased and flattered; generally they sat separately from their guests and were treated like servants.

Gradually everyone drifted off to bed. The boatmen wrapped themselves up in large, animal skin karosses, which kept out the winter chills. Peter and Rafiki sat up for a while longer enjoying the solitude. At this time of year in Botswana Peter knew there was no chance of rain and the sky was indeed completely clear. The only light came from the dying embers of the fire and the stars and moon. Rafiki shone the torch around and picked up a few eyes, some Lechwe and jackal and hyena. Peter made sure that the remains of the buck that Robert had shot were wedged well out of reach in a tree. Peter always loved the African bush at this time of day, when there was no sign of other human presence, and the animals were doing what they had always done without interference. The air smelt fresh and the water unpolluted. He bent down and kissed Rafiki.

A hyena had made a nuisance of itself in the night and eventually the boatmen had chased it away.

Everyone was woken early with the nearby grunting sound of the hippos. When Jessica opened the tent flap she looked straight into a pair of unblinking hippo eyes not twenty feet away.

"Don't worry," said Robert, "it's probably just curious. Hippos can be dangerous if you get between them and the water though."

The hippo yawned, opening its great cavernous mouth, which Jessica could examine in all its glory. She shivered. This Africa, she could see how all the Lawrences, black, brown and white, loved it, with its primitive appeal, its violence, its unpredictability. She wondered if she could ever be part of it in quite the same way that Robert was. Jessica was tall and slim and pretty with long, reddish brown hair, smallish boobs (too small she thought) and a few freckles; she had piercing green eyes and was very bright. She was very successful in her own right as a lawyer but she wanted more, she wanted to make a difference here in Southern Africa. She knew that Kamau was right in what he had said, but why should he get all the glamour jobs; she also wanted to be a heroine, not just some backroom lackey, as she thought of it. Robert kissed her and woke her from her reverie.

"Penny for your thoughts," he said teasingly.

"They're worth a bloody sight more than that," she smiled. She was glad she was back with Robert, whom she now expected to marry. She was thankful for his patience.

Kamau was busy making up the fire and cooking breakfast. The hippo had decided to move away.

"Come on, out, out!" yelled Kamau exuberantly. He started to let the guy ropes down on Robert and Jessica's tent.

"Hey," shouted Robert.

"Come on, come on, enough of that canoodling, half the day has gone already, we must be off," he yelled.

"It's only half past six," Jessica looked out.

"That's right; as I said, half the day has gone."

Eventually Peter, Robert and John tackled Kamau rugby style and tossed him into the river.

"Hey, I might have been eaten by a croc," he yelled.

"No croc would touch you, chum," said Peter. "They'd be put off by the smell. Anyway you are too tough, they wouldn't cope."

Kamau kicked water at all of them and then settled down in a pool to wash.

Robert threw him some soap.

As a precaution Peter fired three shots into the river.

"That'll keep any crocs away for about thirty minutes," he said.

Jessica and Rafiki eventually took over the breakfast duties. Kamau ate two huge breakfasts.

"I'll arrange a worm dose for you when when we get back to Maun," Peter said in mock seriousness.

The mood of the safari had now been transformed by Kamau to one of light-heartedness. They all helped pack up the camp and by nine they were on their way again. They decided to take it in turns to pole the mokoros, making sure that the Yei boatmen would be in a position to take over quickly when they came across game to be photographed. The party spent three nights out in the delta and then found their way back to Maun in the afternoon of the fourth day.

"I know the boys love getting really filthy," Rafiki confided in Jessica, "but I'm really looking forward to a nice hot bath."

Jessica nodded. She hadn't been able to make herself wash in the river much, it was really too public and there was the ever present fear of crocodiles.

The mokoro crew were each given a handsome bonus and bid their farewells. Peter and the boys then made sure all the equipment was dry and serviceable and they repacked the landcruisers.

John and Kamau cleaned the rifles; they then went looking for Tracy and Jemma but were told they had left the day before.

"There was a reporter sniffing around looking for you though," said the hotel owner.

"I hope you told him that I wasn't coming back," said Kamau.

"Yep, he badgered Tracy but she wouldn't tell him anything either."

"Good for her," said Kamau.

The next day they went north out of Maun and made for Savuti.

"Just a few years ago there was a small earthquake in the area which opened up a channel from the Chobe River, which now provides a regular supply of water to this otherwise waterless area," John told them. "Of course, another 'quake could reverse the process and dry it all up again."

The water attracted huge amounts of game of every species. There were large herds of sixty and more elephants as well as herds of up to five hundred buffalo and many thousands of Zebra and wildebeeste.

Rafiki was pleased with the trip; despite the camping and somewhat uncomfortable conditions there had not been a cross word said; everyone had pulled their weight. When Robert got his vehicle hopelessly bogged by going down the wrong track in one place, although he was mercilessly ribbed by Kamau and Peter, the party cheerfully helped him dig the vehicle out. They all fixed punctures without complaining. Peter in particular took hundreds of photographs.

The final stop was Chobe where they camped on the edge of the Chobe River. Both upstream and downstream of the Serondela camp there were watering spots for the game, which was numerous.

On the last evening before the long trek back to Gaborone Kamau decided to have another try at persuading Jessica to abandon her plans for delivering her message for the ANC.

This time he was less confrontational, but put his arm around her and said,

"Jessica, we all love you dearly and really don't want to see you come to any harm. Please reconsider your errand in Jo'burg; it's just not worth it. I am certain that the South African authorities will be looking out for us and will then follow us if we are allowed into the country."

She eased her way out of his embrace.

"Look, Kamau, I hear what you say but I'm going to do this just for my own sake. This is the last time, I promise."

The reply was not unexpected.

"Ok," he said, "can you give me a contact point in Jo'burg? Robert at least will be nearby and if I can manage it so will I."

After some argument she gave them an address of a small hotel in Hillbrow, the crowded flatland of white Johannesburg. She promised to do nothing for forty-eight hours after she arrived in the city.

On the last day of the trip they packed up quite sadly, all perhaps thinking that this was a watershed in their lives.

Peter and Rafiki were staying in nearby Kasane for a few days to visit another Kenyan hunter friend of Peter's who had moved his operations into the area. After that Peter had arranged with the Zambian government to visit some of the facilities in that country. They were to be picked up by a car at Kasane. As neither Peter nor Rafiki wanted anything to do with the white regimes in the south and east (Rhodesia), they decided to make their way back home from Zambia.

It took two days for the rest of the party to drive the approximately one thousand kilometres back to Gaborone across the bone-shaking roads. They all shared the driving.

Kamau had decided that speed was the essence if he was to avoid the South African authorities. The idea was for him to smuggle himself into the country under a false identity. Arrangements had been made for him to stay with a coloured family in Coronationville, which was a designated "coloured" area in the western suburbs of Johannesburg.

Chapter 8

John and Jessica had dropped Kamau and Robert at the office of the car hire company near the President Hotel in the centre of Gaborone. Kamau had a small backpack with a change of clothes, some South African money, a bank account and an identity in the name of Willie Lemmer, born in District Six in Cape Town in 1953 and now living in Coronationville (named at the time of the Coronation of Queen Elizabeth II). He had some water and food and a torch. He was dressed for a very strenuous bush walk.

He gave John a packet.

"This is my British identity; please send it by registered mail." It was addressed to Giles and Louise's address in Belgravia; it would be safe enough there.

John had made a booking at the Holiday Inn in Gaborone for himself and Jessica; he had told the reception staff that their arrival time would be late, after seven p.m.

"Don't book in to the hotel before about six-thirty and only take the vehicle and equipment back tomorrow; if I know anything about them the South Africans will have both places and a few more besides under surveillance." Kamau had taken charge. "Drive down the Lobatse road," he said as an afterthought, "If anyone sees you that will put them off the scent."

Robert had hired a medium sized blue Ford as befitted a reasonably well to do English tourist.

"Any other drivers?" asked the Motswana lady at the desk.

"No."

He arranged to turn the car in to the rental company in Johannesburg a few days later.

John and Jessica had, as suggested, driven down the road to Lobatse.

Robert and Kamau relaxed on the verandah of the President Hotel and from their first floor vantage point watched the world go by in the pedestrian mall below. At about a quarter to six Kamau jumped up.

"O.K., let's go; with any luck I'll be able to walk round the border post while its still light," he said.

They drove the twelve miles to the Tlokweng border post. A few hundred yards from the post Robert stopped the car; Kamau got out and in a flash he had disappeared into the bush. Robert was certain he had not been seen; there were no cars about, just the usual collection of cattle on the road grazing on the verges. The idea was for Robert to enter South Africa legitimately as a tourist; he would then pick Kamau up a few hundred yards the other side of the post. He anticipated the whole exercise would take an hour or two.

Robert dawdled, as he didn't want to draw attention to himself by waiting on the road on the South African side for too long. After about thirty minutes he went to the border post on the Botswana side and filled out the forms. The policeman asked him a few questions and then let him through; the post closed at eight p.m. and all was quiet. Robert drove the few yards to the South African side, filled out the forms and handed over his passport and paperwork to the policeman there.

"Any of those dirty storybooks you get from the Holiday Inn?" he was asked in gutteral English. The men at the border post loved "Playboy" and other similar magazines which weren't available in South Africa due to the censors so they happily confiscated any such publications and enjoyed reading them.

"No," answered Robert.

Then he saw the man suddenly stiffen and become more alert. Robert guessed that his surname had attracted attention.

"Are you alone?" asked the policeman.

"Yes."

There were a few more questions; the policeman then came out and looked in the car. The only piece of luggage was Robert's suitcase.

"We sometimes have roadblocks on this road at night," Robert was told. "Your code is one w blue"

"What's that supposed to mean?" asked Robert.

"Never you mind, just repeat that and you won't get into trouble," said the policeman.

In the meanwhile a colleague had reported Robert's arrival in the country to a security officer in Pretoria. Roux was alerted.

"Only Robert Lawrence you say?" said Roux when he was told, and then almost to himself: "I wonder where the others are?"

Kamau had jogged about seven hundred yards away from the road and then turned east and more carefully made his way through the bush towards the border. He wasn't really sure what to expect or whether there were border patrols. In the event he found a very solid ten-foot fence. He kept watch for about twenty minutes; the light was fading fast but there was no sign of any patrols. He jogged along the fence looking for gaps; he was certain this border was as porous as any in the world and it was bound to have a hole in it somewhere. After about two hundred yards, sure enough there was a freshly cut gap. Kamau smelt a rat; he retreated into the bush and a few minutes later, two men came along dressed in camouflage gear; they had a dog with them.

"No, no sign of anything," they were talking in Afrikaans.

"Ok, let's go home." They went off in the direction of the border post.

Kamau waited ten minutes then pushed his pack through the hole and crawled after it. He then jogged what he judged to be five hundred yards due east and turned south back towards the road. Sure enough there was a car waiting on the side of the road. Robert had the interior light on so that Kamau could easily identify him.

"What kept you?" asked Robert. "I've been here nearly thirty minutes."

"Border patrol," said Kamau.

Robert told him about the code and the probable roadblocks.

"How many cars have passed you while you were waiting here?" asked Kamau.

"Two," said Robert. "Don't worry, neither of them took any notice of me, I pretended to be having a pee on the side of the road as they went past."

Kamau grunted.

"O.K. looks as if it might be a long night," he said. "We'd better get on, but don't drive too fast; I'll need time to jump out and go back into the bush."

Sure enough about ten kilometres further down the road there were some red lights and a torch indicating a roadblock. Without a flicker of hesitation Robert slowed to a crawl and Kamau opened the car door and rolled out. Robert quickly glanced around to see Kamau pick himself up and dive into the bush; a minute later he came up to the roadblock. A torch was shone into his face and round the car.

"Code," barked a voice.

"One w blue," answered Robert.

"What took you so long to come from the border post?"

"I was taken short, I needed a crap," answered Robert.

The man grunted.

"Open the boot."

Robert got out and obliged.

"You may need the code again," said the officer, this time it is: "One w blue eight ten".

"One w blue eight ten," repeated Robert. He was beginning to see how their minds worked. He supposed that the code stood for one white in a blue car at ten past eight—a glance at his watch told him it was ten past eight.

This time Kamau was waiting for him on the road.

"I took a chance and only went a couple of hundred yards into the bush. I kept my eyes open for any side patrols but they don't seem to have any," he said.

Robert really put his foot down for about seven or eight kilometres and then slowed down. Sure enough a short way ahead there was another roadblock. The routine was repeated. Robert gave the code. As he opened the boot he said.

"What are you looking for? There's seems to be an awful lot of security around tonight."

"Mind your own bloody business," was the curt response. The flashlight was shone in his face. "Passport," he was asked.

"What are you doing in this country anyway?" asked the soldier.

"Holiday," answered Robert.

"Where are you staying tonight?"

"Friends in Jo'burg probably," said Robert. "Depends on how many more roadblocks I have to negotiate."

"O.K., you can go now," he handed the passport back and waved Robert on.

Once out of sight Robert drove slowly; Kamau appeared as if out of nowhere

"That was a close one," said Kamau. "This time they did have a side patrol. Luckily for me they were having a smoke break and I caught the whiff of their cigarettes so I was able to avoid them. Whew, I hope that's the end of the road blocks."

"I think so; I was not given any more codes," said Robert.

"According to the map there is a shortcut a few miles from here," said Kamau. "You take a sign saying Lindleyspoort, we then turn south, parallel with the Marico River and emerge on the main Jo'burg road at Groot Marico."

"Is it shorter? I was going to go through Zeerust," said Robert.

"I'm sure it's shorter; the road may be a bit rough though. It has the advantage of missing out Zeerust. They may be looking out for you in Zeerust," said Kamau. "I'm sure they wouldn't think that you would be aware of the shortcut so I guess that road will be clear."

They found the shortcut without difficulty. Robert really gunned the engine and the car flew down the rough dirt road. Kamau was exhausted and went to sleep; he woke up as they turned on to the main road at Groot Marico about an hour later.

"I would try to stop in Swartruggens but I'm sure the hotel is for whites only," Robert said matter of factly.

"Mm," said Kamau, "I don't want to attract any unnecessary attention. We'd better go through to Jo'burg. If you see a phone box anywhere I'll warn my hosts that I'm on the way."

Without having had to directly confront the situation, Robert had become aware that he, with his white skin, would be treated as a first class citizen in this country whereas his brother would automatically be marginalized as part of the coloured community. No consideration whatsoever would be given to Kamau's ability or education.

As if reading his mind Kamau said, "I've been given a job as a waiter in one of the large hotels in downtown Johannesburg; apparently that won't arouse any suspicion. Anything professional or semi-professional would immediately attract the attention of the authorities."

"How long will that go on for?" asked Robert. "What are you actually going to do here anyway?"

"I don't know what I'm going to do here."

"When will you go back to Oxford?" asked Robert.

"I have been given a year off, as a special dispensation," answered Kamau. "I eventually had to get Giles to intervene."

Kamau produced a detailed map and guided Robert into the vast city of Johannesburg. The few phone boxes they found were smashed up and out of order.

"We'll have to just go to Coronationville and knock on the door," said Kamau. "It's on this, the west side of the city."

After making a few wrong turns they eventually found the Coronation-ville hospital and found their way from there.

The suburb even at night was neat and tidy but the small houses gave the place an air of poverty. Robert's heart sank into his boots.

Kamau guided them a bit further.

"This is the street," he said. "Just park here. Let's make sure that I can direct you to the hotel in Hillbrow, and then I'll go in. I don't want them to see you; if I just go inside that's a signal to go. Only the head of the house, Mr. Oakley, knows who I really am; the rest of them think I am Willie Lemmer from Mitchells Plain come to better himself in Jo'burg. Call this number and tell me where you are staying. Only speak if it's an adult male voice. Otherwise just put the phone down." He handed Robert a scrap of paper with a number on it. He got out with his pack and walked the fifty yards or so to the house. Some of the neighbourhood dogs started to bark. He stood by the door of a small cottage for what seemed like ages. Eventually a light went on and the door opened; after another long pause Kamau was allowed in, the door closed and the light went off.

Robert found his way with difficulty to Hillbrow and identified the hotel that Jessica had mentioned. He decided to check into another one nearby. If the security people were tailing Jessica he didn't want them to know he was about as well. A sleepy clerk gave him a room key. When Robert asked where he could park his car the clerk grinned.

"Outside meneer, but it probably won't be there in the morning,' he said cheerfully, 'cars get stolen round here all the time, or just smashed up."

John and Jessica drove down the Lobatse road and then returned to Gaborone just after dark. The hotel provided secure parking for the vehicles and they checked in separately. After dinner they both collapsed into bed and slept until the birds woke them the next morning.

At early breakfast Jessica said, "We'll drop the vehicles off at eight—I'm sure they said they opened early—and then make our way to the airport for the midday flight."

John was going on to Durban to stay with long lost relatives. He had offered to stay in Jo'burg but Kamau had decided that it was likely the authorities would be aware of their arrival and if they split up at least one of the security people might tail John, which would get them out of the way. Kamau had told Jessica she would be certain to be tailed from the airport.

John and Jessica drove their now very dusty trucks to a site in the industrial area of Gaborone and were greeted by the proprietor. They unloaded everything and checked it. They had already returned the rifles.

"All in perfect order," he said smilingly.

"Trucks are a bit dusty," offered Jessica.

"Oh, don't worry about that."

They settled the small amount owing and asked for a ride to the airport.

Unseen, a black man in a worn pair of shorts and shirt had seen them come into the site, had quietly picked up his bicycle lying nearby and had ridden off to make a call to Pretoria from the nearby Gaborone Hotel. He'd been hanging around for almost a week.

"That's three of them," said Hannes Roux when he received the report.

"I wonder where that little shit Kamau is; I'll bet he's given us the slip somehow and is already here."

The flight to Johannesburg was uneventful and the South African customs and immigration took no time to check the ten passengers from the Botswana flight.

The officer checking John and Jessica didn't blink an eye but he did alert the security people as he'd been told to do when he saw who was in front of him.

"Have a nice holiday," he smiled. They looked harmless enough; these security people were always fussing about someone or other, he thought.

They found their luggage and then John helped Jessica find a taxi to take her into town.

Kosie had been designated to watch out for the two of them since he knew what they looked like. He'd been alerted by the customs and was relieved to find them coming out of the customs hall. He was totally at sea when Jessica took the taxi and John went back into the airport building. He followed John and soon determined that John was on his way to Durban. He found a phone box in the airport and phoned Roux.

"You mean you've lost track of the woman," fumed Roux.

"Well, I followed the man."

"O.K., go into town and call me in two hours; I have a fall back plan."

"Ja, meneer."

Jessica found her way to the hotel and was relieved to find a note from Robert when she checked in. She knew enough not to phone from the hotel but went for a quick walk into the bustling shopping area of Hillbrow and eventually in frustration, after finding all the phone boxes unserviceable, made a call from a small shop whose kindly owner took her for an English tourist.

"And how do you like South Africa?" she was asked.

"Oh, it's lovely," she replied, "but I've only just arrived." She made the call and was put through to Robert. She told him where she was staying.

"Have you been followed?" he asked.

"No, can we meet somewhere?" Jessica asked cautiously.

Robert described a small coffee shop.

"I'll be there in fifteen minutes," said Jessica. "I'm sure I can find my way there."

She asked directions from the shop owner.

"It's just two doors down," she was told.

After thanking the shop owner and politely avoiding further conversation Jessica spent the next fifteen minutes walking briskly round Hillbrow, stopping in unexpected places. She was quite certain that nobody was following her. She found the coffee shop and was relieved to find Robert already sitting there. After a quick peck on the cheek Jessica slipped into a chair beside Robert.

They briefly discussed their adventures since they had parted in Gaborone.

"One of those people at the hotel in Maun was at the airport," said Jessica. "He followed us out of the airport building and then followed John back in again."

Robert drew a sharp breath.

"This means they know we are here and will be watching out for us," he said.

"I'm certain that I was not followed here, I've checked," volunteered Jessica.

They drank their coffee.

"I need to deliver this package and then get out of here," said Jessica. "Frankly, I'm scared; it's never been like this before. I've always come in here, done my business and then either had a short holiday or just gone home. This time there's something wrong."

"Why don't you just dump the package and go home?" asked Robert.

"You know I can't do that," answered Jessica. "I've been trying to get Mdantsane and the ANC to take me seriously for years; if I let them down now that would be the end of that."

Robert didn't argue.

"What do you have to do?" he asked.

"Make one telephone call; they will then tell me where to drop the package," she responded. "Normally it's close by. Then I can rebook my flight and go back to England."

"Why don't you call from here," said Robert, "most of these little places are quite helpful. Everyone knows the telephone system is rotten." Jessica called.

"You are to go to the Witbank Hotel at twelve thirty tomorrow lunch-time," said a gruff African voice when she had identified herself.

"Witbank, how…" the phone went dead. She went and sat down again. She was now shaking like a leaf.

"There's something odd going on," she said. "I've been told to go to a hotel in Witbank at lunchtime tomorrow. On all the other occasions it's been a letter-box drop. I don't like it. I'm now really scared."

"Try phoning again," suggested Robert.

She tried four or five times and all she got was a disconnected signal.

"This is a trap," said Robert. "Dump the package and scarper."

Jessica shrugged her shoulders impatiently.

"Phone Mdantsane," offered Robert.

"In England?" said Jessica incredulously.

"Where else?" answered Robert.

"No, I'm going to do what I was told; it's always worked out in the past," she said, 'I'll go straight to the airport from there."

When Roux was told about the call he grunted in satisfaction. Knowing that Jessica was an ANC courier they had always intercepted her messages copied them and returned them for the apparently safe ANC pick-up.

Roux had always left her alone knowing that at some stage she would come in useful.

"Now we've got them," he muttered to himself. "I'll bet those two Lawrence bastards will be following her like bees round a honey-pot." He rubbed his hands.

Robert phoned Kamau. The first two times he put the phone down with a polite, "wrong number." This would excite no comment. Wrong numbers were a way of life in South Africa.

Then the third time he got through to a man and asked for Willie Lemmer. Kamau came on the line almost instantaneously. Robert told him the story.

"Tell her to dump the package and get the hell out," said Kamau.

"I have but she won't listen; something to do with her credibility," said Robert.

"I don't like it, it's a trap; probably for all of us," said Kamau.

"My thoughts exactly," said Robert, "But she won't listen. I think our best bet is for her to deliver the package and then we should high-tail it to the airport and get her out of here."

"If we get that far," said Kamau dubiously. Eventually he said, "I'll be there; you may not recognise me immediately though. You make sure you are also in that dining room having lunch but separately and don't be too obvious. Wear a hat and dark glasses or something." Kamau was totally in control.

"O.K.," said Robert; he was out of his depth now.

"And get another car, don't use the car we came through from Gaborone in," said Kamau.

"O.K., anything else?" asked Robert.

"No, see you tomorrow."

Jessica took the train from the busy Johannesburg station. She went to the white's only ticket booth and eventually was directed to the right platform.

"Change in Pretoria, lady, "said the ticket inspector at the gate.

A quick walk from the station in Witbank following directions given to her by the ticket inspector at Witbank saw her approaching the Witbank Hotel on foot with fifteen minutes to spare. Jessica spent a few minutes getting her bearings in what was a singularly unprepossessing place. Witbank was, she knew, the centre of a major coal-mining district in the Eastern Transvaal; also, for many people it was a stop on the way from Johannesburg to the Kruger National Park and the eastern lowveldt.

The main street had several petrol stations and some dowdy looking shops and fast food cafes smelling of rancid oil. Cans and papers littered the pavement. She hurried towards the hotel and passed a very ragged looking African limping along the road. She nearly jumped out of her skin when a voice, which appeared to come from the African, said, "Slow down, slow down, and don't attract attention." It was Kamau. The African shuffled on.

The Witbank Hotel, typical of many built in country towns in South Africa in the first half of the twentieth century, looked reasonable from the outside but had a seedy, moth-eaten appearance as soon as one stepped through the entrance. Jessica cautiously approached the reception area, where a middle-aged man with thinning grey hair and a worn brown suit and nondescript tie eventually looked up over the glasses perched on the end of his nose.

"Can you tell me where the dining room is, please?" asked Jessica.

"Lunch is at twelve thirty," said the man in heavily accented English. He went back to his work.

Jessica glanced at her watch. At precisely twelve thirty, the dining-room doors were opened by an African dressed in a stained white jacket, dirty grey trousers and unpolished shoes with no socks. She was ushered to a table. The menu was put in front of her; it was freshly typed and currently dated. It was in both Afrikaans and English and the price was R7.50. There was soup, fish, two choices of main course, sweets, cheese and biscuits plus coffee or tea. The waiter sidled up to her.

"Yebo, missus," he said.

"Soup please," she said.

"Main course missus," he asked.

"Lamb, please."

A man came in and sat in the corner; he had on a hat and dark glasses. With a shock Jessica realised it was Robert; he gave no acknowledgment.

The soup arrived with a note. "Please go to room 17 immediately," it said. Jessica finished her soup and while the waiter was out of the room made her way out past Robert's table and without a word dropped the note on it. She then made her way to room 17 with her heart in her mouth.

Room 17 was on the upper story of a two-story building. She walked along the passage and knocked on the door.

"Come in," answered a voice.

She hesitatingly opened the door and entered a sparsely furnished room containing a single bed, a chair, and a chest of drawers with a small mirror on it. At first she saw nobody, then the door closed and from behind it emerged a well-built man with blond hair, piercing blue eyes and a horrible white scar covering the left side of his face. With a half smile he locked the door and put the key in his pocket.

Then she recognised him: it was the man that Kamau and Robert had talked to in the Holiday Inn in Gaborone. She couldn't remember what they said about him. He held out his hand.

"The package please, Miss Hawthorne," he said pleasantly.

She hesitated.

His demeanour changed immediately and he snatched her handbag out of her hands and emptied it out on to the bed.

"Damn you!" said Jessica, reaching out for her possessions.

She was pushed roughly aside; the man picked up the package from the pile on the bed and dumped the handbag on the floor.

"My name is Roux," he said, "I am from the South African Security Police and you are under arrest for cooperating with banned organisations."

Jessica said nothing.

"First though, I want some information and I want it quick," said Roux.

Jessica took one look at Roux's face and felt a shiver of fear; this man would stop at nothing. He had the fixed stare of a psychopath.

"Where is Kamau Lawrence?" he asked harshly.

"I don't know," she said in a small voice.

Roux stood up and backhanded Jessica across the face; she fell over the bed and onto the floor. Roux grabbed her roughly by the front of her dress, which tore.

"Where is he?" he yelled.

Jessica just cowered.

"There's only one thing for you now," Roux said, panting. He ripped the rest of Jessica's dress off

"No, no," she yelled. She could see he was going to rape her.

"Where the hell is Robert," she thought.

Robert was toying with the soup spoon labelled Castle and Lion Hotels and was just about to get up, not having touched his soup, when a very large man came into the dining room and sat next to him.

"Keep very still, meneer or you will get a gutful of lead. Very very still," he said. Robert started to protest, but stopped when a gun was stuck into his stomach.

"I don't want to upset the other diners but I will if I have to," said the man.

There were no other diners. The waiter was hovering next to Jessica's table with the next course, looking perplexed.

"Fuck off kaffir," said the large man.

The waiter scurried off into the kitchen.

There was then an almightly crash from upstairs.

The large man looked around, startled. Robert saw his chance and threw his soup into the man's face and crashed a chair over his head and as he slumped onto the floor, grabbed his gun and for good measure pistol-whipped him across the temple. He stuck the gun in his coat pocket and ran upstairs.

Roux had torn off Jessica's bra and was trying to pull off her panties when the door of the room gave way and Kamau came bursting into the room in a waiter's uniform. He had a knobkerrie in his hand. Roux was despatched into dreamland with one blow to the back of the head. Jessica scrambled to her feet.

"Are you O.K?" asked Kamau.

Jessica nodded.

"Quick, get dressed as best you can," he instructed. He pulled a sheet off the bed and wrapped it round her.

He grabbed the unconscious Roux and tied him up with Roux's own belt and shirt and stuffed some toilet paper in his mouth as a gag. Roux was then pushed under the bed, a rather tight fit.

"Come," he pulled Jessica along; she had had the presence of mind to pick up her handbag and all its contents, including the package destined for the ANC.

They ran out of the broken door, which Kamau pulled shut after them. They met Robert coming along the passage.

"Fire exit," Kamau said as he led them along the passage; the fire exit door led down a short flight of wrought iron steps, which in turn led into the carpark.

Somehow they ran unseen to Robert's hire car, which this time was a white Toyota sedan.

"Keys," yelled Kamau.

Robert handed them over without question. Kamau had already worked out a route out of town, and within less than a minute they had slipped out of the car park and without being seen had left the pandemonium in the hotel behind.

Kamau was plesantly surprised there were no security police or police in the car park.

"Jessica needs some clothes," he said to Robert.

"We have her suitcase in the boot; remember the idea was to take her to the airport after she had delivered the package."

Robert was trying to comfort Jessica who was still shivering in the back.

"Did he do anything to you?" asked Kamau.

"No," she smiled. "You arrived just in time."

"What's the plan?" asked Robert.

"Depends; you both have your travel documents with you, don't you?" asked Kamau.

Robert nodded. He had everything; his objective had been to get both himself and Jessica out of the country as soon as possible.

"O.K.," said Kamau. "Within an hour or so this car will be the subject of a full police alert so we'll dump it and borrow another. I'll see if I can put them off the scent a bit."

He turned north on a road signposted to Groblersdal.

Twenty kilometres down the road Kamau stopped.

"Get some clothes out for Jessica and take over the driving; I need to work out a plan," said Kamau.

Within a few minutes they were on their way again with Kamau poring over a detailed map. Jessica was busy clambering into a new outfit of clothes in the back seat.

Robert drove the remains of the eighty odd kilometres to Groblersdal.

Kamau then said, "We'll find a place to park this thing in a backstreet; hopefully the police will only find it tomorrow. Get everything out of the car and generally wipe it down for fingerprints. Lock it and dump the keys in a dustbin but stay here. I'll be back in twenty minutes." Kamau was in full control.

Robert did what he was told and he and Jessica stood on the pavement and waited for Kamau. Robert as an afterthought wiped the policeman's gun down and dumped it with the car keys.

Kamau went into the centre of town and watched for a few minutes. He was looking for someone who looked as if he or she wouldn't be coming back to the car for a few hours.

Soon a dusty looking V8 Chevrolet sedan pulled up outside one of the hotels. A large man dressed in bush jacket and shorts and boots, looking very pleased with himself, stopped the car and yelled across the street in Afrikaans.

"Hey Piet, come and have a drink, man. I'm waiting for the wife. The drinks are on me; I had a great day at the sale." Kamau presumed that he was talking about a cattle sale; Groblersdal seemed to be the centre of a wealthy farming area.

Kamau waited for the men to go inside and then unobtrusively opened the car door, which was not locked. The keys had been left in the ignition; obviously car theft was not a big problem in that part of the world. He found Robert and Jessica where he had left them.

"Wow," said Robert when he saw the car. "Going up in the world."

"Let's go," said Kamau. "With any luck we will have abandoned this thing by the time the owner is aware that it is missing."

"Where are we going?" asked Robert.

"Nylstroom," said Kamau. "One of the leaders of the Great Trek, I think it was Potgieter, thought he had found the source of the Nile, hence the name Nyl meaning Nile, and stroom meaning river. Unfortunately he was three or four thousand miles adrift. We will drop this bus there; by tomorrow the police will have found your hire car and hopefully shortly after that they will find this thing in Nylstroom, which will point them in the direction of Botswana."

"Yes," said Robert doubtfully.

"However, we will by then have borrowed another car and will be well on our way to Swaziland," said Kamau.

"Swaziland, but that's the other way," said Robert.

"Precisely," said Kamau.

Jessica had recovered from her ordeal and shared some rather revolting pies and cakes she had bought at a nearby tearoom.

It took them three hours to drive the distance to Nylstroom. They parked the car in the main street and Kamau disappeared to find another car. It was now dark; there was nobody about and within ten minutes they were on their way to Swaziland in a serviceable but battered looking Ford FI50 pick-up truck. They drove all night, taking turns at the wheel, stopping only once for petrol. They drove in a great arc: Potgietersrus, then down into the lowveldt at Tzaneen, then Gravelotte.

"There's a big antimony mine there," Kamau informed them. The drive took them through Acornhoek, Nelspruit, and then into Barberton before dawn.

"We need another car," said Kamau.

"O.K.," said Robert.

"For you to drive through the border, I'll be going back to Jo'burg," said Kamau. He stole and hot-wired a Volkswagon Jetta, and they transferred all Jessica and Robert's gear into it.

"We drive up the mountain pass to this border post here, and then you go through to Swaziland and the capital Mbabane via Pigg's Peak. After the border you should be O.K. Fly to Maputo and then Nairobi; the flights are not all that frequent so it may take a few days." Kamau found a piece of ribbon and tied it onto the aerial of the Volkswagen.

"What's that for?" asked Jessica.

"I'll watch you through the border post; if everything is O.K., remove it. If it stays on I will come through the post myself and help you," Kamau answered.

They drove in convoy up the steep, winding, dusty road to the border post. Robert noticed the cable way going all the way into the mountains in Swaziland.

"Some sort of mine," said Jessica. "I think they mine bauxite here, but I'm not sure."

Robert grunted. He was more concerned about safe passage through the border post.

Kamau followed far enough behind to avoid the dust from Robert's car. They had said their farewells in Barberton. Provided Robert and Jessica were not stopped at the border post they would make their way safely to Maputo and then Nairobi and then home to England. He, Kamau, was committed to spending at least twelve months in South Africa helping the ANC.He thought about the contrast between his life of privilege in England—Oxford University, Louise and Giles'establishments in London and Oxfordshire and his celebrity status as a member of the England rugby side—and his current position as a coloured person in Coronationville working as a waiter. That would have been significant enough but he was also in the country illegally. He shivered involuntarily.

Robert and Jessica parked and went into the border post, with Kamau watching. Although they were among the first in the line Kamau watched for a very anxious ten minutes. To his relief they came out of the office and clambered into the Volkswagen; the ribbon stayed firmly attached to the cars arial. There was a long delay at the crossing point with an officious guard re-examining their papers and then insisting on a thorough search of the car and belongings. At last the barrier was lifted and they drove through. About fifty yards past the post, Robert stopped the car and Jessica emerged from the car and removed the ribbon from the arial. Kamau breathed a sigh of relief and was just about to get into the pick-up when to his consternation he was approached by a white policeman.

"Hey kleurling," said the policeman.

"Dear God," thought Kamau, "I've completely blown it; what am I going to do now?"

"Do you have a light?" asked the policeman in Afrikaans. Kamau's thumping heart slowed a bit; he produced a box of matches and lit the policeman's cigarette.

"What time is it?" asked the policeman.

Kamau told him. The policeman sauntered off and Kamau unhurriedly climbed into the truck and drove the dusty few miles to Barberton.

Hannes Roux had eventually come round and managed to make enough noise for the hotel staff to find and release him. It was about an hour before he and the other policeman had had medical treatment and another hour before roadblocks had been set up around Witbank, by which time the birds had flown.

They found Robert's hire car early the next day in Groblersdal and the other car in Nylstroom shortly after that. The border posts into Botswana were alerted an hour after Robert and Jessica were safely in Swaziland. At four o'clock that afternoon John's hosts in Durban were unpleasantly surprised to find a squad of policemen with a search warrant on their doorstep. They spent two hours ransacking the house and were asked by the lady of the house what they were looking for as they left.

"Terrorists, mevrou, terrorists," was the response. John tried to look as confused as the rest of them. 'Must be something to do with that disreputable father of yours,' John was told by his hosts.

Two days later Roux was alerted to the fact that Robert and Jessica had escaped into Swaziland. His agents there could find no trace of them; they had dumped the stolen car in Mbabane and had spent two nights at the Royal Swazi Spa hotel under assumed names. They had then managed to negotiate a lift to Maputo where they had waited two days for the Kenya Airways flight to Nairobi.

Although Jessica had not been badly hurt in the encounter with Roux she had been very badly frightened and spent most of her time at the Swazi Spa sunbathing by the pool; she didn't say much. At dinner the last evening they were there Jessica eventually said to Robert, "I feel such a fool; Kamau is right, I am a white Englishwoman and I don't and cannot possible understand all the emotions in the political situation here. I've put all our lives in danger and could have completely wrecked Kamau's assignment. When he comes back to England I will make sure he knows that I've understood all that."

Robert just held her hand. She continued, "I am still committed to destroying this odious regime, but maybe there is a role for me in England as you and Kamau have said. Robert, I'm sorry, I've caused you much pain; I'll try to make it up to you if you will let me."

Robert kissed her.

"Of course," was all he would say.

During Jessica's period of introspection Robert spent a time exploring the small kingdom of six hundred thousand people. At one time a British colony, Swaziland together with Lesotho and Botswana, had thankfully escaped being incorporated into the Union of South Africa in 1910. The country was now independent and under the control of the traditional monarchy. King Sobhuza II had been the monarch since 1926 and ruled the little kingdom with authoritarian benevolence. Apart from the sugar cane industry and some cattle ranching in the east on the border with Mocambique there was a small industrial area near Manzini where the airport was located. Robert supposed this was because it was the nearest flat area to the capital, Mbabane, which was some thirty to forty minutes by car up a steep, winding road from Manzini. One of the mainstays of the economy was tourism from South Africa, resulting in the creation of resorts like the one they were staying in, which had a large casino attached. The casino was better appointed than the one in Gaborone but from what Robert could see emphasised the same social inequities. Most of the people throwing money around in the casino were white South Africans, with the local blacks generally confined to the slot machines. Robert also had a game of golf on the magnificent Royal Swazi Spa gold course; his companions were South Africans on holiday.

Jessica had phoned Mdantsane in London, and told him of her experiences and asked what she should do with the package, which she still had. "Get rid of it," was all he would say. He was relieved and embarrassed by Jessica's ordeal; if she had been in custody in South Africa she might have given the whole game away including compromising Kamau.

The border at Goba, going into Mozambique, presented no difficulties and Jessica and Robert were dropped off at the Polana Hotel, which was now badly in need of repair and had sunk to a very low level compared to the opulence of previous years; the swimming pool was empty and cracked and the place was overrun with United Nations and military personnel. They spent a little time exploring the town but with no visitors from South Africa and the Frelimo government fighting a civil war in the bush against the South African backed Renamo, the city of Maputo with its hot, humid, tropical climate was literally crumbling. The poverty was all-pervasive because of the large number of people who had moved from the interior to Maputo to escape the war. From what Robert understood, the docks were operating mainly as a result of help from the South Africans, who needed to keep them operating since Maputo was the closest port to the industrial hub of the Witwatersrand. In the colonial time Lourenco Marques, as it was known then, was a haven for South African tourists, who imagined it gave them a flavour of Europe on their doorstep. The Portuguese colonists had never established the rigid racial divides that existed in South Africa and indeed in most of the British Colonies and this had previously given the city its easy air of informality and fun. Now it was nothing but a tip; both Robert and Jessica couldn't wait to get out of there.

Rafiki and Peter welcomed them at Jomo Kenyatta Airport outside Nairobi and they spent a very restful week at Sattimma before going back to England. Jessica had many long chats with Rafiki about her experiences in

South Africa and was now reconciled to the fact that there was a role for her in England but not in the front line in South Africa.

Kamau, now in Barberton, parked the pick-up carefully and then spent half an hour wiping it clear of fingerprints. He bought a third class rail ticket to Johannesburg and eventually found his way back to the little home in Coronationville, just before dusk. He had told them that he would be away from time to time and that they should not worry.

"There was a message for you, Willie, from the hotel I think," he was told by one of the two children in the home. He phoned back. They wanted him to start the next day. All his conversations were now in Afrikaans. His life was going to be very different from now on, he could see.

CHAPTER 9

The Oakley family, Kamau's hosts, consisted of the head of the house Charles, his wife Lettie and a son and a daughter Jannie, twelve and Hettie, eight.

Charles worked as a carpenter for a large construction company engaged in building houses in the new white's only developments to the north of the city of Johannesburg. The names of the suburbs intrigued him, Morningside Manor Ext 3 and such like; to him they expressed the essentially middle class aspirations of the white population. The suburbs were free from Blacks, Coloured and Indians, or if not free, at least these people were only visible as servants or workmen and they never challenged the all white nature of the northern suburbs and the all white nature of the power structure.

Charles also had middle class aspirations so apart from his own wages, his wife, Lettie, worked as a hairdresser's assistant in central Johannesburg. This involved mainly washing the white madams' hair and sometimes setting it; occasionally when the shop was busy she was allowed to cut hair as well but generally this occupation was reserved for the white girls in the salon. In any case most white madams did not want a coloured girl to cut their hair. The two or three black assistants in the shop had an even lower status than Lettie; they were confined to sweeping up, making tea and coffee for customers and running errands. Lettie was not uncomfortable with this situation; she had a defined place in the society, her children were being educated and she was extremely conscious of the family's status in Coronationville, which was at the upper end of the spectrum of coloured society. The contrast between Coronationville and the neighbouring slums of Western Coloured Townships with their dirty streets, illegal drinking shebeens, illegal gambling joints, brothels, and frequent murders was a daily reminder that life could be a lot worse, and indeed was a lot worse even for some members of her extended family. What she had was worth preserving. The fancy white suburbs in northern Johannesburg were so far out of her reach as to be not worth considering and the more modest white suburbs nearer, such as Triomf, she thought were not much better than her own suburb. The Oakleys had recently saved enough money to buy their house so they were well set up as far as they were concerned.

Seven years earlier Charles Oakley had thrown his lot in with the ANC. Although technically, as a skilled carpenter he was in a job category that was reserved for whites, coloureds and Indians, which meant he could not be replaced by a lower paid black person or indeed any black person, he knew he was at least as good at what he did as any white person and the white carpenters were always paid something like fifty percent more than he was. Charles valued his position in much the same way as his wife did and he was proud of the hard work that had brought its just rewards; this was all right for himself but he wanted his children to be full members of society in South Africa, full and equal. That was why he had joined the ANC, although he never told his wife anything about it; he correctly thought that Lettie would have a fit if they even discussed it. Charles was about forty, of medium height, and stockily built; his crinkly hair was greying slightly and was brushed back. He had used his skill as a carpenter to make the most of the small bungalow in Coronationville. He was also a talented musician and played the piano very well.

Lettie was some five years younger than her husband. She had been pretty when she was younger but now she appeared careworn and she walked with a sort of slump, which made her look a bit dumpy. Her hair was turning to grey and although she tried to keep up appearances she looked like what she was, a rather tired, downtrodden coloured woman. Life wasn't all that bad though; she was well thought of in the neighbourhood and she enjoyed the company of the other women in her suburb. As far as Lettie was concerned Willie Lemmer (Kamau) was the friend of one of her husband's relatives from the Cape. She welcomed the additional means he brought into the household and was charmed by his modest ways and the way he immediately and unobtrusively made friends with the children.

To start with Kamau was assigned to a junior waiter's position in "The Thoroughbred", the main restaurant of the very large international hotel in downtown Jo'burg. Most of the waiters were Indian or coloured and there were on occasion some whites. Kamau was pleasantly surprised to find that the place was run with as little racial bias as possible, although none of the whites worked in positions lower than members of other races. Within a very short time Kamau had ingratiated himself with the kitchen staff and the white headwaiter. Within a few short weeks he had a set of tables for which he was responsible and two assistants.

The clientele were exclusively white, mostly business people and their wives and of course many overseas visitors. At the time South Africa was booming and was attracting interest from all over the world. Incongruously, blacks from neighbouring countries were allowed to frequent "international hotels" in the main urban centres, this priveledge did not extend to local blacks whatever their status. The hotel was not a place that Roux or the security police were likely to be seen in; firstly it was in "Engelse" (English) Johannesburg and secondly it was well out of their price range; however, Kamau always kept an eye on the booking sheet and periodically he glanced around the restaurant for any signs of danger.

Once he had mastered the job Kamau was able to hover around tables where diners didn't really seem to be aware of his presence, so he overheard some extraordinary conversations. Many of these conversations concerned the political future of the country; he overheard many prominent people telling their overseas guests such things as, "The blacks could never run this place. The Government is on the right track: let the blacks run their own affairs in their own areas in their own way."

"What about the urban blacks?"

"The Government says that the flow of blacks into the urban areas will start to reverse by 1978."

"That's only three years away."

"Ja, I suppose."

"Do you really think that will happen?"

"Maybe we should discuss our contract."

A typical comment from a woman Kamau took to be a northern suburbs housewife was, "Well, we have six servants: two in the house, a cook, two gardeners and my husband has a driver. We treat them very well but the idea that they could all vote and govern themselves is a joke. They are just like children; I spend my whole life seeing to them you know."

Kamau was especially appreciated by the Afrikaans clients, since he could discuss their needs fluently in their own language, and he often received large tips as a result.

The restaurant was elegantly furnished and the tables all had expensive salt and pepper-shakers. One evening Kamau noticed a very well dressed woman from a large party at one of the tables put a set of the shakers into her handbag. He quietly went to see the headwaiter.

"Are you quite certain they are in her handbag?" he asked.

"Quite certain."

"We'll just add fifteen hundred rand to the bill; that should sort the matter out. I'll be around to help should you need it when the bill is presented," the headwaiter nodded.

Kamau presented the bill and hovered. The guest was about to give him his credit card when he glanced at the total. A look of abject horror came across his face.

"Er, waiter, I think there is some sort of mistake here; the bill seems to be rather higher than I expected." Kamau admired the man's self-restraint.

Kamau just discreetly whispered, "No mistake, sir, but if you can persuade the lady at the end of the table to put the set of salt and pepper shakers back on the table, we can take fifteen hundred rand off the account."

The man went red and Kamau withdrew a discreet distance. The man casually got up and went over to the woman and despite a lot of head shaking the offending articles reappeared on the table. Kamau then processed the reduced bill. Nobody else at the table had the slightest idea that anything was amiss. Kamau was amazed, that these people who to him appeared to have everything still found it necessary to accumulate more by whatever means. The incident convinced him further than the only possible solution to the political issues in the country was a majority government; the blacks had to control their own destiny.

Kamau always worked Saturday evenings and lunch and dinner most weekdays. He was waiting for instructions from the ANC.

One Saturday after lunch he became involved in a game of touch rugby with Jannie and some of his friends in the street. The game was moved to the rock-hard and rather sparsely grassed rugby pitch at the nearby Coronationville High School and very soon more than thirty kids of all ages had assembled, enough for a fullscale game. Very quickly Kamau organised them into two teams with a few reserves and they played a game with Kamau acting as referee cum coach. He showed the forwards how to bind properly in the scrum and how to organise the line-outs. He showed the three quarters how to run the angles. Few of the kids had boots and most of them played in bare feet or "tackies" (gym shoes). At the end of an hour and a half scores were more or less even and the kids had all had a wonderful afternoon. Jannie was very proud of his "oom' (uncle) Willie.

A few adult men had gathered to watch the game; one of them came over to Kamau afterwards and asked in Afrikaans, "Where did you learn your rugby, meneer, you certainly had those kids going."

"Kaapstad (Cape Town)." Kamau smiled.

"You should take on the team here, meneer; they have been very bad the last few years."

"What do you mean, take on the team?" asked Kamau.

"As coach, meneer, they badly need a coach."

A few days later the headmaster of the school came over when Kamau was at home and persuaded him to take on the job as honorary coach of the Coronationville High School rugby team. Kamau had been well briefed and was able to mention the names of a few coloured rugby teams in the Cape, which satisfied the head as to his credentials.

Both Charles Oakley and Kamau had some qualms about this commitment, as they knew it was important to keep a low profile in the community; however being the coach of an obscure school rugby team in the western coloured areas of Johannesburg seemed a modest enough situation. They both independently decided the risk was minimal and didn't discuss it.

Hannes Roux was frustrated. He'd been humiliated by Kamau yet again and although his injuries were not permanent his pride had been badly hurt. Agents in London had traced Robert and Jessica back there, so they were out of the way, and he knew that Peter and Rafiki had returned to Kenya. John had been followed for the two weeks he'd spent in Durban and Roux had decided that John was not involved in any way with the ANC or any other subversive organisations. After his holiday with his South African relations he returned safely to England. There was, however, no trace of Kamau.

Roux's agents had found the cars that Kamau had intended them to find but he couldn't make up his mind whether Kamau had left the country or was still in hiding somewhere in South Africa. His agents had no found a trace of him in Swaziland where Robert and Jessica had left a trail that even the most inexperienced agent could follow; nor in Botswana.

"He has to be here in South Africa, probably somewhere in a coloured area," he thought. "I wonder what the little shit is up to?"

There were many police informers throughout South Africa particularly in the black, coloured and Indian areas. Without exception they were ordinary members of the society who evoked no special response, positive or negative, from the community. They were paid small retainers and were then given bonuses for information they provided. Much of the information was useless and was discarded but every now and then there was a gem, which led to an ANC cell or an arrest or something for the normal police to follow up. A few special agents were entrusted with more delicate missions and Roux had decided that the twenty or so "specials" located in the various coloured areas scattered throughout the country would be given a photograph of Kamau plus a background sketch. Included in the list of Kamau's interests was rugby.

"Bok-bok" Oberholzer was one of these specials. His father was a white man and his mother a coloured and until 1948 when the Nationalist government came to power they were able to live together. Both parents had been completely ostracised by their communities after the Nationalists legislated the Prohibition of Mixed Marriages Act in 1948 and then the Immorality Act two years later. The first made it illegal to marry across colour lines and the second made it illegal to have sexual intercourse across colour lines. Noboy really cared whether blacks, Indians or coloured people had sex across their various groups although they were separate races. The Government's concern was the so-called purity of the white race. Within a few years Bok-bok's father had had enough and he left Bok-bok and his mother to fend for themselves; they were never able to trace him. Bok-bok's mother worked as a prostitute, she felt she had no other option. She tried to look after her son but by the time he was thirteen he was completely out of control and he spent the next ten years in and out of reform school and prison. Now in his thirties, he ran a very successful shebeen (illegal drinking house) where he provided liquor, girls and dagga (marijuana) to his clientele, including the police. The police never bothered him as they were aware of his special status and he was able to pay off anyone he needed to with the profits from his shebeen. He purchased all his liquor openly on credit from the local Administration Board who knew perfectly well who he was and what he did; they welcomed his custom. The liquor companies all had representatives who called constantly; although they were not allowed to sell to him directly they often had promotions in his shebeen and sponsored entertainers. These reps also kept on the right side of the police and were able to warn him if "raids" were planned. These raids were mostly for the benefit of the white owned press and the upper levels of the police to show that the police were doing something about the proliferation of illegal drinking outlets in the black and coloured areas. It was impossible for blacks to obtain liquor licences then and virtually impossible for coloureds. The shebeens therefore provided for a real social need, and none of the clientele had any hesitation in frequenting Bok-bok's establishment, which was very well appointed with plush carpets, good furniture and appropriate music and lighting. Many nightspots in western capitals would not have had better facilities. Bok-bok made a fortune; his margins were high and the police and his own gang of thugs kept the competition away.

Bok-bok deeply resented his social status, that of a second class, voteless coloured man. His way of trying to redress that was to ingratiate himself with the police. He knew Roux personally and had provided numerous tips, some of which the police had acted upon. As far as he was concerned the pay he received from the police was petty cash; the reason he acted as an informer was that this was his way of trying to be part of mainstream white society.

Bok-bok at about five foot six was quite short but he was very broad and strong and nobody ever challenged him physically. He had a close-cropped mop of black crinkly hair and although he didn't say much, his shrewd, piggy little eyes never missed a thing.

Bok-bok was married with two small children; he tried to keep his personal life and his shebeen life quite separate. His mother still lived with the family in one of the better houses in Bosmont, an "upper class" coloured suburb neighbouring Coronationville.

When the notice and photographs of Kamau came into his office he briefly glanced at it and tossed them into a drawer. He'd given Roux enough recently; this issue could wait.

Kamau had done a few little chores for the ANC, delivering messages. He usually did these jobs before he went to work—he was only due at the hotel at eleven in the morning—so after lunch and before dinner he had two hours off. He became very familiar with many parts of Johannesburg doing this. The way the scheme worked was that the message and instructions would be left in his locker in the change rooms of the hotel. He had no idea who put the messages there but they were clearly a test. He delivered the messages without fuss and destroyed the instructions either by flushing them down the toilet or swallowing them.

One morning a more elaborate set of instructions was left in his locker; Kamau read them carefully. This Saturday night the ANC intended to blow up a pylon carrying high voltage electricity wires from the Cabora Bassa hydroelectric scheme in Mozambique. The area chosen was in a remote part of the Northern Transvaal but if successful it would disrupt supplies to Pretoria. He would have to leave for the rendezvous straight after work on Friday night.

"Damn," he thought, "I've taken Saturday night off for the semi-finals of the rugby." Coronationville High was in their first semi-final for years and Kamau wanted to be there to encourage them. "Can't be helped," he thought. "I'll tell them my mother is sick in Cape Town."

At the regular Thursday night practice he told his team that he would not be there on Saturday but he was sure they would beat the opposition. They had a very good practice and the team were left in high spirits.

After work on Friday Kamau rushed to the Johannesburg station, caught a train to Pretoria and then waited for the early morning bus to Pietersburg, where he eventually arrived in mid-afternoon. After another bus ride to a black township on the outskirts of town, by four o'clock he sat exhausted in a beer hall in the place he'd been instructed to wait. The beer hall was a large building made of concrete blocks, with a corrugated iron roof. The tables were concrete and were fixed to the floor and most of the seating was made of concrete. The principle seemed to be to have nothing movable that could be stolen or used as a weapon. The bar had a shutter that could be lowered at a moment's notice.

Kamau ordered a litre of traditional beer served in a white bucket-like plastic container. He sat and sipped it waiting for his contact to appear. Traditional beer was brewed by the local administration board, run by whites. The profits were supposedly destined for welfare in the black townships, but only after the unnecessarily large white staff had been fully compensated. It seemed strange to Kamau that a business, which took a wholly African product and supplied it to a wholly African consumer should be run by white officials. The beer was, however, very palatable and nutritious, being naturally fermented from a mixture of mealie (maize) meal and sorghum which gave it its pinkish tinge. It had the texture of thin gruel and had a low alcohol content.

After about twenty minutes a well dressed young black man came and sat next to him. When the barman had gone for a refill Kamau mentioned the password and received an appropriate response. They finished the beer and unobtrusively left the premises. Not a word was said as they hopped into a small Toyota bakkie (pick-up truck) and as it became dark made their way out of the township. Kamau and his companion pulled on balaclavas, supposedly against the winter cold but the balaclavas also helped to conceal their identities. Kamau also pulled on gloves to avoid leaving fingerprints. A few miles out of town they stopped near a culvert and another black man stepped out of the shadows with a small box. Without a word Kamau hopped into the back of the truck and while it sped on with his two companions in the front he checked the contents of the box.

"Explosives, detonators, fuse wire, timer, and ignition." He identified everything with a grunt of satisfaction. A torch (flashlight) had also thoughtfully been provided. His job was that of explosives expert: he was to blow up the pylon. The equipment was standard rock blasting equipment from the mines, which he had been trained to use in Tanzania. It all seemed simple. He sat with his back to the cab as they drove through the now pitch black night. After an hour the vehicle came to a sudden halt and the two men got out and pointed to where Kamau could see the faint profile of a pylon against the night sky a hundred yards or so away. They carried the box to the base of the pylon and Kamau got to work. Taking about an hour he set the charges so the pylon would fall away from the road. The timer was set at at two minutes and the men hurriedly made their way back to the truck with the box. The bakkie was turned around and they waited a few moments; there were twelve separate explosions. Kamau looked with satisfaction as he saw the great pylon slowly toppling over away from them; the huge cables broke and came hissing down to the ground like great snakes, spurting sparks everywhere. Then all went quiet, although a small grassfire started. They sped off with all three of them in the cab now; Kamau was dropped off at a railway station and some time during the early hours of the morning he stumbled out of his third class railway carriage in Johannesburg. He finally crawled into his bed in the little cottage in Coronationville without disturbing the family and he slept all day.

The rugby had gone well and Coronationville High had won, although they had had to survive some desperate attacks from the opposition in the last ten minutes of the game.

Bok-bok Oberholzer had decided to go and watch; he had no particular loyalty to either side and no real interest in rugby but he had heard that they expected more than five thousand people at the game so he thought it a good idea to check it out. Bok-bok watched unobtrusively through his binoculars from the top of the rickety stand. He surveyed the bench of the home team, as there had been some rumours about a new coach. "Nope," he thought. "It's the same old crew, no new faces there." He then looked across at the opposition bench with the same result. He quietly scanned the crowd but saw nothing to remark on. Shortly after half time he went home.

When little Jannie found Kamau in his bed later in the afternoon he rushed in and jumped all over him.

"Oom Willie, we won, we won!" he yelled.

Kamau looked perplexed.

"The rugby, you pampoen (pumpkin). Coronationville are in the finals and you did it man!" he yelled.

"What was the score?" asked Kamau.

Jannie told him and then gave him a graphic blow-by-blow account of the whole game.

Kamau was pleased.

Later that night after everyone had gone to bed, Charles Oakley sat with Kamau in the kitchen over a cup of tea.

"Over five thousand people there," he said. Kamau nodded.

"I think it's just as well you were not there. The police, man, they always check out these things and they don't like new faces," he said carefully. Kamau looked at him warily.

"I'll make myself scarce for the finals too, I think," said Kamau.

"Ja, it's better to be cautious."

Kamau did actually attend the finals two weeks later but sat in the stands; he had a couple of runners to pass messages on. Coronationville won easily.

Bok-bok had been unable to attend the match but pricked up his ears when he heard some of his staff talking about it. They talked excitedly about a new coach.

"Have you ever seen this fellow?" he asked one of them sharply.

"No meneer, but they said it's true, he's from the Cape somewhere."

Bok-bok thought the issue would keep but it seemed worth following up at some stage.

Kamau continued with his waiter's job, and every few weeks he was sent on another assignment, mostly to blow up pylons. After several assignments only one man came with him; the man never said anything and Kamau never saw his face. The programme was then stepped up, to once every four weeks, then every three and then every two. Much of this activity was not reported in the press and when it was, the extent of the damage and disruption was always minimised. Kamau was becoming exhausted; he feared that sooner or later he would make a mistake and then he'd be caught; but he had no means of communicating upward. Always the careful instructions were placed in his locker and he always followed them to the letter, but he knew he could not go on like this forever.

He decided that he would ignore the next set of instructions and see what happened. Once in the past he had blown up two pylons instead of one and on the Monday morning he had received a very blunt rebuke: "This is a military operation; you will obey your instructions precisely. Do not exceed your authority again."

Nothing happened when he ignored the instructions. The next Friday he found a further set of instructions in his locker. He decided to ignore them as well.

On the following Monday there was a terse note in his locker at the hotel. "Meet at the Pelican Club on Wednesday, 6pm". It gave him a password.

The Pelican Club was a well-known shebeen on the outskirts of Soweto. Kamau managed to swap shifts and take the evening off.

Kamau found the place and made his way uncertainly up a narrow set of stairs. He emerged into a small auditorium, which in the harsh light looked dirty, untidy and unkempt. He sat down in a corner; there was nobody else in the room, although a waiter had scuttled off behind a set of black curtains when he appeared. Kamau looked around, thinking that the place was no different to the few nightclubs that he had seen in London and he judged that the seedy appearance would disappear when the lights were dimmed and the place was filled with people. Someone started to fiddle with the sound system. A man came out from behind the curtains and beckoned, leading the way down a dimly lit passage. Kamau found himself in a small room filled with cigarette smoke. A well-dressed middle-aged black man was sitting in a comfortable chair, smoking, while three younger, unkempt looking men lounged around. One of them was pointedly cleaning a large calibre automatic pistol but no other weapons were visible. Kamau sat down in an upright chair.

"You disobeyed instructions," said the older man in English without any preliminaries or introductions.

"I was unable to fulfil those instructions," Kamau answered. "I've done everything else you asked of me."

"You must obey instructions; we cannot allow the momentum that has been created to slow down," said the man.

"The schedule that you have set makes it impossible to keep up," said Kamau.

"Nonsense, an action every two weeks seems very reasonable to me," countered the man.

"My job is an important part of my cover and even now I am being asked about my absences," said Kamau.

"Get another job."

"This one makes sense. I also hear some very interesting conversations," said Kamau.

"Such as?"

"Commercial discussions, take-over bids, even some security matters," Kamau answered.

"Why didn't you tell us?"

"You know perfectly well there is no mechanism for me to communicate. That is one of the reasons I did not complete the last two assignments. I need regular contact," Kamau countered.

"That will be very dangerous."

"I need to have a sense of what we are trying to accomplish. Why pylons, pylons, pylons, all the time? What about trains, police stations, even army barracks?" Kamau said calmly.

"These decisions are made by a higher authority than you; your job is to obey instructions," said the man.

The youth cleaning the pistol had now finished what he was doing and he pointedly fitted a full magazine into the weapon and a round was levered into the breach. He stared at the gun as if it were the most fascinating thing in the world.

"I am by far your most successful operative in the field," said Kamau. "In order to do what I am doing more effectively I need to be fully in the picture.'

"We have other operatives," said the man defensively.

"Most of whom are either ineffective or have been captured." Kamau was chancing his arm here but one or two things that Charles Oakley had let slip indicated that he, Kamau, was virtually on his own now as a front line operative. Kamau had surmised that the pressure he was now under had resulted from the elimination of other operatives by the security forces.

"You will not talk like that," said the man angrily.

"I am a volunteer," said Kamau. "I am committed to your cause but I am not going to put my life in danger more than I have to. I need to be consulted I need to be able to tell the hierarchy things I have learnt. I do have another life, I can return to that at any time and I am not going to be treated like Jessica Hawthorne."

There was a sharp intake of breath.

"What do you know about Jessica Hawthorne?" hissed the man.

It was clear that the other three in the room only partially followed the conversation; they nevertheless heard the change in the tone of the man's voice. They rose up threateningly. The man waved them down again.

"She is about to become my sister-in-law. I actually saved her from that animal Roux and the security forces and helped her to escape back to England. She got no help from you people at all," Kamau answered evenly.

"Miss Hawthorne was expendable," the man said carelessly and wished he could have dragged the words back into his mouth.

"Like me, you mean?" said Kamau evenly.

There was an attempt at a protest but Kamau had had enough.

"Look Mr.—er… I'm afraid I don't know your name. I am here to help but until I am properly consulted and unless a process is set up where I can pass messages back to the leadership then I will accept no more instructions. Good night."

He quickly got up and left the room before anyone could move. He went out into the nightclub, which was starting to fill up, and clattered his way down the stairs past a startled doorman. He made his way back to the station stopping in an alleyway once to make sure he was not being followed.

Charles Oakley was sitting by himself listening to the radio when Kamau walked in. Kamau was outwardly quite calm. As far as he was concerned they either involved him or he would return to his studies at Oxford. He had no intention of risking his life for people he no longer trusted. He made himself some tea and poured some for his host. The radio was eventually switched off and Mr. Oakley said in Afrikaans.

"What's up?"

Kamau explained the situation, and was told, "I will find out what I can, but you have to be very careful; they have been known to "tip off" security forces to get rid of troublesome elements within their own ranks."

Nothing happened for two weeks; then another instruction appeared in Kamau's locker asking him to deliver a message to an address in Boputhatswana at a place called Mmabatho near Mafikeng. He wondered if this was an olive branch or a trap and he also thought about what he should do.

"Go," said Charles Oakley when he was asked. "These organisational issues take time to sort out; if you go they will take it as a sign of willingness to cooperate, not weakness."

Kamau went by train to Mafikeng and then bus to Mmabatho. As John had mentioned on their flight to Botswana he knew that Mmabatho was to be the new capital of the independent state of Boputhatswana. Mafikeng was controlled by a white town council, and although it was the logical choice for a so-called capital, they had refused to allow this to happen; so the government had extravagantly built the new capital a few kilometres away. Kamau delivered his message safely and then decided to explore. He found his way to the address of a coloured family in Mafikeng provided by Charles Oakley. His genial host, a Mr. Smit, worked somewhere in the administration department of the town council. After dinner he and Kamau went to the local shebeen, which was frequented by both Africans and coloureds. Mr Smit appeared to be well known and within a short time Kamau was involved in a conversation involving the proposed state of Boputhatswana.

Most people were incredulous that such a step was even contemplated; the so-called "state" of Boputhatswana would consist of more than a dozen pieces of land stretching from Mafikeng to Kimberley. All these areas had degenerated into rural slums, where the ever-increasing population were expected to survive on terrain already destroyed by overgrazing and erosion. There was no industry outside Mafikeng although now subsidies were being offered for the establishment of industries in Mmabatho.

Mr Smit was contemptuous. "The education level among the blacks is so low that they will not be able to run this so called country," he said. "All the budget will be provided by the central government and the few jobs they will provide will have to be heavily subsidised. What's more, none of the pieces of land are really connected. The whole thing is ridiculous."

"What about this casino in the Pilanesberg?" asked Kamau.

"Ag man, ja, that will bring jobs but you can't run a country on casinos. The blerry government want to keep their precious white cities like Jo'burg so pure and they're dumping all their problems here; I think it's crazy."

Smit became involved in animated discussions with various people in the shebeen. Kamau listened to the conversations around him; one of the main topics was the independence of Boputhatswana, he learnt from one conversation that the Government was proposing to develop independent "homelands" in all the tribal areas and that this was the official solution to the 'black problem'. The basic idea was that all black people would technically belong to one of these homelands, even if they had lived in an urban area such as Johannesburg for five or six generations, as many had, and had no knowledge of their so-called homeland. The government had forecast that by 1978 the number of jobs created in the homelands would reverse the flow of blacks to the cities and within an unstated number of years the cities would be the exclusive preserve of the whites, coloureds and Indians. The whole thing sounded preposterous to Kamau but government propaganda had somehow convinced the white electorate that what was being proposed was indeed the final solution. Certainly the dusty little capital of Mmabatho had no chance of being the catalyst that would produce thousands of jobs.

Kamau became aware of an old man who shuffled into the shebeen; he came and sat next to Kamau and started to talk in his own language of Setswana. Another neighbour helped him understand what the old man was saying, since Kamau could only pick up a word here and there. Apparently the old man was part of a group who had occupied a piece of land in a designated "white" farming area. Then one day they had all been forcibly removed and dumped in an unfamiliar part of Boputhatswana with few facilities. The old man described how government agents had just arrived one day and loaded the people and all their possessions onto trucks. What was left of the settlement was bulldozed to the ground and he and his people were unceremoniously dumped in their new area. There was no compensation for the years of development in the old place and they had found the new place far worse than the old, with no facilities of any kind. Their old place had been handed over to a white farmer. Kamau found out afterwards that this was no isolated incident but an example of the government policy to remove "black spots" in white areas; several thousand people were dealt with in this way every year and there was no recourse to the courts or any other authority.

Kamau admired the old man's stoicism; there was no sense of self-pity. He told his story with sadness but in a matter-of-fact way. Kamau asked him why he was at the shebeen; he was surprised that a man of this type would spend the hard-earned cash of his group on a non-essential commodity such as beer. The man looked at him as if trying to decide whether he could trust him or not then he quietly said through the interpreter, "For years I trusted the white man and his justice. I had heard many stories, of course, about black people's rights being taken away but I chose to ignore them. Our group was quite well off; we were doing well. But look what has happened to us now; in one day they have destroyed everything. We have been given a piece of desert; it will take years to rebuild our lives, even if it is possible. Many of us will die. I want to find the ANC; maybe they can help us."

Kamau was in a quandary; he could see this man deserved help but it was really out of his line of duty to make any promises or indeed admit to anyone his connection with the ANC. Then he had a brainwave; he told the man to stay where he was and he wandered over to the proprietor and had a brief conversation with him in Afrikaans. The conversation was actually about the train timetable. He then came back to the old man and said,

"Come back here in three weeks, today; I will not be here but the ANC will have a person here to see you then."

The man smiled broadly, said his farewells and scuttled out of the place.

Mr. Smit had obviously done all his business and he and Kamau made their way home by a circuitous route.

"I just make sure I stay in the light," said Smit. "You never know what you might find in some of these dark corners these days. I done some good business tonight, meneer. Those blerry people in Town Council think I can live on my small salary, man. I know what they pay the whites, so if they won't pay me properly I just takes what I can. I arrange building permits for people, meneer; its easy money."

Kamau also understood that Smit owned half the shebeen they had just visited. Smit had absolutely no respect for the law; he had decided that he would get away with whatever he could, and if he paid off the right people the chances of being caught were virtually zero.

"Dear God," thought Kamau, "if this place ever becomes a full democracy it will take fifty years to clean up the corruption, let alone anything else."

There was a message in Kamau's locker when he returned to the hotel the next day. Again the Pelican Club but this time it was for mid-afternoon, which meant he could leave work after the lunch shift and be back just in time for the dinner shift.

As before he was ushered through the curtains and into the same small room. This time the only people who were in the room were the man he had met before and another, slightly younger man to whom the older man deferred. Both men were almost in shadow so it was difficult to see their features clearly, but Kamau immediately had the feeling that he was in the presence of authority.

"Sit down please," his original acquaintance spoke.

Kamau sat in an upright chair in the middle of the room; the chair had been deliberately placed in a pool of light. The atmosphere was tense and uncomfortable. He tried unsuccessfully to move the chair.

"You disobeyed instructions," said the new man.

Kamau said nothing; if they wanted his help they had better be conciliatory or he'd find another way of destroying the white regime in South Africa.

"We run a military operation; we must know that our instructions are going to be obeyed," the man continued.

Kamau felt that this was ground that had been covered already. He decided to keep his peace.

"You have done much good work," the tone was more conciliatory.

This was acknowledged with a small nod of Kamau's head. He still said nothing. There was a full minute's silence from the other side of the room. Kamau just sat still; he wondered why he was there.

"What do you want?" asked the man.

Kamau considered that for a moment and then answered in full.

"I am committed to changing the regime here in South Africa and I am committed to a military solution. I know I am a very good operative but you simply cannot expect me to go out risking my life on more and more dangerous missions and because of the pressure now, risking my cover as well. I need to be part of the consultative process; I also need to be able to report my findings," said Kamau calmly.

"You are not one of us, you are not a South African," said the man.

The implication was clear that they found it difficult to trust Kamau.

"Mdantsane knew that when I was recruited," responded Kamau; "you should also consider two other things. Firstly, this conflict is going to have repercussions far beyond the borders of South Africa and secondly, I have never let you down. I have now completed more than twenty assignments; you cannot have any complaints about that."

There was a grunt from across the room.

"You say you need to report things back to us; please give me an example," said the man.

Kamau described his trip to Mmabatho in some detail, mentioning in particular his conversation with the old man and the commitment for someone to meet him.

"It is dangerous to make a commitment like that; it may be a trap," commented the man.

"It's not a trap," said Kamau. "The ANC needs grassroots support and it is this sort of situation if properly handled that will give you that support."

The man grunted again.

"Please give us the details, but it is inappropriate for you to be involved at that level; we have others who can do that," said the man this time more kindly. The implication was clear; they had more important things for Kamau.

Details were given to the man Kamau had first met.

"You can go now," Kamau was told.

"You will hear from me through the usual channels."

Kamau left the Pelican Club and made as if he was on his way back to Johannesburg. Luckily he had his wits about him and he doubled back on his tracks through an alleyway and watched. Sure enough, a minute or so later the three youths who were at the first meeting at the Pelican Club came running past. Kamau was disappointed; they were obviously trying to follow him but all they had succeeded in doing was making fools of themselves. Kamau nipped out of the alleyway and was lucky enough to find a taxi, which dropped him off at a railway station.

Bok-bok Oberholzer was listening disinterestedly to one of his lieutenants, who was chattering away about his favourite hobby, rugby. Kleinkie Vorster was a very short, thin man with buck-teeth and glasses. He was always shabbily dressed and looked as if he slept in his rags. Bok-bok valued him for his thoroughness and occasionally tolerated these long discussions on subjects in which he had no interest, just to humour Kleinkie. He was shown photographs of teams from New Zealand, Argentina, of course the South African Springboks, and England. He was just about to dismiss Kleinkie when his interest really perked up. Kleinkie was chattering on in Afrikaans and quipped, "Ja meneer Bok-bok, and the strangest thing is this Willie Lemmer who comes from the Cape and coaches the high school here; he looks like this coloured ou [man] who plays for England."

Bok-bok didn't move a muscle but his piggy little eyes suddenly lit up with interest. Much to Kleinkie's delight, he made him go through all the photographs again and spent much time on the rather tattered photo of the England team. Kleinkie pointed out Kamau's picture and repeated, "Ja, just like he is a brother to Willie Lemmer."

"How well do you know this Willie Lemmer?" asked Bok-bok.

"I met him a couple of times," responded Kleinkie.

Bok-bok went out of his office and contrived a small errand for Kleinkie, who started to collect up his photographs.

"Just leave them here; come and collect them when you're finished," Bok-bok told him.

After Kleinkie had left, Bok-bok spent about twenty minutes looking for the photo of Kamau, which he was sure he had somewhere; he couldn't remember any of the details. Eventually he found it. He compared it to the photo Kleinkie had left of the England rugby team. There was no doubt of the strong resemblance. "Could it be the same person?" he thought. "Too much of a coincidence," he thought, "but worth following up."

When Kleinkie returned he collected all his precious photographs and Bok-bok asked him innocently, "Where does this Willie Lemmer live? Maybe we could have him over here for a drink one night."

"I will find out," answered Kleinkie who suddenly realised that he was onto something important. Bok-bok did not invite people over for casual drinks.

The ANC had now decided to humour Kamau. He certainly could not consider that they really consulted him but he was asked to go on an irregular basis to various houses in Soweto, where he received instructions for his assignments. He always met the same two men that he had met at the last meeting in the Pelican Club. He never really saw enough of them to be able to describe them and he was never told their names. He was always given very explicit instructions, which he followed to the letter. He never seemed to have any trouble; but he was also becoming frustrated in that he didn't really have any idea what the strategy was or what the larger picture was. He was slightly better off than before in that he was able to at least tell them what was on his mind. He couldn't tell whether any notice was taken of what he said. There was slightly more variety in what he was asked to blow up, in that apart from pylons there was occasionally an electrical sub-station as a target. All the targets were designed to cause maximum disruption without loss of life.

In order to ensure the authenticity of his cover Kamau decided to change jobs. He was given a very good reference from "The Thoroughbred" and moved to a smaller but equally high-class restaurant attached to a hotel just out of Hillbrow, the flatland of white Johannesburg. The hotel was in a residential area and had large grounds. Travelling was more difficult in that Kamau had to catch a bus and then a train back to Coronationville. Under the supervision of a white head waiter Kamau looked after the tables in one half of the restaurant, with the help of a number of black assistants, and a white Afrikaner, Rita Vos, looked after the other half of the restaurant. Kamau concentrated on doing his job but he tried to keep good relationships with all around him, including Rita. To his surprise, he was treated with kindness and consideration, by Rita in particular. From his short experience in the country, his expectation as far as white women were concerned was that he would either be ignored or treated with condescension, and he usually kept his distance.

One Saturday night after the restaurant had closed, Kamau was hurrying to the bus when Rita came out of the shadows and walked with him.

"I'll walk with you if you don't mind," said Rita in Afrikaans. "It's safer." They walked a little way in silence.

"What happens if you are seen with me?" asked Kamau. "You being white and me being brown."

Rita shrugged.

"People are taking less and less notice of that nonsense now," she said non-committally.

They walked on, chatting about inconsequential things. Rita then stopped outside a large block of flats. "This is me; why don't you come up for ten minutes; I'll make you a cup of coffee."

Kamau hesitated.

"Look, you'll have to use the fire escape stairs, but I'm in Flat 23; the door will be open." Rita showed him the fire stairs and disappeared. Kamau found his way up the stairs and came to the second floor. He looked about him. He waited in the shadows until a couple, who had come out of the lift, went into one of the flats. He then walked quickly to number 23; the door was as promised open and he eased himself into the flat and closed the door behind him.

"Come in," called Rita from the kitchen.

He found himself in a surprisingly spacious one bedroom flat with a dining area, lounge and separate kitchen and bathroom. He wandered into the kitchen; the kettle was boiling and Rita was busy putting a few biscuits out onto a plate. She glanced up. He had always thought she was pretty: she had dark brown hair cut into a bob, brown eyes, and quite a dark skin for a white person, a very full bust and slim, strong looking legs. She blushed slightly under his scrutiny. He guessed she was in her mid twenties.

"Don't you have to be a bit careful, I mean inviting me up here?" he asked cautiously.

They were sitting together on the couch enjoying the coffee and biscuits.

She looked at him carefully, studying him with her big brown eyes, he supposed wondering if she could trust him. She looked away.

"I'm actually a coloured like you," she said quietly. "I just live white."

She did not pull away when he held her hand.

"What do you mean, 'live white'?" he asked.

"Well, I can pass for white in any company, I just try to stay out of the sun and as you know white salaries and wages are higher than coloured. I'm quite sure that if they suspected at the restaurant that I was coloured I'd be shown the door," she said matter of factly.

"And what about living here?" asked Kamau.

"Well they only really check up if you want to buy property in a white area. They obviously think I'm white since that is what I've told them. There are many people like me living in fear of discovery," she said quietly.

"Is it worth it?" asked Kamau.

"I'm much better off, but I miss my friends and community," was the answer.

"Parents?" Kamau enquired.

"They live in the Cape, Mitchell's Plain; I've sort of explained to them what's going on but they've never been to Jo'burg. I keep in touch but they don't really understand the situation. I don't want any of the hordes of cousins coming here; they would spoil everything. I have a brother; he's doing the same as me; he works professionally here in Jo'burg. Maybe we'll both migrate to England or Canada or somewhere; none of this will worry us there."

"Boyfriends, marriage?" Kamau was curious.

"I've had one or two white boyfriends, but they don't last. I don't have much in common with them. Of course at the restaurant I get propositioned all the time," Kamau raised his eyebrows.

"Don't worry; I never mix business with pleasure." She smiled.

"Why tell me all of this?" asked Kamau.

"I don't know, you just look like the sort of person that people talk to." Rita kissed him.

They left a trail of clothes on the way to the bedroom and Kamau stayed the night. In the morning Rita was stroking Kamau's strong, beautiful body and her curiosity was piqued when she saw the ngwati (foreskin knot) on his penis.

"What's this?" she asked.

Kamau was slightly embarrassed.

"It's just the way my circumcision was done," he said. "They left a knot instead of removing the foreskin altogether."

"Never seen that before, or heard about it either; sounds like some strange African ritual," she said jokingly.

Kamau shrugged and they made love again.

✕　✕　✕

Chapter 10

Kleinkie Vorster was waiting excitedly in Bok-Bok Oberholzer's office one morning for Bok-Bok to arrive.

"Ja, what is it Kleinkie?" asked Oberholzer once he had sat down.

"You remember some weeks ago you asked me to find out where this Willie Lemmer lives?" asked Kleinkie.

"Ja."

"Well I found out, meneer," said Kleinkie.

Bok Bok raised his eyebrows.

"Well, this is the address; this Willie, he comes from Mitchell's Plain in the Cape and he stays with the Oakleys."

He handed Bok Bok a card with the address printed out in neat handwriting on it.

"Anything else?" asked Bok Bok.

"Ja, meneer. Charles Oakley is a builder and has worked for the same company for almost twenty years. His wife Lettie works as a hairdresser's assistant in Jo'burg, she has also been there many years. They have two kids, a boy and a girl of twelve years and eight years. They both go to the local school. They own the house they live in, although they are now paying off a mortgage."

"How much is the mortgage?" asked Bok Bok.

"Five thousand, two hundred and eighty five rand and three cents," said Kleinkie.

"Oakley's salary goes against the mortgage. They live off the wife's salary."

As usual Kleinkie had been very thorough.

"You done good Kleinkie, now give me all that stuff," growled Bok Bok. He waved Kleinkie away.

Bok Bok knew that the minute he gave this information to Roux, the Oakley family would be destroyed. Charles would be arrested, along with Kamau, and Lettie and the kids would be out on the street within months when the mortgage payments were not met. He did not really think twice about it; people made their own lives. If Oakley wanted to involve himself with the ANC, then he must have understood the risks for himself and his family.

He phoned Roux and made an appointment to see him in Pretoria. He could tell from the tone of Roux's voice that this was a big fish. Bok Bok was determined to milk it for all it was worth. Bok Bok was ushered into Roux's office. He liked being treated with respect, particularly by white people. He put two spoons of sugar in the coffee one of the assistants brought him and stirred it thoughtfully.

"I've found Kamau Lawrence for you, meneer Roux," said Bok Bok eventually.

Roux was careful.

"Where? How?" he asked.

"In Coronationville, you said he would be in a coloured area," answered Bok Bok.

"Are you sure?" asked Roux.

"Absolutely positive, I have photographs. There is no doubt it is the same person," answered Bok Bok.

"You will be rewarded for this," said Roux.

"Ja, meneer, there is one small, very small thing you can do for me," said Bok Bok guardedly.

"Such as?"

"Well there is this cousin of mine in jail, maybe he could be released," said Bok Bok.

"What's he in for? If its murder, then that might be difficult," answered Roux.

"It was only a very small murder," said Bok Bok.

Roux shook his head.

"Murder is murder, why didn't he hang?" he asked.

Bok Bok shrugged. "As I said it was only a very small murder."

Actually it was one of his hit-men, who had clumsily murdered a prostitute for not handing over the agreed percentage of her takings.

"What's his name and where is he?" asked Roux.

"Kobus Visagie, he's in Pretoria Central," said Bok Bok.

Roux wrote that down.

"O.K, what do you have for me?" asked Roux.

Bok Bok went through all the evidence collected by Kleinkie including several photographs of Kamau taken at the station, outside the Oakley house and whilst coaching the rugby team. They compared them carefully with the photographs Roux had sent him and with the picture of Kamau in the England Rugby team.

"There is no doubt, it's the very same person," said Bok Bok in a very satisfied tone.

Roux nodded.

"Now all the details please."

Bok Bok gave him the Oakley's address and all the other details in the file.

"They will be picked up in a few days, please do not say anything to anyone," said Roux.

"No, meneer, you should know me well enough by now, and please don't forget my cousin," Bok Bok said as he was ushered to the door.

Chapter 11

Charles Oakley was rudely awakened the next Sunday morning at about 3 a.m. with a loud knocking on the front door.

"Open up, open up," yelled a voice. "This is the police."

He quickly put on his dressing gown and amid uncomprehending protests from Lettie opened the front door. A revolver was immediately stuck in his face and the small house was filled with armed police.

"Get Lemmer," shouted the man in command. A few moments later Lettie and the two children came into the lounge looking absolutely terrified.

"Where's Lemmer?" screamed the commander in Afrikaans.

"There's no one else here, meneer," said one of the police. "We've searched."

The commander violently jabbed Charles in the ribs with his pistol.

"Where's Lemmer, we want him as well as you." He had his face right up against Charles's face and the spittle flew in all directions.

"He went out to his job this afternoon, sometimes he only comes back Monday morning," answered Charles.

"What fucking job?"

Charles told him about the waiting job at the International Hotel in central Jo'burg. Kamau had not told anyone in the household about his change of jobs.

"We'll check it out, meantime you are under arrest," the commander said more calmly.

"Arrest, arrest, what's all this about?" Lettie tried to rush to her husband's side. She was pushed roughly to one side and she slumped down on the floor. She was too shocked to cry; suddenly her world had been turned upside down. Her lifestyle had been safe, if rather dull, but now her husband was under arrest and the police seemed to want to arrest their well-behaved and very personable houseguest.

Charles Oakley had kept his head; in the confusion he managed to write a short note and he made sure that Jannie had seen him put it in a flowerpot. All it said was "Warn Willie at the station; don't let him come back here."

The police left as quickly as they had come. The front doors was just left open and with sirens going they screamed out of the suburb, making sure all the neighbours were wide awake and knew what was happening.

Lettie and her two children sat there in stunned silence for almost five minutes. Jannie then stepped forward and shut the door. He retrieved the note from the flower-pot and tried to decipher it. He boiled the kettle and made his mother a cup of coffee. She was still sitting on the floor, where the policeman had pushed her.

An hour later, there was a light knock on the door and Martha, Lettie's best friend from a few doors down, came in and got Lettie to sit in one of her chairs. She and the children eventually haltingly told the neighbour what had happened.

"Why would they want to arrest Charles Oakley?" Martha asked almost to herself. Jannie showed her the note.

"Maybe it's something to do with Willie," said Martha.

"Willie?" said Lettie. "Why, what could he have done?"

"I dunno, but we will find out," said Martha.

"Meantime we had better do what Charles asked. Come, Jannie, help us pack his things," said Martha.

They packed Kamau's few belongings into his small brown suitcase and Jannie was just about to go out of the back door with it.

"Nee, nee, Jannie," said Martha. "There's a policeman outside and another up the street. You'll have to go over the back fence; here let me help you."

They scrambled over the fence into the neighbour's yard without being seen, since it was still early. They looked up and down the street; there were a few figures moving about, probably people making their way to an early shift, but no sign of any police.

"O.K, Jannie, just wait for him at the station. If you come home, come this way, otherwise go straight to school, O.K?" said Martha.

"O.K."

Jannie picked up the suitcase and started walking to the station. He got a terrible fright when a police car came whizzing past, but it took no notice of him. He found a bench outside the station, put the little suitcase underneath it and waited. After a while he noticed that there seemed to be several other men, also all watching and waiting for something. He wondered who they were; he noticed they were all coloured, so they fitted in with the general scene. They were also all quite well dressed, unusual for Coronationville station in the early morning. He noticed that they all became more alert when a train, going into Johannesburg, stopped briefly and then went on its way. Then it dawned on him, these people were probably police looking for Willie. Jannie unobtrusively picked up the suitcase and made his way onto the platform for the trains coming from the city. He wasn't quite sure what he intended to do but he knew he had to get to Willie before the men outside the station did.

After work the previous Friday, Kamau had been sent on his biggest assignment yet. The objective was to disrupt the flow of coal from the Eastern Transvaal coalfields to the port of Maputo (Lourenco Marques) destined for export. As usual he walked from the restaurant with Rita towards her flat. Earlier he had told her that he was not going to be able to stay that night but that he would probably see her on Sunday at her flat. Rita had already decided that there was far more to Kamau (Willie Lemmer as she knew him) than just a waiter at a fancy restaurant in the northern suburbs of Jo'burg. She sensibly kept her mouth shut and her questions to herself.

As arranged, Kamau was picked up in a bakkie (pick-up truck) near a petrol station in Hillbrow. He had been told the registration number. The driver had on a balaclava and said nothing after Kamau gave him the password. Although he found it frustrating, it was better this way; Kamau knew nothing of any of his partners on these assignments and clearly they knew nothing about him.

The truck sped its way through the Eastern Transvaal and they eventually found their way into a very grimy black township on the outskirts of Middelburg just before dawn. They bounced their way along some dirt tracks that passed for roads; then Kamau's companion stopped the vehicle outside one of the small township houses made from concrete blocks, which looked just like all the other houses in the area. He handed Kamau a set of keys and said in broken English, "We take box from back," he pointed to the back of the vehicle. "You check. Food inside, I back at six tonight. No open door to any person." They quickly carried the large box from the back of the vehicle to the house. Kamau unlocked the door and after they had brought the box inside, Kamau found himself alone in the house. He heard the noise of the bakkie driving off. After locking the front door, he looked around. The place was quite neat and tidy but it contained only the barest essentials; there was a sofa and one arm-chair and a small dining table in the main room. Some mealie-pap (maize meal porridge), a loaf of bread and a tin of jam had been left in the small kitchen alcove. There were two bedrooms at the back with old iron bedsteads. The floor was concrete with no covering. Kamau found the toilet out at the back; he assumed there was some arrangement to get rid of the waste as he could see there was no running water or electricity in the place. It depressed him utterly that this was accommodation provided for a family and repeated hundreds of thousands of times right across South Africa. He lit the paraffin stove and made himself a mug of tea; a container with water had been thoughtfully provided. He ate some of the bread and jam and, after making sure the house was secure, checked the contents of the box before he went to sleep fully clothed on one of the beds.

There was a hammering on the front door, which woke Kamau with a start. He looked at his watch. Six o'clock. "Damn," he thought as he leapt off the bed, and after checking he opened the front door. Kamau tidied up the place, they loaded the box into the truck and having locked the little home they raced off into the dusk.

Kamau only had a vague idea of where they were going; he saw several signs saying "Waterval Boven" which he knew was at the top of the escarpment linking the Eastern Transvaal highveld with the lowveld. He could imagine that if a train came off the tracks in this terrain the authorities would have trouble in recovering anything. All his other assignments had been against benign targets such as pylons and substations. This time Kamau knew that although the train would be carrying coal, the driver in the engine would either be killed or very badly hurt. He tried to put the thought out of his mind. "We're fighting a legitimate war and all the S.A.R (South African Railways) drivers are white and if they don't support the National Party Government, they support some other fringe party to the right of the National Party," he said to himself.

They were now on a winding dirt road and then quite suddenly they veered off down a little track through the forest. After what seemed like an eternity, but in reality was only about ten kilometres, they came to a stop and the driver pointed excitedly in the dark to the rail track twenty metres away. "Train, train," he said.

They got out and surveyed the scene. The place had been chosen brilliantly. There was easy access to the tracks and once a train had been derailed it would plunge down the escarpment more than one thousand feet below. As far as he could see, nothing would be recovered from such a situation.

If the information Kamau had been given was correct, a coal train would come past this point in four hours, so there was no time to waste. He and the assistant unloaded the box and then hid the bakkie. Kamau made sure that neither the bakkie nor the place where they were working could be seen from the track. They then worked frantically and dug twenty holes under a twenty-yard stretch of track. Kamau made sure the holes were deep enough and then he laid a charge in each hole and measured off the fuses. He wanted all twenty charges to go off together, which would be enough to blow the engines off the track and then drag the train down the escarpment with its precious load of coal.

Half an hour after they had set everything up, a small, open, two-man rail car came running down the track. This was obviously a check to see that the track was O.K. before the heavy train followed. After a further half hour wait, they could see the big beam of light and then they heard the constant squeal of brakes as the drivers kept the train going slowly downhill. Kamau and his assistant were about one hundred metres from the tracks but Kamau had marked the area well. He would push the plunger to set off the charges just as the profile of the powerful engines came into line with the tree in front of him. He waited and waited and could feel the anxiety from the assistant next to him. The train came on and on, then suddenly the tree and the engines were aligned. He pushed the plunger. There was a blinding flash of light and a huge explosion. Both engines were flung ten feet into the air and then crashed down down down into the valley below. There was a flash as the overhead power supply was torn down. Then the rumble started, as the one hundred or more coal trucks all followed the engine into the ravine. The rumble went on for more than ten minutes and by the time it was over the whole area was covered in a thick layer of coal dust.

After lying there mesmerised for a few minutes, Kamau collected the plunger and threw it in the back of the truck with the explosives box. They leapt into the cab and drove like fury out of the forested area, across the main road linking Johannesburg with the Eastern Transvaal. They then made for Carolina. Before dawn Kamau made the driver drop him off at Bethal and he eventually caught a train into Johannesburg, where he arrived mid-morning. He walked from the station, went down Wolmarans Street and up Claim Street. He climbed the fire stairs and, making sure the coast was clear, knocked on number 23. The door flew open.

"My God, look at you! Where have you been?" Rita was alarmed. She had heard on the news about the coal train being derailed and wondered whether Kamau was involved. It certainly looked as if he had been up to something.

She let him into the flat and quickly closed the door.

"Well, you look as if you could do wit a bit of a wash," said Rita proprietarily, "and those clothes, once I've got you out of them I'll see if I can wash them."

Kamau smiled. He went and ran the bath and tiredly undressed. Rita bustled off with his clothes. He dozed off in the bath but then became fully awake when Rita slipped into the water with him and started to wash him.

Kamau woke up towards evening and wondered where he was. Then he remembered the joy of their love-making and wandered round the flat looking for Rita. He found her in the kitchen, ironing his newly laundered clothes. She looked at him quizzically.

"It doesn't look as if you have had any sleep at all since I saw you on Friday night," she said.

"No, not much," he answered blandly. He started to put on his now clean clothes, which were scattered about the kitchen.

"While you were asleep I went out into the Hillbrow shops. It has been a beautiful day. There were lots of young couples in the café's, all white of course. If you and I went out there together we'd probably be arrested or at the very least set upon by a bunch of white thugs. I wonder where all this will end." Rita finished the ironing and handed Kamau his shirt, which he put on.

"Thanks."

He looked at his watch.

"Sunday, thank God, I thought we would have to go to work soon," he said.

The restaurant was closed on Sundays, as were all cinemas and most places of entertainment. Sunday was preserved for Christian worship.

"There were reports on the radio that a coal train had been blown up in the Eastern Transvaal. Four engine drivers were killed and several thousand tons of coal was lost down a ravine, not to mention the loss of a couple of engines and about one hundred railcars. At least somebody is doing something about getting rid of this odious regime," Rita looked at him shrewdly.

Kamau remained silent but he was thinking. "Sooner or later I'm going to need help; maybe I can trust her. Maybe I should confide in her."

Rita was looking at him with her hands on her hips.

"Willie, maybe we should have a chat. My guess is that you are not Willie Lemmer from Mitchell's Plain. I even wonder if you were born in this country. Your Afrikaans is very good but it's not from the Cape or here. It's clear to me that you could be doing more with your life than working in a fancy Jo'burg restaurant. Also your English is not South African. Be honest with me please; I may even be able to help you."

Kamau took a deep breath. He felt he could trust her and he was certain that he was going to need some help. Roux would see Kamau's hand in the demolition of the coal train and efforts would be stepped up to find him. Maybe, however, she was one of them, part of Roux's battery of spies. If that was so, his cover was already blown and the security police would be on to him anyway.

He took two beers from the fridge, opened them and took Rita by the hand and sat next to her on the couch.

"My name is Kamau Lawrence…"

He told her the whole story about his South African father, Kikuyu mother; his time with his natural grandparents during the emergency in Kenya. The fact that his mother had almost been hanged by the British. He went through the changes that had occurred since independence in Kenya, his final years at school, Oxford and the English rugby team and latterly his few months in South Africa.

"So that's it," he said. "I'm here to try to make a difference. We must get rid of this odious regime and before you ask, I did blow up that coal train in the Eastern Transvaal last night."

She sat in stunned silence.

"Vragtig (truly)! I knew you were different, I did not realise quite how much there was to all this," she said quietly.

"Are you involved in any way?" he asked.

"No, you know how difficult it is for us; all I've tried to do is escape to create another life for myself. It has not been easy," she held his hand tightly.

"I know. If I need help, do you think you can help me?" he asked.

"What sort of help? I can't blow up trains," she answered.

"If they find out about me, even if I escape they will try to destroy the Oakley family. I am particularly concerned with the children. You may be able to help me get them out of the country. Do you think you could do that?" He looked at her intently.

"Probably, but I would have to escape as well," she answered. "Otherwise they would just take it out on me."

"Yes of course, we'd have to include all that in any plans," he said thoughtfully.

They talked long into the night and by the time they had finished Kamau knew he had a strong and faithful ally. Importantly, Rita was unknown to the ANC, and, Kamau hoped, to the security police. Kamau with his usual thoroughness had covered every eventuality. As a final precaution they set up a letter box drop in a space between two bricks on the outside of Rita's block of flats.

"In case we are unable to use the phones," explained Kamau.

CHAPTER 12

As a precaution, Kamau had phoned the Oakley household from Johannesburg Central station. Just as little Hettie nervously answered the phone; there was a slight but clearly audible click. All Kamau's senses suddenly went on full alert. The phone was bugged.

"Damn," he thought as he quietly put the phone down without saying anything, "that's never happened before."

There was a white man gesticulating frantically outside the phone box and as Kamau slipped out of the box, a torrent of abuse was directed his way. He looked surprised and then he realised the problem. He had trodden on the corns of one of apartheid's precious bastions—separate facilities for whites and non-whites. The phone box was reserved for whites. He moved away quickly and then wondered what to do about the call. As a minimum, the security people now had the Oakley establishment under surveillance. After a few moments of thought he went back into the station and phoned Rita from the same "white only" phone booth, this time without interruption. After he dialled he listened for tell-tale clicks, but all seemed clear and he explained to Rita what the situation was. He also explained that he probably would not be at the restaurant that evening. She suggested that he should return to her flat in Claim Street.

"No, no, I can't do that; as soon as they know where I work, you will be followed. Make certain that there is absolutely no evidence of my presence in your flat. I will let you know what is happening." He rang off.

Jannie had hung around the station at Coronationville for what seemed like hours now. The men watching the station were all still there and he noticed that they were very watchful when trains came in. At about mid-morning another train slowly moved into the station and started to disgorge its sparse load of passengers, now that the morning rush was over. He almost cried out when a very ragged, old looking black or coloured man came right up to him.

"Quiet, Jannie, come quickly," he recognised Willie's (Kamau's) voice, and they both hopped back onto the train as it was moving out of the station.

Kamau had been really surprised when he saw Jannie at the station with what appeared to be his (Kamau's) small suitcase. Then it dawned on him, there had to be something really wrong at the Oakley's house for Jannie to be there at the station at all, let alone with the suitcase.

Jannie was just about to say something but Kamau put his finger to his lips and they carried on for two more stops and then left the train. They got off and having made sure that the station was deserted, sat down on a bench. Jannie started to cry.

"Nee, nee Jannie, don't cry," whispered Kamau. "Just tell me what is happening, you're a brave boy."

Jannie told him about the police raid and how his father had been arrested and that they were looking for him, Willie Lemmer. Kamau felt his gut tighten as the story unfolded; he really was a fugitive now and he knew the Oakley family were in danger. He was glad he had briefed Rita; somehow between them they would see to it that at least the children were looked after.

Having made sure that Jannie had the right train ticket he said, "Jannie, go straight to school and tell nobody at all that you have seen me. If they ask you why you are late just tell them your Ma was sick, O.K?"

Jannie nodded.

"Remember, don't tell them you saw me, you will all be in trouble if you do," repeated Kamau.

They got back on the train and Kamau watched Jannie make his way from the platform at Coronationville without any interference.

By mid-afternoon Hannes Roux was beside himself with anger and irritation. They had lost a complete coal train, "Not just a few wagons," as one of his superiors had yelled at him, "but a whole fucking train man! You had better find the culprit, quick!" He had thought he could but the raid on the Oakley's house had only yielded Charles Oakley, not Kamau as he had expected, and now it was certain that Kamau had been alerted to the situation. One of the calls to the Oakleys had been traced to a phone box in Johannesburg station and although the caller had put the phone down quickly, Roux was almost certain that it would have been Kamau. He had two avenues to explore: the family and the restaurant where Kamau worked.

When his men descended in force on "The Thoroughbred", they quickly found out that he no longer worked there; when the manager was asked where Willie (Kamau) had gone he said, "He didn't tell us."

"What do you know about him?" he was asked.

"Really very little. He was always on time and did a great job, but he never told me anything about his private life at all. But that's the same with many people who work here. They come for a few months and then move on."

When Roux was told he yelled, "Search all the so-called high-class restaurants in Jo'burg, he's bound to turn up somewhere." Roux had no time for English speaking Johannesburg in general or its penchant for conspicuous consumption in particular. As far as he was concerned, he wished that gold had never been found in the Transvaal, now almost one hundred years earlier. This was mainly because it had attracted the masses of 'uitlanders' (literally outlanders) to the gold fields. As far as he was concerned Johannesburg was the most sinful place on earth and he hated it.

He thought he had better go and talk to the family himself.

Nobody had taken any notice of the old looking African as he shuffled past the block of flats where Rita lived. Kamau looked about him and stuffed a small piece of paper into the letter-box drop that he and Rita had agreed upon. The note explained what had transpired and that he would be in touch. He asked Rita to alert him when the police came to the restaurant where they both worked.

During his discussions with the ANC in Soweto, Kamau had been given the address of a "safe house", which could in an emergency be used as a refuge if he was in real trouble. The crowded train to Orlando West took about forty minutes and after asking directions from a few people, he found his way down the dirty, unpaved streets to one of the thousands of similar looking houses in Soweto made from concrete blocks. A large, black woman with a friendly, smiling face opened the door and let him in when he gave the password. An hour later her husband arrived from his job in the city. The husband and wife, with furtive glances at Kamau, repaired to one of the two small bedrooms and a furious argument erupted. Kamau tried vainly to entertain the three small children in the front room but they kept glancing nervously from him to the noise in the bedroom. Kamau had never felt more uncomfortable in his life; he was not welcome here, that was clear, but he had nowhere else to go. He waited. The man and his wife came out of the bedroom scowling and the kids were banished to their own room. Speaking in halting English, the man said, "You can spend the night here but only tonight. It is very dangerous, not only for you but for us too. I will find a place for you to go tomorrow."

Kamau shared their rather frugal meal with them. Although the man had what was considered a good job as a driver with a brewery company, the family gave off an air of genteel poverty. However, they did have a roof over their heads and enough to eat and the children were being educated. There was some desultory conversation around this subject, but for the most part the meal was eaten in silence, and shortly afterwards the man went out. Kamau helped his wife clean up and wash the dishes. She was surprised and grateful. An hour later the man came back and gave Kamau a piece of paper with an address on it. By half past eight the household had retired. They had to be up by 4 a.m. for the man to get to his job before 7 a.m.

This process was repeated virtually every day for the next week. There was no contact from the hierarchy of the ANC. Every other day he made the trip back to the letter-box drop outside Rita's flat in Hillbrow. On the Thursday there was a note saying the police had arrived the day before and had interviewed all the staff.

Hannes Roux visited the Oakley house in Coronationville, accompanied by Danie Visser whose leg had now recovered from the crocodile attack in Botswana. Danie had been promoted to Sergeant. Roux had made sure he arrived after school when the children would be at home. Jannie answered the door when Roux knocked. Roux's ghastly appearance terrified him; the soulless blue eyes and the livid white scar on his face made Roux look like the devil himself.

Jannie left the door open and fled into the house. His sister was on the floor playing with a doll and his mother sat looking dazed with a half empty bottle of brandy in front of her. Jannie was really worried; there had been no word of his father, and his mother was drinking heavily. He was aware that some of the neighbours drank, but he had never seen a drop of alcohol in their house. His mother had not been to work since the arrest and she was making no sense. The meticulously prepared meals of their previous existence were now few and far between.

Roux and Visser came in and closed the door. Roux took in the scene at a glance.

"I am Commandant Roux from the South African security police and I need to ask you a few questions," he said.

Lettie looked at him and tried to focus. This was the enemy; these were the people who had taken her husband away and were destroying her life.

Without thinking, she picked up the brandy bottle and hurled it at Roux. He ducked and the bottle smashed against the wall. There was a stunned silence, then she hurled abuse at Roux for a few minutes. Most of it was incoherent but Roux waited patiently for it to finish.

"Your husband has been arrested for belonging to a banned organisation and you are in trouble for harbouring a notorious terrorist," he said.

Lettie looked at him uncomprehendingly

"Notorious terrorist, Willie?" she questioned. "He was a relative of my husband's from Mitchell's Plain and coached the school rugby side."

"I doubt if he has ever been near Mitchell's Plain in his life," said Roux.

Lettie just shrugged. "We know nothing of any terrorist; he is a very good boy."

"Have you seen him since Sunday?" asked Roux.

"No."

Roux noticed Jannie fidgeting.

"Do you know where he is now?" asked Roux.

"No, he has gone; all his things are gone," answered Lettie.

"Gone?" Roux was surprised.

"Ja, gone, go and look if you want," she gesticulated to Jannie who took Danie into Kamau's room.

They came back

Danie nodded.

"Where did he go?" yelled Roux.

"Dunno," said Lettie. "Maybe you people chased him away, back to Mitchell's Plain."

Roux became impatient; he had no tolerance for drunks and he was disgusted with Lettie. "It just shows the weakness of the black and coloured people," he thought to himself, "the smallest crisis and they fall apart."

He got up and grabbed Jannie by the arm and twisted it behind his back.

"And you," he yelled: "have you seen this Willie Lemmer?" Jannie remembered what Kamau had told him and he remained silent. Lettie came rushing over to protect her son. Roux unceremoniously pushed her away. She collapsed on the sofa.

"Kom," said Roux. "We have ways of making little coloured shits like you talk." He twisted Jannie's arm further behind his back, with Jannie yelling with pain, and he frogmarched him out of the house and into the car.

"Talk," he yelled at Jannie. "Someone must have seen him and I think it is you." The arm was twisted more. "Look, your ma needs you real bad; if you don't tell me I will lock you up until you do."

By now Jannie was absolutely terrified, and he had wet his pants in fright. Haltingly he told Roux the story of how he had delivered the suitcase to Willie (Kamau) and how Kamau had told him not to tell anyone. The grip relaxed slightly.

"How was he dressed?" asked Roux shrewdly.

"He was dressed like an old kaffir," answered Jannie. "I didn't recognise him at first."

"Where was he going?" asked Roux.

"He didn't say, he was on a train going back into Jo'burg. I got off here at Coronationville," said Jannie.

"O.K," said Roux. "You done good, real good, now if you see him again you will tell me won't you?"

"Ja, meneer," Jannie was still terrified but was relieved that this man at least thought better of him now.

"Phone this number if you see him, straight away," said Roux. "He is a very bad man and he should be in prison." Jannie was handed a card with Roux's 'phone number.

Jannie nodded. It was difficult to think of Willie as a very bad man.

"Your father will be released if you do this," Roux lied. "So keep your eyes open. Now go back and look after your Ma." He let Jannie out of the car and watched him scamper back into the house.

They drove off.

Jannie went back into the house and he helped his sister clear up the mess left by the broken bottle. He changed his shorts.

"He says Willie is a very bad man and if we see him we must phone him," Said Jannie, "then Pa will be set free."

Nothing was said. None of them knew what to do any more.

Roux was certain that he had got as much out of the interview as possible; they now knew that Kamau used disguises, including that of an old African. He wondered if Oakley would know any more. He doubted it but he would enjoy finding out. He shivered in anticipation.

By the time Roux arrived at the security police headquarters in Johannesburg Charles Oakley had been on his feet in the notorious interview room on the tenth floor for more than twelve hours. He was completely disorientated, and worried sick about his family. He had already told them all he knew about the ANC, which was not that much but would probably lead to a few arrests.

"I've just been to see your family," said Roux unpleasantly. "Your wife was drunk," he added.

Charles said nothing.

"I want to know where your lodger, Lemmer, is," said Roux.

"I don't know," said Oakley.

"What do you know about him?"

Charles gave a few brief details.

"Is that all? We've known all that for months," yelled Roux.

Charles nodded.

"Well, we'll have to see if we can improve your memory," said Roux nastily. "Strip him," he ordered.

Three policemen then held Charles down and another one beat his testicles with a rubber mallet for three or four minutes.

Once he had partly recovered from the excruciating pain Roux asked again, "What do you know about Lemmer?"

Charles remained silent.

The torture went on for hours. They stubbed cigarettes out on his bare skin; they half drowned him.

Eventually Charles croaked through the pain, "I've told you everything, please no more pain." He then slipped into unconsciousness.

Eventually Roux said, "Take him back to his cell; we'll try again another day."

Privately he thought they would not get much more from the man. It had not been a very productive day, he thought, as he and Danie drove back to Pretoria in the early hours of the morning.

"We're looking for an old kaffir," he said almost to himself. "How many old fucking kaffirs are there, I wonder."

Danie said nothing.

Every day or two Kamau was forced to move. He had one meeting with the ANC at the Pelican Club. He blew up a couple of pylons. He wondered how long this could possibly last; escape was imperative but he had to make sure that the Oakley kids were looked after and he needed to see Rita again. The ANC were unsympathetic.

"You cannot concern yourself with such matters," he was told, "what you are doing is of vital importance to the fight against apartheid, you cannot jeopardise that for the sake of your own emotional attachments."

"But they will die, and I can save them," protested Kamau.

"Many people will die in this conflict and you can do nothing to save them," he was told.

"What can you do?" he asked.

"The same arguments apply to us as to you," was the response.

Kamau had other ideas. He had no intention of exploiting people and then just walking away.

The interviews with the staff of the restaurant continued, with Roux intervening from time to time. Rita was particularly nervous. As far as she knew, there was nobody who even suspected that she was a coloured and not a white as she pretended to be, and if that fact ever came to light, she was certain they would eventually find out that she and Kamau were lovers; then she would be in real trouble.

The interviews were no real problem. Sergeant Danie Visser held no fears for her and he, in turn, despite his Botswana experience, could not imagine any self-respecting white girl wanting anything to do with a coloured waiter. The headwaiter said he had a really hard time from Roux, which of course led nowhere. The police spent some hours searching Rita's flat but there was no trace of Kamau or any other male.

"Must be a lesbian," thought Danie.

Giles in London had received a letter from Kamau, explaining his personal situation and that he might have to get the Oakley family out of South Africa and possibly Rita as well. For once in his life, Giles was at a loss. "What is he expecting me to do?" mused Giles. "Set up some sort of refugee camp for all the damaged goods he finds in South Africa?"

"You should bring this up with Trevor Mdantsane," insisted Louise. "They must have some sort of plan for refugees of this nature from South Africa."

Some months passed. Kamau became used to his itinerant lifestyle and the ANC provided him with some funds, now that he wasn't earning anything. He was proving to be a real thorn in the side of the security forces, but he began to feel more and more constrained and in danger.

Rita heard from him at least once a week via the letter box drop. She had told him not to phone since she was certain the phone was bugged, and although none of the staff were being interviewed by the police any more, either Roux or Visser dropped in to the restaurant regularly just to make sure that none of them had forgotten that they were still looking for Willie Lemmer.

In heavy disguise, Kamau returned to the Oakley house in Coronationville. There was no sign whatsoever of Charles and the contacts he had at the ANC had told him that Charles was in jail and was likely to remain there; the authorities had legal devices to lock people up for years without trial if they so wished.

Kamau had become increasingly concerned about the rest of the family though. On more than one occasion he saw Lettie being helped into the house: she appeared to be blind drunk. The children were also looking more and more ragged; Kamau was certain that Jannie only attended school when he felt like it and he had seen him as a member of a gang of street kids. Hettie, the little girl, just got dirtier and dirtier.

Then one week Kamau came to the house, this time dressed as a smart salesman. He had on a wig of longish black hair and he had also grown a moustache. There was still a police presence in the street, but now at a very junior level; it was obvious that the Oakleys had been relegated to small fry. As he watched the Oakley house, he noticed that people whom he had never seen before came and went from the house. Deeply concerned, he politely knocked on the door, and when it was opened he explained that he was a friend of the Oakleys and wondered where they had moved to.

The family that had moved in were in many ways just like the Oakleys, a hard working husband and wife and two young children.

The woman, who did not introduce herself, explained that the previous family had failed to make payments to the building society and the house had been repossessed. She and her husband had now bought the house. She had no idea what had happened to the family. The door was firmly shut in his face.

Roux received a call in his Pretoria office within minutes of the visit.

"Meneer Roux, there was a man here looking for the Oakleys, he didn't look much like the photographs you gave us though. What? An old kaffir, no meneer he did not look like an old kaffir. He was a young, good looking, quite tall and well built. O.K Meneer, and Meneer, thank you for helping us get this house, we will be very happy here."

Roux grunted. He was sure it was Kamau. Somehow there was vulnerability there; if Kamau had any sense he would get out of the country now but Roux could see he would try to rescue those kids first.

When he could find the time, Kamau scoured Coronationville and the nearby delightfully named Western Coloured Township for signs of the Oakley family. He knew that what he was doing was dangerous, even foolhardy, but he also knew that he was the one hope the children had. In a short telephone call to Giles from a public phone, he had persuaded Giles to take the children in, together with their mother. It would be up to Kamau to get them to England, although Giles said he would put a word in with the Foreign Office in London.

In desperation, after some weeks of searching, Kamau went to the local hospital, where he described the family. To start with nobody took any notice, but then one of the older nurses took pity on him.

"What is your interest, meneer?" she asked.

"I am their uncle from the Cape; the father is in jail and I am trying to look after the rest of the family. They moved from the address that we have," he answered.

"There was a lady brought in with that description," she said, "but no kids."

"Well, can I see her? I'll know immediately," he said his spirits lifting.

She went away and came back more than thirty minutes later, and then led him into the bowels of the hospital underground. It took a few minutes for Kamau to realise that he was being taken to the morgue.

The nurse opened the morgue and said, "Not very good news for you meneer, we have two ladies who almost fit your description."

She pulled a freezer drawer open.

Kamau shook his head.

She went to another drawer and there was Lettie lying as if asleep.

Kamau nodded.

"How did she die?" he asked.

"She was sleeping rough and was stabbed. Probably just robbery," was the answer.

"She wanted so little," he said quietly.

"You will need to sign the identification papers," said the nurse in a business-like way.

Kamau did as he was told.

"Any sign of the children?" he asked.

The nurse shook her head.

"You should go to the house," she suggested.

"What house?

"There is an orphanage called St. Joseph's in Western," she said. "They look for kids from situations like this and take them in."

"Who runs it?" asked Kamau.

"It's privately run, there is a white principal and his wife there at the moment," she told him.

"You will need to claim the body," said the nurse.

"Yes, O.K."

That's a job for the ANC, it's the least they can do, he thought.

After a short wait Kamau was ushered into the principal's pokey little office at St. Joseph's.

The principal, a Mr. Jones, was a thin, wiry man with a beard and glasses. He had a pleasant, open manner.

After Kamau had explained the situation Mr. Jones said, "They've been here about three weeks and were in a very bad way. They've spent most of that time in the sick bay. It's most unusual that we know nothing about children who come here. Can you give us some background?" said Mr. Jones.

The principal's face became more and more sombre as Kamau told him the story. Kamau passed himself off as a relative from the Cape.

"How did you find them?" asked Kamau.

"They were in an old car; Jannie was stealing from shops and houses to feed them," was the answer.

Kamau just looked at the floor.

"I'll take you to see them," said Mr. Jones.

Kamau stopped him.

"No, that will just upset them," he said.

Kamau then explained the situation regarding their father and that he would likely remain in jail for a long time. He then outlined his plans to send them to England and explained that in order to obtain travel documents they would have to first obtain Charles Oakley's written permission.

"Can I ask you to do that?" asked Kamau.

"Why can't you do it?" asked Mr. Jones straightforwardly.

Kamau shook his head and answered. "For many reasons, I can't do it. Please don't ask me why but there are reasons.'

"Who are these people in England?" asked Jones.

"My distant relatives; the children will be well looked after there," said Kamau.

Jones looked at Kamau. Clearly Oakley was in jail for some anti-government activity. There was obviously more to the coloured gentleman in front of him, who had not really introduced himself, other than just an interested relative from the Cape. Jones was actively anti-government. The results of their obscene policies were evident to him every single day of the week. The reason he ran St. Joseph's home was to try to redress some of the horrors of apartheid.

"There may be some costs," he said.

"Please don't worry; if you can arrange all the paperwork, then I will ensure a handsome donation to the house from my relatives in England. Please employ lawyers if you have to," said Kamau.

"What did you say your name was?" asked Jones.

"I didn't and it's better that way," answered Kamau.

Jones looked dubious.

"You will receive a donation to the home, ten thousand rand within two weeks. I will phone you from time to time. I will identify myself as Japie," said Kamau. "But you won't see me again."

"The phone is bugged," answered Jones.

"I'm sure it is, but you are doing nothing wrong and I will be using public phones."

They shook hands and Kamau left.

Giles was surprised to receive the letter requesting ten thousand Rand be sent to an obscure orphanage in Johannesburg. Nevertheless he complied with the request. He was more concerned with what to do with two coloured children in London.

Jones had started the legal process to get the children to England and after much haggling had been allowed to see Charles Oakley in prison.

Charles was deeply shaken when he was told what had happened to his family.

"So they've taken everything from me?" he eventually said quietly after Mr. Jones had told him everything.

He signed the papers and wept. They wouldn't even let him out under escort to attend his wife's funeral, which Jones also arranged.

"I know who came to see you," Charles eventually said to Jones. "Please wish him all the best." He was eventually dragged off back to the cells.

✕　✕　✕

CHAPTER 13

After many visits to the lawyers and then to the British Consulate in Johannesburg Philip Jones eventually received travel documents for the children. He had managed in a second visit to get a tearful and despondent Charles Oakley to sign the appropriate papers to allow his children to travel to England. The consulate had been uncooperative and suspicious to begin with but suddenly, much to Jones' surprise, the process was accelerated.

"Word from up high," the lawyers advised, "I hear this has been cleared from the very top."

Jones was even more mystified by the person he now knew as Japie.

Roux was aware of what Jones was doing and allowed it to continue on the grounds that this would encourage Oakley to talk and also that it might expose Kamau. As a matter of routine the security apparatus had bugged the phone at St Joseph's. As far as Roux was concerned any such establishment was automatically suspicious and especially if it was run by an interfering white.

"Why can't these white verligte (literally enlightened) bastards just keep to themselves," he complained to Danie Visser one day. "They have everything they want in the white areas and we have full control over all the other areas."

Danie just nodded. It did not pay to argue with Roux.

There were many phone calls to St. Joseph's, and although the phone was bugged, the regular phone calls from Japie attracted no particularly attention to start with. Only towards the end of the process had anyone in the security police linked the calls at all and it was only when Japie had made arrangements to have the children collected one night that Roux was alerted.

"This was three nights ago, you fucking pampoen (pumpkin). The little bastards are probably in Lusaka by now," he fumed.

"There are something like two hundred phone calls per day to that place, meneer. Many of them are quite hysterical and we have only just linked the four or five previous calls from this Japie to these particular children," one of the technicians explained.

"I've been chasing this blerry (bloody) Japie for months now and all you people can come up with is excuses," fumed Roux. "What else do we know?"

"Well, the British have issued travel documents but they do not wish to be involved in a diplomatic incident. So while the children will be allowed into Britain, we think that rather than risking going through Jan Smuts airport and not being allowed to leave the country, since we have not issued exit permits (all South African born people with foreign passports had to have valid exit permits from the South African authorities to leave the country) they will probably try to smuggle the children into Botswana or Swaziland and then travel from there to London." This was a long speech from Sergeant Danie Visser, who now looked at his chief expectantly.

"When were the children picked up?" asked Roux.

"Two nights ago," answered Danie.

"Who picked them up?" asked Roux.

"We don't really know, the principal was evasive when we asked him, he just said it was relatives from the Cape. We have seen all the papers, they seem to be in order," said Danie.

Kamau had very reluctantly decided to involve Rita in getting the children out of South Africa. He had already established that Rita had a passport and that she had herself been to Gaborone on a previous occasion. The difficulty was getting the children out because of the exit permit problem. Somehow the children would have to be smuggled into Botswana and Rita would have to do the smuggling. Kamau would have to walk across, as he was not living legitimately in South Africa and he had no travel papers at all. He was certain that all the possible exit points would be on high alert watching for him.

Through the letter box drop, he arranged to meet Rita early one morning. He had managed to get the ANC to provide him with a car, which was registered to a legitimate business in Soweto, and he picked Rita up on a street corner some way from her flat to minimise the chance of detection. They had no way of knowing whether Rita was still under surveillance, although they were both certain that the letter-box drop had remained undetected.

They embraced.

"God how I've missed you," said Rita.

"Same for me," said Kamau," but look, me being seen with you is very dangerous for both of us, and the kids. We must be patient or we'll all end up in jail."

They drove off to a deserted, unkempt piece of grassland near a mine dump to the south of the city.

Kamau looked into her liquid brown eyes and her beautiful face and dark brown hair. He shook his head.

"To be safe we have no more than one hour, I want to make love to you with every fibre in my body but we must be patient," he said.

He then explained that she should take the car, park it away from her block of flats and on Friday night, which was two days away, after midnight she was to go to St. Josephs. The principal was expecting them and the children would be handed over to her after she gave the password. Philip Jones, the principal, would have already briefed the children when she picked them up. She was to drive to Mafikeng and was to be at the Ramatlabama border post shortly after it opened on the Saturday morning. She was then to drive to Lobatse and check into the Cumberland Hotel, where rooms had been booked and prepaid for two nights. He would meet her there as soon as he could.

The boot of the car had been organised so that the two children could hide behind the luggage and boxes of samples. Her cover was that she was a representative for a pharmaceutical supply company on a road trip through Botswana. This was usual enough and would arouse no suspicion at the border. They did not discuss what would happen if the children were discovered; it did not bear thinking about.

"How are you going to get across the border?" she asked.

"Walk; I'm leaving today and I expect to meet you in Lobatse by noon Saturday," he said.

Roux had decided to play his hunches. He had alerted all the border posts again, so there was nothing further he could do in that direction. On his own he drove the four hundred odd kilometres to Tlokweng gate and then he checked into the Holiday Inn in Gaborone. He had previously contacted two of his agents in the city, one of whom was to keep an eye on the airport; the other was told to be available on the end of a 'phone in case he was needed.

Roux surveyed the lobby after he had checked in. There was the usual gaggle of people hanging around the entrance to the casino, being kept at bay by the security people. Roux had a deep moral objection to casinos and everything they stood for and he regarded the fact that there were no casinos in "white" South Africa as another sign of the moral superiority of the whites over the other races. He paid no attention to the fact that most of the clientele of the casinos dotted around the independent countries surrounding South Africa and the so-called homelands were white. His self-satisfied reflections came to an abrupt halt when out of the corner of his eye he saw a familiar figure emerging from the dining room.

"My God," he thought, "what is Jessica Hawthorne doing here? This has to be something to do with Kamau Lawrence and those kids." He slipped into the casino entrance without being seen and cautiously watched Jessica, who collected a key from the desk and made off in the direction of her room.

When she had gone Roux went up to the desk and said, "My colleague Miss Hawthorne checked in here earlier today. Can you please give me her room number?"

The clerk gave it to him without hesitation. Phoning from his room he phoned his agent.

"There is a white woman in room 353. I want to know when she leaves the hotel."

"How do I do that?" asked the agent.

"You have a Wayguard security uniform don't you?" asked Roux.

"Yes," was the doubtful answer.

"Then put it on and hang around the corridor; there seem to be dozens of these so-called security people all over the hotel," answered Roux.

"That may be all night," protested the agent.

"Yes, it may be!" yelled Roux. He put the phone down and half an hour later went to check and got a sullen glare from the man as he brushed past him in the passage. His agent fitted in well, and as Roux had assumed looked like any of the several dozen other security people wandering about the hotel.

"Any movement?" he asked. Roux handed him twenty Pula, which placated him a bit.

The man shook his head.

Kamau had gone by train to Mafikeng and then hitched a ride on a large truck making its way to the border post. He hopped off two kilometres from the post and in the gathering dusk he headed off into the bush. He had decided that he would probably have to walk about twenty-five kilometres through the bush round the border post, which he could easily do in the time. He would only travel at night and try to lie up during the day to avoid detection. He would have to keep an eye out for both South African and Botswana border patrols; how extensive these patrols were or even if they existed was unknown to him.

Aided by a small compass, Kamau headed due west for about two hours; he then judged he was five or six kilometres from the road. He then turned due north and walked through the night. This area was good cattle country and whenever he came upon one of the small herds scattered through the bush he deliberately walked through them, using the skills he had learned as a young boy herding his grandfather's cattle in Kenya. Any tracks he left would certainly be covered up by the cattle, and if the patrols had dogs they would lose his scent once it became mixed up with the smell of cattle. He knew that the border was the Ramatlabama River, which, as was usual in this part of the world, was dry except immediately after a rainstorm when it would become a furious torrent for a few hours.

At close to midnight Kamau stopped and ate some mielie pap (maize meal) and an orange that he had brought with him. The bush held no fears for him at all and he enjoyed sitting there with his back to a thorn tree, quietly identifying all the sounds typical of the night in the dry, dusty semi-desert: the yip of a jackal over there and the laugh of a hyena nearby, the crash and squeal of an antelope being caught by a predator. Then there was another sound: first he heard the dogs and then the voices; after a few minutes he picked up the occasional word of Afrikaans. Obviously a border patrol. He wondered what he should do; if he was unlucky, the dogs would pick up his smell in the still, dry air. Quickly packing his small rucksack and ensuring he had left nothing behind, he scampered back through the bush and found a herd of about forty large Afrikander cattle. Collecting them up into a group he drove them towards the border, for he was now reasonably sure the dry river-bed was only a few hundred yards beyond where he had had his meal. Within about thirty minutes he had driven the animals in the direction of the patrol. Keeping down he got the animals to trot towards the river. Suddenly there was a yell and then some dogs barking and then swearing in Afrikaans.

"It's that blerry bobejaan (baboon) Van der Merwe again," said a voice. "He's always trying to move his cattle backwards and forwards across the border to get the best prices."

There was a shot and the cattle scattered in confusion. Kamau jogged away from the noise, found the river-bed and scampered across the border unseen. Waiting in the trees to catch his breath on the Botswana side of the border Kamau smiled despite himself. The noise from the confrontation of the cattle and the patrol had died down. He wondered if the rifle shot would attract patrols from the Botswana side.

After another two hours walking due north, he was exhausted and there were faint traces of light in the sky. He found a patch of bush and after eating more of the food he had brought, he rolled himself up in a light sleeping bag he had with him and went to sleep.

Hours later, when the sun was high in the heavens, Kamau woke and remembered where he was. Suddenly he had an uneasy sensation that he was sharing the sleeping bag with something alive. Without moving he looked about; just at the entrance to his sleeping bag was the very end of the tail of what appeared to be a snake. Kamau started to sweat. "My God, it could be all over right here and now," he thought. "If this is a cobra and it bites me I won't last an hour and the hyenas and jackals will make sure that there is nothing left of me by tomorrow." He didn't dare move; he knew any sudden movement would provoke the animal and it would bite. All the snake had been looking for was a little warmth. Kamau waited ten minutes, wondering what to do. If he waited long enough the snake would get too warm and crawl out of the bag. "When will that be—one hour, two hours, sometime tomorrow?" he thought. He could feel his body tensing up; within a few hours he would be too taut to do anything. Whatever the risks, he decided that action was the only way. He made himself relax for two or three minutes, then in one movement grabbed the tail of the snake and flung it into the bush. The snake hissed angrily as it flew through the air but it slithered off into the bush as Kamau leapt out of his sleeping bag and threw some sticks in the general direction of the snake.

Shivering with fright Kamau examined himself from head to foot. There was a slight nick on his hand, probably from the snake, so taking his penknife he made a very deep cut across the wound and let the blood flow. Even then, his hand and wrist swelled up uncomfortably. He felt very lucky and shuddered at the thought of what might have occurred. To have Rita and the two children holed up in the Cumberland Hotel in Lobatse wondering what had happened to him did not bear thinking about. He put the thought out of his mind. He ate more of the food, drank some water and waited until later in the afternoon. By now he was a long way from the border and the danger from patrols was over. At dawn, now Friday, he crossed a wide dirt road. "That must be the road to Kanye," he thought. He continued north for an hour and then made camp again. This time he lit a small fire and cleared a patch of ground, on which he put his sleeping bag. He knew that snakes would instinctively do anything to avoid crossing the open ground and he wasn't about to take any more chances.

The car that Kamau had secured for Rita looked old and battered but Kamau had assured her that it was in good working order. After she had been left she took the vehicle round Johannesburg to make sure she could remember how to drive. It was some years earlier that her brother had taught her to drive and she wanted to make sure she could manage. There had been no opportunity to drive since she had been in Johannesburg. Twice she made her way to St. Josephs and now on the Friday night she was sitting in her flat with butterflies in her stomach, waiting. As far as she could think, nothing had been forgotten. The car had been filled with petrol. She had money, travel documents; the restaurant had given her the weekend off. She shivered in anticipation; now she was to be part of the struggle even in this very modest way. She gave a brief thought to Willie or as she now knew him, Kamau, finding his way through the bush. Her imagination did not really extend to the dangers he faced and she had never spent a single night in the bush herself. She had every faith that his plans would work.

At about eleven thirty Rita picked up her small suitcase, glanced round the flat before switching off the lights and went out, making sure the door was locked. She went down the fire stairs and as a precaution went round the corner and waited for five minutes to make certain that she was not being followed. The car was as she left it and appeared to be untouched. Car theft was rife in Hillbrow but she could not imagine anyone wanting to steal her old banger. Shortly after midnight she stopped outside St. Joseph's, killed the engine and flashed the headlights twice as she had been instructed. She had driven without incident to the house and had been stopped once by the police but they had assumed she was a white and had waved her on. Five minutes went by and then a man and two young children appeared as if out of nowhere. She opened the car window and gave the password. In complete silence a small suitcase was added to the collection of items in the car boot and Rita made sure that the wide-eyed kids were comfortable in the back seat. The man who had brought the children out shook them each by the hand and wished them well. He gave Rita a package and said in Afrikaans, "Their British travel documents."

For the first hour or more the children sat and said almost nothing. They ate some of the chips and sweets and soft drinks that Rita had provided. Eventually after a stop she invited Jannie into the front and asked him to help her navigate. He'd never seen a map before but he soon got the idea and between him and his sister they excitedly called out of the names of the little towns they went through: Ventersdorp, Coligny, the slightly larger town of Lichtenburg and then Mafikeng. Mostly they were just blots on the landscape, a few shops, a row of silos for the maize crop, a hotel or two, some petrol stations and always two to three kilometres out of town a shanty town for the blacks and coloureds. One even had the unimaginative name of "Kaffir Kraal" (Lit. Kaffir Village). Rita shook her head, thinking that these places were there just to provide labour for the convenience of the whites. She could see that most of them were in deplorable condition.

"What on earth would a person feel about themselves, or the society they lived in if they came from a place called Kaffir Kraal?" she thought.

She found an out of the way petrol station in Mmabatho, which would not worry about coloured children travelling with a white woman. As she refuelled the car, she explained to the children that when they went through the border they would have to hide in the boot. Jannie by now had become more confident and saw it as part of a game. Hettie was more nervous.

"When we are at the border post you must keep very quiet. There will be two stops, one at the South African side and one at the Botswana side. I will then drive for a few minutes on the Botswana side and then you can come out of the boot and sit with me again, O.K?" instructed Rita.

The children nodded.

The car was cleaned up and all the chip packets, bottles and any other debris indicating the presence of the children thrown out. About five kilometres from the border post Rita went down a side road just out of sight of the main road. She carefully packed the children into their little cubby-hole, made sure they had both relieved themselves, provided them with some more coke and chips. She was satisfied that they could breathe and she was certain that unless the car was searched the children would remain undetected.

With her heart in her mouth she shut the boot of the car and drove the ten minutes to the border post, which had now been open about an hour. It was still and the few people at the post were standing huddled in a queue to present their documents. The white policeman spent what seemed to Rita like an unnecessary amount of time on all the blacks. With her he glanced at her documents, stamped them and handed them back without comment. She supposed the attitude stemmed from the fact that blacks were just supposed to stay in places pre-determined by the white administration, and it was beyond the comprehension of the white policeman that they could have legitimate business on the other side of the border. She nervously went back to the car and presented her passport to another policeman manning the barrier. He made her get out and open the boot. Her heart raced, when he pointed at her suitcase. "Open up, please." She did as she was told and he rummaged around among her underwear for a few minutes.

"What is your business, Mevrou?" he asked in Afrikaans.

She explained.

"What is in those boxes?"

"Samples." She gave him a small jar of Vaseline.

He looked at her doubtfully.

"You tell me those kaffirs over there buy this stuff?" he asked.

"Ja, meneer, and the whites too, business is good up there, now with the diamond mines and when the meat factory is working flat out," she answered easily, without betraying any of her nervousness.

"I suppose," was the doubtful reply.

"O.K. mevrou, you may go." The policeman closed the boot, opened the barrier and waved her on.

She drove the fifty or so yards to the Botswana side, where the process was repeated.

The Botswana border guard was intrigued with all of Rita's samples. He clearly wanted something. She was prepared for this and found him a few samples. As the barrier opened it was as if a huge weight had been lifted from her shoulders. She drove not more than a kilometre and then, again out of sight of the road, she extricated the children from their hiding place. They were none the worse for their experience. They ate some of the food they had brought and Jannie was intrigued with the wildness of it all.

"Is this what it will be like in England?" he asked.

Rita laughed, "No, no, England is cold and wet and everything is neat and tidy," she told them. They chatted on about inconsequential things. Rita was surprised how easily she related to the two kids. She was in no hurry, it was still early morning and Lobatse and the Cumberland were less than an hour's drive away. They drove off slowly and watched for game, which consisted of the occasional small antelope. The children were thrilled, as was Rita; none of them had ever seen an animal in the wild before.

Without really noticing, they passed a rather unkempt looking man who waved at them. Rita took no notice.

"Hey," yelled Jannie. "It's oom (uncle) Willie, what is he doing here?"

Rita stopped the car and backed up. Kamau smiled as he hopped into the front seat. The children were all over him in a flash, asking all sorts of questions. He leant over and kissed Rita.

"Everything O.K?" he asked.

They all nodded and related their adventures in great detail.

"And you?" asked Rita. "I've seen you look better and you're all covered in blood.

Kamau explained about his three days in the bush and the patrol and the encounter with the snake.

"Well, let me fix that up for you," she said. "After all, I have a car full of samples for chemist's shops."

She washed and bound his wound and dusted him off proprietorily.

"What will they think when we get to this fancy hotel of yours?" she asked.

"We can tell them the car broke down, I guess that happens often enough," he said.

Lobatse is a small, unattractive place dominated by the Botswana Meat Commission, which has a licence to export meat to the European Economic Community. Kamau knew that this was a great boon to the many cattle owners in the country, who received premium prices for their cattle as a result of the arrangement. They found their way to the Cumberland, which was a surprisingly good hotel on the outskirts of town. They checked in as Mr. and Mrs. Lawrence. The hotel staff did not give them a second glance, much to their relief. The fact that Kamau was coloured and Rita looked white caused no comment, as it would have done south of the border.

"We have no time to waste," Kamau told them.

"We need to get cleaned up and then I will drive the children to Gaborone airport where they will be flown out of the country. I will be back here sometime this afternoon," he told Rita.

She clung to him while the children were playing in the bath. Her body ached for him.

"I will also come to the airport," she said.

"No, I am certain that the South Africans will have agents there, it's much too dangerous. If they see you, you will be arrested when you get back to Jo'burg. We simply cannot take the risk. Make yourself at home here; I will be back as soon as I can," he responded.

Kamau spent a frustrating hour trying to phone the Holiday Inn in Gaborone. At last he got through.

"Jessica Hawthorne please," he asked.

Jessica answered the phone after the first ring.

"Thank heaven it's you," she said after they had greeted each other warmly.

"Well we're all here," said Kamau. "Is everything under control?"

"Yes," said Jessica hesitantly. "I came with the plane from Lusaka and he's ready to take off again. The pilot says he needs to leave by midday to make Kasane well before nightfall and then it's only two hours or so to Lusaka. We're all booked on the BOAC Flight to London on Sunday evening.

"Fine," said Kamau.

"Kamau, there is one other thing," said Jessica.

"What's that?"

"That animal Roux is here in the hotel," Jessica almost whispered, "I caught a glimpse of him yesterday in the lobby and then he ducked into the casino. I suppose he thinks I didn't see him."

Kamau grunted.

"And there's been a sort of security guard outside my door all night," she went on.

"What sort of guard?" asked Kamau cautiously.

"Well, he looks like all the others here, all with the same sort of uniform," she said.

"Yes," said Kamau encouraging her to continue.

"Well, the same person has been there for more than twelve hours now; I'm suspicious, I would expect that if he were on some sort of normal duty he would be on an eight hour shift or something," she went on.

"Hm," said Kamau. "Sounds very suspicious; if I were you I would get the hotel to move him. If he's there for a reason they will tell you; if he's unauthorised I expect they will get rid of him."

"O.K," answered Jessica.

"Look, it's getting on, we will leave here before ten thirty and you ought to be able to take off by noon easily. See you at the airport."

Kamau rung off.

Jessica rang the front desk and asked them why there was a security guard outside her room.

"You are mistaken madam," was the curt reply. "Security guards are not allowed near the rooms."

"Well I've just seen him again and the same person has been there since last night," answered Jessica. The phone was put down. By this time Jessica was furious; after several attempts she managed to get through to the General Manager, who also tried to fob her off.

"Look," she said. "He's standing less than fifty yards from your office, why don't you go and see for yourself."

She waited.

Ten minutes later there was a scuffle outside her room and Roux's agent was frogmarched off the premises.

Roux received a call about two hours later.

"They threw me from the hotel," said his agent.

"What?"

"I was taken out from the hotel and taken to the police. I don't know what happened to the lady," he said.

"Shit," said Roux. "Call me back later."

He phoned the front desk and asked to be put through to Jessica Hawthorne.

"She checked out about an hour ago," was the response.

"Damn, damn, damn," he fumed.

Kamau and Rita and the children went down to the dining room and ordered a huge breakfast. Although they were late, Kamau had been to see the head waiter and had charmed him into keeping the dining room open just for them. The children had never seen anything like it; firstly they were enthralled with the room with their very own bath and now this veritable feast with "Oom" Willie and their new friend Rita. They had noticed a few white people around the hotel, who took no particular notice of them. They didn't really know why but it felt different to South Africa.

By ten fifteen Kamau had told Rita that he hoped to be back by two that afternoon and had packed the children into the car. He drove to Gaborone and the airport.

As he drove into the airport car park, he was relieved to see Jessica standing outside the tin shed that served as the terminal building; together with two men in pilot's uniforms.

He and Jessica embraced as brother and sister.

"You're early," she bubbled. "Great. Well, we'd better get on. We'll have plenty of time to talk on the plane. You must be Jannie and you Hettie," she said to the children. They in turn couldn't understand much of what was being said, but this new aunty seemed friendly enough and she had given them each a wonderful present. Hettie received a doll with innumerable changes of clothes and Jannie a Meccano set.

Kamau picked up their small suitcase and they all went into the customs hall.

Kamau then said to Jessica, "Any more sign of Roux?"

"No, nothing," she said.

"He won't be far away, I'm sure," said Kamau.

"Is this all the luggage you have?" asked Jessica.

"It's for the children, I can't come. I have a few things to do and will follow you on the train in a few days. I'll be in London in a week," he said.

"What?" said Jessica, furiously. "This little jaunt is as much for you as for the children. Trevor told me how much trouble you were in and how valuable you were."

"I can't come," said Kamau firmly. "There is one more little chore I have to do to even things up and then I will be back." The customs people looked at them quizzically.

"You know it's dangerous," said Jessica, "that psychopath Roux is here in town. Even here you're not safe; you must come."

He looked at her and then hugged her. "Please try to understand, I would come if I could," he pleaded. 'Probably on the Sunday night train from Lobatse.'

"Must be some woman," she said knowingly. "Anyway, how will I talk to the children?"

He winked at them.

"This new aunty Jessica will look after you," he said in Afrikaans. "I will see you in England in a week or so; now off you all go." He hugged the kids and Jessica and shook the pilots by the hand.

Jessica tried once more. "You are risking your life," she said.

Kamau smiled.

"So, what's new?" He waved them goodbye. At the last minute Jessica came rushing back.

"Your identity," she tossed him an envelope. "I almost forgot."

It was his British papers.

Kamau stood in the almost completely deserted car park and watched the little plane take off. He knew that Giles had paid all the costs. He felt that part of his obligation to the Oakley family had been paid off. There was no sign of Roux, much to Kamau's relief. He clambered into the battered old car and enjoyed the drive back to Lobatse and Rita. He felt free again. It had been almost eighteen months since he had first gone to South Africa and the anxiety of those months had taken its toll; he was now beginning to relax and unwind.

He knocked quietly on the door of their room in the hotel. Rita opened the door and let him in.

He just managed to get the door shut when Rita leaped on him and started to kiss him passionately. For both of them it was the most joyous weekend, almost like a honeymoon. Rita of course had never stayed in a hotel in her life before, so she enjoyed the luxury, the good meals and the gentle walks. Kamau even taught her to play a bit of tennis and croquet.

On Sunday afternoon there was a call from Jessica.

"We're here in Lusaka," was all she said, "and will catch the flight tonight."

"What about the children?" asked Kamau.

"Fine, they both sicked up the huge breakfast you fed them, but otherwise, O.K." said Jessica.

"What about the language?" asked Kamau.

"Well, since they're going to live and go to school in England I have started teaching them English," said Jessica firmly.

"Can I speak to them?" asked Kamau.

"No, they're watching T.V, they say they've never seen it before," said Jessica.

"That's right, it's only just started in South Africa," said Kamau.

"When are you coming out?" asked Jessica.

"I'm catching tonight's train," was the response.

They said their farewells and rang off.

"The train is at seven tonight. I'll just come to the border post with you and then hitch back here," said Kamau to Rita.

They made love once more and then Kamau checked out and they made their way to the border post at Skilpadshek.

"You can drive straight through to Zeerust from here," he explained.

Rita bid him a tearful farewell.

"When will I see you again?" she asked.

"Soon, but you will have to leave South Africa and join me in England," he said.

"I know, but it's a big step," she said.

"I'll write and phone," he said. "I will not be able to live openly in South Africa again, I've told you all that."

She nodded.

They kissed and he watched her go through the border.

He hitched a ride back to Lobatse and made his way to the station, where he bought a third class ticket to Francistown. He couldn't risk going through Rhodesia, then still in the hands of the Smith regime. He would have to hitch a ride from Francistown to Kasane and then the safety of Zambia.

Roux was fuming. He thought that Kamau had escaped him yet again. Then both agents came to see him just as he was about to check out of the hotel and return to South Africa.

One of the customs officials had told them the whole story of Jessica and the children leaving by air for Kasane and then, as they understood it, on to Lusaka.

"And that Kamau?" asked Roux.

"Well there was another coloured man there who refused to get on the plane although there was room for him," said one of the agents.

"Describe this man," ordered Roux.

He clearly described Kamau.

"Where did he go?" asked Roux.

"Well he drove off in his car, but the customs people said he would catch the Francistown train on Sunday from Lobatse," said the agent.

Roux could now see a glimmer of hope.

"You," he said roughly to one of his agents, "just make sure that we can go through the border post at Parr's Halt sometime between eleven and twelve tonight."

"That gate shuts at six," was the answer.

"I know you stupid fucker, I just said make sure it's open between eleven and twelve," said Roux. "No papers, no evidence, big reward, O.K?"

"O.K." was the response.

"Take my car and meet us at Mahalapye station at about ten thirty tonight," he further instructed.

"Yes, baas."

"Now fuck off."

The agent left.

Roux made one telephone call.

Kamau sat on the hard wooden bench of the third class compartment. He was completely anonymous here, he felt safe. He'd eaten far too much over the weekend, so he had no need of food.

The train stopped at Gaborone, after which he dozed.

The next thing he was aware of was that he woke up. It was completely dark and he was being bumped around and almost suffocated by dust. He vaguely remembered being surrounded by five or six men and then… blackness. His head hurt like hell. He yelled. No response. It was clear that he was in the boot of a car going somewhere. He almost panicked. Then he thought, "Roux, this can only be Roux." His hands and feet were not tied and he still had his backpack on. He fiddled with the boot catch for about ten minutes when the boot popped open. He jumped out just as the car slowed down and lay dazed in the road for a minute, then he started to run down the road. The car screeched to a halt and as Kamau stumbled down the road he was hit from behind with a ferocious rugby tackle. Kamau was still a bit groggy and Roux had caught up with him quickly.

"Got you, you bastard," yelled Roux.

Two others came along and kicked and beat him. They then tied his hands and feet and he was firmly placed between two people in the backseat of the car and they drove on.

Shortly afterwards they came up to what Kamau thought was a border post. The car lights were flicked twice, the barrier lifted and they drove through. The same thing happened on the South African side.

Kamau could not believe it. He had spent months avoiding these very people and now they had abducted him in the simplest circumstances. He knew he was in for a very rough time indeed; he shivered and tried to think.

CHAPTER 14

Nothing much was said during the long drive to Johannesburg. They passed through Ellisras, and Nylstroom, one of the towns that Kamau and Robert and Jessica had stopped at eighteen months earlier during their flight to Swaziland. To Kamau that seemed like a lifetime ago; much water had gone under the bridge since then. The streets of Pretoria were almost completely deserted as they drove speedily through the city just before the dawn. Kamau was roughly hauled out of the car by Roux and his assistants an hour or so later, after they had stopped outside a large, squat, forbidding looking building just west of downtown Johannesburg. Kamau shuddered; he supposed this was police headquarters. He was dragged up the steps and with almost no formality found himself in a small cell in the basement of the building. He had had no food or water since his abduction, and he was having dizzy spells from his knock on the head.

After negotiating the border post, Rita drove slowly and sadly back to Johannesburg. She almost wished she had taken up Kamau's suggestion that she join him in England, but she wasn't really ready for such a large step yet. Her family were still in the Cape; South Africa was her home and she was enjoying the money that her "white" lifestyle brought her. She parked the car, locked it and by midnight was safely back in her flat in Hillbrow, unaware of the drama that was now surrounding Kamau.

More than a week later, she was woken up in the middle of the night by a call from Jessica.

"Japie has not arrived," was the short response after Rita had answered. Jessica had been told that the phone was probably bugged, so she used the same alias as Kamau had used for Mr. Jones at St. Josephs.

Rita's heart beat faster; she wanted to say so much. She presumed that the caller was from England, since Kamau had explained the situation, but she knew she had to remain cautious.

"There has been no contact here," she eventually responded. She guiltily remembered that she hadn't looked at the letter-box drop since her return, since she had assumed that Kamau would be on his way to England. There was silence on the phone.

"Is everything else all right?" asked Rita.

"Yes, all arrived safely," was the answer, then the phone rung off.

Rita was beside herself with anxiety and wondered what to do. She had almost nobody to turn to. She eventually plucked up courage and went to see Philip Jones at St. Josephs in Western Coloured Township. The car in which she had made her trip to Botswana had not been collected by the ANC, so she used that.

At least once a month on Saturday mornings, Philip Jones arranged a sale of some sort in the grounds of the home. This particular Saturday he and a group of volunteers were selling second hand clothes across the fence. Although the home was largely funded by one of the big mining groups in Johannesburg, he felt it was important to do his own fund raising as well, mainly because the home was always short of money, but also to show a willingness to be more self-sufficient. The Government provided nothing.

Jones noticed the battered looking car arrive outside the gates of the home and he couldn't help noticing the very attractive brunette getting out of the car and making her way uncertainly towards the group selling clothes. He thought she looked white but his practised eye saw some mannerisms that made him think she was actually a coloured. He swept the thoughts from his mind. "What on earth does it matter?" he thought. He went over and greeted her in Afrikaans and she whispered a code word to him: the same one that had been used when the children had been picked up a fortnight or three weeks earlier. He excused himself from the group and took Rita to his small cottage on the property.

"You should not be coming here," he said. "Don't you know it could be dangerous for all of us? How are the children, by the way?"

Rita smiled. "The children are fine and safely in England," she said. "It's Kamau I'm worried about."

Philip Jones looked blank.

"You may have known him as Japie," she said.

"Ah yes, the children's relative from the Cape," he answered.

"Well, yes. He was also supposed to be going to England, but he didn't arrive," she said hurriedly.

Philip raised his eyebrows.

"How can I help?" he asked.

"Well I don't know," she almost whispered, "but I had nobody else to turn to."

He thought for a moment. He now had a reason to return to see Charles Oakley in prison. Charles was still being detained, but had not been charged with anything. Philip had been a regular visitor to the jail; he guessed that another visit would raise no further suspicions.

"Look, you had better tell me more; I saw the man I know as Japie only once and then I had a few phone calls from him," he said.

Rita took a deep breath and then told him everything she knew about Kamau. The Willie Lemmer story, sharing the house with the Oakleys and her escape with the Oakley children. She told him nothing about Kamau's membership of the ANC or any of his activities in bombing pylons and railway trains. Philip put two and two together however, and decided that Kamau was probably an agent of the ANC.

"Please don't phone me or anything, but come back here in two weeks; I will see if I can find any information. I'm afraid I don't hold out much hope," he said. "I may need to leave you a message. How do I do that?"

Rather than giving her home phone number, she told him that she could be contacted through the restaurant.

As they went out, Philip said to her, "Just buy something from the sale; it makes your visit look more legitimate."

She bought a very pretty red blouse for a few rand. There was absolutely nothing wrong with it. She supposed that whoever had donated it had just got tired of it and had enough money not to worry. She sighed and wondered if it was the same in other countries.

She did not notice an unprepossessing looking coloured man who appeared to be passing by write something down in a notebook as she drove away.

Much to his surprise, Kamau was left alone in his cell for some days. He was fed twice a day and the latrine bucket in the corner of his cell was emptied periodically. Every two or three days a guard would come and take him to the showers; the water was cold and he was always alone. The guard did not speak to him, except to utter brief instructions. The cell he occupied was very small; there was just enough room for a concrete bed along one wall, which was covered by a thin mattress and two thin, moth eaten blankets. The single electric light bulb remained illuminated all the time and a guard came past the door of his cell, which was an iron grille, approximately every thirty minutes. His cell was draughty and there was no privacy. Worst of all, there was nothing to do; no exercise breaks, nothing to read, nothing.

During the first few days of his incarceration, Kamau had an almost constant headache and he had periodic dizzy spells. He demanded to see a doctor. After a week, he was escorted to a cell at the end of the passage that was set up as a rudimentary doctor's surgery. He was given a perfunctory examination.

"Bit of a bang to the head," the doctor muttered in Afrikaans. "Nothing to worry about, though you will have a headache for a week or more I think. Nothing more than you deserve, I suspect," he added nastily. Kamau was returned to his cell. The routine went on day after day; there was no Roux, no interrogation, nothing.

The block of cells Kamau was in was empty except for one cell at the far end of a row of twenty or more cells, where there appeared to be one other prisoner. He tried to call out to him.

"Shut up, shut up," yelled the guard. "There is to be no talking, you hear."

Kamau lapsed into silence.

After a few days, when his headache had subsided, Kamau started a strict regimen of exercises. Push ups, sit-ups, running on the spot. All in all, within a week he was exercising for three hours a day.

One day a new guard came and watched him.

"Hey Kleurling," he said in Afrikaans. "What's all this exercise for? From what I hear about you, all that body of yours will be doing soon will be feeding the worms. Better fatten it up a bit man; there will be nothing left for them to eat." He chuckled at his own humour and ambled off. Kamau took no notice.

More than two weeks had passed and the routine of the prison was really getting on Kamau's nerves. Meals, exercise, the occasional shower. He had not been able to communicate at all with the only other prisoner in the block, but he was sure he was a coloured. Then one day there was a flurry of activity and all the other thirty eight cells in the block were filled up, in some cases two to a cell. The new inmates were all black Africans and mostly children in their mid-teens. The guards found it impossible to keep them all quiet and over a day or two Kamau heard that there had been major riots in Soweto led by the schoolchildren. These were the supposed ringleaders. The riots had started a few days earlier on June 16 (1976) and the jails all over the Witwatersrand were full of young black schoolchildren. Over a few days Kamau managed to listen to many of the stories surrounding these young people. The reason for the riots was that suddenly the government had insisted that the only medium of instruction in the black schools throughout Soweto and indeed South Africa was to be Afrikaans. The standard of instruction was poor at best and this further insistence on the hated language of the oppressor was the last straw. The police had fired on large crowds of youths, killing many. Others had fled across the borders to neighbouring countries and still others had gone into hiding. Kamau wondered whether this was the beginning of the end of the regime.

Kamau continued his exercise routine and within days had almost everyone in the cell block following his example. All, except the coloured man, who was, apart from Kamau, the original occupant of the cell block, and whom Kamau had never seen.

"Ask him why he won't join in." Kamau passed the message on to his neighbour.

"He has nothing left to live for," was the eventual answer.

"Why?" Kamau asked.

"His wife has been murdered and his children have gone to live in England," the answer came back.

Kamau felt his gut tighten.

"Ask him his name." He passed the message on.

The answer came back.

"Charles Oakley."

"My God," thought Kamau.

"Tell him this is Willie Lemmer and that his children are O.K.," said Kamau.

The conversation went back and forth. Kamau understood that Charles had been tortured and interrogated regularly now in the months since he had been arrested.

Rita had been back to St. Joseph's twice since her last visit. On one of the occasions she had been stopped by police, who had stepped up security enormously since the riots had started. Again, because of her apparently white skin they did not concern themselves much with her. "Just be very careful, lady," said the policeman: "these blacks are getting out of hand."

On the third visit Philip Jones had more news for her.

"I've at last been able to see Charles Oakley," said Philip, "he's in a bad way, both mentally and physically. He's been tortured, I'm sure. I gave him the news about the children, which cheered him up. But guess what, the biggest news of all. Willie Lemmer is in there with him."

Rita's worst fears all seemed to bear down on her all at once.

"Oh no," she wiped some tears away, "how did he end up there?"

"Some garbled story about being abducted from the train in Botswana," answered Philip.

"Oh my God," said Rita. "What can I do now?"

Philip shook his head.

"Not much," he said. "He may need some looking after if he ever gets out of there though."

Rita wrote Jessica a note on a standard air letter form telling her the news. She felt safe and was certain that only a very small number of letters were actually intercepted. She also told Jessica that it was too dangerous to phone and that she should not attempt it except in dire emergency.

Kleinkie Vorster was sitting in Bok-Bok Oberholzer's office when he arrived there about midday.

He looked at Kleinkie, who was very animated and excited about something. He wondered how much chatter he would have to listen to before Kleinkie would tell him why he was there. If anything, Kleinkie was looking and smelling worse by the week. Bok-Bok turned up his nose. Kleinkie made him wade through several newspaper clippings of various rugby teams, including one of the English team.

"See, no Willie Lemmer this time," said Kleinkie.

Bok-Bok grunted.

"O.K., Kleinkie, what have you got now? I know it has nothing to do with Lemmer and the rugby this time," he said patiently.

"O.K.," said Kleinkie. "You know that house for orphans, St. Joseph's?"

Bok-Bok nodded.

"Well, I go there sometimes to buy clothes, they sell them over the fence," he started.

Bok-Bok looked at the state of Kleinkie's clothes and thought it must be some months since he had bought any clothes at all.

"Ja. Well I've been there a few times now, and a couple of times this pretty white woman comes in a really old looking car and talks, you know, privately with the boss there, that blerry (bloody) communist Jones," Kleinkie continued.

"Ja. So what? Jones has pretty white friends; white with white, that's O.K Kleinkie." Bok-Bok was getting impatient.

"Nee, man, just listen. I was interested so I wrote down the number of the car," said Kleinkie.

"So?" said Bok-Bok.

"Ja, well the blerry car is registered to a butchery in Soweto," said Kleinkie triumphantly.

Bok-Bok forgot the smell and looked at Kleinkie in admiration.

"So what's a white woman doing driving a car registered to a butchery in Soweto? Meneer Oberholzer, I would say there is something strange about this," said Kleinkie rather formally.

Bok-Bok patted him on the back.

"You done good Kleinkie just give me the details and I'll pass it on. You have a photograph of the woman, well done," said Bok-Bok.

"Oh, and Kleinkie," Bok-Bok added.

"Ja meneer?"

"Go and have a fucking wash will you, and get some clean clothes," said Bok-Bok. He handed him fifty rand.

"Dankie (thank you) meneer, dankie," said Kleinkie obsequiously.

Kamau was conscious of the fact that Charles Oakley had been taken away by the guards and had been gone for some time. He supposed it was for interrogation. Kamau had been there for more than three weeks and there had been no sign of interrogation.

Then, just as the boring routine of the day started, two guards came for Kamau. This time it was different, he could tell. They put handcuffs on him, which was never done when he went for a shower, and he was whisked up in the lift to the tenth floor. He stepped out of the lift, walked down a short passage and entered a large room with white, gloss enamel walls, a tiled floor and a large window, which was open. The room was bright and light and airy, its appearance totally belying the use it was put to. The sight that greeted him was the most horrible and grotesque he had ever witnessed in his life. There was Charles Oakley, completely naked, bleeding from the nose and mouth and crawling in what appeared to be his own faeces and urine. He had cigarette burns all over his body.

Roux was supervising and there were half a dozen other men standing around with an assortment of clubs. There was a charcoal brazier with some cattle branding irons next to it. From the appearance of his friend, he had been branded in several places on his body. Roux paid no attention whatever to Kamau. There was a fixed, psychopathic stare from Roux's steely blue eyes.

"Get on with it, get on with it," he yelled. "I've just signed this press release to say that Charles Oakley, a man detained under the suppression of Communism Act, jumped to his death from the tenth floor of police headquarters in Johannesburg whilst under interrogation. The time given for his death is 10:15. It is now 10:15; get him out of here."

Two burly policemen picked Charles up and dragged him towards the open window. Charles had clearly understood what was planned for him and, despite his depleted physical condition, fought like a tiger for a few minutes. It was all too much and with a final shove, Charles was pushed out of the window. There was a deathly hush in the room and then, faintly, the sound of a body hitting the pavement. Charles had made no noise at all. All the men in the room rushed to the window and watched for a few minutes while Charles's body was picked up and the pavement cleaned up. Kamau's guards, however, kept a firm hold on him so he couldn't move even if he had wanted to. The horror of what he had just seen started to sink in. Clearly the fact that he had been forced to watch Charles Oakley's grisly execution was no accident, and the likelihood was that the same fate was planned for him.

Roux and his cronies came back from the open window. It was clear that Roux was in an extreme state of excitement and that he got enormous pleasure from the power that inflicting pain and death gave him.

Roux's eyes glistened; he seemed on the verge of insanity.

"Kamau Lawrence," he said pleasantly, "we have a little party in store for you too." Then he screamed like a maniac, "Get those fucking clothes off him, now! Strip the dirty little fucker naked."

Kamau was stripped naked.

"Clean the place up!" Roux yelled again at Kamau. "He was your friend; you clean his piss and shit up."

He came over and kicked Kamau in the groin. Kamau doubled over. Some cloths and a bucket were shoved into his hands and over the next fifteen minutes, amid kicking and beating, Kamau managed to clean the floor of what he was now thinking of as the torture room. By the time he was finished, he in turn was covered in the mess that he had cleaned off the floor. He started to wipe himself down. Roux snatched the cloth from his hand. "You can stay like you are, all covered in piss and shit. That's what you are, piss and shit."

Kamau had taken his beatings stoically, although he was hurting all over from the blows. He remained standing, fighting off waves of nausea. He now noticed that Danie Visser, sporting his Sergeant's stripes, was part of the group. He walked with a pronounced limp from the crocodile attack and he would not meet Kamau's eyes.

Kamau didn't think that Visser had joined in the beating he had just received. From the appearance of Charles Oakley, he knew that was just the beginning and he tried to steel himself for the extreme pain he was about to endure. He started to go into a self-induced trance, something he had learned from his grandmother in Kikuyu land. He suddenly became aware that Roux was yelling at him again.

"Hey you, Kamau fucking Lawrence, these papers are yours."

Roux was waving his British passport and citizenship certificate at him. Kamau said nothing.

"Well, as far as we are concerned you don't exist, at all. There is no record of you entering the country, none. No stamps in this Rooinek[1] piece of shit." Roux threw the papers onto the now very hot charcoal brazier and watched them burn to ashes in a few seconds. Roux then continued.

"We want information from you, and we are certainly going to get it. There will be no mercy; for me you are double shit, black and British. Here, hand me those tongs."

Kamau could see that Roux was on the verge of blowing up. The excitement of the grisly Oakley execution and the prospect of extracting the maximum revenge from this coloured man who had bested him in every confrontation they had ever had, was almost too much for him. Then an extraordinary calm appeared to come over Roux; Kamau could see him making an enormous effort. He picked up the tongs and walked over to Kamau, who was standing between two guards. Roux said, quite calmly, "We know you were at the ANC training camp in Tanzania. We know what training you had there and we know that you were part of a firing squad that executed one of our agents there." Kamau said nothing. Roux went on, "Most of the other incompetent fools who went to that camp have been dealt with and are either dead or in prison."

"You abducted me from Botswana. You have absolutely no rights in this situation. Both the British and Botswana governments will have more than a little to say about this," answered Kamau.

"Neither of them know anything about you; you entered this country illegally and when we have finished with you, you will simply disappear; nobody will be any the wiser."

"My family know exactly what is going on," countered Kamau. The more

1   Derogatory Afrikaans word for English due to the sunburn they suffered in the Boer War

he could keep Roux talking, he thought, the better his very slim chances of getting out of this alive would be.

"Your bloody family. Your father is a traitor to his race, and as for your stinking black mother, the British had the right idea: they should have hanged her but as is typical they chickened out at the last minute. As for that mob in England, talking to the ANC one minute and our shameful, so called verligte (enlightened) traitors, the next…" his voice faltered for a minute. "They will get what's coming to them."

"You can't kill and imprison everyone, you know," said Kamau evenly. "Sometime, somewhere you will have to deal with the majority in this country on terms they come to understand and accept, otherwise there will be a bloodbath which you cannot win."

The incongruity of the situation struck Kamau; here he was, naked and covered in his dead friend's excrement, having a high level conversation with this maniac.

"You just watch us! A bloodbath we would welcome; it would mean there would be fewer blacks to send back to the homelands. Maybe the uitlanders (foreigners) would also go home, then we could be true to the volk (people) and the dreams that our forefathers had for us, where we relied on ourselves, our guns and our cattle." Roux had a faraway, dreamlike look on his face.

"You mean try to turn the clock back something like one hundred and fifty years, to the time when your illiterate, peasant forefathers started the rape of this country?" countered Kamau.

"They were not illiterate," yelled Roux.

"They were mostly illiterate; even your famous President Paul Kruger could barely sign his name," Kamau said calmly.

"The fact that you even speak the name of such a great man is an insult to the volk; you are not fit to eat his turds," yelled Roux and he swung the tongs he was holding at Kamau's head. Kamau ducked and Roux almost lost his balance.

One of Roux's sycophants prevented him from falling over and whispered something in his ear. Roux nodded and looked sideways at Kamau. He came over and held Kamau's penis with the tongs.

"So this is the dirty thing that fucks white women. Well Mr. fucking Kamau Lawrence, not only will we stop you abusing God's law in future but this thing will never fuck again, never again," he said harshly.

"God's law, what are you talking about? Most of the coloured population here in this country are the result of relationships between your precious volk and the indigenous population in this country. Even the people in this room, all of whom claim to be pure white, have inevitably got black blood in them, even you." Kamau looked Roux straight in the eyes.

Roux looked at Kamau with a half smile on his face and replied, "I'm holding your disgusting prick with this pair of tongs and you talk nonsense like that. Now let me see, what is this little knob on the side of your prick here?" He had just seen Kamau's Ngwati knot. "The result of some disgusting African ritual, I suppose; it just looks like the witchdoctor did a bad job. Well, I can fix that for you right now; pass me that scalpel, will you," he waved at one of his assistants.

At that moment the phone rang. Roux picked it up and listened for a minute or two.

"Ja, meneer commandant, right away. I will be in Pretoria as soon as I can get there," he responded.

"Visser," he yelled at Danie Visser.

"Ja meneer."

"Take this animal back to his cell; I will deal with him later." Roux then walked out, muttering about the interfering Western press. Apparently there had already been reports on the international news media about a detainee being thrown from the interrogation room on the tenth floor of police headquarters in Johannesburg.

Kamau struggled back into his clothes. Visser handcuffed him and alone escorted him back to his cell. Kamau was wondering how he had managed to escape so lightly and how he would survive the next session, when on the way down in the lift Visser said in a surly voice: "You saved my life once so I will give you a chance. Give me the address of someone who can help you and I will see what I can do."

Kamau looked at him; he was totally surprised that help should come from this direction. He supposed it was based on some sort of biblical injunction. He responded quickly, "Rita Vos," and gave Visser her address and telephone number, watching him write it down. He hoped it was not a trap.

"Ah yes, the lady in the restaurant. That surprises me, I thought she was clean," said Visser.

"She is," responded Kamau.

The lift arrived in the basement and Kamau was escorted back to his cell by a guard.

"I need a shower," pleaded Kamau.

"You had one yesterday," was the response, "your next shower is in three days' time."

Kamau's cell was occupied by a very large, imposing Zulu.

"Who the fuck are you?" asked Kamau. The last thing he needed was to share his already cramped quarters with someone else.

"Randolph Zuma," was the response.

"Randolph, what kind of a name is that?" said Kamau uncharitably.

"My father was Winston Zuma so he named me after Winston Churchill's father," was the easy response.

"My God," said Kamau. "Two of the best known colonials of all time. Whose side are you on then?"

"These are just names," was the response, "they do not necessarily reflect political affiliations."

Kamau looked at his newfound companion. Randolph or Zuma as he preferred to be called was a huge man, at least six foot six, and he must have weighed two hundred and fifty pounds. His bullet like head was clean-shaven and a pair of sparkling, intelligent eyes looked out from his open, smiling face. A flat nose and thick lips completed the picture. Kamau was given the impression of calm intelligence coupled with enormous physical and mental strength.

"I'm…" Kamau was about to introduce himself.

"I know who you are and I am very pleased to meet you," responded Zuma. Kamau looked surprised.

"All those bombs on the pylons and trains," said Zuma.

"Yes," said Kamau hesitantly.

"I planned them all and arranged for the supply of equipment," said Zuma.

"They went without a hitch," said Kamau.

"Good planning I think," Said Zuma, "but also brilliant execution, according to the debriefings I had from my people."

Kamau could tell he was going to like this Zuma, given half a chance.

"My God, but you do stink," said Zuma.

Kamau explained what had happened upstairs and his unsuccessful attempt to have a shower. After half an hour of arguing the guard was persuaded to bring another mattress and blankets. One of them would sleep on the floor and one on the concrete bunk.

The ritual of the exercise routine was then explained to Zuma. This was now kept going for six hours every day since most of the cells had two people in them. The effect on morale was tremendous; the exercises gave people something to do and introduced an element of competition into the otherwise ghastly place.

Rita was more than a little taken aback when Danie Visser phoned her at the restaurant. Visser had to use all his powers of persuasion to be allowed to talk to Rita.

"Lemmer is in prison at police headquarters," said Visser.

"Who… who is speaking?" asked Rita anxiously.

"Never you mind," said Visser, "Just listen. If you want to save him, be at the corner of Fox and West Streets at one a.m. this morning."

"Is this a trap?" asked Rita, now even more anxious than ever.

"Trap, who is speaking about a trap?" said Visser, "If the police wanted to pick you up they could come right now. No, it's not a trap."

"O.K., I'm sorry, I'll be there," said Rita.

"Do you have a car? If so, please give me the licence plate number," said Visser.

Rita gave him the number of the ANC car; she fervently hoped the ANC had not repossessed it.

Rita spent the rest of her shift worrying about the phone call and what it was all about. At least there was a promise of being able to see Kamau again and she now knew where he was.

"So what was all that about now?" asked the head-waiter, when the restaurant was about to close. "It was that policeman Visser again, wasn't it?"

Rita nodded.

"I think they are still following up on that Willie Lemmer," said Rita. "I would help them if I could."

"That's my girl," he said comfortingly. "See you tomorrow then."

Rita went home, and just after twelve thirty went out to the car, which she had established was still where she had left it. She didn't really know what to expect, and she took a small suitcase with her. The car was still stacked with the samples from her Botswana trip.

Having parked the car in the spot indicated, Rita got out and waited in the shadows of a nearby building. She wanted to have a chance to get away if the whole thing turned out to be an elaborate police trap.

Although Kamau had given Danie Visser Rita's details, he didn't really hold out much hope. He and Zuma talked quietly into the night about the ANC and what should be done next. He knew nobody could help him with his forthcoming ordeal with Roux; he was completely on his own in that regard. It was also fortunate that he knew very little about the organisation of the ANC in South Africa, so even if he was persuaded to talk he had almost no information to give.

The slight rattling of a key in the door of his cell woke Kamau up with a start. For some reason the whole place was in complete darkness. A flashlight was shone in his face.

"Kom, Lawrence, quick." It was Visser. Kamau scrambled up from his mattress on the floor. Zuma was also awake. Kamau followed Visser out of the cell and was followed by Zuma. Visser relocked the cell and they quietly slipped past two sleeping guards. They then went up the back stairs and after going through three more sets of security doors to which Visser had keys, they found themselves out in the street. It was so dark that Visser had not noticed Zuma until that moment.

"Hey, who is this fucker?" said Visser anxiously. "I owe you my life, but I have no intention of being part of a general jail break."

"There's nothing we can do now," whispered Kamau, "you will not get into trouble for this, will you?"

"No, I have an alibi in Pretoria and those guards will sleep for at least another two hours," he whispered back.

Visser told them where to go and pointed out Rita's car. "Now Lawrence, we're quits O.K? If you get caught again I will not help you and I won't expect anything from you. Tot siens (goodbye)." Visser walked away.

Rita saw two figures moving quietly down the street, keeping to the shadows as much as they could. They came and stood next to the car. There was one enormous African and then another person who had a familiar profile.

"Rita, where are you?" whispered Kamau. Only then did she recognise him and came out of the shadows.

They embraced briefly. Rita noticed the smell.

"This is Randolph Zuma," Kamau said to Rita, "and Rita Vos," he said to Zuma. "We must go quickly now, back to your flat. I must get rid of this appalling smell before we go anywhere."

It took them ten minutes to get to the flat in Claim Street. The city streets were almost deserted. Zuma stayed with the car and unpacked the samples and left them on the footpath. Kamau and Rita raced back to the flat and Kamau dived into a nice hot bath while Rita washed his clothes.

"What happened?" she asked.

"We must hurry," was all he would say. "You are now in trouble as well; you will have to come with us."

"Come with you where?" she asked.

"I don't know; we'll have to discuss it with Zuma, maybe he will have some ideas."

His clothes were soaking wet so he borrowed a large sweater from Rita and a dressing gown. He had his own shoes and his clothes would eventually dry. They raced out of the flat. Rita barely gave the place a second glance. The events of past weeks had reconciled her to having to turn her back on what was a contrived life; another South African lie forced on her and thousands of others by the rigid enforcement of racial prejudice under apartheid.

Kamau and Zuma had a brief discussion in the front of the car. Rita packed the boot and made sure the food and water she had brought was accessible.

Zuma only had his passbook, which he had to carry and produce whenever a policeman in a white area demanded it. Kamau had no papers at all, Roux having burned his British passport. Rita had a full set of papers, including an exit permit.

"Well, you can go by plane then," said Zuma, who had become increasingly uncomfortable with Rita's presence, despite the role she had played in their escape. He did not want to be burdened by what he saw as an irrelevant white woman. Kamau eventually took him aside and explained the situation, leaving nothing out.

"Well we all have to leave South Africa," said Zuma eventually. "None of us will survive if we are caught again."

"They will expect us to make directly for Botswana," said Kamau.

"Then we should go the other way," said Zuma.

"What other way?" asked Rita.

"To Mozambique through Northern Natal," answered Zuma. "We will have to walk for four or five days maybe when crossing the border.

He looked at Rita disparagingly.

"If you can manage that," he said.

Rita smiled at him and said, "Of course."

They decided it would be two or at the most three hours before the authorities discovered that they had escaped, so it was important to get moving. The mixture of people travelling together would also draw attention: a black man and a coloured man travelling with an apparently white woman.

With Kamau driving, they went South East across the Transvaal and towards Natal and made good time through Heidelberg to Standerton and then into Natal at Volksrust. After refuelling at Dundee shortly after the dawn broke, they were able to travel on minor roads which were all dirt and which gave them a stronger sense of security. They passed the turn off to Isandlwana.

"The first battle of the Zulu/British war," Zuma pointed out. "The Zulu won a comprehensive victory with more than twelve hundred dead on the British side."

Rita had never heard of it. Her education had been very skimpy regarding history and most of that had dealt with the Great Trek and various Boer victories over black tribes in the interior.

Zuma had now taken over the driving and they went through Nqutu. Zuma amused them by insisting on their pronouncing Nqutu with a Zulu click after the N. Kamau managed it easily, but Rita found it impossible. At Babanango Zuma parked the car under a tree and dashed off.

"I will only be a few minutes," he told them.

After an hour and a half, Rita said to Kamau, "Do you think he's coming back? We are starting to attract attention."

A collection of children had gathered and were staring at them.

Kamau went over and tried to talk to them and handed out a few sweets.

One of the children had an old soccer ball, filled with grass since the bladder had burst some time before. Kamau started an impromptu game, in which some of the children took part.

Three hours later a beaming Zuma arrived in a battered old pick-up, with another man.

No mention was made of the time he had been away.

"Our escape is the number one news item on every news programme in every language. They even have a description of the car and its licence plate number. This is my brother; he will hide the car and then take us in his pick-up to Ndumu," Zuma told them breathlessly.

Roux had driven to Pretoria in a fury and had then had a very stormy meeting with his own boss.

"Have you any idea how much damage this sort of incident does to the government?" the boss fumed. "You can't just throw people out of windows and expect nobody to notice."

"He jumped," said Roux defensively. "I have ten witnesses to prove it."

"Ja, sure," said the commandant sarcastically. "Nobody believes that. Anyway, with the riots and now this, you have sparked a major crisis. The government is afraid that foreign investment will dry up."

Roux wished with all his being that foreign investment would dry up and that he and the volk could just be allowed to return to their nineteenth century ways. He went back to his office fuming, and was sitting there thinking about what he would do to Kamau when the phone rang.

"Bok-Bok Oberholzer here, meneer," said an obsequious voice.

"Ja, well, what is it then?" asked Roux roughly.

Bok-Bok told him all about the car. Roux wrote it all down.

At five a.m. Roux was woken with another call from the Johannesburg police headquarters which made his blood go cold.

"Kamau and Randolph Zuma escaped," he said disbelievingly. He hurled abuse at the caller for five minutes and then rushed to his Pretoria office. People had already started to gather.

"Make sure it is on all the news bulletins as soon as you can and see if you can find this car." He described the car that the fugitives were believed to be using and gave quick instructions.

"And we're looking for a coloured, a black, and possibly a white woman. Concentrate on the Western Transvaal and the Botswana border," he said, playing his hunches.

Within an hour there were reports coming in from all over the country. He supposed the ANC were behind many of the reports, trying to cause confusion.

At midday there was a very firm report from Zululand saying that people matching the descriptions had been seen, as well as the car.

"Forget bloody Zululand," he yelled. "What do you think they are going to do there, catch a boat? Concentrate on Botswana."

Following Zuma and his brother, Kamau and Rita were bumped over some very rough tracks and eventually came to a small village, which consisted of a dozen beehive shaped huts made of thatched grass in the traditional Zulu fashion. The villagers crowded round. Zuma was obviously a hero in this, his home village. Rita had never seen anything like it in her life; she had to crawl on hands and knees through the small entrance to get into one of the huts. Inside, was clean but rather smoky from a small fire in the centre of the establishment. They were all made a big fuss of and a meal was miraculously provided. After two hours Kamau started to get anxious.

"Shouldn't we be on our way?" he said to Zuma.

"Better to travel in the dark," was the response.

Rita crawled out of the hut. She needed time to herself. The events of the last twenty-four hours had been overwhelming. The village was surrounded by a fence made of thorn bushes and there were a few young boys tending some very scrawny looking cattle. The village was near the top of a hill and the view was spectacular, with the hills rolling off into the distance. The air was clear and there were patches of forest in many of the little valleys. She could see the occasional small village in the distance.

She was quite depressed at the apparent poverty of the people in the village. Even to her unpractised eye, the land was overgrazed and the people in the village had no resources. It was also noticeable that there were no young men around at all. The place was populated by women and children and a few old men. She supposed all the young men had gone to the towns to find work, leaving behind the women and children and those too old to work. Despite its natural beauty, it was a sad, sad place. She was thankful when the men emerged and they set off again in the pick up. The men took it in turn to drive; Rita had to sit in the back with the luggage.

They turned north at Melmoth and made their way through the un-prepossessing Kwa-Zulu capital of Ulundi.

"The final battle of the Zulu/British war," said Zuma to Kamau despondently. "They just machine-gunned us down. We did not have a chance and we had not learned anything from other battles with the Boers and British." It was almost as if he felt personally responsible for the disaster that had befallen the Zulus at the time.

"This time," he said determinedly, "it will be different. We will win; we will get it all back."

After Nongoma they had to travel more slowly since only one of the headlights on the pick-up functioned and it was getting dark. Kamau and Zuma dozed in the front while Zuma's brother drove and Rita slept, despite the discomfort in the back. They crossed the main Durban to Swaziland road at Candover, went past the vast Pongola dam at Josini and by midnight they were close to the boundary of the Ndumu Game Reserve, which bordered the southern boundary of Mozambique.

"From here we walk," announced Zuma, as they said farewell to his brother and started off into the bush.

Rita had no experience of the wild. It was completely dark, and there wasn't a light in sight; she was terrified of all the night sounds.

Kamau and Zuma seemed perfectly at home. They ate some of the food they had brought from Zuma's Kraal (village) and lay down as if to sleep.

Kamau gestured to her to join him. "You want me to sleep here?" she asked.

He shrugged.

"There's nowhere else, it's quite warm and safe and we can't go anywhere in the dark."

She cuddled up to him and tried to remember their last night together in the Cumberland Hotel.

The sun had already risen when they woke up. Some monkeys were looking at them curiously from high in the trees above them.

After eating some more of the food they had been given, they set off. Rita was reasonably well dressed in strong walking shoes and suitable clothing. Kamau and Zuma had only what they had escaped in. Within minutes, both of them discarded their shoes and carried their few belongings as best they could. To start with they were able to use the roads provided by the Natal Parks Board, who ran the reserve. They had to jump into the bush whenever they heard a vehicle.

Zuma and Kamau confidently led the way, finding their direction by looking at the sun. It was hot and after the first two days there appeared to be no more tracks, so it was very hard going.

Once Zuma stopped and pointed to a small gathering of antelope.

"Nyala," he said. "This place is well known for them."

During the third day their food had almost run out and they were all scratched and bleeding, with their clothes torn from the thorns. Kamau said, "We're over the border now; we need to find a track and we'll be O.K."

Not long after that they came across a small, dilapidated village.

"Stay here," Zuma told them.

He came back an hour later with food.

"These people are Shangaan," he said. "The language is similar to Zulu. We can walk to the main road from here in about two days."

They were allowed to sleep in the village that night and then, after two days walking, found themselves on the main road into Maputo. Zuma managed to get them a lift on the first truck that came along and when they arrived in Maputo, the capital of Mozambique, he found his way to an ANC safe house in the city.

After several days of hanging around, they eventually managed to get a flight on a Kenya Airways plane bound for Nairobi.

Rafiki got the surprise of her life when a smiling Peter walked into Sattimma accompanied by her precious son and a huge Zulu and what Rafiki had determined was a pretty white girl.

When the party had arrived at Jomo Kenyatta Airport, Kamau had had no papers and Zuma only his South African passbook. It was difficult for

Africans to get passports at all under the apartheid regime, and whilst Rita had a complete set of papers, the Kenya government, as with most black African countries, refused entry to people with South African passports. The immigration people were in a quandary and it took a great deal of explaining from Kamau, first in English, then in Kikuyu, to get them to understand what the three were doing there. In the end he was able to persuade the authorities to let him 'phone Peter and some hours later all three were released into Peter's custody. Their intention was always to go to England and join the struggle against apartheid there. It was evident, however, after a few enquiries, that apart from Kamau, who was entitled to a British passport, it would take some weeks, if not months, for Rita and Zuma to gain refugee status in Britain.

CHAPTER 15

Kamau and his guests did virtually nothing but sleep and eat for three days after their arrival at Sattimma.

For Kamau, of course, it was home and he had no trouble in settling into the normal routine of the household. Zuma and Rita found it the strangest possible experience. Zuma was used to township life in South Africa, with the mean, unpaved streets, rows and rows of houses all precisely the same, the litter, the violence and, in many cases, the hopelessness of the lives that the apartheid state had created for the black population in South Africa. He had never been inside a white person's home anywhere and the middle class comfort of Sattimma made him very uncomfortable. He also could not believe that Rafiki, this elegant black woman, could be happily married to and living with a white man. To Zuma, Peter looked no different from the hundreds of white men he saw on the streets of Johannesburg; the white oppressors, as he thought of them. It took all of Peter's considerable charm and much patience to engage Zuma in any kind of sensible conversation.

Rita was, if anything, in a worse position. All her upbringing had taught her that as a coloured she was socially superior to the black population, and yet here was Rafiki, an educated, charming, courteous black person, infinitely more sophisticated than she, Rita was. All her life Rita had aspired to a white lifestyle, but she did not really know any white people beyond working with the other whites in the restaurant in Johannesburg, and, of course, all the diners were white; she had never been to a white home or had much social interaction with whites. So for her, Peter was frightening, at least to start with.

Although Peter and Rafiki were busy with their own lives, they were thrilled to have Kamau back home, even for a short time, and they were intrigued by their other guests and very sensitive to their feelings and attitudes.

At one of the first meals they all had together, Peter addressed Zuma in fluent Zulu. Peter was a very good linguist and had been brought up on a mission station in Zululand, so Zulu was almost his first language. Zuma nearly fell off his chair in surprise and delight and after that, treated Peter like a long lost relative. Peter also spoke some Afrikaans and tried his best to put Rita at ease, but she tended to be preoccupied with Kamau and for the first few days she and Kamau spent almost all their time in bed.

After finding Zuma one day disconsolately throwing a ball for the dog, Peter took him in hand and except where Peter had official duties in Nairobi, Zuma accompanied him everywhere. They conversed mainly in Zulu, much to the astonishment of the local people, especially the Kikuyu, who regarded Peter as one of their own.

On one occasion Peter took Zuma back to Naseby. He had returned only once to Naseby since he had left it in 1963. It was almost as if he had been born again when he left the farm, and that part of his life was cut off and compartmentalised from his present life as a minister in the Kenya government; so it was with some trepidation that Peter drove the hundred miles to the little village of Ol'Kalou and up the familiar five winding miles to what had been his life for seventeen years. Although he had a government vehicle, the visit had not been announced, but when Peter arrived at the old house he was immediately recognised by the Kikuyu now living there and he and Zuma were given what could only be described as 'royal' treatment.

Some years earlier Peter had arranged for the boreholes on Naseby and some of the surrounding previously owned 'white' farms to be repaired and run periodically to provide water for the new settlers. This water was supposed to supplement water from the local rivers and streams during the dry seasons. As he now well knew his dreams of returning Naseby and the other previously owned 'white' farms to their productive best had not materialised and with few exceptions the land provided nothing more than a basis for subsistence agriculture.

He also knew that, as with many of the resettlement areas, people had started to consolidate their holdings. Naseby's fifty acre lots were already being consolidated into holdings of one hundred to two hundred acres. Peter, of course, knew from his personal observations in other areas and official statistics that productivity in the resettled areas was low.

He also knew that many of the larger landowners contrived to live in towns and only paid an occasional visit to their landholdings.

In general, the stock looked reasonable and there was some pyrethrum growing, so the farm wasn't completely unproductive.

The locals couldn't get enough of Peter and, apart from consuming copious amounts of food and 'pombe' (beer), many people came just to see him. For them he was a hero: he was seen as having been instrumental in rescuing Rafiki from the gallows and the people who had been resettled on Naseby with their families believed he was personally responsible for their good fortune.

When Peter and Zuma eventually left, late in the afternoon, they were silent for the first few miles.

Zuma broke the silence: "As you know, we have the same problem in South Africa. When we eventually take over there will have to be resettlement, I think on a very large scale. How successful has this project been?"

Peter glanced at him. "The official line, of course, is that it's been a great success, and we can produce statistics that prove that."

"But you are in charge," insisted Zuma. "What do you really think?"

Peter sighed. "Politically, we had no choice. There were huge numbers of people, many of them Kikuyu, packed into the so-called reserves, the result of an enormous population growth. They had to be moved out."

"But, by doing that a significantly productive sector of the economy was almost eliminated," said Zuma.

"Yes. You have to remember, though, that many of the white farmers here, like me, were first generation settlers. Under the circumstances they were unlikely to be long-term citizens of an independent Kenya. I still think it was the right thing to do from a political viewpoint. Firstly, we released the pressure in the Kikuyu and other tribal reserves and then, as a result of being paid out in London, many of the white farmers chose to leave. It's arguable whether this is a good or bad thing. In the short term this may have had a negative impact economically, but it has forced us to put programmes into place that educate the peasant farmers to be more productive. As I said, in the short term we had no option."

"What about the programme, on the ground I mean?" Zuma persisted.

"Well, you saw for yourself. The use that is being made of that farm is poor. We still have a long way to go. I'm totally frustrated by what I see there, but we are making progress. Training is what is needed," said Peter.

They drove on in silence.

"What is the biggest problem you face?" asked Zuma eventually. He was expecting the response 'lack of training' or something similar.

"Corruption," said Peter, as he negotiated a sharp corner on the dusty road.

"What?"

"Corruption," Peter repeated.

"But that's inexcusable," said Zuma heatedly. "The people in power have a sacred duty to do their best to reverse the worst excesses of the colonial era, not to make it worse."

"My sentiments exactly," said Peter, "but it is not working like that."

"Corruption, what sort of corruption?" asked Zuma.

"You name it—providing relatives and constituents with jobs, kickbacks on major contracts. I've been under enormous pressure from colleagues to resettle relatives of ministers and officials, many of whom are not suitable or qualified. And it's from the top down. It can only get worse, in my opinion," Peter went on. "Part of the problem, of course, is that ministers and high officials expect, maybe not unreasonably, a western or first world standard of living, also they are expected to provide largesse to their home villages. Their salaries, again not unreasonably, do not provide for that, so they help themselves. You will have the same problem, I can assure you. Rafiki and I have been instrumental in stopping some of these schemes. With one of the schemes that we actually stopped Kamau was kidnapped, aged about fifteen, and they threatened to kill him unless we ceased what we were doing. To cut a long story short all the perpetrators are still in jail for that particular crime but we had to break a lot of rules, even laws to achieve that end. Rafiki played a major part in all that, you ask her sometime."

Zuma was silent for a few minutes:

"Never," he said sternly. "Never; we will punish anyone who is found stealing very severely."

"Maybe," said Peter, "but the history of post-colonial Africa is not en-couraging."

"Well," said Zuma, "I can assure you there is no corruption in the ANC; we are all dedicated to the cause."

"I'm happy to hear it," said Peter non-committally.

"And you?" asked Zuma aggressively. "You have a first world standard of living. How do you manage that?"

"I am lucky," said Peter. "Firstly, I was paid out for Naseby, which paid for Sattimma, and secondly, for years now I have been able to sell, at quite good prices, photographs that I take all over Kenya and indeed other places to international magazines. I can assure you that we put more into the society here than we take out. Rafiki, for example, operates clinics in Pumwani, on a voluntary basis. I will arrange for you to visit them."

Peter continued: 'We were privileged to spend a few days with Seretse Khama and his English born wife in Gaborone, last year. They seem to have it all sorted out in that country. Corruption in that country is down to a bare minimum. Seretse has established a very tough regime in that regard and he personally has no need to take anything from the central treasury: his status is assured being a hereditary chief and I presume that he has large herds of cattle in his home village. Also I think that he has little interest in wealth for its own sake. His concern is for the welfare of his people and nothing else, but then the Khama's have always operated like that.'

Zuma grunted. "Corruption," he almost whispered. "I will kill anyone who I find stealing from us."

Peter had no doubt that he meant it.

Rita spent most of the first days at Sattimma re-establishing her relationship with Kamau. Rita had spent all her life, firstly as a child, being rejected by the white community in South Africa and then, as an adult, she lived almost between the coloured and white communities, working as a white on a white salary but not really being part of either community. She had never given a thought to the plight of the black community. Her only motivation had been personal survival. The atmosphere at Sattimma was, therefore, a complete surprise to her and opened her eyes to a whole new world. She was accepted unquestioningly in the household and the discussions at the dinner table often dealt with the plight of the less fortunate and what was to be done about them. She had also been persuaded by Kamau and Rafiki to go to the clinics in Pumwani that Rafiki ran. She had no idea that such a world existed. She had never been to a black area in South Africa and although the coloured township where she had been brought up was poor, she had never seen such poverty as in Pumwani. It was even worse than her brief experiences of Western Coloured Township in Johannesburg. Hesitantly she asked Kamau: "Is it as bad as this in South Africa?"

"The scale is much bigger in South Africa," Kamau answered, "but it is a big problem and it will get worse."

Rita was still focussed on her own plight; she had now left her home, South Africa, unofficially, and the government had linked her to Kamau's escape from gaol. Kamau, as far as the government was concerned, was a 'notorious terrorist', so should Rita now ever contemplate returning, she would certainly be arrested on arrival and end up with a lengthy gaol term. Nevertheless, her experiences in the three months they spent at Sattimma had a big impact on her and were stored away in the back of her mind.

Kamau had no difficulty in renewing his British passport. Rita had valid travel documents but she needed to establish refugee status in Britain, otherwise she would only be allowed to stay six months at the most, and Zuma had no papers at all. After much to-ing and fro-ing with no result, Peter took the matter into his own hands and made an appointment with the British high commissioner. Kamau, Zuma and Rita went with him. To start with, the high commissioner was dismissive and words and phrases like 'impossible' and 'not within our policy' flowed freely from his lips. Peter then became angry and said:

"You, sir, of course are aware of my personal history and that of my family."

The man nodded.

"You realise that these three," Peter indicated Kamau, Zuma and Rita, "would almost certainly be executed if they returned to South Africa under the present regime. Is that what the British government wants?"

The high commissioner tried to look impassive and said, "Surely you exaggerate."

"No, I do not exaggerate," said Peter firmly. "The South African government is executing two or three people a week for just the sort of offences that these people are supposed to have committed. And if they are unable to find the evidence they think they need, they either manufacture the evidence or kill them anyway."

The high commissioner raised his eyebrows, as if to say, "This is nonsense."

Peter went on, "Kamau, tell the high commissioner about Charles Oakley and your experiences in prison in South Africa."

Kamau told the story of his kidnapping in Botswana and imprisonment and his witnessing Charles Oakley's death.

To start with, the high commissioner fidgeted at his desk and appeared to want to dismiss the whole interview. At the end of Kamau's short speech he was silent and the blood had drained from his face.

"I will see what I can do," he said curtly.

"Before we go," said Peter, "so far we have kept all this out of the British press, but we will go there if we have to, and please remember that I do have some connections
in Britain."

The high commissioner did not need reminding of Peter's history or of the time, many years earlier, when he had pulled strings with Giles in London to get Rafiki freed.

"Don't threaten," said the high commissioner.

Peter said nothing.

When they were back in the car, Peter let out a sigh and said, "These people are all the same; they resist you until you threaten them with connections in high places and then nothing is too much trouble."

Within a few days all the appropriate papers were delivered by hand to Sattimma, granting both Rita and Zuma refugee status in Britain.

Rafiki shed a silent tear or two as she and Peter waved goodbye to her son and Rita and Zuma at the airport. Kamau's escapades had gradually and haltingly emerged, mainly at the dinner table at Sattimma. In her heart of hearts as a mother, she wished Kamau was not involved, but mindful of her own history, she remained silent.

"Louise said she would pick us up," said Kamau, once they had cleared immigration and customs at Heathrow airport.

"Who is Louise?" asked Zuma.

Kamau explained.

They spotted Louise patiently waiting outside the customs hall. Kamau ran up to her and hugged her. Zuma looked on impassively; he still wasn't used to all this intimacy between races. When he was introduced, she greeted him in Xhosa, which he understood since the language was very close to Zulu. He responded warmly in Zulu. Rita was greeted in halting Afrikaans.

Both Rita's and Zuma's eyes stood out on stalks when Louise and Kamau confidently marched up to the Bentley in the airport car park. Louise tossed Kamau the keys.

"You drive," she said. "Then I can talk to our guests."

Zuma walked round the car twice, muttering, "Hau!" before he heaved his huge frame into the back seat.

Louise tried during the forty-minute drive to the Belgravia house to put Zuma and Rita at ease. Kamau was amused and caught Rita's eye in the mirror and grinned. Zuma was too busy staring in wonder at the traffic as they whizzed down the motorway and into the Cromwell Road.

The two Oakley children, Jannie and Hettie, rushed out to the car when they arrived; Hettie jumped into Kamau's lap as he opened the car door and hugged him. Then she climbed over the seat and jumped on Rita. Clearly they were completely at home and uninhibited. Kamau looked at Louise and smiled gratefully. The children were slightly wary of Zuma, mainly because of his size, but Louise asked them to show him his room and this helped to break the ice. Although they came from the same country, they did not have a common language. The Oakley children's native tongue was Afrikaans, the language of the oppressor as far as Zuma was concerned, and he spoke it badly. Neither Jannie nor Hettie spoke any Zulu at all but their English had improved greatly in the months they had been in England, so they spoke that, despite Zuma's heavily accented, but quite fluent, command of the language.

Both Rita and Zuma found the house even more intimidating than Sattimma. Dinner that night was an extraordinary affair as well. Giles, Louise, Kamau, Zuma and Rita and Jannie and Hettie were there. Robert and Jessica, now married, were invited and the Dingley-Ferris children, Belinda, now 21 and Angus, now 19, were also present. The conversation touched lightly on many subjects—the journey over, the weather and so on—but steered clear of the political situation. Although there was a cook in the kitchen, Belinda, Angus, Robert, Jessica and Kamau did all the waiting at table. Rita glanced shyly around and caught the eye of Zuma, who was amused.

"It would be the other way around in South Africa," he said to Giles. "Rita and I and Jannie and Hettie would be waiting, with all the white people sitting down.'

Giles laughed. He was starting to like the big Zulu. At the end of the meal Zuma insisted on carrying a few plates to the kitchen and he started to stack the dishwasher, having insisted that Kamau show him how it worked.

"Just leave that to me, sir," said the cook.

"You call me sir," said Zuma, smiling. "No white person has ever called me sir in my whole life."

"If you are a guest in this house, you are sir, that's for certain," responded the cook. "Don't care where you come from. Anyway, sir, where do you come from?"

"South Africa; I am a Zulu."

"Ah yes, the same as the madam, I suppose," was the response. Zuma just raised his eyebrows.

Later, when the Oakley children had been put to bed, Kamau gave them all a brief rundown of what he had done since Robert and Jessica had escaped into Swaziland. He dealt with the deaths of Charles and Lettie Oakley in some detail.

"Please leave it to me to deal with Jannie and Hettie," he said. "Do they have any idea that their parents are dead?"

"They know about their mother," said Louise. "That man at the home in Jo'burg told them, I think."

"Mr Jones?" enquired Kamau.

"Yes, they speak quite fondly of him," said Louise.

Kamau talked about Rita's bravery in helping the children escape and her role in getting himself and Zuma out of South Africa. Rita had said very little over dinner and she blushed at the attention.

"What do you think you will do here?" asked Louise.

"Well," replied Rita, "I helped run a very good restaurant in Jo'burg. I expect I can do something similar here. But maybe I just need to look around first. Perhaps I should think about Jannie and Hettie as well."

"You do not have to feel responsible for them," said Kamau. "You have already done your bit for them."

"My thoughts exactly," said Louise.

"What education do you have?" asked Belinda, rather insensitively. "There are plenty of opportunities here."

"Only high school; anything beyond that is very difficult in South Africa unless you are white," said Rita.

Belinda looked puzzled.

"Rita is actually what they call coloured in South Africa," Kamau explained, "although she passed as white in the last few years."

"Passed as white—what does that mean?" asked Belinda.

"In South Africa, all the races are segregated," explained Kamau. "White, coloured, Indian and black—and this means that areas are also segregated, as are schools, buses, hospitals, post offices—everything. There is a coloured university in Cape Town, but Rita went to Jo'burg and started work. Since she could pass as a white, her salary was higher than it would have been if she had been employed as a coloured."

"How horrible!" said Belinda. "This has got to change."

"And blacks are paid less than coloureds or Indians," chipped in Zuma, "and it will change. That is why we are all here," he added meaningfully.

"I see I have a lot to learn," said Belinda.

"I did think of university," said Rita, "but then I think I would have been stuck in that community, being one of the relatively few educated coloureds. I wanted to move on. Anyway, the standards at the coloured university are lower than those for whites."

"And lower still for blacks, I presume," said Belinda.

Zuma nodded. "You are learning fast," he said humorously. They all laughed.

Everyone gradually drifted off to bed, leaving Kamau with Robert and Jessica.

"What are you going to do?" asked Robert.

"Well, I think that for a start, I should finish my degree," Kamau smiled, "and then we'll see."

"What about Rita?" asked Jessica.

"We need to get that into perspective," said Kamau. "She has helped save both my life and the Oakley kids' lives. Life needs to be based on normal, everyday things and then we will see," he answered evasively.

Once they had been in the Belgravia mansion a few days Kamau, Louise and Rita decided it was necessary to tell the Oakley children what had happened to their father. Since nothing had been said, Jannie knew in his heart of hearts that all was not well.

"We'll talk to them when they come home from school," said Louise. "They're at a small private school round the corner which specialises in common entrance."

"Common entrance?" asked Kamau.

"Yes, to the public school system," said Louise.

"Public school means private school here," Kamau explained to Rita.

"If they get in they will go to the same schools that Belinda and Angus went to," said Louise.

"You don't have to do that, you know," said Kamau, but before he could continue, Louise waved him away.

"It's the least we can do; Giles is completely committed to it."

"How are they doing?" asked Rita.

"Jannie will make it easily; although he is a few months too old, we have established with the school that he will be accepted. Hettie needs to work a little harder, but we have more time with her, so I hope she will get in. She misses her mother."

"Boarding school?" asked Kamau.

"Yes, of course," said Louise.

"Well, they need a bit of luck after all the shit they've been through," said Kamau.

"Quite," said Louise.

There was a moment's silence.

"Giles thinks we should go the whole hog and adopt them," said Louise.

"I'm sure that would be wonderful for them," said Kamau. "We will have to introduce the idea slowly. First they'll have to get used to the idea that they will never see their parents again. We can get the paperwork done, though, in preparation."

The children came bouncing into the house as usual, just before four in the afternoon, and after they had had some tea and scones in the kitchen they all gathered in the sunroom. Hettie sat on Rita's lap, Jannie on his own, facing Kamau. Louise made up the group.

"Jannie, Hettie," Kamau began, speaking in Afrikaans, "you know about your ma."

They nodded.

"Mr Jones in the home in Western (Western Coloured Township) told us. He said you and the ANC would go to the funeral," said Jannie.

"I did, but only from a distance; the security police were there. I was lucky to escape arrest," answered Kamau.

Hettie started to cry.

"And Pa?" asked Jannie.

"He's dead too, said Kamau quietly. "I was there when he died. He was a very brave man."

A tear trickled down Jannie's face.

"It's all your blerry fault, Meneer Lawrence," he yelled. "If it wasn't for you and the verdomde (damned) ANC coming to live with us, they would both be alive today. Damn you to hell, Meneer Willie fucking Lemmer, damn you!"

He then burst into tears, with Louise trying to comfort him.

Kamau was silent.

"Tell me how he died then," sneered Jannie.

Kamau told them, leaving out the fact that Charles was naked and had been made to slip about in his own excrement.

"Why were you there?" asked Jannie aggressively.

Kamau explained how he had been kidnapped by the security police and taken to Johannesburg. "I would have been thrown out of the same window, the next day or the day after, if I hadn't escaped," he said.

Jannie said nothing, but he glowered at Kamau.

"I have a letter here, from your father," said Rita. "Mr Jones at the home gave it to me." She handed it over to Jannie; he recognised his father's handwriting. He tore open the envelope. It was written in Afrikaans and dated a few days before his death:

"My dearest Jannie and Hettie,

If you ever receive this letter, I will be dead, killed probably by the South African security police.

I hope you understand this, but I have been a member of the ANC now for many years. My original reasons for joining were the same as they would be today. The society that we live in has to change; it cannot continue to be based solely on the colour of a person's skin. I sincerely hope that both of you join up and continue the struggle as soon as you are old enough to do so.

I never told your Ma anything about this and I blame myself entirely for her death. She was a good woman but would not have understood why I was a member of the ANC or what I did for the organisation.

As for your futures, you will have to rely on God and your own hard work. Trust Willie Lemmer; he will get you to England, I am sure. He is also in a position to see that you are looked after there. Do not blame Willie for anything; it was entirely my own idea that he should come and stay with us.

Your ever-loving father,
Charles Oakley."

Jannie flung the letter down and ran out of the door and up the stairs. Rita picked it up and read it quietly to Hettie.

Hettie cried. "He was a good pa. Why did they kill him?" she asked.

"They are very bad men from a very bad government," Rita replied. "You will begin to understand as you grow up."

Kamau looked at Louise.

"I'll go and see how he is in an hour or two," said Louise. "He only went to his room."

Over the next days and weeks, with Louise and Zuma's help, Jannie gradually came round to the idea that Kamau was not evil and was not the direct cause of his father's death. In particular, Zuma managed to get Jannie to show him some of the sights of London, and during these expeditions Zuma managed to praise Kamau's selflessness and bravery.

One evening at dinner, Louise asked Jannie:

"None of us were able to go to either your mother's or your father's funeral. If you would like me to, I can arrange for all of us to have a memorial service either at our local Church of England or at the Presbyterian Church, which is Calvinist and is a bit closer to the Dutch Reformed Church you are used to."

"What is a memorial service?" asked Hettie.

"It is almost the same as a funeral," said Louise, "for people to say goodbye to someone special who has died, and where they were not able to go to the funeral."

Jannie nodded: "We would like that. Maybe the church we have been going to with you is better. We know the people there. Anyway, the church we went to in Coronationville was only for…non-whites,' he said hesitatingly, almost as if he couldn't believe what he was saying, 'maybe it is better to go to a church where everyone is allowed."

A few Sundays later, the large contingent from the Belgravia mansion, plus Trevor Mdantsane and a cohort from the ANC and Robert and Jessica came to the memorial service.

Apart from the priest, both Kamau and Mdantsane spoke and then, much to everyone's surprise, Jannie insisted on speaking.

"I know my father was a brave man," he said to the twenty or so people gathered. 'I don't know why they killed him, but when I am bigger I will try to find out, and Ma she was really killed by the same people, those police and that horrible man Roux.'

"Hopefully that will create some sort of platform for them to go on with their lives," said Louise to Kamau afterwards.

Within days of the service, Zuma moved to a flat in Finsbury Park and he continued to work full time for the ANC under Mdantsane. Kamau went back to Oxford to finish his degree and Rita found a well-paid job in a restaurant in the west end of London. She stayed for a few more weeks at Louise's insistence, "Just to make sure the children are settled properly." Whether that was the real reason Rita didn't know, but it helped her establish herself. She moved to a small flat in Earl's Court and dropped in to see the children at least once a week.

Chapter 16

After the action and excitement of the previous two years Kamau found it difficult to settle back to his life in England. He did however spend a year completing his studies at Oxford and graduated with a first class degree.

Without thinking Kamau had assumed that while he was at Oxford he would be able to continue his very good relationship with Rita; he had no idea where the relationship was going but had assumed that she would automatically fit in with his plans. In the year that it took to complete his degree he saw Rita when he could, although within a few months he was beginning to get the feeling that his visits were less and less welcome.

Rita had made no effort to join the ANC, and as she had done in Johannesburg, she worked hard and was quickly promoted to 'maitre d' at an exclusive restaurant in Knightsbridge. She really wanted nothing more than to escape her past and make the most of the opportunity that had now presented itself. Nobody questioned her racial origins, and she never discussed them. If anyone asked her where she was from she vaguely mentioned 'South Africa' and left the questioner to assume whatever they liked.

On one of the few evenings that Kamau was down from the university and was able to get Rita to go out with him, they were having supper at a small bistro and Kamau was unthinkingly describing in boring detail some minor initiative of the ANC, when she stopped him and told him:

"Look Kamau, I know how you feel about the situation in South Africa. I'm afraid that I do not really understand why you want to be involved at all; you were not even born there and if you think that you will ever be part of the inner circle then you are dreaming. As for me, I want to settle down; I want a family and children of my own. I know that with you, you will always be chasing off to heaven knows where in support of the impossible dream of changing things in South Africa. We all know that the government there is very powerful and I don't see big changes for fifty or one hundred years. I only have one life and I am truly grateful to you for having brought me to this place, but I know you, probably in a few months you will be off again somewhere and I will spend the next weeks and months wondering whether you are alive or dead." Kamau tried to interrupt, but she went on breathlessly, knowing that if she did not say everything she needed to, his charm would persuade her to go on with this relationship that she knew was never going to give her what she really wanted: a secure, first world existence.

Rita firmly withdrew her hand when he tried to hold it and she continued her speech, which she had practised now over many weeks.

"Just hear me out," she almost shouted. A few people in the restaurant looked over at them curiously. "Please, look I've been seeing someone else, an Englishman who I'm happy to say barely knows where South Africa is. I am so happy just doing ordinary things with ordinary people and not worrying about the millions of poor people around the world that I can do nothing to help anyway." Kamau looked at her in astonishment, he had not really considered Rita as having needs and wants of her own, he really had assumed that she would always fit in with whatever plans he might have.

"What about your people in the Cape?" he asked.

"I may be selfish, but I separated my life from theirs, years ago. I'm still in touch but I'm going to make my life here in England with the opportunity that I now have. My children will be English and I'm not going to even think about grubbing about in some South African township set aside by a harsh and unthinking government for so called coloured people like you and me. I may marry this person, I don't know, I'm certain he is in love with me."

She burst into tears; somehow this had come out all wrong. What she had envisaged was a gentle and civilised conversation with her friend Kamau. They would then part ways and stay in touch as friends. She knew that she sounded like an uncaring, selfish bitch and was almost ashamed of herself; she wondered whether Kamau would ever talk to her again. Kamau, for his part, had no idea what to do; he moved around the table and put his arms around her and tried to wipe away her tears with a napkin amid curious stares from other diners.

"Please don't cry," he said, "let's talk about it."

Rita could feel her resolve weakening, it would have been very easy just to have folded herself into his strong arms and let things go on as before.

"No, dammit" she thought to herself "I've come this far, I'm going to finish it off and to hell with the consequences." She tore herself away from his grasp and glared at him and said furiously in Afrikaans, so the other diners could not understand:

"You just don't bloody understand, do you? You with all you fancy relations and political connections. I have dragged myself up by my fucking bootstraps; it's tough for me just to make it in white society without having the complications of trying to change governments in far off countries, or whatever you are trying to do." She paused for breath.

"Please, just listen for a moment "he pleaded, still in Afrikaans.

"No, no you stupid pampoen [pumpkin], I'm bloody well not going to listen, I know that you will try to talk me round. Just understand, I've made up my mind and I do not want you as part of my life any more." With that she finally struggled out of his embrace and without a backward glance ran out of the bistro.

Kamau sat where he was for a good ten minutes then, amid a concerned frown from the proprietor, he got up and paid the bill and made his way sadly back to Belgravia. He wasn't sure whether he was in love with Rita but they had got along well. He supposed that he had been insensitive but her outburst had amazed him; he thought he would phone her in a few days.

On one of his regular visits from Oxford he had as usual arranged to see Zuma. The big Zulu had a troubled expression on his face. They settled down in a corner of a local pub in Finsbury Park. Zuma looked at his pint of English bitter and grinned:

"Maybe this is better than utshwala [traditional beer]" he said "but I still think that I prefer a nice cold Castle."

Kamau sipped his beer. "How are things?" he asked.

Zuma frowned and then looked away. "O.K., I suppose, I don't really know," he responded heavily.

"Come on, what's wrong? You look as if you have all the worries of the world on your shoulders" said Kamau. He was really concerned about his normally very cheerful and ebullient friend.

Zuma looked thoughtful. "I had a conversation with your father," he eventually said, "and he told me that the biggest problem he had to deal with was corruption, you know government officials just helping themselves to money that does not belong to them. I never thought that could ever happen in the ANC."

"So has anything changed your mind then?" asked Kamau.

"Well, I think." He hesitated. "No, I know that Trevor is stealing ANC funds for his own use."

"How do you know?" asked Kamau.

"He owns a number of flats in the Finsbury Park area. All of them were originally funded from ANC sources," answered Zuma.

"Has he paid the money back?" asked Kamau.

Zuma laughed mirthlessly. "Does the hyaena ever pay back the meal he has stolen from the lion? No, the deposit is always paid from ANC sources," he said.

"How did you find this out?" asked Kamau.

"I saw a cheque made out in the name of an estate agent. Trevor had gone out of the office for a minute and it was lying on his desk," said Zuma.

"So?" asked Kamau.

"It was from an ANC bank account and when I checked later it was entered as funds for five cells we have in Tanzania and Zambia. There is no doubt, I checked it several times."

"Are you absolutely sure?" asked Kamau.

Zuma nodded. He finished his beer, hesitated and then went up to the bar and fetched two more pints of the flat warm beer.

"I'm going to kill the bastard," he said angrily.

"Just be careful, we need to work this out together. Murder is still an offence here in England," said Kamau carefully. "Do you think that he has any idea that you know what he is up to?"

Zuma pondered and then said: "Maybe he does, he's locking all the books up now and when I asked to see something the other day he made some excuse; the net result was that I no longer have access to the books and accounts any more."

When they parted both had agreed that Zuma would just continue to do his job, keep his eyes open and try to gain Trevor's trust. Above all they needed more evidence.

Shortly after Kamau and Zuma had arrived in England, Roux in his large basement office in security headquarters in Pretoria was sitting there fuming.

"You mean that coloured baboon Kamau is back in the UK." he yelled at Danie Visser.

"Ja, meneer," said Danie. "We lost him for a while but I understand that he has gone back to Oxford to finish his degree."

"Those pampoen rooineks will regret the day they ever allowed the blacks to be educated," grumbled Roux, "they are not the same as the white man and they will destroy us if we are not careful."

"Ja, meneer" said Danie. Privately he thought that Roux was mad and he hated these conversations.

"I had that little fucker," Roux said almost to himself, "I had him in these hands." He looked at his hands as if they were something alien. "Another two days and we would have had all the information we wanted from him and then he would just have disappeared."

Danie was silent.

"I said all we needed was another two days and then we would have finished him off," shouted Roux.

"Ja, meneer, just another two days."

"And now the fucker is back in that rooinek capital just wandering about as if nothing had happened here," said Roux.

"He is still working for the ANC," said Danie helpfully.

"Of course he is, are you a moron or something, the only time he will stop is when we have fed him to the hyaenas," yelled Roux.

Roux paced up and down and then appeared to calm down a bit.

"And that big Zulu, Randolph Zuma, or whatever his stupid name is. Why can't these kaffirs stick to their own kaffir names and leave the blerry rooinek names alone. Randolph blerry Zuma, what an abortion of a name. I suppose he is also working for the ANC in London?" asked Roux.

"Ja meneer Roux, here are the photographs, there is no doubt it is him," said Danie.

Roux knocked the pack of photos out of Danie's hand.

"I've seen enough of that big black kaffir to last me a lifetime," said Roux unhappily as Danie retrieved the photographs.

"The question is, how do we kill them both?" asked Roux. "Any sign of that coloured woman Vos?"

"No meneer, said Danie.

"We had her too, or you did. How did she get away?" asked Roux.

"I followed her for days, weeks even, she seemed clean to me. Worked at the restaurant in Jo'burg, went home, no boyfriends, nothing." said Danie defensively. He was glad that the subject of Kamau and Zuma seemed to be behind him, at least for the time being. He still felt guilty about helping Zuma escape, although saving Kamau's life was, for him, a matter of honour.

Roux looked evilly at him. "You didn't try to get your leg over there, did you now Sergeant Major? [Danie had been promoted again.] You fancied a little bit of coloured fanny, did you?"

Danie was genuinely shocked. He drew himself up to his full height.

"Meneer, I am a happily married man, now with two children. How could you think such a thing of me? Anyway at that stage we thought she was white."

Roux laughed and said: "So that makes it all right then does it, the fact that we thought she was white." He got up and patted Danie on the shoulder.

"O.K., O.K., so you didn't poke her, we just left that to Kamau Lawrence" Roux continued nastily.

There was silence for a few moments.

"I said, how do we kill those two fuckers?" said Roux.

"Well, meneer, we can't do it in London. If we did the British would expel our agents and we don't want that," said Danie. "Somehow we have to get them to Africa."

Roux looked at his subordinate with a mixture of contempt and admiration. Sometimes he made the most obvious statements but sometimes those obvious statements held the solution, as this one did.

"Ja," said Roux, "that is what we must do, somehow get them back to Africa, then I will deal with them."

Some weeks later when Danie was well out of the way, Roux made his way to a small room known only to him and one technician. It was behind a large bookcase in his spacious basement office. He rang a number and, as he knew it would, the number rang ten times and then rang out. He waited ten minutes and rang again. This time the 'phone was picked up almost immediately.

"Hogs Back," said an obviously African voice.

"Maclear" was Roux's response. There was silence at the other end, eventually punctuated in Afrikaans by a very reluctant "How are you". These were the codes that Roux and Trevor had agreed on years and years before when Roux had recruited Trevor into the South African security system, when they had both lived in the Eastern Cape. Roux was then a young security policeman, and Trevor a student at the University of Fort Hare. The significance of the codes was that they were two small towns in the Eastern Cape. Roux had only activated the arrangement once before, but he had continued to make sure that it was live and in fact it was the South African security budget that had funded Trevor's first flat in London and not the ANC as Zuma thought.

"I need your assistance," said Roux.

There was a grunt at the other end. "There is a limit as to what I can do," said Trevor.

"Maybe, but I think that you can help in this case," said Roux.

"Tell me," said Trevor, without any enthusiasm. In his view he had really established himself financially and no longer needed the assistance of such people as Roux, whom he now regarded with distaste.

"There are two people in your organisation in London, who are troubling me greatly and I need them somewhere in Africa, where I can get at them," said Roux.

"What's it worth?" asked Trevor.

"Ten thousand," answered Roux.

Trevor laughed. "You can do better than that," he said.

They eventually settled on fifty thousand pounds.

"Who are these people, anyway?" asked Trevor. The fact that he had not asked this question before surprised Roux; it certainly told him that Trevor was a very powerful figure in the organisation now.

"Lawrence and Zuma," answered Roux.

A flutter of excitement swept through Trevor's chest. These two were getting too big for their boots anyway. If he played his cards right he could get the South African security forces to deal with what he now saw as his problem, and he was going to score fifty grand into the bargain. He was certain that Zuma knew about his property dealings and where much of the funding came from. He'd kicked himself many times for carelessly leaving the information around that he was certain that Zuma had seen. As for that little shit Kamau, he was much too clever and Lusaka was taking too much notice of him. Trevor had been wondering what to do about him anyway and this would certainly act as a catalyst for him to do something.

Trevor was all business.

"Pay twenty five grand into the Swiss bank and phone me in two months. You can pay the other twenty five grand when those two arrive in either Lusaka or Luanda, but please be patient; I can't act too quickly. Zuma has only been here a short while and I need to make sure that Lusaka feels that his training is complete, and as for that pretentious little bastard Kamau, I think that he will have to be allowed to finish his degree at Oxford before he is moved again, otherwise it might look suspicious," he said. Roux made sure that he had the correct details of Trevor's bank account and they rang off.

Trevor knew that Roux would deliver and based on experience Roux expected that both Kamau and Zuma would be somewhere where he could 'get at them' within a few months.

The Oxford University rugby fraternity welcomed Kamau back into the fold with open arms and he played regularly for the university. He also rejoined his London club.

"Helping my mother establish clinics in Nairobi," was what he told anybody who asked him where he had been in the past two years. If anyone in the rugby world had known what he had actually been doing, they would probably not have believed the story. He was never recalled to the England squad and Kamau sometimes wondered whether the small world of international rugby had its own way of communicating; although the South Africans had been banned from international rugby, there were still continuous contacts between all the major participant nations, including South Africa, and the England management had probably been told enough to completely exclude him. Not that any of this worried him. The main business as far as he was concerned was the fight in South Africa. To this end, therefore, he had made contact with a small legal firm in Lincoln's Inn fields in London, who specialized in human rights issues. He spent parts of his vacations there but mainly focussed on helping the ANC. The plan was for him to join the firm when he graduated from the university.

Towards the end of his sojourn at Oxford Kamau had an excited phone call from Zuma.

"I've really found something now," he said.

"Where are you calling from?" asked Kamau.

"A call box; what I have here is dynamite, I need to see you urgently," he said breathlessly.

"I'm in the middle of exams, so I can't come right now," Kamau told him, "Do you have any papers?"

"Yes, and I'm in trouble if I'm found with them on me," said Zuma.

"Will they be missed?" asked Kamau.

"No, they are old," was the response.

"Take them to my law firm in Lincoln's Inn and make certain that you make a list of what you have. If they find that the papers are missing, will they think you are involved?"

"No. They have no idea that I have access to them."

Kamau gave Zuma the address and the name of the firm in Lincoln's Inn, and who to contact there.

"There is one other thing," said Zuma hesitantly.

"What's that?" asked Kamau.

"Trevor is behaving strangely. He let slip something the other day, it was almost as if he wasn't expecting me to be here in a few months' time. I think he is planning something."

"What did he say?" asked Kamau.

"Something like 'when you are in Angola' and when I asked him to elaborate he made some excuse and said he was only talking theoretically. Since then, however, he has been very friendly, which is very different from the last few months. I am certain that something is going on. He wants me out of here. You too probably."

"What does he say about me?" asked Kamau.

"Not much, but what he does say is generally some snide remark about clever dicks at Oxford."

"Just keep your ear to the ground, but you still have not told me what was in the papers you have," said Kamau.

"Difficult to tell you on the phone, but apart from ANC money, it looks as if Trevor had some money transferred from a Swiss Bank account as a deposit for at least one of his property investments. This was some years ago."

"How did you find all this out?" asked Kamau.

"I have made friends with one of the office girls at the estate agent who looks after Trevor's affairs."

"Oh yes," said Kamau non-committally. "Does Trevor know anything about that? If he does you may be putting her life in danger."

"We have been very discreet," was the thoughtful response. "I have never been to the offices when there has been anyone else there. Most of the time I go to her place."

"Why is she doing this for you?" asked Kamau.

There was a chuckle from Zuma. "She says she likes big Zulus," was the answer.

"Just be very careful. You do realise that you may be putting her life in danger, don't you? If Trevor got wind of this, he would not hesitate: I'm sure that he would kill her, or at the very least she could lose her job," said Kamau.

"Her father owns the agency," said Zuma, "so I do not think that she will ever lose her job. I also think that her father is more than capable of looking after himself and his own. The feeling that I have is that they are all into some pretty shady deals and that is why Trevor went there in the first place. If Trevor starts to get heavy then I think that it is him that is in danger as much as anyone."

"OK, I hope you know what you are doing. I'm sure that you can look after yourself even in the wilds of North London," said Kamau.

Zuma chuckled as they rang off.

During periodic contacts and calls in the past the ANC leadership in Lusaka had consulted Trevor on the management and manning of the various facilities that the organisation had in different parts of the world. Trevor was very careful not to send out negative signals regarding Kamau and Zuma; in fact he went out of his way to praise them when he had a chance. Lusaka had actually become used to the idea that they were his protégés. Trevor knew that the leadership of the various training camps was always an issue and that there was considerable conflict between the providers of the training, such as the Russians and Chinese in Tanzania and the Cubans in Angola, and the ANC leadership in those camps, so he thought that one or other of these positions would come up for discussion in the near future. He was not disappointed.

Only a few weeks after Kamau had started full time with the law firm in Lincoln's Inn, he was called in to Trevor's office in Finsbury Park together with Zuma. There was almost a look of triumph on Trevor's face as he told them that because of their good work they were going to be given a major promotion and this involved both of them going to a training camp in northern Angola, with Kamau as commandant and Zuma his deputy.

"I thought it was regarded as important because of my legal qualifications that I should stay here in London," argued Kamau.

"Lusaka has changed their mind for the time being," said Trevor. "Anyway, all I do is to follow instructions." He smiled disingenuously. "You can ask them the same question when you arrive in Lusaka."

"When will that be?" asked Zuma.

"Within a few days actually, I have the tickets here."

They were ushered out of the office.

A detailed examination of the papers that Zuma had taken from the estate agent's offices had revealed that Trevor owned at least six flats in various parts of North London. Where the information was available, the original deposits for the purchases had come from ANC sources. This was the case except for the first purchase, where it appeared that the deposit had come from a Swiss bank account.

"He has been very clever with all this," Zuma pointed out. "You see he has sold a couple of the flats when prices were right and he now owns at least two of the flats outright; the others all have mortgages."

"I see all that, but what is worrying me is where he got the initial deposit from. Do you think that his family in South Africa is wealthy and smart enough to have somehow got money into a Swiss bank account so that he could make his initial deposit on the first flat?"

"I know that he went to Fort Hare but it would be very unusual for an African family in South Africa to have found a way to get money into a Swiss bank account," said Zuma.

"My feeling exactly," Said Kamau. "So where do you think this money originated?"

"I just don't know, the only possibilities are that it came from his family, he stole it, or it came from the South African security people," responded Zuma quietly.

"You think he is playing a double game?" asked Kamau in a surprised voice.

"Maybe; if he is then we really do have to watch our backs," said Zuma.

"We know that South African security have infiltrated some of our camps; we are going to have to be very careful," said Kamau. "I wonder how much Trevor had to do with both of us being transferred to Angola. He claims it was on instructions from Lusaka, but it would not surprise me if the original recommendation did not come from Trevor himself. I will make a point of finding out when we get to Lusaka."

Roux had kept in touch with Trevor over the months and when Trevor told him that Kamau and Zuma would be going to Angola he found it hard to contain his excitement.

"I will get you bastards now," he said to himself.

He made another secret call from the little back room. This time it was a radio call that he used much more regularly. It was part of a routine and he made the call once every two weeks.

"Cabinda," answered a familiar voice. Roux answered with his own call sign of: "Mocamedes." The call sign was changed regularly but both parties were familiar with the other's voice that this was almost unnecessary. "Colonel Roux how are you?" said a warm voice in heavily accented English with a South American flavour to it. "What can I do for you this time?"

"Ah, Colonel Hernandez, thank you for the information you sent us. We have picked up about 80% of the people on the list; you have been most helpful."

"It is only a pleasure to do business with you, but your call is a little early this time. I still have a few more months before the sheep will be ready for shearing again," said Hernandez, laughing at his own rather clumsy attempt at humour.

"I have some other information that I think you will find most interesting," said Roux.

"It is always interesting talking to you, Senor Colonel Roux; my Swiss bank account is also very appreciative of the attention it receives," said the Cuban, laughing again.

"I hear that your so called commandant is to be replaced," Said Roux.

"As usual the Senor Colonel is very well informed," Said Hernandez. "The last one, well he became a little too curious and he met with rather a bad accident, which unfortunately proved to be fatal. We could, of course, do without any kind of commandant, especially the ignorant black fools they usually send me, but I suppose it is a cross we have to bear."

"Well, this time you are getting two, and I am sorry to tell you that they are not ignorant and they are not fools," responded Roux.

"I have been informed that there are two baboons on the way, Senor Colonel. Since you have made this call, am I to assume that you have a special interest in, let me see if I can remember their names, ah yes, Lawrence and Zuma? I was informed a week or so ago," said Colonel Hernandez.

"I have a very special interest in both of them; I need them both alive and in my hands, Colonel Hernandez. You will of course be well rewarded when this happens," said Roux.

"I am flattered by your confidence in me," said Hernandez, "but delivering them alive to you will be very difficult."

"We can arrange a pickup by helicopter somewhere in the south." said Roux.

"OK, what is it worth?" asked Hernandez.

"Fifty grand US apiece delivered alive, paid after delivery." said Roux.

"Phew, these really are big fish," said Hernandez. "I will be able to retire after this one. You said they were not the usual type of fool they send me; perhaps you would explain."

Roux then went on to give Hernandez a history of both Kamau and Zuma, leaving nothing out.

"You say they both escaped from security headquarters in Johannesburg, together!" Hernandez was incredulous.

"Yes, they did, and even now we do not have the slightest idea how they got out. If they hadn't escaped they would both be feeding worms by now," said Roux.

"And this Lawrence, he ran around your country blowing things up for eighteen months and you were unable to catch him?" Hernandez was almost disbelieving.

"Colonel, I would not be telling you if it were not true; believe me I am not proud of any of this," said Roux.

"O.K., fifty grand US apiece delivered alive to your helicopter in the South of Angola," said Hernandez. "I am sure we can do that; give me a few months."

They rang off.

Before they caught the 'plane to Lusaka Kamau had a brief telephone call to Rita.

"I don't suppose you can tell me where you are going and when you will be back," said Rita.

Kamau laughed. "I'm sure that you know the answer to that," he said.

"I particularly want you at my wedding, so don't get yourself killed," said Rita.

"Wedding?" asked Kamau in a disbelieving voice.

"Yes, the Englishman I told you about; we'll be getting married within a year I guess. I sent him to the Cape to see my people; I of course was not able to go since I assume that I'm still on some wanted list."

"I'll be back," said Kamau with more confidence than he really felt.

They kicked their heels in frustration for a week in Lusaka. There was very little information regarding their destination or their objectives and no real information about the fate of Kamau's predecessor.

Kamau, after some delays, made contact with a senior officer in the Zambian armed forces.

"I am not able to tell you much, but I can tell you that that camp appears to us to be out of control and from what we hear the casualty rates of the trainees once they return to South Africa are much higher than from other places and they are higher than we would expect."

Kamau looked at him expectantly.

"If you get into trouble I suggest that you get in touch with a Colonel Carvalho in Luanda, he seems to have his feet on the ground. You cannot expect any help from us or from the ANC here, who really have no real resources to help you anyway," said the colonel.

"I would say we are in real trouble," said Zuma thoughtfully once they were on their way back to the house they were staying in.

"I've spoken to many people here," said Kamau. "They all seem to think that our friend Trevor is some sort of hero. We happen to know different, but I have not met one person here who thinks anything but good of him; I wonder how he does it? Also I get nothing but silence and, from some people, sympathy, when I talk about Angola. I always thought that Angola was one of their prize training facilities; now nobody wants to even mention it. I would say that you are right. Maybe this Colonel Carvalho will be able to help. Also I did check with the leadership and they see both of us as Trevor's protégés, and, yes, it was Trevor who recommended that we be sent to sort the problem out in Angola, and I quote, "If anyone can sort the problem out it will be those two". The quote is attributed to Trevor. So much for his statements that he was merely obeying instructions from the people here in Lusaka."

"I think we are being led into a trap," observed Zuma, "and that trap has been baited by Trevor, he wants to get rid of us." He then smiled. "He's right, we are the best people to sort the matter out, and we'll sort him out while we are about it."

Glancing at his friend Zuma, Kamau was at once encouraged that Zuma was as determined as he himself was to "sort the matter out". Despite the now obvious danger they were not going to back off.

The rickety Zambian military 'plane that took them to Luanda did not even turn off its engines after they landed. They were let out near to the airport buildings and then the 'plane turned around and took off again.

There was a sergeant and a driver from the Angolan military who took them into Luanda and dumped them outside a seedy hotel. The sergeant spoke no English at all; so on the way into the city Kamau took the opportunity to look around. The ramshackle city was dominated by the military, with people in a variety of uniforms on every street corner. He particularly noticed the Cubans; they were there at the behest of the Russians, who were funding the "proxy" war against the west, basically, the Americans and the South Africans. He knew that most of the instructors at the ANC camp in the north of the country were Cubans. The other most noticeable thing about the city was the heat and the undeniable smell of Africa, which he could not have described, but which made him feel at home, despite the fact that he spoke none of the local languages nor Portuguese, the language of the former colonial oppressor.

Zuma smiled at him and sniffed the air without saying anything.

Kamau nodded.

They were dropped at the hotel and the driver drove off, wordlessly and without any sort of sign.

"Now what?" said Zuma.

"I expect we will hear in due course, but I think we should use the time well; perhaps we should go and see our friend Colonel Carvalho," answered Kamau.

Smartly dressed and not looking at all out of place in their military style uniforms, Kamau sporting a colonels' insignia and Zuma that of a major, made their way to the Angolan military headquarters. They hung around for more than an hour and were then told to return at ten o'clock the following morning.

There was still no sign from the camp.

"I expect they are trying to send us some sort of message," said Kamau. "It is obvious that there is a discipline problem at the camp which we are going to have to deal with very quickly."

"The Cubans make me feel very uncomfortable," said Zuma "and it is not only a language thing; they are behaving like the whites in South Africa, as if they are superior to the black people we see on the streets, and yet they seem poor specimens to me and none of the ones that I have seen do their military units any credit at all. They are all scruffy and poorly turned out."

"It's not really their war," said Kamau. "They probably do not want to be here at all, except that I understand they get some sort of cash bonus when they go home at the end of two years."

They ate in a little restaurant near the hotel, which had seen better days and might have been one of the smarter watering holes in the colonial era. The food still had a Portuguese influence.

The following morning saw them at the Angolan military headquarters at the appointed time. As they expected, they were kept waiting for a good hour, so were able to observe the passing parade.

"Plenty of very senior Russians and, as one would expect, Cubans," said Kamau. "It looks as if the Russians have a very big influence," said Zuma. "I have seen several generals. The Cubans all seem to be relatively junior officers."

Kamau nodded. A corporal with an Angolan uniform on ushered them into a large office, where they were greeted by a tall, coal black Angolan with colonel's insignia on his epaulettes. The colonel had an open face and a broad smile. Kamau and Zuma saluted.

"Colonel Carvalho," he said and shook their hands. He ordered coffee. Kamau introduced Zuma and himself.

"I have been briefed with regard to your mission," Carvalho said in very good English. "How do you think I can help you?"

"Well," answered Kamau, much relieved on account of the English, "we have very little information with regard to camp Tambo [named after one of the leaders of the ANC] but we hear some very ugly rumours about what has happened there in the past. We were given your name and wondered if there was anything that you would be able to tell us."

Carvalho was cautious. "What have you heard?"

"For one thing, that the previous commandant was killed in rather mysterious circumstances, and also that the graduates from that camp do not last very long when they get sent into the field in South Africa," Answered Kamau. "That must worry you too; after all we are both fighting the same enemy."

"All of what you say is true," said Carvalho. He looked at them quizzically and then seemed to decide that he could trust them.

"Are you not concerned?" asked Kamau.

"Of course we are, but with the shortage of resources…" his voice trailed off. "Frankly we have other priorities."

"I see," said Kamau. "Is there anything you can do help us if we get into trouble, and is there any other information you might have that you think could help us? For example, transport. We have been here two days and there is absolutely no sign of the people who are supposed to come and fetch us. I think they are playing the fool frankly, trying to intimidate us, but it would take the wind out of their sails if we just arrived under our own steam. Also, have you any information on who is supposed to run the camp and what we might expect? Do you have any suspicions regarding the high casualty rate from the camp?"

Carvalho looked uneasy.

"Well," he said slowly. "We have been intercepting radio calls, which appear to come from the south somewhere, probably South Africa. They are usually short but not always, every now and then there is a much longer call. All the calls are answered in the vicinity of camp Tambo. Most probably from the camp, since we have no other facilities anywhere near there."

"What language are the calls made in?" asked Zuma.

"We think English, but so far when we have intercepted calls the radio operator has had no English language skills and we don't have the resources to tape all calls."

"We have some radio equipment with us," said Zuma. "Do you have a frequency?"

"I will get it for you, but it changes I think."

Zuma nodded. "Any information you have would be helpful."

Carvalho made a call.

"Did you have anything to do with the previous ANC representatives in the camp?" asked Kamau.

"No, frankly they came nowhere near us, I do not know why."

"Is there any chance that you could provide us with transport and perhaps a small escort?" asked Kamau.

Carvalho looked at them warily. "It is probably in our interests to take more notice of what is going on in that camp," he said. "Please wait here for a few minutes, I need to consult."

They waited about an hour, and the colonel returned looking very pleased with himself.

He handed Zuma a piece of paper with two radio frequencies on it.

"The Cubans in the camp are in charge of a Colonel Hernandez. We do not know much about him except that he has a very good record in the Cuban armed forces. Our people say that he really runs camp Tambo."

Handing over a piece of paper he continued: "Those are the frequencies of the mystery calls we have intercepted; the last one was some time within the last two weeks," Said Carvalho.

"Thank you," said Zuma.

"Regarding transport," he smiled, "an army truck and six of our people under the command of a sergeant will take you up to the camp tonight. They will collect you at the hotel at six this evening; the journey will take most of the night."

Kamau was overwhelmed by the turn of fortune.

"Thank you, thank you," he said to the Colonel. "Is there any way that I can keep in touch with you?"

"Yes there is, call this frequency," he wrote down another frequency on Zuma's piece of paper. "The escort I am giving you will stay with you; they are from my tribe and are completely loyal to me. They will not let you come to any harm up there. Please call if you need anything."

They were ushered out of the office.

When they returned to the hotel they were given a message that a driver would come and fetch them in the morning.

"Who left this message?" asked Kamau.

The clerk said something in Portuguese. A bystander translated it as "a rather dirty Cuban."

"Those must be our friends from the camp," observed Zuma.

"Well, they will find that the bird has flown, when they get here in the morning, if indeed they do get here at that time," said Kamau.

He had a conversation with the desk clerk and gave him a handsome tip. They left the clerk beaming.

"I just told him, through our friend here," he indicated the bystander, "to tell them to get their idle backsides back to the camp and that we had already made our own way there. We'll see if they return within a week."

An old but well kept Angolan Army truck arrived just before six under the command of an immaculately turned out sergeant and six men. All were armed with clean Kalashnikov AK47 rifles. The sergeant drove and Kamau and Zuma were asked to get in front with him. Zuma thought for a second and then indicated that he would like to be in the back with the men. The men then gratefully took it in turns to sit in the front. Once they had made their way out of the potholed, badly lit streets of Luanda, the roads gradually deteriorated again from potholed tar to good dirt roads and then eventually to nothing more than a track that was given the once over with a road grader every year or two. Kamau guessed that during the rains the track would become impassable so that obtaining supplies would be difficult. It was hard to converse with the sergeant since he spoke no English and had to concentrate on the driving. After a few hours Kamau's offer to take over some of the driving was gratefully accepted.

Zuma in the back had in the meanwhile found a man who had spent a few years in South West Africa [now Namibia] and spoke some Afrikaans. So after some hesitation Zuma turned on his charm and for the rest of the journey there was much hilarity and laughter from the back of the vehicle.

As the dawn came up they were driving quite slowly along the track; they had seen no other vehicles for the past two or three hours.

"How much further?" asked Kamau, in sign language. The sergeant held up two fingers, which Kamau eventually gathered meant two more hours.

The countryside was flat and uninteresting and the red dust was everywhere. They passed an occasional village and often large and small antelope charged across the road in front of the vehicle and were immediately lost to view in the thick bush. The bush was mostly what Kamau thought looked like the mopane in Botswana, with the occasional large tree. There were signs of larger game such as elephant and buffalo. There was certainly a deepening sense of remoteness; Kamau thanked his lucky stars that they had called on Colonel Carvalho in Luanda and that if he got into real trouble he had something to fall back on.

Almost without warning, as they negotiated a bend in the road they came across the camp. The road skirted the camp and continued on to heaven knew where. The driver turned off the road and was stopped at the barrier by a very unkempt looking guard. Zuma and the men hopped out of the back. Zuma spoke briefly to the guard, who turned out to be a fellow Zulu and was one of the trainees.

"I've told him to go and find this Colonel Hernandez," said Zuma.

While they were waiting Kamau looked about with a growing sense of irritation. The camp itself appeared to be well constructed. There was a row of mud-brick cottages up the one side, separated from the main camp by a row of eucalypts. The main camp had a dozen barrack like buildings made from a combination of wood and corrugated iron.

There was a large, dusty parade ground in the middle and there were many big shade trees scattered round the camp. Some attempt had been made to grow vegetables in one corner of the camp. The guard house and what Kamau took to be an armoury to house the weapons were also in the vicinity. The place could have looked good, or at least reasonable, but it had an air of neglect; there was rubbish all over the place, the few visible trainees were slouching around as if they had nothing to do and there was no sign of any training at all.

After about fifteen minutes a tall, well built Cuban with colonel's insignia came up to the truck and saluted in a desultory fashion. Kamau responded with sharp, crisp salute.

"Colonel Lawrence, I see," said Hernandez in good English. "I sent an escort to Luanda to fetch you." He sounded offended.

"They were late, so as you can see, Colonel, I made my own arrangements. My escort will be staying here so I would be grateful if you would provide them with suitable accommodation."

"We are rather short of accommodation, sir," replied Hernandez.

Kamau looked at him.

"Colonel Hernandez, please do not question my orders. I told you to find suitable accommodation for the sergeant and his men. Is that clear?" said Kamau firmly.

"Yes sir," was the surly response.

"And Colonel, one other thing. There will be a parade at two o'clock this afternoon; only those who are bedridden have my permission to be absent."

Kamau could see that Hernandez was just about to object, but in view of Kamau's stern-looking demeanour he clearly thought better of it.

"Two o'clock it will be, sir," then he paused and added "in the heat of the day."

Kamau chose to ignore the comment.

"Please show us to our quarters, Colonel."

Kamau and Zuma were shown to a pleasant cottage that was clearly the best of the cottages in the complex. Hernandez appeared to have a similar cottage at the other end of the row, as far away from the Commandants' cottage as possible.

"I will join the trainees for the midday meal, Colonel, if you could tell me what time that is."

"Twelve thirty, sir," Was the curt response.

The cottage was quite comfortable and there was a maid hovering around the kitchen. Kamau had trouble in making himself understood so Zuma fetched the Angolan sergeant who was able to translate.

"Apparently, our escort all come from the local tribe; your Colonel Carvalho really does have his head screwed on the right way, doesn't he? I'm sure that we will find out what is going on here very quickly indeed as a result of that. I'm sure that all the instructors will have servants of their own and there will be no secrets from them," said Zuma, as a result of a fairly long conversation between the sergeant and the maid.

At the appointed time Kamau and Zuma made their way to the large central dining room and entered the building.

There was a table of Cuban officers and NCO's, already eating. About half the young trainees were at tables, eating, and the rest were still queuing up at the serving hatch. There was another rather subdued looking group of Africans at another table. Nobody moved or took much notice.

"BE UPSTANDING," bellowed Zuma in Zulu. The whole dining room froze and stood up hastily, all except one of the Cubans, who pointedly kept on eating his lunch. Zuma waited a few seconds and then noisily marched over to the man's table and stood in front of the Cuban sergeant. The man looked up insolently.

The huge Zulu quietly said: "Stand up, sergeant."

The sergeant was, by this time, wholly intimidated by Zuma's presence. He rose sloppily to his feet.

"Name?" asked Zuma. The man looked blankly at Zuma.

"Gomez, he speak no English," said a man to his left.

"Sergeant Gomez, I am putting you on a charge of insubordination. Report to me in full battledress after the parade at two o'clock. In the meantime you will stand to attention in the centre of the dining area here until the meal is over."

Zuma removed the man's half-eaten plate of food, turned on his heel and took the plate to the serving hatch.

He went back to where Kamau was standing. There was a stunned silence. Nobody had ever dared to treat one of the Cuban instructors like that before.

Zuma said:"This is Colonel Lawrence, your new commanding officer, and I am Major Zuma, his second in command."

The message was repeated in Zulu, Xhosa, and Tswana as well as English and Afrikaans.

At the end, when they were told to continue with their lunch, the trainees all spontaneously clapped.

Kamau went into the kitchen and completed a general inspection. He asked the chief cook to clean up certain things, but was generally quite pleased with state of the facility. He tasted all the dishes.

The parade was a shambles. Although the three hundred trainees were organised into ten squads of thirty each, they seemed to have no idea how to march and did not know any of the basic drills. The Cubans looked unkempt but were able to respond to the commands that Zuma gave them. The more senior Africans, who turned out to be the ANC contingent at the camp, looked quite good and were able to complete the drills, but they were obviously still completely intimidated by the Cubans.

Kamau, having completed a basic inspection of the people on parade, stood impassively, together with Hernandez, watching Zuma attempt to put the troops through their paces.

"How long have the trainees been in the camp, Colonel?" asked Kamau.

"Almost two months, sir," was the answer.

"And they can't even march!"

Hernandez was silent and furious.

"Immediately after the parade, we will review the training programme, Colonel; what I see here is frankly a disgrace. How long is it since my predecessor, er, was killed?"

"He was killed just prior to this intake arriving."

"So you have effectively been in charge for the last two months."

"Yes, sir."

"And you are proud of this shambles?"

The colonel remained silent.

"While this parade continues we, that is you and I, will visit the three sick people, all Cubans I see, on the list here," said Kamau.

One of the three was genuinely sick; the other two were horrified to find the new commanding officer on their doorstep.

"Those two will be sent back to Luanda today, Colonel, is that clear?" said Kamau.

The Colonel hesitated. "I ask you to give them another chance. If they get sent back to Luanda they will either go to the front line against the South Africans or be sent home, in which case they will lose their bonus. Either way it will cause hardship."

"They should have thought of that when they decided not to attend the parade. I saw both of them in the dining room at lunch. Frankly they deserve what is coming to them. I want their names and rank and I will advise Luanda." Kamau turned on his heel. "Oh and there is one other thing, Colonel. All weapons will be turned in to the armoury this evening. I noticed that many of your people brought weapons directly to the parade. The weapons will be in the charge of Major Zuma or his designate."

They returned to the parade ground just as Zuma was about to dismiss the troops.

Kamau addressed them:

"Colonel Hernandez and I are going to rearrange the training programme after parade this evening, but I can see there is much work to do, so as from tomorrow morning the first parade will be a training run at five a.m. sharp, followed by breakfast at six thirty. Any instructor who is late will find himself on his way back to Luanda and probably Cuba, which means that bonuses will not be paid. Any trainee who is late will be put on a charge, and you will see shortly how people who get put on a charge are dealt with."

The parade was dismissed, all except Sergeant Gomez who stood forlornly on the side of the parade ground with a full sixty-pound pack on his back.

Zuma arranged for one of the other ANC personnel to take charge of the weapons being returned to the armoury.

"There are to be no weapons, even private ones, kept in the living quarters. If I this rule is disobeyed the guilty party will be dismissed forthwith, and sent back to Luanda, and any private weapons will be confiscated," Kamau told the parade.

It took more than an hour for all the weapons to be returned to the armoury. The Cuban instructors kept machine guns plus live ammunition and their normal service rifles in their houses. He was told later that many of the Cuban men used camp weapons to hunt game.

Zuma was quite merciless when it came to dealing with Sergeant Gomez. Apart from the sixty pound pack he was made to carry his rifle above his head and march at the double.

After half an hour Gomez was in a state of complete exhaustion and looked as if he was about to collapse.

Hernandez started to get agitated. He could see what was happening from the office where he and Kamau were busy rescheduling the training programme.

"Colonel, are you trying to kill him?" asked Hernandez.

"Colonel," said Kamau, icily, "if you wish to join your colleague, just say the word." He went on with his work.

After an hour Gomez collapsed on the parade ground.

Zuma went over to him and tore off his sergeant's stripes.

"Corporal Gomez from tomorrow," he announced.

Hernandez looked sick. Some of Gomez' colleagues picked him up and took him away.

"When the escort that was supposed to pick us up in Luanda arrives," Kamau instructed the guards at the gate, "they are to be arrested and locked up. I will deal with them."

Kamau sat with the ANC cadre at the evening meal and they started to open up to him. Their stories were full of tales of abuse at the hands of the Cubans and of the generally slack programme, which Kamau now assured them had been addressed.

Zuma pointedly sat with the Cubans and although to start with there was considerable hostility, he made it plain that if they behaved and did what was expected of them they could expect nothing but fair treatment from him. Communication was not easy, but by the end of the meal, the Cubans had relaxed slightly and seemed to partially accept his goodwill.

Both Zuma and Kamau made a point of attending some of the barracks at lights out. "Many of us have no running shoes," one of them said. "What should we do in the morning?"

"Did your father provide you with running shoes when you went out to herd the cows or the goats in the morning?" Asked Kamau, amid laughter from the other trainees. "I spent years herding cows and goats for my grandfather and I do not remember one pair of shoes for anything.

Use what God gave you; that is what I will be wearing."

Nevertheless Kamau was thankful for the intervention and he went the next morning with all the others on a barefoot run. Soon it was the standard practice and any trainee who attended the run in anything but bare feet, was jeered at by the other trainees.

Within weeks the camp was clean and orderly; every day except Sunday the whole camp went on a training run, which Kamau led himself. He started with runs of less than five kilometres but that built up to regular runs of ten kilometres with one longer run every week. Once Kamau and Zuma were satisfied that the training was on course they introduced regular games three or four times a week. Football was a natural activity, and Kamau introduced rugby which eventually became popular. They also constructed a four hundred metre athletic track.

With the help of the Angolan army sergeant, who was still with them, Kamau made contact with the local chief and made sure that the camp was seen as a benefit and not a burden to the local economy. The chief was always invited to functions at the camp, such as the finals of the football or rugby competitions, which he much enjoyed. Most of the Cuban instructors actually welcomed the changes that Kamau and Zuma had wrought, they just got on with their jobs, mostly very competently and when the time came for them to leave they took their bonuses and left happily. Hernandez was forced to cooperate but he obviously did not like the change of regime and the loss of power it represented as far as he was concerned.

Roux had radioed Hernandez impatiently once or twice to ask what was going on.

"You will have to be patient, Senor Colonel Roux," he was told. "I am making my plans and the pair will be delivered as I promised."

Zuma had listened regularly to the frequencies given by Carvalho, but to no avail. On more than one occasion he was sure there had been a call that he had missed.

During their regular weekly calls to Carvalho in Luanda he confirmed that calls had come through but they had not been able to trace them.

Eventually Zuma found six trainees that he trusted implicitly and they undertook to man the radio on a permanent round the clock basis. He made certain that none of the Cubans were aware of the activity.

After two months they intercepted a very unusual call.

One of the trainees was reading a magazine and wondering what all the fuss was about, since neither he, nor any of his colleagues had heard anything but a crackling sound coming from the radio. Still, they liked and trusted Kamau and Zuma, so they went on manning the radio in an uncomplaining fashion. Then one night after midnight the radio suddenly crackled to life and he heard a conversation that made his eyes almost pop out of his head.

Once the call signals had been dispensed with he heard a very South African voice talking to none other than Colonel Hernandez, who was only a few doors away. He kicked one of his colleagues awake and told him to fetch Zuma.

A very sleepy Zuma emerged, who suddenly became fully alert when he heard Roux's voice.

"I hear that the regime in the camp is rather more disciplined than before," said Roux.

"As always, the Senor Colonel is very well informed. Yes, your friends have put their stamp on the place. Everything you told me about them has come to pass. As you know, I saw no value in training people who would immediately fall into your hands so we deliberately ran a rather lax regime. It gave us plenty of time for hunting and such like. Nothing like that any more; we start with a run at five a.m., if you can believe it. I can assure you that I am very much motivated to return to the more leisurely arrangements we had in the past."

"How are you going to do that, and when will you let me have the list of the trainees in the camp?" Asked Roux impatiently.

"Patience, Senor Colonel. I have not yet heard that the money is safely in my Swiss bank account. I have the lists, though, and will give you the first fifty tonight," responded Hernandez.

Then to their horror Zuma and the two trainees heard Hernandez read out fifty names of trainees in the camp, together with their addresses in South Africa and the names of next of kin.

"Quick, get Colonel Lawrence," whispered Zuma to one of the trainees.

When Kamau arrived they just sat there in stunned silence as Hernandez virtually handed out a death sentence to fifty of what Kamau now thought of as his precious trainees.

"Good," Roux grunted. "What about Lawrence and Zuma?"

"Ah, that will be more difficult," said Hernandez, "but I have arranged with some of my colleagues for a helicopter to be available to take them to the south, as we discussed, when I have captured them."

"And when will you capture them?" said an obviously impatient Roux.

"Patience, my dear Colonel, patience. But I think that we will have an opportunity within the next few weeks. Our gallant commandant," he said sarcastically, "has arranged a field firing exercise some way from here, in fact halfway to the south and the whole camp is going. I and a few of my Cuban colleagues will capture them and bundle them into the helicopter and send them on to you. I will radio the details when I can."

Roux grunted.

"We will talk next week then?" he said.

"Yes," answered Hernandez.

Kamau, Zuma and the two trainees just sat there for ten minutes in stunned silence.

"Nothing is to be said to anyone about this," Kamau eventually broke the silence, and to Zuma, "We can get the bastard before he does any more damage; somehow we have to get the lists that he has and replace them with others that will just lead the South Africans astray."

"What about the field exercise?" asked Zuma.

"That will go on as planned," answered Kamau. "We will get Hernandez, his colleagues here and any other bastards in the Cuban military who want to play this sort of game. I am going into Luanda shortly and I will fully brief Carvalho. I am sure that we can arrange a very unpleasant surprise for Hernandez and his friends."

Much to Kamau's surprise, Hernandez asked him if he and his family could accompany Kamau on his proposed trip to Luanda.

Kamau agreed; in fact it suited both him and Zuma; they needed to find a way of gaining access to Hernandez' house without him knowing.

So within a few days Kamau, Hernandez together with his wife and two young children went to Luanda in the Angolan army truck that had brought them to camp Tambo in the first place. The Angolan army sergeant insisted on accompanying them with two of his men; by now he was a confirmed fan of Kamau's, and he almost dogged his every footstep. Apart from the way Kamau handled the responsibility of running the camp, the sergeant had been given much kudos in the local district with his tribe, since Kamau had seen to it that the local people had benefited from the existence of the camp.

Kamau dropped Hernandez and his family off at a place near the Cuban military base and drove into town.

He and the sergeant had found a way to communicate over the previous few months.

"The Colonel must be very careful with that hyaena, he will kill you if he can," said the sergeant.

"Why do you say that?" asked Kamau.

"There are rumours going around the camp that he has a plan to capture you and then kill you."

"What rumours?" asked Kamau sharply.

"One of the Cubans he come to me and told me."

"Which one?"

The sergeant identified the person.

Kamau smiled. "You are right, we need to watch out."

Kamau spent two days with Colonel Carvalho, basically planning the field exercise of his trainees with some elements of the Angolan army.

They also dealt with the threat from Hernandez.

"Why don't we just go and pick him up and then shoot him?" asked Carvalho.

"Well, we could, but I think that this conspiracy goes further than just Hernandez. I want all of them, including some of the people here who can authorize the use of a helicopter for such nefarious purposes."

"O.K." said Carvalho. "I will brief my commanders, and they will expect some orders from you. Best of luck."

"You won't be there?" asked Kamau.

"Maybe not," was the evasive answer.

Kamau feigned surprise when he picked up Hernandez without his wife and children.

"They will stay with friends for a few weeks," said Hernandez. "They will come back after the field exercise."

"This snake is planning something big," said the Angolan army sergeant to Kamau when Hernandez was out of sight. "This is what the Cuban told me would happen."

When they returned to camp, Zuma told Kamau that he had found Hernandez' radio transmitter in the roof of his cottage. He had managed to replace the list that was found next to the transmitter with one that looked the same but contained false information. They had taken the trouble to ensure that all the little marks that Hernandez had made on the list looked the same.

A few days before they were all due to take off for the field exercise in Central Angola they intercepted another call from Roux to Hernandez.

This time Hernandez gave Roux another fifty names; false ones as it turned out. He then proceeded to give Roux details of the field exercise and how they were to capture Kamau and Zuma.

"They are not suspicious at all?" asked Roux.

"No. We are getting along famously," answered Hernandez. "I even went to Luanda with him last week."

The call was finished off by giving map coordinates for the pickup point where Hernandez expected to drop off Kamau and Zuma. Kamau made a note to pass the information on to Carvalho.

In great excitement the convoy, made up of trucks provided by the Angolan Army, wound its way out of the gates of the camp. For most of the trainees it was the first time they had been allowed to leave the camp since their arrival five months earlier. There were about forty vehicles in the convoy. Kamau had made sure that Hernandez was not too carefully monitored, so that he would have a chance to sneak his heavy transmitter onto the truck in which most of the Cubans were travelling. He did notice that there was a truck backed up to Hernandez' cottage. He also made sure that their own transmitter accompanied them and was in good working order.

It took three days to find their way to a very remote location some three hundred kilometres east of Huambo. They were camped near a river in tents, provided by the Angolan army.

Despite the fact that Kamau knew that there was to be a showdown with Hernandez, he really enjoyed the remoteness of the camp and the exercises went very well into the bargain. As far as he was concerned he had inherited a group of raw, mismanaged recruits and in a few months had made them into a cohesive unit, which would give a good account of themselves in any circumstances. Now he had to deal with the unpleasantness of Hernandez, which he knew he would do with absolute ruthlessness; he just hoped that not too many innocent bystanders would get hurt.

On the second night at the camp they intercepted a very brief call from Roux, which confirmed their present position and the date, time and place of the pick-up for Zuma and Kamau. "And you have not forgotten me, have you Senor Colonel Roux? My wife is already on her way to Europe; I need to escape this place as well."

"Of course we have arranged to pick you up as well, Colonel Hernandez. I look forward to seeing you face to face in Pretoria and treating you to a good meal."

Kamau was almost certain that Hernandez and his cronies would strike on the last night before their scheduled departure for camp Tambo. This had been arranged as a party night and the Cubans had promised them all something special. Both Kamau and Zuma had to pretend to participate but they made certain that the Angolan Army sergeant and his men had been fully briefed, as well as thirty five of the trainees; they were all secluded in a spot well away from the festivities. Every time Hernandez or one of his people came and filled up a glass for either Zuma or Kamau, they made sure that they tipped the contents away behind a bush and they ate only their own food. The rest of the troops were not so fortunate, and Kamau could see that from as early as 11pm they were collapsing all over the camp. Kamau was sure that none of them would have much more than a sore head in the morning, and all they had been given was a sleeping draught that would keep them out of action for a few hours. So just after midnight Kamau made his apologies to Hernandez, said something about feeling a bit woozy and made his way back to his tent. Kamau primed a number of flares, made certain that his twenty men all had their weapons fully functioning and that they all had clear fields of fire. Zuma had taken another twenty men to the clearing, which was destined to be the pick-up-point for the helicopter. He also primed some flares and made sure that each of his men was fully prepared. He had unearthed a fearsome looking anti-tank weapon, which he had tested once with great effect on a Baobab tree. He thought that if the helicopter showed any chance of getting away he would have the last say with the anti-tank weapon.

They waited and waited and then at the very darkest moment of the night, just when Kamau had thought that nothing was going to happen, there was a slight movement in front of him. He hoped that his men had seen the movement; they had all been told to hold fire until the flare went up and then to keep firing until there was nothing left to shoot at. In the darkness Kamau became aware of many figures surrounding his tent, which was no more than twenty yards away. He pulled the wire, which shot the flare up into the air. There were at least fifteen men surrounding his tent, and as soon as the flare went up Kamau and his colleagues put up a murderous fire. Almost all the men around the tent were caught in the first burst. Kamau put up another flare and instructed three of his men to go forward and investigate; most of the insurgents were dead with one or two badly wounded. There was no sign of Hernandez though. Kamau left ten men to collect the bodies and took the others cautiously through the still sleeping camp to where the Cubans had their tents. It was almost deserted; there were three or four very sleepy Cubans who had obviously played no part in the attempted abduction. Kamau left two of his men to guard them. There was still no sign of Hernandez.

Zuma heard the firing from where Kamau had ambushed the attempted kidnappers. He quietly moved among his men. "Keep quiet until I tell you to fire and not one second before. They may try to gather here just before the helicopter arrives. Let them light their fires and flares. I want the helicopter on the ground and then we can capture all the treasonous bastards involved in this nonsense."

So they waited and waited. Kamau for his part knew that Zuma would have his area under control and spent the time scouring the encampment looking for Hernandez, with no luck.

Just as the sky started to lighten up in the east they heard the sound of a helicopter coming in over the trees to a spot more than five hundred yards away where a flare had just illuminated the sky.

"Shit" yelled Zuma and then he had an idea. So he sent up his own flare.

"That should confuse the bastards," he said to no one in particular.

It did. The helicopter was seen to hesitate, then the engines revved up again and the helicopter was seen briefly through the trees quickly gaining height.

Some of Zuma's men fired a few shots in the general direction of the machine, but by that time it had moved away and the shots flew uselessly into the air. Zuma thought of using his anti-tank weapon but decided that it would be wasted and in any event he was short of ammunition for it.

He gathered up the men and quickly went back to the camp. He found Kamau.

"Any sign of Hernandez? The 'copter did not land so he must be somewhere around here, unless you shot him in that first burst of fire," said Zuma.

"No, we have not seen anything of him, he left the dirty work to his mates, most of whom are dead or wounded," answered Kamau.

"We had better protect the vehicles," said Zuma. "That will be his next avenue of escape."

"I just did," said Kamau. Then they heard the sound of a vehicle racing away, but from the opposite side of the camp from where they had parked the convoy.

"He really thought of everything didn't he," said an exasperated Kamau.

"He is not getting away with this," said Zuma heatedly. "I am going after him."

Kamau thought for a second.

"O.K., you go. Take two trucks and fifteen men and make sure that you are prepared for a long chase."

An hour later two well-prepared vehicles under the command of Zuma started to give chase; they had enough fuel for a week and food for a few days. Kamau said he would inform the Angolan army what was going on.

Far to the south Colonel Carvalho was talking to the head of an artillery unit there. He had given him the coordinates for the helicopter pick up planned by Hernandez. "You will see a helicopter coming in from the south and then one from the north; I want you to plaster the area with as much high explosive as you can when they land."

The man looked dubious. "As soon as we start pounding them we get it back, very accurately within about fifteen minutes," he said. "If we don't move the guns immediately we will all be blown to pieces."

"This is important," Said Carvalho. "As soon as we see the helicopter, give them all you can for seven or eight minutes and then get the hell out of here."

"Si, Senor Colonel," said the man and he proceeded to give instructions.

Carvalho kept watch through his binoculars and then just before ten in the morning, as Kamau told him it would, a helicopter came into view as a speck on the horizon and then disappeared among some trees.

"O.K." he said, "that is it; give it your best shot."

The artillery-man barked some instructions and each of the ten 105MM howitzers he had under his control thundered away. They were told to fire five shells each and then withdraw a kilometre away. The men needed no encouragement. They fired their five shots and then quickly withdrew to another prepared position.

Carvalho from his jeep saw where all the shells struck; initially there was no other sign.

"Ah well," he thought, "at least we will have given them a very bad fright."

Then he saw a plume of smoke as if from the fuel tank of an aeroplane or helicopter.

"Got you, you bastards," he thought.

There was no helicopter from the north, but then he didn't expect one.

In his basement office in Pretoria, Roux was trying to piece together what had happened.

On the one hand he had the military yelling at him that they had told him the pick-up point was too close to the front line and now their worst fears had been realised and they had lost a helicopter and one of their best crews. He had been told that no sooner had the 'copter landed than a ton of shells had followed it in. "They were waiting for us, they seemed to know exactly where to put the barrage down."

He had been frantically trying to contact Hernandez and only in the last few minutes had had a very brief contact with him.

"They were waiting for us, Senor Colonel Roux; I am now trying to escape into Zambia in a truck. We had it all planned and we had drugged the whole contingent, but they were waiting for us and we were shot to pieces. I am escaping with five of my brave compatriots. You may not hear from me again." The contact was broken but Zuma had heard it and he redoubled his efforts.

Zuma gave up the chase after three days when it was evident that his quarry had escaped over the border into Zambia.

He made his way back to their encampment, where two of the trainees were waiting to tell them that Kamau had packed up the camp and had made his way back to camp Tambo and that they were to follow.

Months later a forlorn group of Cubans was picked up in the remote northern Transvaal, they had a garbled story about escaping from Angola. They insisted on being taken to see 'Senor Colonel Roux,' who actually was not at all pleased to see them.

Kamau in the meanwhile had handed over his responsibilities to Zuma at camp Tambo and was back in London, determined to expose Trevor.

Chapter 17

Kamau's expectation was that he would present his report to the leadership on his way through Lusaka and then go back to London and continue with the legal work that he had so briefly started. He was still passionately committed to the ANC objective of ridding South Africa of its oppressive government.

His feelings when he went back to Lusaka were of satisfaction that he had really cleaned up a very bad facility, which had been feeding raw, poorly trained recruits straight into the arms of a ruthless and well-trained enemy. Almost all of these previous recruits had been killed within days of returning to their homeland and most of them had had no idea what hit them. He also had a feeling of frustration in that Hernandez had got away, presumably to haunt him another day, and Roux was still an ever-present danger. And there was the cancer of Trevor. Kamau and Zuma had no doubt that Trevor had somehow put them in harm's way, and although his objective of eliminating both Zuma and Kamau had not come to fruition, Trevor was still in place and would undoubtedly try again sometime. Kamau was therefore determined to speak his mind in Lusaka and try to have Trevor removed.

During his discussions with the leadership they made all the right noises and congratulated him on a job well done, but he was left with a feeling of insincerity; it was almost as if they wished he had not been quite so successful. Many asides were spoken in Zulu and Xhosa, which Kamau understood quite well, unbeknown to the hierarchy. All they saw was this too clever coloured man from Kenya of all places, who seemed to be totally committed to their cause but who was not really one of them. Kamau smiled to himself at one of the disparaging comments. He was almost tempted to say a few words in Zulu, to embarrass them, but decided it was in his own best interests to keep his own council and see what transpired.

After the interview was over Kamau asked if he could raise one other important point and was told: "Yes, but we actually have another critical assignment for you, before you return to assisting us with our legal issues in London."

All Kamau did was to raise an eyebrow.

There was another aside, this time in Xhosa, and another man was ushered into the room.

Kamau had gathered that the assignment was a major target in South Africa somewhere.

"There are some major dams along the Orange and Vaal rivers," he was told vaguely.

"And a storage dam high up in the Drakensberg, near the source of the Orange, which releases water to the dams lower down when there is a shortage or a drought," added Kamau.

The men round the table looked at him with a mixture of admiration and distaste. He really was too clever for his own good, said some of the expressions. Kamau sensed the hostility but was tired of constantly pandering to their sensibilities and he went on:

"So what is the assignment?"

"Well, blow up the dams," he was told. Then the man who had been brought in went into some detail about what was wanted and the resources that he thought Kamau would need. The briefing was impressive and very thorough.

"When?" asked Kamau.

"The best time is after the rains, in say April or May when all the dams are full and there is no prospect of them being filled up for another six months," he was told.

"Maybe August or September would be even better," said Kamau. "Then there would also be no prospect of any of the dams being repaired before the rain starts again."

"Yes, but they would have the use of the water during the dry season. It would probably be better that it is done early and if they repair the dams, maybe we could blow them up again," was the thoughtful reply.

"We will not be able to do it twice," said Kamau. "Once we blow up a facility, their security will make it very difficult for us to get near those targets again."

The debate went round the table and most of the leadership forgot their hostility to Kamau and enjoyed the discussion, which resulted in a very good outcome: they would blow up the smaller storage dams high in the mountains of the eastern Orange Free State in the early part of the dry season and then concentrate on the larger ones in August.

Although he was aware of the danger, the prospect of such an assignment really excited Kamau and he soon immersed himself in the details.

"I must have Zuma," announced Kamau.

"No," he was told firmly. "Zuma will stay in Angola: that place is now under control for the first time in years and we cannot afford to compromise that again."

Kamau saw the sense in that and then carefully nominated eleven men, all of whom he had trained in Angola. They were a mixture of Zulu, Xhosa, Tswana, Sotho and two coloured men from the Cape. Some eyebrows were raised at the inclusion of the latter but nothing was said. Kamau had chosen them all for the various competencies they each had. One was an expert on explosives, another was a very good mechanic and so on. He was also determined, where possible, to have a mix of different people in the group since they might need help from different communities once they were on the ground in South Africa.

The discussion took some hours and when Kamau was satisfied that he had every detail attended to, the group relaxed and the man who had briefed them was ushered out.

"You had another issue that you wanted to raise with us?" said one of the leadership. They all looked at Kamau inquiringly, completely unprepared for the bombshell he was about to drop on them. Some of them had softened their attitude towards him, as a result of the previous discussion, and they were thankful for his very thorough approach.

Kamau wondered if he should say anything, then he thought: "I have to; Trevor has been stealing from the organisation and he is a double agent and has deliberately put Zuma and me in danger."

"It is about Trevor Mdantsane," he said.

There were some uneasy glances around the room.

"I will show you all the evidence that I have," said Kamau, "I know that Trevor has been with the organisation for a long time."

"And he has served us faithfully and well," chimed in one of the men, emphatically.

Kamau looked around; all he could see was a number of now very closed faces. "This is not going to be easy," he thought.

"I am afraid to tell you that I have evidence here that Trevor has been acting as an agent for the South African Government," said Kamau. There was a sharp intake of breath and then silence.

"He has also been stealing from the ANC; he has acquired a number of flats in London, all financed with our money."

Still nothing was said. There were looks of stunned disbelief on the faces of the six people in the room, who represented the highest echelons of the organisation.

"He also deliberately put Zuma and me in the way of the South African security services."

There was a silence for almost a minute.

"These are very serious allegations; what evidence do you have?" said a very angry voice.

Kamau produced copies of all the documents that Zuma had found and he went through them in detail.

"How do you know these are not forgeries?" he was asked.

"I have the originals," was Kamau's answer. "I also have a report from the law firm I work for in Lincoln's Inn. They say the evidence is incontrovertible and he would be convicted of fraud in a court in the UK if it was ever presented." He gave them a copy of the report.

"What about this nonsense that he is a double agent?" asked another hostile voice.

"This payment made from a Swiss bank account some years ago the only possible source is the South African security people," said Kamau reasonably. "There is no other possible explanation. Has he ever told any of you that he owns at least six flats in London? If these properties were acquired legitimately you would all know about them. I doubt if he has ever mentioned them."

There was silence.

"This is all nonsense," said one of the men angrily. "Why are you saying these things?"

"Because they are true," it was now Kamau's turn to be angry. "I risk my life every day for this organisation, and I am about to do it again. This man wants me and Zuma dead and if he gets to hear about the operation we are about to embark on, I have no doubt that there will be a reception committee on the other side of the border waiting."

Everyone in the room looked uneasy.

"Why do you say that he put you and Zuma in harm's way?" he was asked.

"He knew that there was a problem there in the Angolan camp. The previous commandant had been murdered, we now know by Colonel Hernandez, and he hoped that we would suffer the same fate. Luckily we got wise to his trickery and were prepared for the trouble when it occurred. I have told you about the radio contact between Roux in Pretoria and Hernandez. It would be just as easy to have similar contact with Trevor in London."

"This is just fantasy," said one of the men. "I have had enough of this." He made a move to leave.

"Sit," he was told by the leader. "This is a serious matter; evidence has been produced; what are we going to do?"

"You should have his office and his flat in London searched," said Kamau. "I think that you will be surprised what you might find."

There was another silence. People looked uneasily around. There were signs that they wanted him to leave.

"We will look into the matter," he was told rather lamely. "Please leave your evidence with us, and the best of luck for your venture. We need those dams blown up."

Kamau stood up to leave. He was very unhappy with the response.

"I suggest that you ask Zuma what he thinks; if you don't believe me ask him," said Kamau.

The response was a stunned and hostile silence.

April was still five months away, so Kamau returned to London and his duties with the firm of solicitors in Lincoln's Inn. He had some contact with Trevor and when he did, Trevor was all charm and smiles. He always mentioned the good job that Kamau had done in the camp in Angola and said how pleased they, the hierarchy of the ANC, were with the progress that Zuma was making. Trevor never mentioned any knowledge of Kamau's assignment to South Africa during the dry winter period, but gave him many assignments that would take him until long past the time when he needed to go to the south.

During his stint in London Kamau was able to attend Rita's wedding, where he was asked to give the bride away. Rita looked stunning in her white wedding dress and Kamau was impressed with her husband, who seemed to have his feet on the ground and clearly understood what he was getting himself into. Kamau was greeted like a long lost relative by Rita's parents, whom he met for the first time at the wedding; they obviously thought that he was some sort of saviour as far as their daughter was concerned. The fact that he could converse with them in Afrikaans was a great relief to them as well; whilst they spoke some English they were less than fluent in the language and struggled to converse with their new in-laws.

In early March Kamau flew out to a training facility on the outskirts of Lusaka, where the men he had chosen were gathered. There he had planned to complete a final month's worth of training and briefing. He had finally persuaded the hierarchy that Zuma should be made available to him for this month. Between them they created a very close knit team, with early morning runs at five a.m. in bare feet, intensive weapons and explosives training, as well as living together for the whole month and making certain that every team member knew what his job was and how he fitted into the team. They built up total trust in one another, partly created previously during the basic training in the camp in Angola and then reinforced at this facility. Kamau had chosen well and the team worked together like a dream.

There was a great deal of concern in Kamau's mind in regard to the security of the operation and he and Zuma discussed this at length.

"Did they talk to you about the evidence I gave them about Trevor?" asked Kamau when they were alone one evening.

Zuma nodded.

"Yes, briefly; I told them that it was our view that Trevor had been stealing from the ANC for years and that it was likely that he was an agent for the South Africans. I said that he had put our lives at risk and that if they were not prepared to deal with the issue, they should be aware that others probably would."

Kamau smiled. "And the response to that?"

"They said I should be careful what I said, that Trevor had been a trusted servant of the organisation for many years and in their view the matter needed further investigation. I also asked them, if that was the case, what they had done in the intervening months since you had presented them with evidence."

"And then?" asked Kamau.

"They said they were at present further investigating the evidence and that I should keep quiet," was the response from Zuma. He added: "It was almost as if I had done something wrong. We are the people who have been wronged; I do not like this at all. You should be very careful who knows about your plans and where you are going to make the crossing into South Africa."

Kamau grinned. "They all think they know that I am crossing the Molopo on April 3rd just after midnight. I have no intention of being anywhere near there on that date; by then we will have split up into groups of two or three and I have arranged safe houses from our crossing from Botswana near Parr's Halt in the Northern Transvaal all the way through to the Free State. That is actually all I have been doing for the past few months. It is clear that the hierarchy are at best unreliable. When I saw them in Lusaka it was obvious that they had no intention of doing anything about Trevor, so I have made my own arrangements. I will blow up the dams, but in my own time and in the order I choose. I have also sent in my own supply of high explosive and it is being stored in a cave in the Drakensberg, just inside Lesotho. What you can do is to confirm with the leadership that the plans we arranged all those months ago are now firmly in place. That should keep them happy."

A week before the training camp was officially complete, Kamau gathered all his men together.

"We are now going on our journey. You will tell not one other person where or how we are travelling; if you do I will shoot you. It is very important that this operation succeed, and to succeed we will have to be very flexible and we may have to change our plans frequently."

Each man had an AK 47 rifle and a hundred rounds of ammunition. They were all dressed in army gear with proper boots and a rucksack each. This was for the first part of the journey. Once they arrived in South Africa they would all be given civilian clothes and a suitcase and of course each of the blacks in the group would be issued with a much used pass of the type that all blacks were required to carry at all times. Each man was also given a thousand Rand in cash. Kamau felt that he could trust them all and that none of his trusted accomplices would do anything with the cash that would draw attention to themselves.

A Zambian Army truck was waiting.

"How did you manage that?" asked Zuma, indicating the truck.

"Influence, and of course personal charm." Kamau smiled.

Zuma looked surprised.

"When you arrive in Lusaka please just tell them that all the plans are in hand and I will let them know if I need any help." Kamau was talking to Zuma. They embraced warmly.

"You have some more tricks up your sleeve, don't you?" asked Zuma.

"Of course," said Kamau, but then I always do."

They dropped Zuma off at a point where he could either catch a train or cadge a lift back to Lusaka.

He was due to spend a week in Lusaka and then return to his post in Angola. He was not actually due back in Lusaka for a few days and he had plans of his own.

Colonel Roux in his basement office in Pretoria had had a very frustrating few months.

During one of his infrequent calls to Trevor in London he had learnt that Kamau was due to come back to South Africa, and that obviously meant trouble. Trevor had promised to tell him how and when Kamau was planning to return. He had not been told what Kamau intended to do, but he decided that although that information would be useful, he would have arrested him prior to anything happening so it was a lower priority.

He decided to make a further attempt to contact Trevor.

Much to his surprise the phone was picked up almost immediately. "Hogs Back" was the answer and as soon as Roux gave his own call sign of "Maclear," Trevor said: "April 3rd Molopo," and gave some map coordinates. Roux wrote all that down. Then Trevor said: "I think that I am in trouble here; someone has tumbled to this scheme and I am in trouble. The best chance is that we suspend operations for at least two years; after that you can call me again here. I am sure I will have sorted the problem out by then." The phone was put down and when Roux tried to phone back there was an engaged signal. A few days later he received a discontinued signal when he tried to call Trevor on that line.

Roux had no choice but to follow the lead he'd been given and he commandeered a company of army regulars. April 3rd was just a few days away so he had precious little time. In his briefing to the troops he told them that Kamau was the most wanted man in South Africa and that the country would be put in jeopardy should the man escape. He was asked if the information he had was accurate and reference was made to the loss of the helicopter and its crew in Angola the previous year.

He responded angrily in Afrikaans: "This is the best information we have; I have run this agent now for more than twenty years and all the information he has produced has been accurate. There are only twelve of them crossing over and we have heavy weapons in case they resist, but please, we want them all alive, particularly their leader, this man Kamau."

No mention was made of the fact that he now had no way of contacting his agent.

The company made their way to the area that had been described to them and had five days to reconnoitre. The area was very remote and an ideal place to cross from Botswana to South Africa. The only activity apart from game movements was from the occasional herd of cattle which strayed across the border in search of better grazing amid the sparse grasses and thorn scrub. There were a number of possible crossing points, so Roux and the company commander sent out patrols throughout the area and quickly concluded that in the dark, a small group could with luck slip through any cordon they might be able to establish with a company of one hundred men. Roux did not hesitate; he quickly managed to secure the services of a full brigade from the army depot in Kimberley, this time commanded by a general. "Meneer," the General said to Roux in Afrikaans when he arrived, "this exercise now has a very high profile in Pretoria; your information had better be accurate." There was a steely glint in his eye. Roux took a deep breath and said quietly: "Yes, sir, I understand."

Simon Molofo was twelve years old and he spent some of his time at a school set up by the government in the south of Botswana, not far from the Molopo River, and some of his time herding his father's cattle. He much preferred the latter and he knew, by name, each of the one hundred animals his father owned. On more than one occasion he had chased away a pride of lions and he took considerable satisfaction in looking after the herd. From time to time the family was able to send a few beasts to the meat factory in Lobatse; it took about ten days to trek the animals to the factory. Simon knew that his father received a good price for the animals and he understood that the meat went to Europe under a clever deal, which the government had made with the Europeans. This arrangement made the family quite well off and Simon could see that it was worthwhile to look after the cattle properly. He saw less value in the time he spent at school, but he did acknowledge that it was useful to be able to read the receipts from the factory and understand how much money he was going to put in the bank for his father, who could not read or write.

His knowledge of the area surrounding his father's village was extensive and from time to time he allowed the cattle to stray across the border into South Africa, but only after he had made certain that the coast was clear and there was no sign of the infrequent South African patrols.

On a recent visit to Lobatse with his father, when they had delivered ten of their best and fattest cattle, Simon had been approached by a very big smart looking man. Simon thought he was from the north, perhaps a Kalanga from Francistown, since the man had a very black skin, whereas his own people were a light brown like the Kalahari Desert they lived in. The man had told him that some, perhaps many, South African soldiers would be coming to a place across the border from his village and that he, Simon should give them an envelope, which the man handed him, to one of the soldiers when they came. The man gave him fifty Pula {about fifty US dollars at that time] and said that next time he was in Lobatse, if the envelope was delivered properly he, Simon, would get another fifty Pula.

Simon thought about this for a while and decided that he would not tell his father and on the day mentioned or the day after he would go across the border, and if the soldiers were there he would give them the envelope.

On the evening of April 3rd Roux and the general briefed the troops and told them that if at all possible, the people coming across the border should be captured rather than killed, but that none of them should be allowed to escape. All one thousand troops were deployed in predetermined positions in the border area.

"This time he will not escape," thought Roux to himself.

He went back to the local headquarter tent to await developments. They waited all night and then all day the next day and then all night on April 4th. Roux was beside himself with fury and humiliation.

Simon Molofo had slipped across the border during the day on April 3rd and had watched the soldiers from various hideouts that he had used during his own incursions across the border. He was reluctant to approach the soldiers since he did not know what they would do to him; he doubted that any of them would speak his language and he did not want to get into trouble. He started to follow, at a safe distance, a small patrol until he became used to their pattern. His hope was that he could put the envelope in the pocket of one of the soldiers when they were asleep, but to start with they kept a very strict watch and he could not get near them. On the second night towards dawn in the very darkest part of the night Simon crept up to the patrol. This time they were all asleep; they had had a very tiring two days with no sign of the enemy and they were bored as well as tired. Simon crept up to the man on the edge of the group of five and carefully placed the envelope on his rucksack with a small stone to weigh it down so it could not possibly be missed. He then started to creep away, but there was a rifle propped up against a tree, just yards from the fire. Simon hesitated but it was too tempting, so he nipped over and grabbed the rifle and ran, and in so doing he kicked over a billy-can of cold tea, which made a terrifying noise and woke the small patrol up.

Simon ran about one hundred yards to an old ant-bear hole in which he had been hiding and waited a few seconds. The men in the patrol started shooting at everything and nothing, and Simon crept further down the hole. He was thankful for the cover and that he was not walking about, when he might have been hit by a stray bullet. The shooting lasted about ten minutes, with the whole brigade joining in.

"There you are," said Roux to the general as they scrambled out of their respective sleeping bags. "We've got them now."

The shooting eventually stopped. Simon grabbed the rifle he had stolen and ran. He was glad to see that it had a full magazine. He was sure that his father would be pleased with the new acquisition, as it would be used to help keep the lions away from the cattle. Within an hour he was across the border and back home.

The patrol that Simon had disturbed were in a high state of panic; private Gerber was the unfortunate whose rifle had been stolen; he knew he would have to endure at least a month in a military prison, where the regime was harsh to say the least. When the light started to filter through the eastern sky Sergeant Viljoen came across a small envelope placed on his rucksack. The envelope was clearly marked for the attention of Colonel Roux and it gave the map coordinates that had been the centre of their operations. He made a radio call to the headquarters. The patrol was told to double back and report to the headquarters as soon as they could.

Roux was pacing up and down in frustration and the general could not help smirking at Roux's discomfiture. There had obviously been another botched piece of intelligence from their colleagues in the security services and the general was enjoying every minute of Roux's sense of impending failure.

As soon as the patrol arrived, the envelope was delivered to the now shaking hands of Colonel Roux, who tore it open and read, in perfect Afrikaans:

My dear Colonel Roux,

I trust that this note finds you well. I know that the weather in the Molopo is particularly fine at this time of year, with the summer heat having passed on, and the winter not yet having fully arrived.

Unfortunately, I will not be joining you, as had been planned, due to other more pressing engagements. Perhaps another time.

Trevor has turned into a rather unreliable travel agent; perhaps next time we should consider using someone else.

Yours sincerely,
Kamau Lawrence [COL. ANC]

P.S. This note will be delivered by a small boy. If you happen to apprehend him, please do him no harm; he is only a messenger and knows nothing of me.

Roux almost wept as he handed the note to the general, who read it with grim relish.

"Well Colonel," he said unsympathetically, "I hope that you enjoy the music in Pretoria; rather you than me. I will now make plans to get my men out of here and into more productive occupations than chasing fictitious terrorists in the Molopo."

He marched off brusquely and started to give orders.

Zuma reported back to the leadership of the ANC one day before he was actually due. The same group that had seen Kamau ushered him into a meeting room. They were all ashen faced.

Zuma looked about him.

"What's wrong, what's the matter? You all look as if you had seen a ghost or something." He was handed a newspaper cutting from an English daily.

It was a very short article from a few days previous. It read:

'The body, thought to be that of a Mr. Trevor Mdantsane [sometimes known as Simon Molefe] was found hanging from a beam in his garage in the block of flats where he lived in Finsbury Park. Mr. Mdantsane was well known in the area and was believed to own a number of properties in North London. Police expected to confirm the identity of the victim today; they also stated that they did not suspect foul play."

Without a word Zuma handed the article back. He looked grim faced.

There was silence for a few seconds.

Then a small bespectacled man looked at Zuma and said:

"What do you know about this? There were rumours circulating that you have been seen in London in the last few days."

Everyone looked at the man in surprise; Zuma stood up, walked quickly over to him, grabbed him by the front of his shirt and slammed him against the wall. His glasses fell off. Zuma crushed them under his large boot.

"You, stinking son of a thieving jackal, have a few questions to answer me-all of us here actually. Did you tell Trevor of the expedition to the south that Kamau is now leading? If you didn't, perhaps you can tell me why there was a reception committee of more than one thousand South African troops waiting for Kamau at the exact place where he was due to cross, on the exact date that had been set in a meeting in this very room. A meeting that you attended."

The man's feet were about a foot above the ground and he was panting.

Zuma looked at the leader.

"If you do not believe me about the South African troops, phone your friends in the BDF [Botswana Defence Force]; they will confirm what I have just said."

On a signal from the leader a man scurried out.

'Now, just answer the question, instead of making all sorts of unfounded accusations relating to things you know nothing about. Tell me, tell us, did you tell Trevor about the scheme to blow up the dams?"

"I did not tell him about the dams, no," was the evasive answer.

Zuma impatiently slammed him hard against the wall again.

"Did you tell him about where and when Kamau was to cross the border?"

There was silence from the man.

Zuma slammed him even harder again, and the others watched in silent fascination.

"Answer, did you mention the border crossing to Trevor?"

"Yes, I might have done, it was part of another conversation though," squeaked the man.

Zuma dropped him as if he were something unclean. The man crashed to the ground whimpering.

The person who had been sent out came back into the room and nodded.

"I just talked to the BDF; they were notified rather unexpectedly that the South Africans were to hold exercises in the Molopo area from April 1st to 8th. Our contact said it was very unusual; normally they receive at least two months notice of any such activity. Apparently there was a lot of shooting on the morning of April 5th and then the troops all went away very quickly."

"When did you speak to Trevor, son of a piece of hyaena turd?" Zuma toed the man with his large boot, who was now sitting up.

There was no answer.

"Answer!" Bellowed Zuma. They all jumped.

"Maybe early March," was the weak answer.

"I can tell you exactly," said Zuma. "It was February 26th at 10 p.m. here, when everyone else had gone home. 9p.m. in London. And, yes you are right; I had the call monitored in London. I have a recording here, should you wish to listen to it. The only subject of discussion was the crossing point and the date. I have no doubt that Trevor, or whatever his name is passed that information on to the South Africans and that is why they were there."

"Are you trying to tell us that Kamau has been shot or captured?" asked the leader in a weak voice.

Zuma laughed mirthlessly.

"No, I am not; Kamau realised after his conversation here six months ago that you people would do nothing about Trevor, and that somehow Trevor would get to know what the plans were, so I am happy to tell you that he made other arrangements. He went into South Africa a few days before the appointed date and he took a completely different route."

"You mean he disobeyed our explicit instructions?" said another voice.

Zuma went over to the voice, lifted him to his feet and punched him as hard as he could. The man flew across the room and collapsed unconscious against the wall.

"Any more clever comments?" asked Zuma threateningly.

Nobody stirred. Despite their seniority, they were all completely intimidated by the big Zulu. He was one of them, they saw sense in what he said, and none of them could even dream of matching him physically. He did cause deep and lasting resentment though.

"This man," Zuma toed the person who had now admitted telling Trevor about Kamau's expedition, "has admitted treason. He should be executed forthwith; we really cannot tolerate this kind of behaviour." He looked at the leader. "What are you going to do about it?' he asked. "We risk our lives every day; you cannot allow this to go on."

"It is for me to deal with," said the leader quietly, "not you. The matter will be dealt with."

Zuma looked around him.

"There are many brave men out there. Like me, they risk their lives everyday. If this man lives you are betraying the trust of thousands. If you don't do it, you can be sure that someone else will."

"Like Trevor, you mean," said the leader.

Zuma went up to him and looked him in the eye from a few inches away.

"Maybe, maybe like Trevor. He was the worst traitor we have ever seen, and you would do nothing about it."

To his credit the man did not blink.

Zuma pulled out from his pocket a small tape cassette and handed it over to the leader.

"This is all the evidence you will need. I think that you will be very surprised at the conversation. Both participants in the conversation thought they were sending Kamau to his death."

Zuma then excused himself. He waited a few days and then found his own way back to Angola. Months later he was told that a senior member of the leadership in Lusaka had been executed for treason. He wondered. He had his own methods of following up.

The Zambian military vehicle had been persuaded to drop Kamau and his group just a mile out of Kasane, which is where South West Africa's [now

Namibia's] Caprivi Strip, Zambia, Botswana, and Rhodesia [now Zimbabwe] all meet. Once they had unloaded they made their way east and south and came across a small Zambian army post whose job it was to monitor the military activity on the Rhodesian side of the border. Kamau had a bit of explaining to do to establish his credentials but once that was done the Zambians were very helpful.

There were talks going on in London at that very moment, which would lead, within months, to elections and independence for the new nation of Zimbabwe. The Zambians said that as a result of that the military activity both from the Rhodesians and from Joshua Nkomo's fighters was at present very low. They thought that crossing the Zambezi and making their way down the eastern side of Botswana would be relatively easy at that time. After spending two days reconnoitring the area the group embarked in two canoes, to which the Zambian military directed them. The canoes had been used by illicit travellers to the south on many other occasions, to cross the strongly flowing Zambezi River, which at that point was about two hundred yards wide. Kamau had decided that it would be too dangerous to attempt the crossing in the dark, so they set off at first light. The group had thought that if they launched the canoes some way up-river from where they intended to disembark on the other side, and paddled hard, they could easily reach their destination.

They had decided that the canoe commanded by Kamau should go first and when they were safely across the other canoe would follow. As soon as Kamau and the five other men guided the canoe into the swirling river, it was clear that they had misjudged and that even with superhuman efforts they were going to land on the other bank at least five hundred yards downstream from where they had intended. Kamau signalled to the men in the other boat to stay where they were, but his signal was misinterpreted and to his horror he saw the other canoe launch itself into the fast flowing river and immediately get into difficulty. Although the river should have been benign at that time of year, since the normal floods that came down from Angola and feed into the Chobe through Botswana should only have arrived in Kasane in July or later, Kamau noticed large tree trunks and other debris swirling down the murky torrent, making it doubly dangerous. If any one fell out of the canoes, apart from being swept away, they could also expect to draw the fatal attention of crocodiles, which abounded, and of course Kamau had warned all his men to be on the look out for hippos which would not take kindly to any human presence in their territory.

Kamau decided that his best hope was to make sure that his own canoe made it to the other shore as safely and quickly as possible, and then he would turn his attention to the second boat. Urging the other five in his boat on as hard as he could they paddled frantically and managed to get their boat into a much calmer backwater. Kamau then glanced round at the other boat, which was completely out of control and appeared to be going round in circles at the whim of the current. He saw that he had one chance and one chance only to save them. He dropped his paddle, tore off his clothes and without any concern for his own safety, dived into the river and swam strongly to the other boat, which was now less than twenty yards away. He struggled through the current and somehow managed to get a hand on the gunwale of the now almost swamped canoe. Willing hands pulled him into the boat and he quickly took charge. Two people were directed to bail the water out of the canoe and the rest of the crew, together with Kamau, paddled in unison and soon managed to get the boat facing downstream and in control again. Within twenty minutes they landed on the south bank of the Zambezi amid a tangle of roots.

The first canoe appeared within minutes, having crept along the bank of the river, keeping out of the current. Kamau looked around him, and hoped that the rest of his hazardous journey did not offer quite such tough challenges as this part had.

Kamau's obvious concern for the safety of the rest of his men further cemented his leadership and none of his men had the slightest doubt from then on as to his credentials.

Kamau made them pull the boats up the bank and hide them in the well-wooded banks of the river. They were now in enemy territory, Ian Smith's Rhodesia, and they knew that they would be given no quarter if they were ever seen by the security forces. Sentries were immediately posted and Kamau and one other went out on patrol to see if there was an obvious way out and if there was any danger. Less than fifty yards from where his men were making a makeshift camp, they found the fresh bootmarks of a patrol. Kamau sent his companion to tell the men not to make any sound and not to light a fire. He waited a few minutes for his companion to return and they carefully followed the trail left by the patrol, stopping every few minutes to listen. Kamau thought that the patrol was only about half an hour ahead of them, moving along a well-worn game trail. Soon the trail meandered its way back towards the river and then they heard voices. They crept up to the source of the voices and saw the patrol, consisting of one white, who was obviously in charge, and four black soldiers. They were camped in precisely the spot that Kamau's group had originally planned to land their canoes. He thought that somehow all the trauma of the crossing had had some purpose and that there must be a God after all, watching over them. After about an hour observing the patrol it was clear that they would not be going any further that day and Kamau and his companion backed off and without a sound they made their way back to their own people.

Having briefed the group, they made certain that the canoes were well hidden and then Kamau led them away from the river. The very last thing he needed was any sort of contact with the Rhodesian security forces, so when they came to the game trail he made all the men take off their boots and walk along the edges of the trail without leaving any marks. After a few minutes they came across another trail branching off and away from the river. After an hour on this trail Kamau allowed boots to be put on again and then, setting a very fast pace, he led them as far as possible from the river in a due south direction. By nightfall they estimated that they might have covered a good fifteen miles and so were well out of range of the patrol they had seen. Exercising caution they only made a small fire, and kept a watch, changing every hour throughout the night.

For the next two days Kamau kept up the furious pace from dawn to dusk, first travelling south and then southwest. Most of the time he directed himself and his men with reference to the sun, but he did have a small compass, to which he referred occasionally.

His intention was to move into Botswana and the main road between Kasane and Nata in Botswana, which had some heavy vehicles travelling on it. The idea was to stop a vehicle and (either willingly or unwillingly) persuade them to give the group a lift.

After four days they saw a plume of dust in the distance and another two hours found them on the edge of the road. Kamau estimated that they were about eighty or so miles south of Kasane, where the road was only about five miles from the border between Rhodesia and Botswana. The road was dirt but had been properly made with a camber and it was metalled with stones that had been rolled into the surface. Vehicles would be travelling at high speed. Two cars went past, which Kamau let go. They would not have room for twelve people. Then he saw a truck barrelling down the road. He stepped out into the road and held up his hand. The truck driver's response was to accelerate, move onto the other side of the road and keep going. This seemed like action based on advice from the police in Kasane; obviously others had used this route and the regular travellers would not stop unless they had to. They then cut down a large tree, which they dragged across the road as a road-block. Kamau hoped that there would be no official vehicles, since that would almost certainly provoke a response from either the military or police, which he could well do without. The first vehicle was travelling north and was a well-equipped Toyota Land Cruiser driven by a white man who had his wife and three small children in the vehicle with him. The driver was was quite unconcerned and offered Kamau's group packets of cigarettes. Kamau took them since to do otherwise would raise suspicion in the man's mind. Kamau explained that the road was being used by "infiltrators" from the north and that he should not stop if at all possible. There was a loud sneeze behind him; the men were obviously finding the situation hilarious and had trouble containing themselves.

"I would not have stopped for you except for the tree," said the man. "The police in Nata told me the same, not to stop for anyone; he did not say that the BDF [Botswana Defence Force] would be on the road."

"The police do not always know all our movements; we have to be flexible," answered Kamau, amid another loud guffaw from behind him.

"Quite," Said the man.

The tree was pulled out of the way and the vehicle allowed to pass.

The next vehicle was driven by a very garrulous black man, who much to the consternation of the group got out of the car he was driving and proceeded to pass the time of day with the few men that were visible.

He was eventually persuaded that he should get on with his journey.

Towards dusk, when Kamau was getting desperate and wondering what his next move should be, he saw the dust trail of a large vehicle, travelling south, which came to a grinding halt just in front of the tree, covering itself and its surroundings with dust.

The African driver knew exactly who and what Kamau was.

"How many?" was all he asked.

"Twelve." Answered Kamau.

"There is room for six at a squeeze in the sleeping quarters at the back. I will want five hundred Rand [about five hundred dollars US at the time] as well," he added.

Kamau contemplated this request. It was better to keep these people sweet. The less they told the authorities the better and if they were able to make money on the side without their employers knowing, they would probably keep quiet. Kamau explained that if he wanted that sort of payment, he would have to take the group within a few miles of the Parrs Halt border crossing with South Africa. The driver nodded and six of the group were squeezed into the vehicle, two in the front and four in the sleeper cab. Amid protests, he made the drivers' two assistants sit on the load. One of the Xhosa in the group, Aaron, was designated as leader of the group. Kamau gave him a map and the money.

"Wait for the rest of us here," he pointed at a place on the map, "do not pay this driver until he has dropped you off and don't let him out of your sight. Any nonsense, just shoot him. We cannot afford any problems at this stage."

He said this within the hearing of the driver. Aaron then took charge. He had a quick word with Kamau and then indicated that one of the assistants should travel inside the cab and one of his group should travel on the load of rather smelly cattle hides with the other assistant. They would all take it in turns to be in the back, and as he explained he did not want the assistants to get ideas and jump off and report them to the authorities.

The truck drove off.

It was almost twelve hours before another suitable vehicle came along. Only one car passed during the night and scooted off when Kamau waved him through the road-block. If nothing arrived within an hour or so of the dawn, Kamau had decided that he would have to go back into the bush, keep quiet for a few days and then try again at another spot. He felt that by now the authorities would have been told of the road-block and while they would not necessarily want to do anything about it immediately, if he continued to flaunt their authority they would certainly take action.

The vehicle was another large truck, this time, much to Kamau's surprise, carrying a load of maize meal from Zambia. Crops must have been good in Zambia if they could afford to export any food at all.

The arrangements were much the same as with the other truck.

When Kamau asked the driver if he had taken other people south, he was answered with a short laugh. "At least one group every month; it is good for us, we can earn many Rands doing this and we also support what you are doing."

"Who owns this truck, and does he know what is going on?" asked Kamau.

"I have a partner, a white man in Gaborone; he knows nothing about these arrangements. It is better that way; he might want to tell the government. I do not think that is a good idea."

Kamau grunted.

By dusk they had arrived at the spot that Kamau had indicated to Aaron on the map. He paid the driver, who with some difficulty turned his big articulated rig around to resume his journey down the main road to Gaborone. He had had to go a hundred miles or more out of his way.

There was no sign of Aaron. They were in a very isolated spot and Kamau knew that the border crossing, which was about ten miles down the road, closed at dusk so the possibility of detection was low. He cocked his AK 47 and fired three shots into the air, a signal that he had agreed with Aaron. There was no response. They waited half an hour and then started to walk along the road towards the border. Every thirty minutes they stopped and fired three shots into the air. They had to duck off into the bush once when a car came past. They walked until midnight. It was obvious to Kamau that there was something amiss, so he sent two of his men back up the road the way they had come and another two on towards the border.

"Don't be seen, under any circumstances. Keep hidden during the day. We will wait here until you return, even if that is a week or more away," he said, and to the two going towards the border post: "Don't get too close. You should be back here within a day at the most. This piece of cloth will tell you where we are. Go now." He tied a piece of dirty old cloth to a thorn bush on the side of the road.

His one remaining companion, Abraham, was slightly older than the rest of his companions and that was why he had kept him back. They took it in turns to keep watch on the road, two hours on and then two hours off under a shady thorn tree where they could try to get some sleep. Abraham was a trained builder and according to him was a very good one. He had joined the ANC because despite his training he could not become a registered builder in "white areas", which comprised at least eighty-five percent of the area of the country and more than ninety-five percent of the economic activity. He always had to work under a "registered builder", who according to the law had to be a white, a coloured or an Indian. Abraham would have liked to start his own building company but that was impossible except in some impoverished homeland. "You could be a registered builder," joked Abraham.

"Yes, but I could not be a partner in a law firm in a 'white' part of town, even if I wanted to," Kamau had responded. Abraham looked at him thoughtfully; he still did not really understand why Kamau had chosen this fight. After all, his country was independent and had been for some time.

They waited a day and a half and the two, now very tired, members of the group that had been sent in the direction of the border post came back empty handed. They collapsed exhausted under the thorn tree that had become their temporary base. Kamau was becoming concerned about supplies, and also the longer they stayed in one place the more likely it was that they would be seen. He suggested to Abraham that he might go off and shoot a buck for the pot and also see if there was any water in the vicinity. Kamau did a four-hour stint on the road and then asked his two other companions to start taking their turn. Abraham returned with a springbok. Petrus and Lucas told Kamau that there was a windmill at the border post and if they were careful they could probably get water there. Kamau did not want to go anywhere near the border post.

After another two days of anxious waiting, at last a very tired and bedraggled group of eight men came in sight.

After a meal and some water, which Abraham had found in a dry river-bed nearby, by digging, Aaron explained that the driver had misled them and had dropped them off about twenty miles from where they were. "We only realised what had happened, when we saw what must have been your truck go past, and then an hour later the same truck returned. Then we started walking and came across the men you sent to find us yesterday."

After a brief discussion Kamau realised that the men needed a break before they embarked on what was to be the most dangerous and difficult part of their journey.

Abraham told the group that when he was out shooting he had seen a farmhouse and a small village, which obviously housed the workers employed on the farm. The group felt that they had no choice and they decided to take a chance and see if they could stay there for a few days to recuperate. When they reached the farmhouse, Davis, a South African Tswana, who spoke the local language, was directed to go and make contact with the people in the village. The rest of the group took cover; Kamau went with Davis but waited out of sight with his gun at the ready in case of trouble.

After a few minutes Davis emerged and waved. All was well; the white owner was away and the group could easily be accommodated for a few days, provided they were all gone by the time the owner returned. They stayed at the village for four days and having paid the people in the village handsomely for their hospitality went on their way, carefully directed by the headman. Kamau spent two weeks guiding the group through the bush in a south-easterly direction. The border was easily negotiated since there was just a small fence; the difficulty lay in the fact that all the land on the South African side of the border was all owned and farmed by somebody, and if they were seen they would certainly attract attention, so they had to walk at night and rest during the day.

Roux was sitting in his office fuming; he had just spent the last two days fruitlessly explaining to the higher-ups that he had no choice but to follow up his leads and try to apprehend Kamau crossing the border. He explained that his contact in London had always supplied reliable information and that there was no reason to believe that what had been supplied on this occasion was any different.

"I have recently been informed that my contact has committed suicide, so there may have been something wrong in the first place, but I was not to know that," he explained.

"Was this the same contact that succeeded in getting our helicopter crew blown up in Angola a few months ago?" he was asked belligerently.

"No sir, it was not, but the people involved, including Colonel Hernandez, came here, and were sent to deal with some explosives that we were told had been stored in the Kimberley area." Roux hesitated; he found it too painful to continue.

"And?" asked the same belligerent voice.

"The information regarding the explosives was correct; unfortunately the site was booby trapped and Hernandez and his people were all blown up and killed."

"These were the Cubans you were looking after?"

"Yes."

The man shrugged; to him a few more or less Cubans in the world did not matter, it was when South Africans were killed or hurt that the politicians came down on them.

Even Roux was slightly taken aback by the man's callous attitude.

"You had better be more careful, we simply cannot waste resources like this in future," he was told and then dismissed.

Danie came in, very excited, and with a note in his hand.

"What is it man, what is it? Can't you see that I am busy?"

Danie ignored him.

"Just in, meneer, just in, our man in Naboomspruit sent us this report, and it says that a farmer just over the border in Botswana found his labourers with a lot of Rands and after much questioning found that these labourers had been looking after a group of twelve terrorists, who crossed the border about a week ago. The man went to the border and found tracks. They disappeared near Naboomspruit, but, meneer, just listen to this, after questioning shopkeepers in Naboomspruit they found that one shop had sold twelve of those cheap cardboard suitcases that the kaffirs all use. It must be the same group."

"When did all this happen?" asked Roux.

"More than a week ago, meneer; our man in Naboomspruit was very careful to check his facts after the instruction you sent out," said Danie helpfully.

Roux almost tore his hair out.

"You do realise, don't you, you stupid fucker, that this group of twelve is almost certainly that coloured baboon Kamau. The timing is right, and now you have let them go running around for a week," shouted Roux

"If the Colonel would give me a minute, I was just coming to that," said Danie defensively. "The Colonel is of course correct, this group is probably Kamau Lawrence; we do know that the group was led by a coloured man whose description fits Lawrence."

"Why has it taken so long to get the report to me?" asked Roux angrily.

"It has not taken so long," was the answer. "I have only had it five minutes myself."

Roux calmed down.

"Those fuckers are in that cess pit of Ga—Rankuwa, [a large black township near Pretoria] I'll bet you," said Roux. "I wonder what they are up to. It must be something big if that coloured baboon is involved. Something involving explosives. Could be any bloody thing." He was almost talking to himself.

Kamau was pleasantly surprised that the long hike through the bush to the outskirts of Naboomspruit was so uneventful.

They managed without trouble to re-equip themselves to appear like civilians and set out in groups of two for the sprawling township of Ga-Rankuwa, where Kamau had set up safe houses for them all. The guns and military uniforms were all in their suitcases so if any of them were searched they would be in trouble, but other than that there was nothing to attract attention to themselves. They just looked like the millions of other migrant workers who had flooded so called "white" South Africa over the past several decades, but particularly since the Second World War. They far outnumbered the whites in every part of South Africa and despite Government propaganda the so-called homelands were just rural slums with no prospects, which were becoming more and more overcrowded as the years went by. Kamau was amazed that the white government could not see any of this, or that they were sitting on a time bomb. "If there was a fully democratic state," he thought to himself, "this situation would have adjusted itself over the years and maybe this conflict would not have been necessary. Anyway, what ever happens I am going to help change all this. South Africa is the land of my father's birth, even though he hates it so much."

They were to spend no more than two or three days in the township and then each group of two had separate plans to make their way to Ladybrand in the Eastern Free State and wait for each other there.

Roux had not been idle.

"Get every fucking operative and informant that we have in that disgusting township and let's find that coloured baboon. I'm going to have to do all this without calling in extra resources. I doubt if they would give me any anyway. We've had a couple of disappointments in the past few months, so they are pissed off at me and probably will not listen. Just to protect my arse I will send this report with 'urgent' written on it to the boss."

"Ja, meneer," said Danie.

The group had strict instructions from Kamau not to leave the safe houses that they been assigned to and in particular not to go to any of the numerous shebeens that abounded in the township. "The police have informers all over the place and that is one of the places that they will go; you will be spotted within minutes of entering a shebeen, so don't do it," he said.

Moses and Jacob were young, they had escaped South Africa at the time of the 1976 riots started by schoolchildren in Soweto, in protest at being made to learn in Afrikaans, the language of the "hated oppressor", and they hadn't returned until this visit. They were really excited by being back home.

After they had found their way to the safe house and had spent one night there, there seemed to be nothing to worry about, it was all very quiet. Jacob said to Moses on the second evening, "I know this place very well; I used to go to school near here, until I escaped in 1976. There was a very small shebeen close by; surely we can just go round there for one beer and then come back. Kamau will never know." Moses needed no second invitation and the pair popped out into the poorly lit street. There were beer cans and other garbage scattered around and the unpaved road had large washaways, making it necessary for the occasional rickety old car to bump its way carefully and slowly along to avoid damage.

"Here, this way," said Jacob, and the pair excitedly went down a side street, found the shebeen and after some discussion with the proprietor were allowed inside. They ordered a Castle Lager and sat down. The shebeen, although just a small township house, was well furnished and had seating for most of the customers. It was crowded and no notice was taken of the pair.

Elias had been a police informer for most of the years since the 1976 riots. He had not been a very bright student and had participated very briefly in the disturbances. The police had arrested him and he had been lightly beaten up. When the police realised that he did not really understand what was going on and had been persuaded to join the riots just so as not to be left out, they ceased the beatings and Elias was very easily persuaded to become an informer. That morning one of the black policemen who kept in touch with him had told him that a particularly dangerous bunch of terrorists had infiltrated the country and were believed to be in Ga-Rankuwa. So Elias was the happy recipient of enough money to visit a number of shebeens in his area. He had been in this particular shebeen for about an hour and as far as he could see, all the customers were regulars. He was about to go when two newcomers entered the place. He could see by the way they behaved that they were not regulars. His instructions were clear; anything suspicious should be reported and quickly. He left as soon as he could, ran to the police station and reported what he had seen. The African sergeant made one call and then he, a constable and Elias returned to the shebeen. They waited in the shadows outside and after not more than twenty minutes Jacob and Moses, who had stuck strictly to their one beer promise, came out and walked back to the safe house. Elias and the police followed carefully in the shadows and when the two went into the house, the sergeant made a call on his police radio. Half an hour later a squad of twelve black police surrounded the house. Without ceremony the sergeant smashed the door down and all the inhabitants were arrested. Jacob and Moses' suitcases were found and searched, and then the game was up. Neither was given a chance to escape. They had been quickly handcuffed and when the search revealed the contents of their suitcases, they were bundled into the police van and taken to security headquarters in Pretoria. There was no ceremony. They were both stripped and first Jacob and then Moses found themselves in front of a blond haired white man with a very ugly scar across the whole of one side of his face.

No questions were asked, but three policemen came in and for fifteen minutes beat each of them mercilessly with sjamboks [Rhino hide whips].

The white man then asked them questions. There were more beatings. It took twenty-four hours and by then Moses was dead and Jacob would die within another day and Roux had the whole story.

"Of course," he muttered to himself. "The fucking dams, why didn't I think of that before?"

Kamau, of course, did not suspect that anything was amiss and he found his way, as did the other pairs, to the black township near Ladybrand, in the Orange Free State, from where he thought that they would enter Lesotho to collect the explosives to blow up the dams.

As they got off the rickety old bus that dropped them off in Ladybrand, Abraham, whom Kamau had chosen as his companion, pointed out what appeared to be an enormous police presence. Kamau quickly took him behind a bus shelter. "I think this is it," said Kamau. "It looks as if they have tumbled to our scheme, but we still have hope, as they do not know what any of you look like. So you, Abraham, must get all the others out of here as quickly as possible and into the mountains in Lesotho. They may catch me, so wait a few weeks and then carry on with the scheme. You have all the maps. Now go."

"What are you going to do?" asked Abraham.

"Try to get on the bus to Bloemfontein, over there," he gesticulated in the direction of another dilapidated bus, "and then I will find my own way into Lesotho. Do not worry about me; just get yourselves into Lesotho as quickly as possible. The only way they could have found out about this scheme is by picking up one of the groups, so if someone is missing leave them; they will be past caring anyway. I will wait here for ten minutes, so get going."

Abraham reluctantly left.

There was a Bloemfontein bus waiting, which would leave within half an hour. Kamau pulled his hat down over his eyes and nonchalantly wandered over to the bus. He left his suitcase where it was. If he was caught, the contents would be no good to him but would provide incriminating evidence.

A black, plain-clothes policeman spoke quietly into a hand-held radio. "I think I have spotted him. Yes I am certain it is him, and he appears to be alone. I think he is getting on to the Bloemfontein bus."

Roux was at the other end of the radio link in a vehicle just out of sight.

"Keep an eye on him; he will lead us to the others; but do not make a move until I tell you. If he gets on the bus you do the same thing-understand?"

"Yes, boss," was the answer.

Kamau purchased a ticket and sat down towards the front of the bus, trying to be as unobtrusive as possible. A few minutes later he noticed a man who was slightly better dressed than most of the other passengers, who came and sat immediately behind him.

"They can't help themselves," he thought, "that must be a policeman."

Kamau decided to move right to the back of the bus and see what the man would do; as soon as he did, the man looked around and then got off the bus for a minute, having spoken to the driver. Kamau decided to get off the bus himself; he had seen the policeman go in one direction, so he went the opposite way and clambered onto another bus in the large bus station. A few minutes later all hell broke loose as about two hundred police came into the dusty depot. All traffic was stopped and the police began a methodical search. Kamau noticed a few people unobtrusively slipping through a hole in the corrugated iron fence and he slowly made his way in that direction. He looked around; there was pandemonium and not much attention was being paid to him, so he quietly slipped through the hole with several others and started to walk away and move into the township. "They have definitely got wind of something," he thought. "I will get out of here while I can."

Unluckily he slipped down a little alleyway, most of which was blocked a police Land Rover with a man frantically giving orders on a two way radio. As he tried to slip past, there was a yell and his worst nightmare was suddenly in front of him with a very large revolver aimed straight at his stomach.

"Hands up! "Yelled a large white policeman in great excitement. Speaking in Afrikaans, he said: "We've been looking for a coloured like you for hours; just back up against the wall there; keep those hands up now."

Kamau was backed up against a wall and the policeman, who appeared to be alone in the vehicle made a desultory effort to frisk him.

"You had better not try anything," he said. "It would give me a great deal of pleasure to put a bullet in you; I'm sick of all these searches."

Kamau remained silent. The last thing he needed was to provoke the man. His main thought was to see if he could get away, or at least keep all the attention onto himself so that his companions could escape into the mountains. Kamau had kept his head down and adopted a pose of complete subservience. "You don't look much like a dangerous terrorist to me," continued the policemen. "Just another drunken coloured, I suppose."

"Ja, meneer colonel," said Kamau in a snivelling tone.

The policeman laughed and his guard came down for a few seconds.

"Look, look at these pips, I am"…he was going to say a mere lieutenant, but instead all that came out was a strangled gurgle as Kamau hit him in the windpipe. Kamau seized his revolver and with it gave him a big whack on the head. The man collapsed, whimpering. Kamau threw the weapon as far away as he could and then ran, out along the alley and further into the seething township. The bus station was no longer an option, by now it would be teeming with police. He would not go near the safe house he had arranged for himself. As he walked further into the dusty, dirty township, he came across a small café and he stopped there and bought himself a coke and a very nasty pie. The African proprietor was quite friendly and kept up a conversation with him, trying both Afrikaans and English. Kamau had not noticed that the proprietor had nipped out to the back of the shop for a few seconds as Kamau was selecting his purchases. The proprietor was quite personable and asked where Kamau was from, to which he answered: "Cape Town." He questioned the proprietor about the number of police in the township and all the fuss at the bus station. "We have always had fuss here," was the answer. "Ever since they sent that Mrs. Mandela to Brandfort for house arrest, so many years ago now there have always been many police here." He laughed. "Actually it is quite good for business."

A small boy came in from the back and called him.

"Excuse me a minute," he said.

There was a lot of whispering in the back and just as Kamau's suspicions were starting to be raised, three large policemen came in the front and another two from the back. Kamau had a pistol stuck in his face and his arms twisted behind his back.

"Got you now," said a rough voice. "We will stay here until Colonel Roux arrives, that is the instruction." One of the police finished off Kamau's coke and another ate his pie.

"This won't be much use to you where you are going," he joked.

Kamau said nothing.

Within ten minutes a police car arrived and none other than Roux leaped out of the front seat. He stormed into the small shop.

"That's him!" he screamed. To Kamau he seemed more unbalanced than the last time he had seen him.

The proprietor stood there beaming.

"I told you it was him," he said proudly.

"Ja, dankie [yes thank you], kaffir," said Roux. "Now let's get this animal [gesticulating at Kamau] in the car and back to Pretoria, where he will be dealt with. I will go with him and you sergeant. I want two vehicles in front and two at the back, and any funny business just shoot him; we have had more than enough trouble from this monkey to last several lifetimes."

Within minutes the convoy set off set off at high speed for Pretoria, with sirens wailing

In the six hours it took them to get back to the capital, Kamau was offered no food and drink. Once, when he wanted to go to the toilet, he was taken off into the bush with three policemen watching him.

They arrived in Pretoria and without ceremony Kamau was dumped in a cell and the door banged shut.

Based on his previous experience in Johannesburg in the hands of Roux, Kamau was expecting very harsh treatment indeed, and this feeling was exacerbated by the personal animosity that now went back many years. So he was surprised to be left alone for more than two days after his capture.

When he was taken into an interrogation room there was just Roux, albeit in a high state of agitation, Danie Visser and Kamau and none of the instruments of torture that had been in evidence before.

Kamau refused to tell them anything.

"I want to be formally charged, I want legal representation, and I want to see the British Ambassador. Otherwise release me. You have absolutely no evidence; if you have, produce it," was all he said over many hours of interrogation.

"We captured some of the people who came across the border with you; we know all about your schemes to blow up the dams in the Free State."

"Produce the evidence; where are these people? I have a valid British passport with a valid entry stamp in it. You have no right to hold me," Kamau said.

"We know that entry stamp is forged," answered Roux.

"Then bring me before a magistrate and charge me," Answered Kamau.

"You will be charged all right, the charges will not be these Mickey Mouse things you suggest, but the charges that I will bring will demand the death penalty," said Roux.

"Then provide the evidence," answered Kamau. "If you can't produce the people that you said came across the border with me, where are they? If you captured them, produce them, otherwise you have no evidence."

"So you admit coming across the border illegally."

"I admit nothing of the sort. Look at my passport."

To his amazement nothing was said about the Molopo incident.

They tried everything apart from physical torture. He was starved for a few days; they tried to keep him awake for more than a week. Kamau could see that Roux was getting more and more frustrated.

In an aside he heard Roux say to Visser. "If they would only let me really interrogate him for two days, we would have everything we need. Then we could hang him."

It was clear that the authorities were preventing Roux from harming Kamau but were prepared to let him continue to interrogate him for as long as he wanted.

A junior official from the British Embassy came to see him after he had been incarcerated for more than three weeks. The man was unsympathetic.

"They say that you entered the country illegally and that you are a wanted terrorist," he told Kamau.

"Then tell them to charge me. What evidence do they have? They have not shown me a thing."

"They say that the entry stamp in your passport is a forgery and that they have no evidence that you entered the country legally."

"Maybe they lost the papers. Have you seen the entry stamp and if so, does it look OK to you?" asked Kamau.

"I have not seen your passport."

"Get me a lawyer; why am I not able to see a lawyer?"

"I'll ask."

"Could you also do me a favour and contact Giles Dingley-Ferris; he will want to know what has happened to me."

The man laughed unpleasantly.

"You really do suffer from delusions don't you? What on earth would such a man want with scum like you? He's white; he's a white Englishman, and a pillar of our society. I am sure that he has no coloured or black members in his family at all. Quite unthinkable."

"His wife is related to my father by marriage, I have been a guest in his house in Belgravia many times and I am sure that when I report this conversation to him, there will be repercussions." Kamau said evenly. Even the representatives of the British in South Africa were racists at heart, he thought.

"Rubbish," was the response. "We do not need people like you causing trouble for our embassy. I will of course report all this to the Ambassador."

Kamau nodded.

"But don't expect much sympathy from us; if people break the law in foreign countries, then they must expect to take the consequences."

"Then tell them to charge me with an offence; so far I have not been charged."

"I expect that you will be, and soon. They think that you may have to face the death penalty."

Kamau remained silent.

There was no activity for a few days and Kamau managed to get a complete night's sleep for the first time in weeks. He saw nothing of Roux and he was still not brought before a court.

A more senior person from the embassy came to see him.

"We did report your arrest to Mr. Dingley-Ferris; to our absolute surprise he said that he knew you very well and that you were an outstanding young man and that he would do anything to have you released."

"So am I to be released or charged?" asked Kamau.

"I don't know, but I do know that Mr. Dingley-Ferris has a powerful influence on events here in this part of the world. You may be surprised at the outcome."

Several more days passed and there was still no sign of Roux. Then one night when Kamau was fast asleep in his cell, he was woken by the noise of his cell door opening and before he knew what was happening he was handcuffed and a hood was put over his head. Some very rough hands yanked him out of the cell; he was dragged up the stairs and found himself in the back seat of a car, which was soon travelling at a high speed.

"Where are we going, what is all this?" he muttered through the bag.

His only response was a fist through the bag, which made him all the more concerned. The South African government did at least make an attempt to operate in a legitimate way; this had all the hallmarks of a completely illegitimate operation.

The car travelled for some hours and Kamau dozed. He was woken when the car bumped its way onto a dirt road, and after another hour or so they came to a sudden stop.

"Get the bastard out of there." It was Roux's voice and he was roughly bundled out of the car. It was quite cold, so he thought they were in the mountains somewhere.

"Put these fucking shoes on, we are going for a walk," he was told.

The hood was removed and he was handcuffed to a very large, rough looking man, wearing a police uniform.

"Any fucking nonsense and it will give me great pleasure to send you into the next world," said the man. "Come with me."

They started walking up a narrow path with Roux and another man following. All three were carrying rucksacks and they were all heavily armed with revolvers and sub-machine guns.

'What are you doing, where are we going," asked Kamau.

The response was a sharp jerk on his handcuffed hand, which unbalanced him and he fell over. He was dragged to his feet again and the journey continued.

Kamau could see that they were in the Drakensberg, and as the dawn came up he thought he recognised the outline of one of the resorts in the mountains. It seemed that they had parked in the hotel car park and had then started walking.

Roux and the others talked about heading for a cave high in the mountains.

"We can give this baboon everything he deserves and when he admits it all, perhaps Pretoria will believe what I tell them," said Roux.

They walked and walked and it was mid-afternoon when Roux said: "Just round the next corner."

There was a large rock a few yards ahead and behind it a spacious, dry cave. Unless one was close to it, the interior of the cave was hidden from view.

"Ideal for a siege," thought Kamau.

He was dragged inside. One man, whom the others called "Oom", was detailed to keep an eye on the prisoner and Roux and "Andries" collected some firewood and water from a nearby stream.

"Tonight we sleep," announced Roux. "Tomorrow, we deal with this monkey here," he indicated Kamau.

Kamau looked around. If he could get out of the cave he was certain that he could outpace the three men. Roux looked as if he was still quite fit, but the other two were older and had puffed and blowed their way up the mountain.

Roux came over and cuffed Kamau across the head.

"I saw you looking around, don't get any ideas. We will shoot you if we have to."

The men cooked themselves a meal, but Kamau was just given a cup of water.

"We will not waste our food on you. We came here to get information, not to feed terrorists," said Andries.

Kamau was handcuffed and had some leg irons put on him. His captors kept as far away as possible. They talked in low voices hoping that Kamau was out of earshot. He kept very still and was able to hear almost every word they said.

"Those idiots in Pretoria, they just do not understand," Roux confided in the other men.

"If I had been allowed to deal with this fellow in the way I wanted, I would have had all the information I needed and then we would have had a case. They said that I could not torture this man because he is a British citizen, and also in the last week or so they said that some high-up in Britain had threatened to withdraw investments from South Africa unless this baboon was charged or released." He waved his hand vaguely in the direction of Kamau's prone body.

"The bloody rooinek British, they are the cause of all the trouble here in the first place. If they had not found diamonds and then, the curse of all mankind, gold, we would have been left alone with our cattle and farms and we would have been able to keep the kaffirs under control in our own way. I don't want any of the rooinek investment here; I wish they would all go away," said Roux. It was one of his favourite themes.

The others made sympathetic noises; for them, Roux was a hero who could do no wrong; his Springbok rugby credentials were sufficient to assure complete loyalty.

Kamau kept still; the man was quite mad and apparently capable of doing anything. He wondered what delights they had in store for him in the morning.

The next day, after a very fitful and disturbed sleep, Kamau woke to find Andries stoking up the fire and making breakfast. He was given another cup of water and they removed his leg irons so that he could go outside to relieve himself.

"After all, we don't want him to piss and shit all over this cave when we start to deal with him; we might be here for a few days yet," said Roux.

Kamau shivered despite himself.

While they were outside a helicopter came over, followed by another one. It seemed clear that they were looking for them. He assumed that the police vehicle had been found in the hotel car park and the mountain would soon be teeming with military and police.

The question was, how to direct them to this place soon enough to rescue him.

Roux and the others were concerned. "I did not think they would find out where we had gone quite so quickly," said Roux. "Never mind, it just means that we will have to sort this traitor out sooner rather than later." He built up the fire, and put two branding irons normally used for cattle in the fire.

"I have never had anyone hold out for long when I use those," he said and grinned his maniacal grin.

They had forgotten to put the leg irons back on Kamau, so he swiftly dashed to where the men had been sleeping picked up two of the sleeping bags they had used and threw them on to the now blazing fire. They immediately caught alight, sending out clouds of smoke, which Kamau thought would waft out of the cave and show up in the clear mountain air, hopefully quickly attracting the rescue party. He then made a move to run out of the cave, while his captors strove to put out the now strongly burning fire. They were all choking on the smoke. As he dashed out of the cave, Andries grabbed his sub-machine gun and in turning and trying to shoot Kamau at the same time, he pulled the trigger too soon and emptied the magazine into Oom's midriff, almost cutting him in half. A look of absolute horror came over Andries' face and in the split second it took him to recover Kamau was out of the cave and running as fast as he could, given that his hands were still handcuffed, down the path, where he hoped that he would soon find the rescuers.

He had not reckoned on Roux. Kamau had only gone about fifty yards when he was rugby tackled from behind. He smashed his face on a stone and Roux pistol-whipped him.

His next memory was being back inside the still smoky cave, with Roux again busy with the branding irons.

Roux dashed some water into Kamau's face. "We need you fully awake for the next phase, Mr fucking Lawrence. You are going to tell me all about your latest little escapade with your friends the ANC. If you tell me now, we can save you much pain. If you won't say anything, I promise that the next few hours will be very painful indeed."

"Confessions given under duress are not legal, even in this country. You are wasting your time. The military will be here soon and you will be on your way to jail. Give yourself up man, be sensible," responded Kamau.

Almost simultaneously there was the sound of a loudspeaker from outside and Roux rushed at Kamau with a red-hot branding iron, yelling at the still very shaken Andries to hold Kamau down. The branding iron grazed Kamau's leg, causing him excruciating pain, but he pushed Roux away, who stumbled toward the fire.

Roux, to Kamau's relief, then grabbed his sub-machine gun and went outside, firing. "I'll deal with these fuckers first and then come back for you; just hold him down, Andries."

As Roux went outside he sprayed a full magazine, from his sub-machine gun all around him.

The man in charge of the security forces was an old friend and colleague who in the past had had a great admiration for Roux, for his prowess on the rugby field and for his police work in the early days.

"Hannes," he said through the loudspeaker in Afrikaans, "this is your friend Kobus Meiring here. Put your gun down and we can talk. You are surrounded and you cannot get away with any more…"

Roux aimed the gun in the direction of the voice and fired another full magazine at the sound.

Meiring tried again. Roux seemed to have an endless supply of ammunition. Meiring's instructions were explicit. "No casualties, but if you have to shoot Roux to achieve that, then so be it."

He put his head in his hands and then called up the sharpshooter. "What a waste, what a fucking waste," he said to himself. "All for a coloured terrorist."

"Take him out," he instructed the sharpshooter, "although my instructions are to kill him, I will not authorise that; there is no need to kill him, just disable him-try to shoot the weapon out of his hands. One shot if possible." He could not bear to watch.

There was one shot from a high-powered rifle and a scream of pain and frustration from Roux. Roux was quickly overpowered, his smashed right arm hanging uselessly and pouring blood. He was placed on a stretcher and carried out of sight.

Meiring picked up the loudspeaker.

"Andries, Oom, come out with your hands up. Leave all the weapons inside the cave and walk very slowly."

A very shaken Andries came out of the cave with his hands high above his head. He was whimpering. "Don't shoot, don't shoot."

"Where is Oom?" demanded Meiring through the loudspeaker.

"Dead, he is dead, in the cave," came the mournful response.

Meiring made a gesture and ten men moved into the cave. They came out less than a minute later with Kamau.

"Oom is dead," they confirmed.

Looking around him Kamau was surprised at the lack of security at the hospital to which he had been taken in Bloemfontein. The chopper had landed in a nearby field and he was now in a private ward, isolated from the rest of the hospital. He supposed that the facility was reserved for whites and the authorities did not want the other occupants to see that they were sharing it with a coloured. There was one young white policeman at the door, the windows were not barred, although the room was on the third floor, it looked to Kamau as if they almost wanted him to escape. He had been told that 'the British' would come and fetch him in a few days.

Kamau felt there was very little wrong with him physically apart from a bruised face and a slight burn on his leg. He could see that Roux would be out of the way and completely discredited. He surmised that the intelligence Roux had gathered which led to his arrest would now be discarded. He felt responsible for the welfare of the people he had brought in from Zambia, and he thought that in all probability the protection of the dams would have now taken a back seat, if indeed the authorities had taken any notice of Roux's reports and requests at all. So he decided to act.

The revolting hospital meal was as usual brought to him at five thirty in the evening. The normal hospital routine was to have a final inspection at about seven and then it was lights out at eight thirty. As soon as the final inspection had been carried out, from the pillows and blankets he made a shape in the bed to look like a sleeping body, dressed himself and climbed out of the window. He eased himself over towards the drainpipe at the corner of the building and climbed down to the ground. The hospital grounds were still busy and not much notice was taken of a lone coloured man in the dark as he nonchalantly wandered out of the complex.

The hospital was in a busy part of the town and Kamau watched for a few minutes having left the hospital grounds and made his way to a small local shopping centre. Soon a white woman came rushing up to a shop in her car and leaving the engine running, charged into the shop opposite. Without hesitating Kamau ran over to the car, leapt into the driving seat and drove off. He was relieved to see that the fuel tank was full. Orientating himself in the city took about half an hour and before ten o'clock he was rapidly covering the one hundred or so kilometres to the border with Lesotho. He abandoned the car in Ladybrand after spending an uncomfortable night trying to get some sleep in it. At five in the morning, having wiped the car clear of all fingerprints, he set out on foot to cover the remaining twenty kilometres to the Lesotho border. He soon managed to thumb a lift and arrived at the busy post just as the first bleary-eyed travellers were making their way past the already bored people manning the post. Kamau watched and waited for a while and then, hoping that he was unseen, nipped into the back of a small pickup truck and covered himself with a tarpaulin. He had determined that the white owner of the vehicle crossed the border at regular intervals and, being well known at the post, would not provoke any kind of a search.

There was no problem on the South African side of the border post but he became really apprehensive when there was an extensive delay on the Lesotho side and some sort of argument took place between the driver of the vehicle and the border guard. The argument subsided and the pick-up went tearing off towards the nearby dusty little city of Maseru, the capital of Lesotho, located in the foothills of the great Drakensberg range, which provided the border between South Africa and the impoverished mountain kingdom. While he was lying underneath the tarpaulin he became aware that there was a very good reason that the driver of the pick-up did not want the border police to search his vehicle. Kamau was sharing the space under the tarpaulin with a quantity of dagga [marijuana]. This meant it was doubly important for him to remove himself, without being seen, from the vehicle. He had no interest in the few kilos of the weed that were in the back of the vehicle, but he had to make certain that the driver was not provoked in some way that would draw attention.

The vehicle stopped, and the driver got out and slammed the door. Kamau then heard footsteps scurrying off into the distance. He peered out; the vehicle appeared to be parked in what passed for the main shopping street of the city. There were almost no people around. Kamau got out and clambered over the tailgate of the vehicle; he had just started walking when there was a yell and he saw the driver of the vehicle running towards him. Kamau needed no second invitation and sprinted away from the scene and around the corner. Kamau waited in a doorway, but there were no further signs of pursuit and he then made his way to the local bus station.

The lady whose car he had stolen in Bloemfontein had thoughtfully left her handbag in the car, with more than five hundred Rand in it, which Kamau had taken.

He hoped the police would assume that the motive for stealing the car was purely theft and would look no further. He established that the daily bus into the mountains south of the capital left at midday, so he went off in search of a store. He needed boots and some warm clothing, and something to eat. It was till too early for the stores to open, but Kamau noticed a Holiday Inn where he knew he could get a meal. As was the case in Botswana and Swaziland, the hotel contained a casino as well as providing accommodation, mainly for visiting South Africans. As he was seated in the dining room, a white man came up to him and said truculently: "You were the bugger that was messing around in my truck this morning; what the hell do you think you were doing?"

Kamau looked at him as if he were completely mad and said in his best Oxford accent: "I beg your pardon, sir. I have not the faintest idea what you are talking about."

The man was slightly taken aback, and showed signs of hesitation and Kamau followed up with: "Your attitude, sir, maybe acceptable over the border, but not here. If you like we can take the matter up with the police; otherwise I suggest that you back off."

The man walked away muttering. Kamau finished his breakfast and scanned the newspapers. There was no mention of him or his escape. He went into town and bought some boots, warm clothing a rucksack and a detailed map and went off in search of the bus.

The bus wound its way slowly through the mountains. From his vantage point at the back, Kamau could see bedraggled villages with some scrawny cattle and a few goats. The country looked barren and overgrazed; there were patches of weedy looking maize growing. He looked at it all in a rather depressed state of mind: "Much of Africa is like this, what do we have to do to improve the situation?" he thought. "This is an independent country, and it seems to be worse off than across the border in South Africa. I suppose like Trevor the leaders expect to steal the country blind once they get into power." He then started to reflect on Trevor and wondered if he were really dead; it seemed too convenient. He had made Zuma promise that he would not take the law into his own hands and there was no fundamental reason that Trevor should take his own life. If he ever returned to England he would make sure that he got to the bottom of the situation.

The bus stopped frequently at all the little villages, with people getting on and off with their myriad possessions, amid much disorganised but good-humoured shouting. Many of the travellers were migratory workers, returning from jobs in South Africa, and were temporarily, at least, comparatively well off with cash in their hands. From a fellow traveller he had determined that he needed to leave the bus at a small village about eighty kilometres from Maseru.

To start with, he was treated with a great deal of suspicion by the villagers, but after a very long discussion the headman, whom he plied with packets of cigarettes, told him he would provide a guide. He knew where Kamau wanted to go but had not heard of any strangers in the area. Kamau avoided any mention of his mission, although he imagined it would have been obvious to the headman that he was connected to the struggle in South Africa. He shared a frugal meal with the headman and his wife; all their children were employed as migratory workers in South Africa and came back to the village once or twice a year. The headman was worried about who would take over his responsibilities in the future. None of the young people had any knowledge or interest in the life of the village, although they provided money from time to time. They conversed in Afrikaans; the headman in his youth had worked on a farm, owned by an Afrikaner, in the nearby inaptly named Orange Free State.

They marched west towards the border, into the remote parts where the land was bare and rocky and there were few villages. One night was spent wrapped up in thin blankets, trying to keep warm with the help of small fire. At about midday on the second day of their trek, there was a crack as a bullet whistled over their heads and from the subsequent report of the gun, Kamau determined that they were being fired on from a vantage point about three hundred yards away. He stood still, assuming that this was a warning shot and that if his assailants had wanted to they could have shot him dead. His companion cowered behind a rock.

After a few minutes Aaron emerged from behind a nearby rock, and Kamau was surrounded by the nine survivors of his expedition. They all grasped Kamau excitedly by the hand and started to talk all at once. The guide was paid and happily returned to his village. Kamau hoped that he had enough sense to keep his mouth shut; he felt the chances of any one in authority becoming aware of their presence was remote, as generally all the action was in Maseru and the outlying villages rarely received a visit of any kind.

The group had found the cave and the hidden explosives. The last two had only arrived at the hideout within the previous few days. Aaron had taken on the leadership role and he had persuaded his companions that they should wait another week to see if any of the others would find their way to the hideout. They were very surprised to see Kamau, since they had heard from several sources that he had been captured by the authorities in South Africa.

They spent much of that day and the night excitedly catching up with each other's stories. Kamau eventually managed to get them to focus on the job at hand, and he went into meticulous detail on their objective to get to the nearby Welgedacht storage dam and how they could blow it up.

Two days of moving during the night and staying hidden during the day saw them close to their objective. The bleak but spectacular scenery of Lesotho had given way to the well-ordered farms of the eastern "Free State" with their well-fed cattle and sheep. The group had decided that there was a possibility that at weekends there would be people at the dam, since it was in a designated recreation area, and that they would therefore only attempt to blow it up on a Tuesday or Wednesday to reduce the risk of injuries to innocent people. This meant that they had two days to wait. They used the time well, and during the following two nights they reconnoitred the wall and established that there was no evidence of any security at all. There were a few people in the area during the days but it remained deserted at night and after Monday the area was completely deserted.

They started just after dusk on the Tuesday and with Kamau's expertise, laid twenty five charges at the base of the wall. Kamau made the group stand more than half a mile away and he allowed Aaron to light the fuses. A few seconds later there were several flashes of light and then they heard all twenty five explosions. As if in slow motion the fifty foot wall fell slowly down, followed by a sudden wall of water, as the dam quickly started to empty. The water thundered down the Caledon River. There was some light from the moon and the group stood there in awe, wondering what havoc they had wreaked or were about to wreak downstream. Kamau wondered if the walls of the dams downstream could withstand the sudden inflow of water. After ten minutes the group was gathered together.

"We should split up into three groups and meet in one week. Aaron and Joseph will come with me and by the time we see each other again, we will know what damage has been done and what security has been put into place at the other dams." He gave each member of his group a different address in a black township on the outskirts of Bloemfontein and arranged to meet in one of them. The two other groups headed back towards Lesotho, expecting to reach the safety of the border before dawn. Kamau knew that within hours the area would be crawling with police and security people.

Roux was rudely woken up in his hospital bed in Pretoria, just before midnight, by a very angry Kobus Meiring. Roux was groggy with the drugs he had been given to deaden the pain from his shattered arm. The surgeons had spent countless hours in putting the arm together again, and promised Roux that he would have some use of it when it was all healed.

"Why the fuck did you not tell us what that lunatic Kamau Lawrence had planned? He has now blown up one dam and heaven knows what is planned next!" yelled Meiring.

"What, what is going on, what dam? I thought Lawrence was in custody. What are you talking about?"

"They have blown up the fucking Welgedacht dam and I am sure that there will be extensive damage all the way along the Caledon; why for Christ's sake did you not tell us what was going on?"

"I did tell you; there is a report that was filed some weeks ago now. We picked a couple of them up in Ga-Rankuwa and got the full story out of them." Roux was now fully awake. He told Meiring where to find the report.

"Where are the two that you picked up?" asked Meiring.

"They died; we had to beat them to get the information. It is the only way."

Meiring turned away in disgust. He shook his head and thought: "I should have had him shot dead in the mountains there; what has this country come to when we kill almost for the sake of it."

He turned on his heel and walked out.

"Wait, wait! "Yelled Roux. Now he would be vindicated, did the fools not see, that his way, Roux's way, was the only way? Get rid of the Rooineks and then all the Kaffirs and the land would belong to the volk again. Meiring did not even break his stride.

He found Roux's report and by dawn he had read the very thorough document at least twice.

Within twenty-four hours there was a brigade of troops guarding all the large storage dams along the Vaal and the Orange. A massive manhunt had established that most of the 'terrorists' had escaped into Lesotho, although there was some indication that some of them had made their way further into the Free State.

At three in the morning Kamau hot-wired a car in the small town of Wepener and by dawn they were in Bloemfontein, with all the remaining explosives and equipment. Kamau abandoned the car in the centre of Bloemfontein, making certain that all evidence of who had used it was eliminated. The morning papers had no mention of the incident, but by mid-morning there were already massive troop movements going south from the bases round the town. The afternoon papers had a full report, which mentioned Kamau by name and had a very bad picture of him on page one. He went back to the township.

The newspaper reports had tales of extensive damage down the Caledon River, including at least two farmhouses that had been completely swept away with all the occupants. There was a sense of outrage in the press and the white world at large. The politicians all vowed that they would 'get the perpetrators of this heinous crime'.

Kamau could see that it would be some time before the storm died down; in the meantime he had his colleagues to think of. It was clear that there would be an intensive manhunt through all the townships in the country and the chances of them being able to lie low and reappear in a few months to bomb another dam were remote. The only chance was that they should go to a neutral country and wait there.

There was now great danger for all of them if the seven who had returned to Lesotho entered South Africa as they had arranged. He decided that Aaron and Joseph should risk no further delays and should escape through Botswana as soon as they could. They were to steal a car, drive as near as possible to the border with Botswana and make the rest of the journey on foot through the bush. The probability was that border patrols would be at a minimum with most of the troops concentrated on protecting the dams. Kamau decided that he should go a soon as he could to Lesotho and try to prevent the others from coming to South Africa at all. Having seen Aaron and Joseph on their way—"see you in Lusaka" was their cheery farewell—he then headed for the border post near Maseru. There, much to his surprise was the small pick-up in which he had hidden previously. He was confident that the vehicle would not be searched so, he again hid under the tarpaulin, among the now expected cargo of dagga, and within an hour of arriving at the border post he found himself in Maseru. All seven of his colleagues were surprised and delighted to see him in the safe house that was their base in Maseru.

"We have seen the press reports," Riempie, one of the coloureds in the group told him, "and we decided that it would be foolhardy to attempt to go to Bloemfontein, so we have all booked on the weekly flight from Maseru to Gaborone, which goes tomorrow. We thought that we would get to Lusaka from there and see what happened. We did not book for you, obviously."

Kamau was pleased with the initiative shown. "You all still have all your papers; mine were taken away when I was arrested. I expect it will take some time to get them back, so I'll see you in Lusaka or London."

The actions that Kamau had taken further cemented the loyalty of the group to him. He had further risked his life to ensure their safety; he could easily have crossed the border with Aaron and Joseph and left his colleagues in Lesotho to their fate. The group were aware that in most cases this was what they could have expected of their leaders.

After many delays Kamau was eventually given a new set of papers by the British authorities. They were quite unsympathetic to his situation and many of the people in the Maseru mission heartily wished that he was in the hands of the South Africans. Some weeks later he found himself in the ANC headquarters in Lusaka. A message had been sent to Zuma in Angola to meet him there.

✕　✕　✕

Chapter 18

To his utter amazement, far from being treated as a hero in the ANC organisation, Kamau was castigated and vilified. "You deliberately disobeyed explicit instructions," he was told.

"But those instructions would have led us into a trap, and we would have all been killed," he protested.

"If you had doubts about the plan, you should have come back and asked for further instructions," was the unreasonable response.

"And had those plans immediately passed on to the South Africans in the same way? We would have been led into another trap."

"You have no proof of that."

Kamau looked at the leadership blankly. It was clear that they no longer wanted him around, but he made one last attempt to get the leadership to see his point of view.

"I am your most successful operative by far, now over some years. The bombing of the Welgedacht dam was the most spectacular incident in this whole war; what else could you possibly want? I've constantly risked my life for this organisation, but I get no thanks for it at all, just this nonsense. None of you have ever been in the line of fire; all you want to do is to sit on your fat arses and issue stupid and very dangerous instructions."

"The objectives of your mission were not accomplished. You only blew up one dam; our instructions were for you to blow up several dams. Also, you lost two highly trained operatives. To suggest that this was a successful operation is exaggeration; all you succeeded in doing was to put people's lives in danger."

Kamau shrugged. He had never been allowed into the inner circle of the organisation. He presumed this was because he was not a South African, more particularly not a black South African. His record in the organisation was exemplary, he knew. There was something going on that they did not want him to know about and they seemed determined to sideline him because of it. Was it jealousy, he wondered? Jealousy and one or two other things.

He decided he would return to his legal firm and if this organisation did not want him, there were plenty of others who would welcome his level of skill and commitment.

Before returning to London he had many discussions with Zuma. "For some reason I am on the outer as well," Zuma told him. "The training camp in Angola is still doing very well and we can manage when the Cubans all leave. We provide many good recruits for the organisation. I think that all this nonsense you and I are getting from the people her in Lusaka has something to do with Trevor."

"Did you have anything to do with death of Trevor?" asked Kamau.

"No, I did not, absolutely not," replied Zuma, and then he hesitated. Kamau looked at him expectantly. Zuma shook his big, bullet-like head.

"Come on, what is it, what is it?" asked Kamau. "You are hiding something from me."

"It's impossible—no it's too far fetched forget it—I'm sure I'm wrong," said the big Zulu, fidgeting.

"Out with it! If you know something that could explain all this nonsense I have to go through, tell me now," demanded Kamau.

Zuma sighed.

"I don't think Trevor is dead, it is just too convenient. I think he is alive and well and is still living in London, probably under another name."

Kamau also had the same suspicions but he decided to get all he was able out of Zuma.

"The reports of his death seemed pretty clear to me; what are you talking about?"

"Maybe I'm wrong; just forget it," said Zuma quietly.

"No, I will not forget it. Come on, let's talk it out."

They talked for hours, and then made a plan.

Two weeks after Kamau returned to London to pick up the pieces of his life, Zuma joined him.

"I left the Angolan camp in the hands of my deputy, who is now very competent. I have two months leave," he told Kamau.

Peter and Rafiki had bought a flat in Belgravia, not far from where Giles and Louise lived. They used it very little, so Kamau had made it his home. Zuma stayed there during his period in the British capital.

Very soon after his arrival Zuma made a call:

"This is the big Zulu here, Julie, how are you?" he said in a friendly tone.

There was hesitation at the other end.

"I'm married now, and I have a small child. I hope you understand, I really can't see you."

"Just a drink, that can't do any harm. Maybe lunch time; I know you have to get back to your family in the evening," cajoled Zuma.

"Please, it's very difficult for me, you must understand."

Zuma turned on the charm.

"We had such good times, in that old pub in Finsbury Park. For old time's sake, meet me there for lunch."

"O.K., just this once though; if I'm found with you, my life will not be worth living, you have to understand that."

They agreed to meet the next day.

"If I'm not there it means something has come up and I won't be able to make it. If that happens come at the same time the following day; it's dangerous for me, you have to understand." The phone was put down before Zuma could say anything.

Zuma deliberately arrived early and selected a dark corner of the pub. He bought a beer and watched and waited. A man came in; taking no notice of Zuma he bought a half of bitter and sipped it; he appeared to be waiting for something. The man went out and then twenty minutes later came back into the pub and did the same thing. After an hour Zuma left. It was only on the third day that a very nervous looking girl came in. She was all wrapped up and had dark glasses on; he barely recognised her.

They embraced warmly.

"I have very little time, but it's great to see you. Sorry about the other days. Was there a man in here?" asked Julie. She described the man that Zuma had seen in the pub on the previous two days.

Zuma nodded.

"Not today, but yesterday and the day before." Zuma described him.

"He's been told to keep an eye on me, to see that I don't get into any mischief." She smiled.

"What about today?"

"He's gone up north; he will only be back tomorrow."

"What is all this? You seem to be in some sort of trouble."

"It's Dad that is in trouble. I wish we had never set eyes on that friend of yours, Trevor; he's brought a whole heap of trouble in the past few years.

Dad could manage the odd scam, but he's right in over his head now. They keep an eye on both of us. They need us to make the operation look kosher. I don't know where it will all end up." Julie shivered.

"I thought that Trevor was dead," said Zuma innocently.

She shook her head.

"He's not dead," she whispered.

"Do you know where I can find him?" he asked quietly.

Julie hesitated.

They drank their beer and ate the pie and chips that they had chosen.

"Richmond; try the Waterman's Arms there, it's a small pub down a laneway near the river. He goes there sometimes. I really can't tell you anything else." She shivered involuntarily. "If they knew that I had even told you that, I'd be dead."

Zuma turned the conversation to more mundane matters. He had the information that he had come for. He felt sorry for Julie, and wondered what trouble she and her father had got themselves into. Julie finished her beer, put her arms around Zuma and kissed him.

"Don't phone again, I will be in big trouble if you do." And then she muttered to herself. "Someone has to fix that bastard."

She put on her hat, dark glasses and scarf and without a backward glance left the pub. Zuma noticed that she went out the back way.

"Well, you can't go anywhere near the place," Kamau told him when Zuma broke the news. "If he saw your size and shape two hundred yards down the street, you wouldn't see him for dust." He thought for a minute.

" I have used many disguises; I' m sure if I did a proper job Trevor would not recognise me even if he were standing right next to me."

"So, what do you suggest?" asked Zuma.

"First, we need more information. You may have to break into the offices of the estate agent, which Julie and her father run and see what you can find. I will see if I can find Trevor."

"What do think that we are looking for?" asked Zuma.

"I don't know really, but it's more than the six or so flats we thought Trevor owned. It is much bigger than that; I think we will both be surprised at what we find."

The publican at the Waterman's Arms had always kept a watchful eye on his clientele. Generally he catered for working class men and was happy doing that. In recent months there had been a subtle change though. Richmond, in London's south-west, had always been a 'posh' suburb, but latterly it seemed that the young and wealthy had completely taken over. Also, there was this very well dressed black man who came to the pub at least twice a week. He often had a companion with him and they sat unobtrusively in the corner and held what appeared to be intense conversations in hushed tones. He wished the black man would go elsewhere. Not that he was racist; he just didn't want to have anything to do with blacks. He did not like the conspiratorial nature of the conversations either. And now there was this tramp who had started coming in. He had nothing against tramps, but this fellow truly stank, although he was not a nuisance and surprisingly, appeared to have money.

The publican was wondering what he could do to return the situation to what he considered to be normal when he noticed a subtle change in the tramp's demeanour. The black man had just come into the pub. That was really strange; why would the tramp be any more interested in the black than anyone else? He thought he had better keep an eye on the situation.

Zuma had spent a few days unobtrusively monitoring the movements in and out of the offices of the estate agency run by Julie and her father. There was a great deal of activity and he saw the man he had seen at the pub come and go many times. He also identified a number of others who were regular visitors. One, at least, he was certain was a black South African. Otherwise, there was the normal mix of people of all hues. The agency always shut at midday on Saturday, and as far as Zuma could see, nobody went anywhere near the place until it reopened on Monday morning. He only had two precious months, so time was important. So, one Saturday afternoon when he thought the coast was clear, he slipped up the back stairs and without any effort picked the lock and let himself in. He locked the door behind him and set to work. He worked right through the night and all through Sunday and eventually let himself out at three in the morning on Monday. He had a bundle of photocopies with him. Exhausted but elated, he hailed a cab and returned to Belgravia. He fell into bed and slept. Over the next few days he and Kamau pieced together details of what appeared to be a very large operation owning flats all over London. Some of the funding came from existing operations but there were mysterious deposits from Swiss bank accounts; one came directly from South Africa and several appeared to come directly from the Soviet Union. Certainly the abolition of exchange control had meant that more payments came from a variety of sources than before. An address in Richmond featured prominently, and was the registered office of many of the companies. Each property was registered in the name of a different company.

"You will have to go and search all the company files for these companies; I think it will be extremely interesting to see who the shareholders and directors are," said Kamau.

One quiet evening at the Waterman's Arms to the Publican's amazement the tramp came up to him and said in an educated voice: "I'm not sure what you make of me, and I'm sorry about the smell, but I am not what I seem."

The publican kept his mouth shut.

"I need a little information from you, and I can really make it worth your while. You will not be in any danger and you will deal only with me." At that point two fifty pound notes were pressed into his hand.

"What do you want, I mean what do you want me to do?" stammered the Publican.

"That black gentleman who occasionally comes in here, you know the one I mean."

"Yes," he said dubiously. "Are you a copper or something? I don't hold with coppers. Is he in some sort of trouble?"

"I'm not a copper, and no, the man is not in trouble; I am more interested in the companions he brings in here. All I want is a description, the best you can do. One hundred quid for each description. And they had better be genuine."

"O.K., money for old rope," muttered the publican. "A hundred, tax free, no problem." He watched the tramp sidle out.

To start with Zuma's searches yielded very little. The shareholders were other companies; all had the one director, a Mr. Simon Molefe at the address in Richmond.

"You had better go on searching, my friend," said Kamau.

Zuma looked unenthusiastic.

"It is the only way. I will find out who this Simon Molefe is," said Kamau, "and you can't do that; there is no disguise that could possibly give you cover for more than five seconds."

"That tramp outfit you have, is it necessary for it to smell so bad?" asked Zuma laughing.

"I am the one who has to wear it," said Kamau. "It means that almost nobody looks past the smell, if you see what I mean. I expect to be quite to close some of the people we are looking for, and there must be no chance that they suspect who I am."

"How do you get it to smell like that anyway?" asked Zuma.

"State secret." Kamau smiled.

When Zuma dug deeper he found that there were two or three layers of companies before he found anything of value.

"Just look at this," said Zuma to Kamau one evening at their flat. He had all his papers spread out over the floor. "Look at the names," He whispered. "Just look at the fucking names."

Kamau bent down and spent the next ten minutes following the trail that Zuma had laid out.

He stood up and said almost to himself:

"All of them are in this, every one of those bastards in Lusaka are in this, as well as Trevor. No wonder they wanted us out of the way, and of course they would not do anything about Trevor himself. Shit! Shit! Shit!"

"And I believed in this organisation," said Zuma. "Think of all those kids, all the people who have gone to their deaths willingly, thinking they were doing it for a cause, and then these fuckers, stealing large sums of money so they can live like fat cats whatever the outcome in South Africa and however long it takes." Tears of shame and humiliation coursed down his cheeks.

"You wait, I will get my hands on that animal Trevor; he will really wish he had died." He shook with anger.

In his tramp's outfit Kamau spent several days outside a Richmond address which Zuma had unearthed in his searches.

"Nothing short of half a million pounds there, for each flat," he told Zuma later. "None of this slumming in Finsbury Park for our Mr. Molefe or whatever his name is. Our Mr. Molefe has come up in the world by the looks of things."

The first few visits back to the Waterman's arms yielded very little.

"He's brought in a few other black people in the past week or so," the publican confided in Kamau, the tramp. "But they all look the bloody same to me; I can't tell one from the other."

"Well, you will have to try a little harder," said Kamau kindly. "Look at their hair for strands of grey, are they fat or thin, how black is their skin and so on."

After that, he started to get better descriptions, and over a period of about six weeks he identified almost the whole Lusaka leadership group. He was not able to positively say that Simon Molefe was the same person as Trevor. He had not seen Trevor either come out of, or go into the block of flats.

Kamau had not been back to the pub in Richmond for a few days, and when he went in, the publican was bubbling with excitement. "He had a white man in here a few days ago," he whispered. "The bugger had a nasty white scar all down the side of his face. And horrible blue eyes, they seemed to look right through me. That any good to you?"

Kamau nearly fell off his barstool. He nodded.

"Yes, yes indeed," he said as he paid the man double.

"Roux," he thought. "Roux, I might have guessed it."

He went back to the flat and told Zuma what he had found.

"I just do not believe this," said Zuma. "I am going to sort this out if it is the last thing I do. Dealing with that traitor."

"Careful, careful," said Kamau. "We still do not know who this Simon Molefe is."

"No, but we have a bloody good idea, don't we?" Said Zuma.

A week later as he was shuffling into the pub, Kamau almost fell over a portly black man coming out. The man backed off, holding his nose. It was Trevor. Kamau followed him at a distance in the shadows. He went into the nearby luxury block of flats, which Kamau had been so painstakingly monitoring, walked into the underground garage, and minutes later emerged driving the latest, top of the range, BMW.

"I might have guessed it," thought Kamau.

A long discussion was held between Zuma and Kamau as to what they should do.

"I' m going to kill the fucker," said Zuma.

"I have a much better idea. The police will not act, as we have discussed. As far as they are concerned, all these transactions are legitimate, having been sanctioned by the proper authority. They will cooperate, however, and if we play our cards correctly we can sort this matter out completely."

"How?" asked Zuma.

Kamau explained.

Kamau and Zuma waited in the shadows near the Richmond address. Trevor had established a pattern; for the previous two weeks he and Roux had met for an hour or more every Wednesday at the Waterman's arms.

Kamau was waiting at the pub, in his disguise. Trevor and Roux walked in.

He nodded to the Publican and went out.

"Are you sure about the number, and that there is nobody else, like a girlfriend, in residence?" asked Zuma anxiously.

"Quite sure," answered Kamau. "I have made a number of telephone calls to the concierge and have been in there in the guise of a plumber, when Trevor was out. There is only one occupant and that is Trevor."

They moved quickly, entered the flats through the underground garage and made their way up to the third floor flat overlooking the river. Kamau picked the lock and they slipped quietly into the darkened apartment. Zuma was carrying a large briefcase, packed with papers.

"Whew," breathed Zuma. "Nothing skimpy about our Trevor, is there?" He looked out onto the Thames, snaking its way into the distance with the moonlight reflecting on the water.

"Once they start stealing they don't seem to be able to stop. A person can, after all only sleep in one bed," he reflected. "Still, enough of this, we need to get on."

An hour went by, and then another.

Zuma started to fidget.

"Maybe they've gone away for the evening,"

"Shh. Here they come."

A key was eased into the lock and the lights were switched on.

Zuma grabbed Trevor and Kamau ruthlessly knocked Roux out with a rolling pin that he had found in the kitchen. Roux was gagged and trussed up like a chicken and left lying on the plush carpet.

"We won't be hearing from him for a while," muttered Kamau.

Trevor started struggling.

"Police, I will call the police," he mumbled through Zuma's large hand over his mouth.

"Soon enough, soon enough," said Zuma. "First we have some business with you, and you had better cooperate. As you know, Trevor Mdantsane was certified dead, now some months ago. So he won't be missed if you see what I mean." Zuma grinned evilly into Trevor's face.

"What do you thieves want, what do you want? I should have had you killed long ago. I knew that you were no good," yelled Trevor.

Trevor was now tied up in a chair. The only muscle he could move was his mouth.

"You tried hard enough, but you were too greedy, weren't you?" said Zuma triumphantly.

"What do you want?" Trevor's eyes bulged and he wet himself.

"Actually all we want is for you to sign some papers, but there are rather a lot of them; you have been a busy boy," said Zuma.

"What papers?"

"These." Kamau waved a sheaf of documents before Trevor's eyes.

"O.K., I will sign them," Trevor said unthinkingly.

They untied his hands and brought a table and put it in front of him.

His legs were still firmly tied to the chair.

"No, no, not these, I will not sign these," said Trevor, throwing the papers on to the floor. "How dare you! The leadership will have you executed." He glared around him.

"Bring the body-bag," said Kamau; he was standing behind Trevor and he looked up at Zuma. "I presume the boat is ready; we can have his body dumped in the ocean by midnight, and after all nobody will miss him, since he is already dead. The cleanest thing is just to suffocate him. Shooting and stabbing are so messy. We have practised forging his signature enough times anyway; it would have been better to have the real thing but if he won't cooperate, forgeries will have to do." He sighed and winked at Zuma over Trevor's head.

Zuma moved menacingly over to where Trevor was sitting.

"No, no," Trevor whimpered, cringing. "I will sign anything." Zuma noticed a bad smell. Trevor had crapped himself.

"I just need to change," He muttered.

"Plenty of time for that. Start signing".

Zuma started putting papers in front of him.

Three hours later it was all finished.

All the properties had been transferred back into the name of the ANC, and Zuma and Kamau had been given authority to sell the properties and transfer the monies back into the legitimate bank accounts of the ANC.

Roux was given another bang on the head when he started moving and then Kamau spent another hour checking everything.

"One more thing."

"What is that?" asked Trevor, now completely exhausted and intimidated.

"A document that says you signed all these papers willingly and voluntarily; it has already been witnessed," said Kamau.

There was hesitation, but he signed it when Kamau shook the body bag again.

"Get him cleaned up," suggested Kamau. "I will call Inspector Pride."

"What, what's this?" asked Trevor.

"You will find out soon enough. Murder is still an offence here in England, even if it was your own brother," said Kamau.

Zuma took Trevor off to the bathroom and Kamau made a brief call from Trevor's telephone.

"Took you long enough," said the voice at the other end. "We've been waiting for hours, it's nearly morning."

"They spent too long in the pub," explained Kamau.

"They?" asked the voice.

"Yes, we have another beauty for you; he is just waking up."

"I'll see you in ten minutes."

Zuma brought a very forlorn looking Trevor into the lounge. He was now all spruced up and had changed into another of his many suits. The smell had gone.

"Bit of a change from your traditional goatskins,' observed Zuma.

Three policemen arrived, headed by Inspector Pride.

He faced Trevor.

"Mr Trevor Molefe, you are under arrest for the murder of you brother, Mr Simon Molefe. You do not need to say anything, but if you do it will be taken down in evidence and used against you in court."

Trevor looked absolutely shattered at the turn of events.

"What about him?" asked Kamau, indicating Roux, who was now sitting up.

"Ah, yes, Mr. Roux. We'll take him, of course. He is wanted for various offences; in all probability he will just be deported. The South Africans are also looking for him. We'll probably let them look after their own scum."

The pair were led out by the other two policemen.

"Got everything you want?" asked the inspector.

"Oh, yes. Thank you and thank you for you help. The right people are going to get the money and this scum will end up where they deserve."

They shook hands.

A few days later a triumphant Zuma marched into the offices of the ANC in Finsbury Park and to the ongoing amazement of the people there, unloaded hundreds of documents, which gave the ANC title to properties all over London.

"I will be dealing with this," he said authoritatively as he moved everything into the office that had belonged to Trevor. "And for the time being, Lusaka is to be told nothing—nothing is that clear?" He looked round belligerently.

A few heads nodded; the office had been denuded of people in recent months, and most of the people still there had not been paid for at least six of those months. This at least gave them some hope. They were glad to have Zuma back and it looked as if the finances would be healthy again for a while.

✖   ✖   ✖

Epilogue

February 1990. Paarl. Cape Province. South Africa.

The crowd were getting restless. The great man, Nelson Mandela, had been due for release at least one hour earlier, and still there was no sign of him. The news teams from all around the world wanted to witness the release of the man who had spent twenty-seven years in jail for his political beliefs. He had been encouraged to compromise many times but he was now being released on his own terms. The political transformation in South Africa was about to start.

Suddenly there was a cheer and the crowd tried to surge forward but were kept in place by the small and unobtrusive cordon of police.

The Lawrences: Peter, Rafiki, Kamau, Robert and his wife Jessica were in a little enclosure away from the main crowd.

Kamau's friend Zuma had arranged for them to be there and said to Kamau, "Don't move and I will bring him to you. If you move I won't be able to find you. He was most insistent that he wanted to meet you, almost above everyone else."

In the intervening eight years Zuma had played a more and more prominent role in the ANC. He had started off by firmly controlling the decimated finances of the operation. He was able to do this by keeping all the property dealings under his control and by personally authorizing any major expense.

He had found many different ways of easing the members of the hierarchy that had been in league with Trevor out of the organisation. Every one of them had been dealt with. None now had positions of any significance in the organisation.

Kamau had helped with all the legal issues and had played a major role, together with his brother Robert, in creating a haven at Dingley Hall for the protagonists in the South African morass to meet and negotiate the beginnings of a settlement out of the public eye. Giles had handed over most of his responsibilities to the Lawrence brothers, as he had envisaged all those years earlier. They still went to him for advice, though.

Trevor was serving a life sentence in England. Roux was confined to a lunatic asylum.

The crowd was getting closer. It parted and Zuma, as large as life, brought the great man forward and introduced him to the Lawrence party. All the introductions were made.

" Before we move on I want to say, publicly, to you, the Lawrence family: you have done as much now over many years and have made as many sacrifices as any family I know for the cause of political equality and freedom for the black people of Africa. I hope that we can work with you in the future and I thank you from the bottom of my heart for all that you have done."

He shook each one again by the hand.

"I now have to move on." He sounded reluctant. The crowd engulfed him and the cheering rose to a crescendo. It was a moment South Africa had been waiting for, for a long time.

✳   ✳   ✳

About the Author

Guy Hallowes was born and brought up on a farm in the so called 'White Highlands' of Kenya (described The first book of the 'Winds of Change' trilogy—'No Happy Valley'), and attended school in Nairobi.

He lived for many years in South Africa and Botswana as well as the UK

He now lives in Sydney, Australia.

* 9 7 8 0 6 4 8 4 7 9 0 7 9 *